FOREVER
MAN

By
Brian W. Matthews

JournalStone
San Francisco

JOURNALSTONE
YOUR LINK TO ARTISTIC TALENT

JournalStone books may be ordered through booksellers or by contacting:

JournalStone
www.journalstone.com
www.journal-store.com

The views expressed in this work are solely those of the authors and do not necessarily reflect the views of the publisher, and the publisher hereby disclaims any responsibility for them.

ISBN: 978-1-936564-65-1   (sc)
ISBN: 978-1-936564-66-8   (ebook)

Library of Congress Control Number: 2012953064

Printed in the United States of America
JournalStone rev. date: February 15, 2013

Cover Design: Denis Daniel
Cover Art: M. Wayne Miller

Edited By: Dr. Michael Collings

DEDICATION

For William S. Matthews, Jr., and Andy Matthews
The reasons are obvious,
the sentiment is real.

ENDORSEMENTS

"Matthews's debut, a supernatural thriller with a smalltown ethos, drops a lot of tantalizing hints and brief scares into a story centered around family relationships. The novel wisely focuses on the human 'distractions' who would normally be glossed over in favor of the monster, and it presents their emotional pain and fears in a manner that maintains the suspense throughout." - *Publishers Weekly*

"Brian Matthews has written an intriguing story enriched with unique characters intertwined within a plot full of mystery, crime and horror. Strap yourself in and hold on tight." – K. Trap Jones, Award winning author of *The Sinner*

"With his debut novel, *Forever Man*, Brian W. Matthews has turned me into a major fan. Layering horror, mystery and an eternal battle between good and evil, Matthews tells his story with assured, luxurious prose and develops his plot with the skill of a master craftsman. *Forever Man* is a chiller of the first order. I loved it!"
– Joe McKinney, Bram Stoker Award-winning author of *Flesh Eaters* and *Inheritance*

ACKNOWLEDGEMENTS

My heartfelt thanks go out to the many wonderful people who helped in the creation of this novel. To Diane Clancy, Mark Foley, and Devon Hornberger, who read an earlier version of *Forever Man* and provided valuable feedback. To Tamra Leclaire, for handing out blunt but honest commentary, and for saving Katie Bethel from backstory limbo and bringing her to the forefront of the story. To my brother, Robert M. Matthews, Sr., for advice on police procedures, and any mistakes in the story are mine. To Christopher Payne and the crew at JournalStone, for believing in me. To Dr. Michael Collings, for his editorial acumen. To Wayne Miller, for the kick-ass cover. And to my good friend and fellow author, Jeff LaSala, who recognized something in me that I couldn't see in myself. I know it sounds like hyperbole, but without him, you wouldn't be reading this book.

My biggest thanks go, of course, to my wife, Jill, and my daughter, Dana. They put up with my crazy hours, my shirking of various household chores (cough, cough), and my state of perpetual distraction as I concentrated on my writing. Without them, I wouldn't be the person I am today.

PART ONE

THE TWILIGHT
OF
OUR DREAMS

The Greyhound bus shrugged to a stop.

The old man glanced up from the paperback he'd been reading. Lifting a hand to the window beside him, he rubbed away some of the grime and gazed out at the prosaic landscape of yet another town.

Bartholomew Owens sighed. After so many cities, the stores and homes and people had run together until everything looked much the same.

Still…there were bright spots, images of people he'd met and places he'd seen that were so special—so *vivid*—that they burned like signal fires along the paths of his past, guiding him back to his younger days, days which now seemed so long ago he doubted whether he could even remember them correctly.

But that was a lie. He could remember them.

They burned the brightest.

From the front of the bus, the driver barked out, "Newberry!" and the exit door swung open with a snaky hiss.

Bart rose to his feet. Stretching, he retrieved his guitar case from the overhead bin, then his canvas duffel. With the bag slung comfortably over his shoulder, he started forward. Even after all these years, he still sat at the back of the bus, a blunt reminder to himself and others of how far the world had come. Besides, he preferred the bumpy isolation of those back seats.

Easing his way past the more congested front sections, Bart approached the exit and was surprised when the driver held up a hand, clearly trying to get his attention.

Bart had traveled from Nashville through St. Louis, Chicago and Milwaukee, with his final transfer having occurred less than an hour ago in the town of Escanaba in Michigan's Upper Peninsula. After spending the last twenty-four hours on a bus, he wanted to be on his way.

"Is there a problem?" he asked, frowning.

The driver gave a curt shake of his head. "No, but do you mind if I ask you a question?" He was in his late fifties, with broad shoulders, a bull neck and close-cropped white hair. Sitting ram-rod straight in his seat, he had the familiar bearing of a military veteran. The name badge sewn onto his shirt breast pocket said "Frank."

"If you can make it quick," Bart replied. "I'm in kind of a hurry here."

"That." Frank gestured to the insignia stitched into the green canvas of Bart's kit bag: it was the head of a panther emblazoned upon a golden shield, with the motto 'Come Out Fighting' embroidered below. "I noticed it when you got on, but I don't recognize the unit."

With the easy smile, Bart said, "That would be the 761st Tank Battalion—the Black Panthers. They fought with Patton's Third Army in France."

Frank returned the smile. "My granddad served back then. All the men in my family serve." He glanced back. In a low voice, he added, "My first tour was 'Nam. Guess I got lucky. All I lost were these." He held up his other hand. Two of the digits ended in fleshy stumps.

"Let me guess," Bart said. "Marines. Infantry?"

"Damn straight. How 'bout you?"

"We're all soldiers in some kind of war."

Frank's brow drew together in a puzzled frown. Then he gave a dismissive shrug. "Anyway, sorry to have kept you. It's just…I don't see many people who remember what the word 'sacrifice' means." Frank took a final, meaningful look at the kit bag. "The man who used that, he must've been pretty special."

Bart stepped onto the sidewalk, the brassy autumn sun warming his face. He thought about the young boy who had once owned the kit bag, a boy whose life had been cut short on a rainy battlefield in France.

"Yes," he said sadly. "He was."

After a respectful nod, Frank closed the door and drove off. The bus diminished into the distance, fading like a neglected memory until it melted away into the shimmering heat reflected off the tarmac.

Bart turned around. On the other side of the street, a prison sprawled across several acres of land overlooking the town proper. Locked away behind twin electrified fences topped with concertina wire, young black men strolled the exercise yard, played ball, and lagged farther behind the rest of society. Most looked barely out of high school, if they'd finished school at all. The consequential by-products of a culture which had largely forgotten its roots.

Quit sermonizing, old man. You need to get moving. You've got a job to do.

With a heavy sigh, he turned his back on the prison and hitched the kit bag high on his shoulder. Renewing his grip on the guitar case, he started up the road.

Kinsey was still a few hours away.

PROLOGUE

Friday Night

Natalie ran faster, her long legs quivering from the surge of adrenalin.

Looming high over her shoulder, the full moon shone through a canopy of dying leaves, speckling the ground with ghostly coins of pale light. But there wasn't enough light, not *nearly* enough. The darkness seemed to bleed into everything, making it difficult for her to find her way.

She ducked under a thick bough. Paused to catch her breath. Before her, the hiking trail from Black Pine Lake campgrounds unwound like a dark ribbon. Trees crowded the edge of the path, hemming her in, reaching for her....

Behind her, Jimmy shouted. Called her name. Pleaded with her to stop. When a cry floated up the trail, she grinned savagely. Maybe something got the bastard.

She took off again. Her white Skechers pounded hard against the ground, propelling her forward. The path stretched east for nearly fifty yards, only to veer north; beyond, the forest waited patiently, a hedge maze of oak, pine, and maple. It may as well have been a brick wall.

She'd run about half the distance when she heard Jimmy shout her name. Turning, she caught sight of him, not thirty yards back. He had stopped, his lungs heaving as he tried to catch his breath.

"I said...I was sorry," Jimmy called out. "I'm not gonna...hurt you."

"It's a little late for apologies!" Natalie yelled, her voice carrying through the still night.

"Look," he said, his breath coming in slow, shallow gulps. "Let's stop running...and talk.

"About what? How you're a knuckle-scraping Neanderthal?"

Jimmy nodded. "Okay, maybe I deserve that. But don't forget, this is as much your fault as it is mine."

"What? Oh my God, you are such an asshole!"

He took a few cautious steps forward. "You honestly thought we came up here to look at the stars? That maybe I'd spent all this money and would get nothing in return?"

"All we did was go to a dance together," Natalie said. "Coming up here wasn't an invitation for you to—to—"

With a frustrated cry, she grabbed her necklace and gave it a yank. The chain broke, and she threw the necklace at him. "Screw you and your presents. Just go. Leave me alone. I can find my own way home."

Jimmy continued toward her, his large frame silhouetted by the cold, blue moonlight. Now Natalie matched each step with a cautious step backward. Twigs snapped under her feet. She almost tripped on a root.

When he reached the necklace, Jimmy stooped to picked it up. The thin metal chain dangled from his hand. He stared at it for several seconds, then his gaze found her. He didn't say a word.

Natalie started to wonder if Jimmy was more than angry. Maybe he was a little crazy. Her insides did an unpleasant roll into her pelvis. Sweat trickled down her spine like ice melting down a windowpane.

Girl chased through woods by psycho boyfriend. Didn't this shit only happen in the movies?

"Neither of us is leaving," Jimmy said, shoving the necklace into his pocket. "Not until we work this out."

The words were out of her mouth before she could stop them. "It's 'neither of us *is* leaving,' you idiot!"

Jimmy's face twisted into a snarl. He charged after her.

Natalie turned and fled, panic pushing her to run faster. She'd almost reached the curve in the trail when she slipped on a patch of damp autumn leaves. Her feet flew out from under her and she landed hard on her side, her breath exploding from her lungs. Momentum carried her forward. She rolled and rolled and then collided, back first, into a tree. For a moment she lay stunned, trying to draw a breath. Then she felt something wet trickling across her stomach. Looking down—well, sideways—she saw a stick protruding from her abdomen, near the edge of her waist. It was thin, no wider than two of her fingers, the sharp tip extending about four inches beyond a tear in her shirt. Blood seeped from the small wound, coated the bark. Her blood. She tried rolling forward, but the stick pulled at her. She cried out. The world spun as pain wracked her body.

"Jesus, Nat."

Lifting her eyes, she saw Jimmy standing over her, his face pale. "Get help," she said weakly. "My mom. My dad. Anybody. Just go."

He bit his lip. "I can't...at least, not yet."

His words stunned her. "Look at me, Jimmy! I'm stuck to a *fucking tree!*"

"I'll get you out, but only after we get our facts straight."

The ground started to tilt. Would he really let her die out here? Glaring at him, she said, "Fine. I'll agree to whatever you say. Just go get—"

An ululating howl punctured the night, followed by the sound of breaking wood.

Jimmy frowned, glaring into the forest. Branches cracked like rifle shots as something crashed toward them.

"Damn, that sounds big." His eyes found hers. "Change of plans," he said, digging into his pocket. "You're on your own." Fishing out the necklace, he tossed it at her. "I hear if you play dead, a bear won't maul you too badly."

Panic gripped her. "Wait! You can't do this! *You can't leave me here!*"

He gave an embarrassed shrug, then started back up the trail.

Something issued a horrid, otherworldly scream—it sounded like two different animals howling at the same time—and out of the woods burst a dark shape. It headed straight for Jimmy.

He hadn't gotten far when it hit him. His shrill cries cut through the night air. There was a wet, tearing sound that reminded Natalie of deer hunting with her dad: it was the sound of someone dressing a kill.

"Oh god," Natalie whimpered, turning her head away from the carnage. "Oh god oh god."

She had to get off this branch. Her fingers clawed at the dirt, scrambling until they found a wiry root sticking up from the ground. She wrapped her hands around it, gritted her teeth against what was to come, hesitated, swallowed hard, and pulled.

Her scream soared high above the treetops. The branch slowly scraped through her abdomen. Rough bark lifted from the wood like tiny knives and carved bloody grooves into her flesh. Trembling, tears running down her face, she jerked forward again. The wood pulled, snagged on something deep inside her *oh god it HURTS* and she threw her head back, sobbing, yanking, yanking…and slid free of the branch.

Up the trail. A zipper of sharp snaps. Bones breaking. Jimmy's screams turned to shrieks and then silence.

Run, she thought. Get away.

Natalie wedged one hand against the ground and pressed the other over her wounded side. She'd gotten her legs under her when she heard a guttural hiss. Warm, fetid air washed over her face. Her eyes flew up. There, crouched down before her—

—Natalie opened her mouth to scream. A large, taloned hand clamped over her face. Razor sharp nails punctured her sweaty skin and she was lifted off the ground. She struggled as fangs, wet and dripping with Jimmy's blood, snapped at the air. The creature made a whooping sound, like a hyena's laugh.

Overwhelmed by pain and fear, dangling helplessly from the creature's hand, Natalie had one fleeting thought before she passed out: as a little girl, her mother had told her there was no such thing as monsters.

Oh, Mom, you were so wrong.

CHAPTER
1

Saturday

It was dawn.

At least, Izzy Morris thought it was. Trying to judge time from the hazy sunlight filtering in through the blinds was way too much work for…well, for this early in the morning.

Yawning, she squinted at the alarm clock on her nightstand.

Oh, yeah. Dawn. And then some.

With a groan that was part regret, part resentment, Izzy rolled onto her back. She'd wanted to be up by six but had forgotten to set the alarm. Now she was almost half an hour late starting her day.

She turned her head. Lying beside her, Stanley slept soundly, his face half-buried in a rumpled pillow. Sometime during the night, he'd kicked his foot out from under the comforter, exposing it to the cool air. Once she might have thought it cute, her husband laying there, sleeping, his toes twitching as he dreamed whatever men dreamed. Back then, she might have crawled across the bed and run her fingernail lightly along the arch of his foot. And when he woke, with his sleepy gaze peering down at her, she might have grinned lasciviously, slipped her hand under the covers, tickled another part of him until she had his full attention. Then she'd slowly, teasingly, crawl up his body, sharing touches, sharing kisses, until they were loving their way to lunch.

But that was years ago. Too many years and too many hard emotions. Now the sight of the pale fleshy limb struck her as irritating.

Slipping out of bed, she pulled the comforter down until it covered his foot.

Quietly, Izzy stepped into the bathroom, did what she needed to do, then changed into a pair of shorts and an old Michigan State sweatshirt. Pausing at the sink, she stared at her reflection in the mirror. Hazel eyes stared back. Beneath a slender nose dusted with freckles, her pale lips could use a touch more color, but that was a vanity she could do without. Her auburn hair was a mess, though, and using a hair tie, she worked her unruly curls into a kind of controlled chaos.

Before she stepped out to begin her day, she hesitated, her gaze lingering on her reflection. When she couldn't bear the scrutiny any further, she turned away and moved back into the bedroom.

Stanley had woken while she was in the bathroom. He lay on his back, scrawny arms crossed behind his head, his gray eyes following her across the room. He waited until she'd almost reached the hallway door to speak.

"Kind of early to be up, isn't it?"

Reluctantly, Izzy halted. She caught a hint of cinnamon from the air freshener plugged into the wall. It was one of her favorite fragrances.

Turning to face him, she smiled. "I wanted to get my run in before Natalie comes home."

"She'll be at Katie's for hours. And besides, it's your day off. Why not take it easy?"

Izzy almost laughed. "Tell that to the three loads of laundry sitting in the hamper. In between which, I still have to clean the house and get dinner together. So, either I get started now, or come Monday, you'll be wearing dirty shirts to work."

"Oh God, please," he said, a bit too harshly for her liking. "I'll do what I can to help before I leave for work. And Nat always does her part. That'll free up a few hours of your time." He brought his arms from behind his head and crossed them over his chest. "You worked hard this week. You've earned some relaxation."

"For me, running *is* relaxing." She stepped up to the bed and bumped it playfully with her knee. "You could join me, you know. Work on losing that muffin top of yours."

Stanley patted his belly. "Sometimes less isn't more, Iz." He reached out to embrace her. "Besides, I have a better idea."

She stepped back before he could wrap his arms around her. "I'm serious. The doctor—"

"Roger Linden's a nagging ass," he said. "*And* he likes the Yankees. Never trust an A-Rod fan."

"Your weight's up," Izzy went on patiently. "So is your blood pressure. And don't forget what happened last spring." Back in April, she'd called EMS after Stanley started complaining of chest pain. It had only been angina, but Stanley had received the standard speech about exercising more and eating better.

Of course, he hadn't changed his lifestyle at all—like doctors and nurses, pharmacists made terrible patients.

"I'm fine," he said irritably. "And I hate running."

"All right, then. We can walk. It's still exercise."

He patted the empty side of the bed. "I can think of another kind of exercise."

Izzy closed her eyes...and saw that foot again, pallid and fleshy and disgusting, sticking out from under the covers. She had been trying to get along with him, trying hard. And she might have even joined him in bed. But any amorous feelings she had, or could have faked, fled from the image of that foot.

She had been silent for too long. It was as much a rejection as if she had spoken her refusal out loud.

"What?" he said, his tone prickly. "Is there a problem?"

Sighing, she opened her eyes. "No, there's no problem. It's just—"

"Just what, Iz?" He leaned forward. "Just what exactly is going on? Explain it to me, will you, because I sure as shit don't understand."

Izzy opened her mouth to speak, but the words caught in her throat. How did you tell someone you'd been with for almost twenty-five years that you weren't sure if you loved him anymore?

She couldn't do it. 'Sticks and stones' be damned: sometimes words did hurt.

"Look," she said. "I'm going for my run. We can talk about it after I get back."

"It?" he asked incredulously. "What the hell is *it*?"

"Please, I don't want to fight."

Stanley continued as if he hadn't heard her. His hands were balled into fists. "How about I tell *you* what 'it' is? 'It' is the fact that I want to have sex and you don't want to have anything to do with 'it.'"

"That's an oversimplification—"

"That's a goddamn fact," he snapped, his face was hot with anger.

"It's not about the sex," Izzy said, her eyes meeting his. "It's about love. It's about sharing. Not just getting your rocks off." She turned toward the door. "I tried, Stanley. I tried to get us to go running. To do something together, something other than…that. And not to make too fine a point, you're the one who turned me down first."

"God, when did you become such a bitch?"

"When you started caring more about yourself than us," she said, slamming the bedroom door shut on her way out.

At the front door, Izzy laced up her running shoes, shoved her cell into her pocket, and inserted the earbuds of her iPod. Then she was outside and running.

While Green Day waited for September to end, she headed west on Windmere, each long, leisurely stride carrying her further from her fight with Stanley.

The early morning air was chilly. On either side of Windmere, large maples shaded the lane, blocking what meager warmth the sun might have provided. Identical two-story bungalows lounged indolently behind the trees. The houses had been young once, vibrant, brought to life by families living and loving in them. Now, most showed their age. Where the paint had peeled away, bare wood dotted their skin like liver spots. Boards sagged here and there. And every so often, there was the occasional angry cataract of a boarded-up window.

On her iPod, Aerosmith replaced Green Day. Steven Tyler launched into a tale about child abuse and a young girl who couldn't take it anymore. Izzy skipped it. Loved the song, but she had to be in the right mood for the subject.

The shuffler brought up an old Moody Blues tune. She breathed deeply, wanted to clear her head of negative thoughts. Warmth flowed into her legs as her muscles loosened up. She pushed herself, lengthened her strides. Four more miles.

Izzy veered right onto Overbrook. Her route carried her past Wooliver Park, a small rectangular patch of grass that sported a three-person swing set, a slide, and a merry-go-round with the base painted brick red. A halo of wood chips ringed each play set: modern-day guardian angels for the overly daring or the eagerly litigious. Modest steel benches flanked either end of the park, giving parents a place to sit and watch their children play.

Before she'd discovered dresses and dating, Nat had loved to visit Wooliver Park. As a family, they would walk the short distance to the playground. Izzy and Stanley would sit together on a bench, sometimes holding hands, sometimes simply talking about their respective days, while Nat scurried from swing to slide and back again. Then it would be time for the merry-go-round. Stanley would grab the steel handles and spin Nat around and around until she was laughing so hard he had to stop so she could breathe. And, like any kid, she'd want to do it all over again.

The memory brought a fleeting smile to Izzy's lips. At one time, their lives had been good. They had been happy.

What had gone so wrong?

And why had they allowed it to happen?

Izzy ran harder, picking up the pace as she neared Asher Boulevard, the main road through town. Her heart beat a steady, predictable *thub-dub* in her chest. Sweat caused her shirt to stick to her skin.

She angled left on Asher, cutting through Sclater's Gas and Go. It was early October, but the station's Labor Day pennants were still on display and snapping smartly in the breeze.

A block down Asher, Izzy had just decided to skip making dinner and take everyone out to eat at the Lula when she saw blue and red lights flashing in the distance. Soon they resolved into a Kinsey police cruiser heading her way. She slowed down. When the unit pulled up in front of her, she stopped, removed the earbuds and flipped them over her shoulder.

Sgt. Bob Talbert got out of the car. He was the Saturday morning shift supervisor. "Good, I found you. We've got a problem."

Izzy smiled. "So I gathered. What is it this time? Someone found Chet Boardman passed out under another bush?"

Talbert looked shaken. "A call came in. Two people were hiking the trail up at Black Pine Lake. You know, the one off the campgrounds." He paused. "They found a body."

Izzy smile faded. "A body? A *dead* body?"

Talbert nodded. "Guess it's pretty bad. Looks like an animal attack."

"Is Carlton up there?" Carlton Manick was the patrolman on duty this morning. That is, if he'd managed to show up for his shift. Officer Manick was a work in progress.

"Yeah," Bob said. "He's there."

"Okay, call Sten Billick. Have him head over and take charge of the scene. Then pull in Al Hamilton to cover Carlton's patrol. I want you up there helping Carlton. He's going to need it."

"Izzy." Bob's tone stopped her—it was flat, bleak. "There was a car there." He wiped a hand across his mouth. "It was Jimmy Cain's Mustang. Carlton found a purse in it. There was a driver's license." He paused. "It was Natalie's."

Her stomach fluttered, and she suddenly felt cold. "But...that's not right. She's at a friend's house. She spent the night there."

With a slight shrug, Bob said, "It was definitely her license."

"But I don't...." Then it hit her. "Oh God, the body, is it—?"

Bob quickly raised his hands. "No, it's not her. The DB's male."

Izzy's mind churned. The Homecoming dance. Nat went there last night with Jimmy Cain. But she was supposed to go to Katie Bethel's house afterward. She shouldn't have been anywhere *near* the campgrounds. Yet, Jimmy's car was there. And now Izzy had a dead body. Was it Jimmy? Or someone else? And if the body was Jimmy, then where's...?

"Chief?" Bob was staring at her. "Should I call Stanley? Have him come pick you up."

Izzy shook her head. "No. Take me to the station. I'll grab a cruiser and head up to the campgrounds. But first I'll call Stanley. Then the Bethels."

"And if Natalie's not there?"

Chief of Police Elizabeth Morris hurried over to the cruiser.

"Then nobody rests until we find her."

CHAPTER
2

The road leading to Black Pine Lake Campground was a relatively straight, hard-packed dirt lane barely wide enough for two-way traffic.

Izzy Morris eased off the accelerator and braked into the last of the road's few curves; the tall trees crowding either side of the road fell away to reveal a small parking area with a large lake in the background. Two Kinsey PD units were there, both with their bar lights flashing. One had parked near the south end, where the campground's trail began. The other unit idled near the entrance to the lot, partially blocking the road. Not surprisingly, she saw Stanley's Audi. After she'd called him about Natalie, he'd said he would meet her here.

Parked next to the Audi was Detective Billick's pickup. Four other vehicles occupied various spots in the lot. Three were SUVs with trailer hitches and probably belonged to campers.

The fourth was Jimmy Cain's Mustang.

It sat at the far end of the lot, near the path that led down to the beach and Black Pine Lake. At night, with its unfettered view of the water and the sprinkling of cabin lights that decorated the shoreline, the parking lot was a popular gathering place for teenagers. That's why she had a unit run through here nightly to break up any parties.

Which made her wonder what had happened last night. Why wasn't Jimmy's car spotted then? The situation investigated *then*?

Izzy rolled to a stop next to the unit blocking the exit. Patrolman Carlton Manick heaved his bulk out from behind the steering wheel. His uniform was wrinkled, the flesh under his eyes puffy, giving him a wounded, sullen look. One hand held a large take-out coffee container.

"Chief," he said, nodding slightly. "Hope you don't mind I let your husband in. Said he was with you last night." He smirked.

"Figured that's as tight an alibi as anyone's gonna get."

Izzy ignored his innuendo. "Has anyone found my daughter?"

"Nope. Just the DB. James Elijah Cain. Age seventeen. Chewed up real good, too. Probably a bear."

Izzy frowned. "How'd we get the positive ID?"

Carlton opened his mouth to speak, but then hesitated, his expression growing uncertain. After a few moments, he said, "Well, I...uh...turned the body over. So I could get to his wallet."

"You did wait for Sten, right?"

"Um...no."

"Damn it, Carlton. What were you thinking?"

"Come on, Chief. It's not like we're dealing with a homicide. Wait'll you see that kid. Seriously, only an animal could've done that to him."

Izzy clamped down on her frustration. Now wasn't the time. Later, when things settled down, she'd deal with his incompetence. She waved a hand as if she were shooing away an annoying fly. "Just stay here and don't let anyone in or out until I say so."

"Sure," Carlton replied, sounding relieved. When he took another pull at his coffee, his hand was trembling.

She nodded at the coffee. "And what'd I tell you about coming in to work hung over?"

His smirk returned. "It's lack of sleep. Al Hamilton needed last night off. Stacy had her ten-year reunion, so I took his shift." She must have looked confused, because he quickly added, "You approved the overtime."

Yes, she did, though she'd only just now remembered. And her look wasn't confusion about the overtime. It was the realization that—

"You were the one on patrol last night."

It was Carlton's turn to frown. "You sure you're all right, Chief?"

"What time did you swing through here last night? Through *this* parking lot?"

There was a flicker of hesitation as Carlton put the pieces together. "Oh, I dunno. Nine-twenty. Maybe nine-thirty, tops."

"And you never saw that bright yellow Mustang? The one over there, with the driver's door open? The one sticking out like a sore thumb?"

He shrugged, his eyes drifting over to Jimmy's car. "Must've arrived after my drive through."

"And when was that again?"

"Nine-thirty."

"Little early for a drive through, given there was a school dance last night. You sure about that time?"

"Positive," he said, then added with a note of asperity, "Something you want to say to me, Chief?"

Izzy nodded. "Only the obvious: my daughter was last seen with the guy driving the Mustang you *claim* you didn't see when you *claim* you swung through here last night—the same guy I'm told is lying dead up in those woods. And now my daughter is missing." She gestured to the trail. "I don't know if she's back in the forest somewhere. I don't know if she managed to escape what happened to Jimmy. I don't know where she is—but I do intend to find her. So when you tell me you were up here around nine-thirty and that car wasn't parked there, I'll have to take your word for it. Conduct my investigation accordingly." She leaned her head out the window. "And if I find out you're lying—that you're putting my daughter's life in danger—I will make sure you never work in law enforcement again.

"Now, you still want to stick to your story?"

Carlton Manick stood motionless, his coffee seemingly forgotten. He was glaring at her, his jaw clenched, the muscles beneath his thin skin bunching like fists.

Long moments passed, the silence thickening the air between them.

Izzy said, "Something you want to say to *me*, Officer Manick?"

Carlton pulled in a deep breath, his nostrils flaring. He held the air for a moment. Izzy thought he was going to start shouting, and in her current mood, she would have welcomed it.

Then his muscles relaxed. He seemed to deflate as his breath seeped out from between lips that had spread into a solicitous grin.

"Sorry, Chief. I understand your daughter's missing, and that's got you on edge. I really do. But yes, I was up here last night. At nine-thirty. And no, the Mustang wasn't here."

He took a casual sip from his coffee cup.

Izzy cocked an eyebrow at her patrolman. She kept silent and simply stared at him.

Carlton Manick held her gaze for several seconds. Then his eyes drifted downward. A slight frown eroded the edges of his grin. Swirling the coffee in his cup, he tried to nonchalantly bring it up to his lips for another sip, but his hand was trembling again.

When he looked up, Izzy made sure her eyes were locked onto his.

His smile was gone—he looked completely subdued. Like the small child he was inside, Carlton couldn't stand the silent reproach of an authority figure.

"Radio Sten," she said tersely. "Ask him to meet me at the Mustang. I want him to walk me through what he has so far."

Carlton hesitated, only a moment, and then nodded.

"Sure, Chief," he said. "And...good luck finding your daughter."

"You and I are not done with this," she told him. "Not even close."

CHAPTER

3

Izzy had just completed her first circuit around the Mustang when Sten Billick emerged from the trail.

Even this early on a Saturday morning, he wore dark slacks, a sport coat, and an unassuming blue tie. His face was all sharp planes and angles, giving him a gritty, tenacious look. White hair fell casually across his brow. Beneath eyes like flakes of granite, he had a sharp nose, ideal for cutting through bullshit and getting right to the point.

He saw her, gave a curt nod, and made his way across the dirt parking lot. They met at the open driver's door of the Mustang.

"Chief," Sten said. He gestured to a group of people huddled together near the drive down into the campgrounds. "These campers didn't see anything. You mind if I release them?"

Izzy nodded her approval, then pointed at her husband's Audi. "Where's Stanley?"

"Up at the crime scene. He was looking around for signs of your daughter. We're keeping him away from the evidence."

"Any sign of Natalie?"

He didn't answer. Simply stared at her.

She felt a stab of fear. "What is it? What'd you find?"

"First of all," he cautioned, "it may have nothing to do with Natalie. But there are two sets of footprints around the body. One—"

"What do you mean, 'the body'? Don't we have a positive ID?" Maybe the body wasn't Jimmy's—maybe this was a horrible, nightmarish misunderstanding.

Sten glanced back up the trail. "Most likely it's Jimmy. His car's here. The body seems the right size and age. And thanks to Carlton's blunder, I have his ID."

"But you're not certain?"

"That's the point. It's impossible to tell." He grimaced. "He's—well, you'll see. The damage is significant."

"All right," she said, her spirits sinking. "What about the footprints?"

"There are two different sets. One's larger and looks like the vic's. The other's smaller, probably female. But that doesn't necessarily mean they're Natalie's." He paused for a moment. "Let's work under the assumption that the body is Jimmy Cain. Even though he and Nat went to the dance together, maybe she didn't come up here with him. Sometimes dates go wrong—"

Izzy raised a hand to stop him. "I already talked to Katie Bethel. She confirmed that Jimmy and Natalie were coming up here after the dance. They were supposed to meet back at Katie's house but never showed." She blinked back tears. "That was the last time she saw my daughter. Driving off with Jimmy."

Sten took a moment to process this information. "But the other prints, they weren't a woman's dress shoe."

Izzy wiped at her eyes. "She took a change of clothes. Jeans, a white shirt, and her Skechers."

Sten looked lost for a moment, his hand absently scrubbing the top of his head, his eyes tracking the few fishing boats trawling for pike along the surface of Black Pine Lake. Finally, his shoulders slumped.

"This is some fucked up shit, Izzy."

She and Sten were approaching the bend in the trail where Jimmy's body had been found.

This deep into the woods, the trees practically surrounded them; only a narrow swath of blue sky could be seen above the boughs. And while the trail was wide enough for them to walk two abreast, they occasionally had to duck under low-hanging branches or step over deadfalls. In the daylight, hiking this trail would be challenging; at night, even with the full moon, it would be damned treacherous.

By Izzy's estimate, they had covered about half a mile.

Up ahead, Bob Talbert walked along the tree line, searching the ground. Jimmy's body lay several yards before the bend, a dark plastic tarp covering him.

There was no sign of Stanley.

Stopping at Jimmy's body, Izzy said, "Bob, where's my husband?"

Bob Talbert stopped and gestured to where the path continued beyond the bend. "Took off that way. When he realized I wasn't going to let him get close and contaminate the crime scene, he headed out to see if he can find some sign of your daughter. He was shouting her name, but I haven't heard him for a while now." He got that uncomfortable look again. "I'm not sure he should be up here, Chief."

Izzy nodded. "I know, but what was I supposed to do? He's my husband. I couldn't tell him to stay away."

"Bob's got a point," Sten agreed quietly. "It's bad police procedure to have a civilian here, let alone the father of a missing girl."

"I'm her mother," she said, frustration creeping into her words. "Should I stay away too?"

"See what I mean?" Sten replied. "You're trained for this, and already it's getting to you."

Izzy forced herself to relax. "I understand what you both are saying, but for now, he stays. We'll deal with the rest as it comes." Her eyes strayed to the plastic tarp. "Let's get this over with."

"You sure you want to do this?"

She swallowed past a lump in her throat. It would be difficult seeing Jimmy's remains, knowing that her daughter was last seen with him. "I have to. It's my job."

"We're going to have to call his parents soon. See if Jimmy's actually at home."

"I know," Izzy said. She hated making these types of calls, but this one would be especially rough. She and Stanley had known the Cains for years. Denny worked as the assistant manager at Stanley's drug store. And while he had some rough edges, he was generally a likable man. Maddie, on the other hand, was a sweetheart. News of her son's death was going to crush her.

Sten crouched down and grasped one edge of the tarp. "You ready?"

Izzy nodded, and Sten lifted the tarp away from the body.

She stiffened. Jimmy had been ripped to shreds, his face reduced to a pulpy mass of lacerations. A large flap of skin had been peeled back near the hairline, exposing part of his skull. One blow had torn clean through both cheeks—his jaw hung obscenely open, his tongue poking through the destroyed flesh like some kind of pink slug. His eyes were missing, taken either by whatever had attacked him or by forest scavengers.

But it was his chest—

"Where's...?"

Sten nodded toward the tree line. There, lying among the trees like a piece of discarded trash, was Jimmy's ribcage. Something had torn it completely out of his body.

"Jesus," whispered Izzy. "What could have done this?"

"No idea." Sten lowered the tarp. "I've never seen anything like it."

"Animal tracks?"

"A few. I've marked them off."

"We'll need DNR up here. Maybe they can tell us what we're dealing with."

"I've already put in the call."

"Hey." Bob Talbert was waving them over. "You guys are gonna want to see this."

"What've you got?" Izzy asked as they walked over to him.

"There," Bob replied, pointing to a spot on the ground.

Izzy crouched down. Sten followed suit.

There was a small amount of dark fluid mixed in with the dirt. Its shape was uneven, as if it had been rubbed or smeared by something. Part of a leaf was stuck in it, making her think the fluid was viscous. To Izzy, it looked like congealed blood.

She glanced over at Jimmy's body. It lay several feet away. And the ground showed no evidence that he'd been dragged there.

"And here," Sten added, pointing to a low, sharp branch coated with blood.

Izzy stared for a moment, trying to puzzle together the meaning of the blood and the branch. "Where's the ME?"

"On his way," Sten answered. "Apparently he'd gone fishing. Muskellunge Lake. No cell coverage. Someone had to boat out and get him."

"Make sure he types this. Nat's is A negative. I don't know Jimmy's blood type."

Sten paused. After an uncomfortable silence, he said, "You got it, Chief."

Izzy frowned. "What? What's the matter?"

"Nothing. I'll tell the ME to put a rush on the blood typing. Make sure the results are forwarded to your office."

Forwarded to my—? That's when she realized she'd been issuing orders as if she were taking over his investigation.

"Sten…look, I'm sorry. You're lead on this. Everything goes through your office." She made a helpless gesture with her hands. "I wasn't thinking."

"You can run this, Chief. I'd understand."

"No, I want you on it. I'd be too close, too emotional. I might miss something. Really, I'm sorry."

"No worries. I understand. Hell, I'd behave the same if it were one of my kids." His face grew serious. "We'll find her, Izzy. Whatever it takes, we're going to bring her home."

She gave him a grateful smile, then heard a rustle of leaves. Turning, she saw Stanley round the corner of the trail.

His appearance shocked her. He must have been running through the woods for some time. Sweat had moistened his skin until he glistened. His damp hair hugged the contours of his skull. Branches had scratched fine lines across his cheeks. His clothes were a semaphore of torn fabric.

But it was his eyes that disturbed her the most.

She had expected the bloodshot, puffy glare of a panicked father. But Stanley…his eyes had a darker cast, more bruised, as if they had been battered by his worst fears.

"I want to know," he said evenly, his eyebrows drawing together, "where the hell you've been."

She felt Sten go still. Next to him, Bob Talbert shifted slightly, eyes cast down, his hand settling casually on the butt of his gun.

"I've been here." She stepped forward, putting her body between him and her officers. "Trying to figure out what happened."

"What happened?" Stanley said. "Who the hell cares *what happened*? The only thing that matters is that Natalie's missing. Our little girl is gone."

"Stanley, please. We're doing what we can to find her."

"By standing around?" he exploded, throwing his arms in the air. "Why aren't you out there, searching the woods? Don't you have dogs that can track her? Or—or a helicopter? Something that can fly overhead and look?"

"You're jumping to the end of this. There's a process to an investigation. We follow specific procedures because they work. It's the quickest way to—"

"Quit talking to me like a cop! Talk to me as my wife—as the mother of our missing daughter."

"—to *find* Natalie," she finished, her voice climbing. "I want that, too. More than anything, I want to find my baby. But if I waste resources on an assumption, then I do more harm than good. I need to know what happened before I can decide where to look."

"Oh, come on," Stanley said, his frown deepening. "It doesn't take a Columbo to figure this out. Jimmy and Nat came up here after the dance. For whatever reason, they decided to take a walk. Something attacked Jimmy. Now Nat's missing. She probably ran away from whatever"—he gestured toward Jimmy's tarp-covered body—"did that. Now she's lost in the woods, which is where we should be searching. How goddamn complicated is that?"

Izzy nodded. "Okay, let's say you're right. Let's say she got away from whatever killed Jimmy. As soon as the sun came up, she'd have her bearings. She'd know that if she walked west, she'd either hit the trail or the lake. Either way, she should be able to find her way out."

Except, she thought, for the blood and the branch. They bothered her.

If the blood turned out to be Natalie's, that meant she was hurt, possibly seriously. She might not be able to get out. Then again, if she was hurt, how could she have gotten away from whatever attacked Jimmy? Nothing about this made sense.

"So all you're going to do is sit and wait?" asked Stanley. "Hope our little girl shows up?"

Izzy looked at Sten. He gave her a "go for it" shrug. Turning back to Stanley, she said, "We're going to continue our investigation. Sten'll wait here for the crime scene people. And Carlton will stay down by the lake. If Natalie shows up, we'll know. I'm going to go talk with J.J. Sallinen. He was one of the last persons to see Natalie and Jimmy together. Maybe he knows something."

Stanley's hands clenched into fists. "That's it? You're not going to search for her?"

"I'm going to put the word out. If she doesn't show up in the next couple of hours, we'll organize a search party to comb the woods. We may be able to get a few hours in before nightfall. But it'll probably be tomorrow morning before we have enough people to really go through those woods."

"And what am I supposed to do?"

"I want you to go home." She put up her hands to forestall another outburst. "I need you there in case she calls."

"I'm not leaving her alone in these woods."

"Dr. Morris." Sten Billick stepped up next to Izzy. "If your daughter managed to get away from whatever killed the Cain boy, then she's also likely to find her way out of here. And what do you think she'll do first? She'll call home." He nodded his head toward Stanley. "She's going to need her dad. And you'll want to be there for her."

Stanley shot the detective a look that could've chipped paint from a wall. His body tensed, and Izzy thought he was going to throw a punch. Then he began to tremble. With tears spilling from the corners of his eyes, he started walking stiffly down the trail.

"I'll let you know if I she calls," he said. "Find her, Iz. Please, just find her."

Izzy watched until he disappeared from view. How could she be so uncertain about her feelings for him, yet still ache to see him hurting?

Turning to Sten, Izzy said, "Keep looking. I'll let you know what J.J. has to say."

"Good luck with that one," he grunted. "I hope for your sake his dad isn't home."

CHAPTER
4

Izzy's police cruiser slowed as it approached the Sallinen house at the end of Ryanwood Street. She saw Jack Sallinen's black Mercedes CL 600 parked in the driveway and swore under her breath. Her day was about to get worse, if that were even possible.

She parked behind the Benz, then headed up the front walk.

Two large oaks shaded the expensive colonial. Along the front of the house, manicured tea roses mingled with designer shrubs. Jack Sallinen had even replaced the concrete walkway with red paver stones. The landscaping alone had to have cost at least fifteen grand.

Must have been nice.

At the front door, she pulled out her notepad and rang the doorbell.

A few moments later, the door opened. Instead of Jack, his son Kevin stepped out onto the porch. The eight-year-old wore blue pajamas that ended about two inches shy of his ankles. Unruly black hair framed his face. His eyes roamed the landscape, skimming over everything but her. In one hand, he held a Pop-Tart. In the other, a piece of paper with a drawing on it.

"Hello, Kevin," she said gently.

"Pop smart." He held out the half-eaten pastry.

"Yes, I see. It looks yummy." Pointing to the paper, she added, "Did you draw that?"

At first Kevin didn't respond. She was about to repeat her question when he lifted the paper toward her. On it was a crayon picture of an animal. Although the drawing was limited to brown and black smears, Izzy could make out four limbs and an elongated body. The head looked a little wolfish. He'd added raindrops and lightning bolts.

"That's wonderful. What is it?"

"Fickle-fek."

His answer puzzled but didn't surprise her. The boy's autism made conversations difficult.

Izzy heard a door shut and looked up. Jack Sallinen had emerged from a room and was striding down the hallway toward them, his face a mixture of anger and resentment.

At the doorway, he crouched down next to his son. "Hey buddy, why don't you go watch some TV? Or maybe draw me another picture? I think I can find a spot on the fridge."

Kevin nodded, turned—then stopped. He held out the drawing to Izzy.

She frowned slightly. "Yes, I saw. It's lovely."

He gave the picture a little shake.

Finally understanding the boy's intent, Izzy nodded and took the picture. "Thank you."

Wordlessly, Kevin retreated into the house.

Okay, she thought. Time to deal with the dad.

Jack Sallinen stood. He was dressed casually in beige chinos, a polo shirt, and deck shoes. His brown hair was neatly combed, his cheeks clean-shaven. Even though he had put on a few extra pounds over the years, Izzy couldn't help but begrudge how handsome he was. At least, on the surface.

"Chief Morris," he said, glancing at her shorts and sweatshirt. She hadn't had time to change. "Can I help you with something?"

"I'd like to talk to J.J.. Is he here?"

"He just got back from the gym," he said, a puzzled look on his face. "He's in the shower. Why? What's this about?"

"Something happened last night."

Jack stepped outside and closed the door behind him. "And this 'something' involves my son?"

She briefly summarized the events of the morning.

"The Cain boy's dead?" Jack said, sounding amazed. "But I still don't understand. What's this got to do with J.J.?"

"He was Jimmy's best friend. He and Katie were at the dance with Jimmy and Natalie. Maybe he saw or heard something last night that can help us understand what happened."

"I see," he muttered, apparently lost in thought.

"Jack, this is serious. I've got a dead boy, and my daughter is missing. She could be hurt. I really need to hurry on this. So please, could you go get your son?"

"Tell me," said Jack. "Have you determined whether the Cain boy's death was accidental or intentional?"

"What? I don't see how—?"

"Please bear with me. Do you think his death was an accident or not?"

Where the hell was he going with this? "It's too soon to tell. And that's all I'm going to say at this point."

"So, it *could* go either way. We could, at some point, be talking about a possible homicide?"

"I'm sorry," she said, irritated at the man's persistent stalling. "I'm simply not going to discuss an ongoing case. Now, if you wouldn't mind, I'd like to talk to J.J.."

Jack was silent for a moment, then he shook his head. "I'm sorry, Chief Morris. I can't let you involve him in this. Just being questioned by the police...people might get the wrong impression. I won't risk the taint of a criminal investigation getting attached to his name. And I do have my own reputation to consider."

Izzy slowly lowered her pad and pen. "You're worried about reputations? Okay, maybe you didn't understand me, so I'll say it again, this time in short sentences." She spoke her next words with exaggerated clarity. "My daughter is missing. J.J. might know something. I need to talk to him."

Jack's expression darkened. "Do you think he's involved with your daughter's disappearance? Or the Cain boy's death?"

"Of course not. I'm just trying to—"

"So he isn't a suspect of any kind? This isn't part of an official investigation?"

"I still have a missing person. I need to know what your son might—"

"Is it or isn't it a formal investigation?"

Izzy paused. Reluctantly, she said, "No. Not yet. Natalie hasn't been missing long enough. But I am asking for a little cooperation here."

"Then this conversation really needs to be over, doesn't it?" He turned to open the front door, then stopped and glanced back over his shoulder. "I do understand how important this is. And I will talk with my son. I promise. If he has anything to add, I'll let you know." He gave her a sympathetic look, stepped into his house, and closed the door. The muted click of the deadbolt signaled an end to their discussion.

Izzy Morris stood there a moment, debating if she should push her luck and start kicking the door. But as much as she hated to admit it, he did have a point. She had no authority to demand an interview. Not yet. Not until she knew more.

She looked down at Kevin's drawing, stuck it in the back of the notepad, and turned to leave.

From inside the Sallinen house, Jack watched as Chief Morris climbed into her cop car and drove off.

He despised Morris and her ilk—the Be Nothings that infested the world.

Long ago, when Jack was young boy sitting at the dining room table doing his homework, his father would often plop down next to him, beer in hand, and preach about the perils of the Be Nothings: *Don't let 'em get the better of you, son. They're everywhere. Mostly coloreds, like that uppity King fella down south, but they can jus' as easily be real God-fearing Americans. They're the vermin of the world, Jacky, scurrying 'round like rats and spreading diseases called* welfare *and* equal rights. *And they hate us. They hate us with a fervor passion! They see what we got and they want it. But are they willin' to work for it? Hell no! They stand 'round with hat in hand and that gimme-gimme look on their faces and never say so much as a thank you and then call it* progress. *Stay sharp, son. Never let the Be Nothings stand in your way.*

It was one of the few lessons his father had tried to teach him that made any sense. Despite the man's distasteful prejudices, his concerns about the Be Nothings had resonated with Jack. And Jack had come to understand them better than his old man: no one was born a Be Nothing—the condition wasn't based on race or creed. A person *chose* to be *nothing* in life. Chose to ignore the opportunities the world had to offer. Refused to take what he wanted and seize it for his own.

In Jack's opinion, a Be Nothing lacked ambition, plain and simple.

And the thought of anyone living like that galled him.

Moving away from the window, Jack walked down the short hallway into his office. He closed the doors and engaged the lock. At his desk, he pulled out a key, unlocked a drawer, and withdrew a locked, gray metal box. Inside that box were color photos. He'd found them this morning in a large unmarked envelope, exactly where he'd been told to look: wedged between the front left tire of his Benz and the steering assembly.

He grabbed his cell, thumbed the buttons.

A man answered on the third ring. "Yes, Jack?"

"Morris was here. She's looking for her kid."

"Excellent. It's started already."

"This whole thing's got me nervous. I don't want to lose everything I've worked for."

"*Again,* what you have is small compared to what you can attain. Keep that in mind."

Jack fanned the photos out on his desk top. "I have the gift you left me."

"Yes," the man said trenchantly. "And I'm already regretting it."

"Why?" He traced his finger over the glossy surfaces, then lifted one to his nose and inhaled deeply. "I like them."

"Just be careful. If anyone sees them, you *will* lose everything— and more."

Jack ignored the threat. "So what's next?"

"I'm early. Pulled in last night. Right now I'm trying to find a place to stay."

"Is there something you want me to do?"

"Not at the moment. Later, yes. But for now, just sit tight."

"I hope you don't plan on waiting too long. You've promised me a lot."

"Relax, Jack. I'll call you when it's time to move." The man clicked off.

Jack closed his cell, then picked up the photos, feeling his heart accelerate.

It was finally going to come to him. Everything he'd worked for.

The thrill was almost too much to contain.

* * *

Eugene Vincent thumbed the switch on the old Budweiser sign that hung in the front window. The circuitry stuttered and hitched like an old man's heart, and he wondered briefly if the Big Red Bow Tie was finally going toes up on him—or in this case, tubes up. But then the electrodes sparked, the gas flared, and he heard the high, hard hum of electricity surging through the sign. He smiled. In the afternoon sun, the neon glow would be nearly invisible—a chemical ghost. At night, it would blush pale red, almost pink. Not exactly the most masculine color for a bar, but that didn't bother him. He was never one to worry about what other people thought.

He walked gingerly to the front door, navigating around white laminate tables with their shiny metal napkin dispensers and wire condiments racks filled with bottles of catsup and mustard and A-1 sauce, and disengaged the lock. He flipped the sign over so the CLOSED side faced him.

Three o'clock sharp. The Lula was open for business.

He turned, careful not to aggravate his back.

While the Lula wasn't very different from other small town bars—booze and burgers were still his moneymakers—he had worked hard to make it unique. And with a name like Gene Vincent, picking a theme hadn't been difficult.

Instead of the typical beer memorabilia hanging on the walls, he'd hunted down and framed vintage concert posters. There was one for Bill Haley and the Comets at the Old Orchard Beach Pier, another for Little Richard at the Armory Dance Center. And his personal favorite, a poster for Buddy Holly with the Big Bopper and Richie Valens, all performing together at the Laramar Ballroom. The gig took place four days before they would die tragically in a plane crash outside Clear Lake, Iowa.

He also knew he would need music, so he'd installed a digital jukebox filled with oldies. And not oldies as in 70s oldies, either. He was talking *real* oldies, with songs by guys sporting nicknames like Fats and Killer and the King—people with real talent, belting out hit after hit, long before the advent of vocal tuning gimmickry.

In keeping with the motif, Gene had installed a small stage for live music. The sound system consisted of a vintage Music Man amp and a mic connected to two speakers mounted from the ceiling; basically enough for someone to sit on a stool and noodle around on a guitar. He kept putting out ads for musicians, but so far all he'd gotten were long-haired Metallica wannabes and crusty old farts whose musical repertoire ended before Chuck Berry first duck-walked across a stage.

He had a musician coming in next weekend, but he'd given up hope of finding anyone good. The pay simply wasn't sufficient to attract real talent.

Across the room, a bar ran the length of the wall, an elegant oak construct with old 45 rpm records inlayed into the surface and treble clefs carved into the wainscoting. He'd bought half a dozen old-fashioned, square-ringed bar stools with the thickly padded seats covered in bright red vinyl. He'd even replaced the draft beer pull-handles with customized guitar necks, the style of beer printed along the fret board.

Cool, daddy-o.

The kitchen door to the right of the bar creaked open. Sam Burkardt poked out his head, his long black hair tied into a ponytail and held back with a hair net.

"The grill's ready to go, boss. Deep fryers still need about fifteen. Other than that, we're ready to rock and roll."

Sam was his cook, and a pretty damn good one. Years ago, he had left Kinsey behind to attend culinary school. Then, as the excesses of the 90s came crashing down, the job offers fell faster than a bad soufflé. So he decided to move back to Kinsey. When Gene ran into him years later, Sam had been working odd jobs to make ends meet. And when Gene decided to open a bar, Sam had jumped at the chance to cook again.

Two Kinsey ex-pats had come home to roost and had ended up working in the same coop.

"Let's hope we get an encore," Gene said, smiling.

Sam kept staring at him, lips pursed.

"Something on your mind, Sam?"

"Sorry. You were standing there, you know, real still. Like maybe you'd jacked your back up again."

"I'm fine. See?" Gene did a quick soft-shoe shuffle, his hands scissoring in front of him. The movement sent a wave of pain washing down his left hip and leg, but he kept his smile. "Now quit playing Mother Hen and go work on the chili. And cut back on the peppers this time. My blisters haven't healed from your last batch."

Sam nodded solemnly. "Sure, boss. But you ain't fooling me. You're sweating." Then he retreated into the kitchen.

As soon as Sam was gone, Gene grabbed the nearest chair for support. Breathing heavily, he pulled several napkins from the dispenser and mopped his face. It took a minute or two of standing still before low tide returned and the pain receded to a dull throb.

Keep moving. Don't let your back stiffen up.

He stepped carefully to the bar, flipped up the swing top, and maneuvered behind it. He didn't want to sit; that only made his back worse. Instead he found a damp rag and began wiping down the bar top.

He was almost done when the front door opened. Through it stepped Chet Boardman, one of his regulars. He was followed by another figure, a black man carrying a guitar case and some kind of large duffel.

Chet strolled over to the bar, his boots scraping against the linoleum. He slid comfortably onto one of the bar stools. "The usual, Gene."

As Gene started on the bourbon and cola, the stranger took the seat next to Chet. He leaned his guitar case against the bar and set the duffel on the empty stool beside him.

Chet scooted one seat over—away from the stranger.

With a puzzled look, Gene placed the drink in front of Chet, followed by a bowl of snack mix. He turned to the stranger. "What can I do you for?"

The man studied the bottles lined behind the bar. "Whiskey and water?"

"Sure thing. Premium or house?"

"House is fine."

Gene grabbed a bottle and quickly placed the drink in front of the man. "Four-fifty."

The stranger pulled out a five and laid it on the bar. "Keep the change."

Nodding his thanks, Gene set out another bowl of mix.

The man sipped his drink, then asked, "You the owner?"

Gene extended his hand. "Eugene Vincent."

The man shook it. "Bart Owens." He gestured to his guitar case. "I'm here for the job."

Gene had to think for a moment. "The stage gig?"

Owens nodded. "I'm a little early."

"I'm sorry, but—" He stared at the man. "You're the guy I talked to? The one who's supposed to start next week?"

"That'd be me," Owens said with a quick grin. "I was hoping to start *this* weekend, if you don't mind. You know, earn a little extra cash. Make it worth the trip."

Gene gave the man a closer look. His black hair was shot through with gray, his dark skin smooth with only hints of the usual crow's feet or laugh lines. His eyes were an unusual bright blue, like sapphires. But what caught Gene's attention was the teardrop-shaped mark under his left eye. He'd seen gang members and ex-cons with similar tats.

"When we talked on the phone, you said you'd be traveling to get here. I'd assumed you meant from somewhere nearby, like Traverse City or Marquette."

Picking up his drink, Owens took another sip. "No, I meant from out of state."

"Wisconsin?"

"Nope. Nashville."

"You came all the way from Tennessee? To play here?"

Owens shrugged. "A job's a job."

"But...?"

"The pay's still the same, right? Friday and Saturday nights. Fifty a night, plus tips."

Before Gene could respond, Chet signaled from two seats away. "Running on fumes here, Gene."

Reluctantly, Gene turned away from Owens. After fixing a new drink, he leaned over and set the bourbon and cola in front of Chet. It wasn't much of a bend, but that was the pisser with bad backs: it often doesn't take much. Pain drilled into him like an auger.

Chet must have caught his expression. "You all right?"

"I'm fine," Gene said, grimacing. Then he slid a menu over to Chet. "Why don't you order something? I don't want to see you drunk by six."

Chet snorted. "Dodge and evade. You'd've made a good politician."

"And your concern is?"

"I understand pain," said Chet, holding up his hands. His fingers were gnarled and bent. "See these? Forty years of fishing—day after day, haulin' in nets of Menominee and lake trout. Me and pain, we know each other well."

"Chronic pain can be stressful," Owens added quietly.

When Chet scowled at the old man, Gene leaned in and whispered into Chet's ear. "Whatever your problem is, get over it. Or you can find somewhere else to drink."

Chet shifted his scowl to the depths of his drink, but he kept quiet.

"I have back problems," Gene explained to Owens. "And hip. And leg. A few years back, a drunk driver ran a red light. Plowed right into me. I got pretty messed up." He'd spent weeks in the hospital, and then months in rehab. He'd lost his construction job in Chicago, and his injury had made him too much of a liability to other employers. It was a memory he'd love to forget. "It still gives me trouble now and again."

Owens sipped at his drink. "You have my sympathies, sir."

"Anyway," Gene said, wanting to change the subject. "Back to business. You're okay with two nights a week? Hundred bucks plus tips?"

Owens nodded. "I can't afford to be picky."

"How long do you want the gig for?"

"Can we try the next two weekends? Then see what happens from there."

"You want to leave this open ended?"

"Spontaneity keeps me young."

"Spontaneity doesn't pay the bills," Gene returned. "I don't see how you can survive on a hundred a week."

"I believe that's my concern."

"I just don't want you skipping out because you've run out of cash."

"I'll be here," Owens insisted. "I'm a man of my word."

Gene stared at the man, and then shrugged. "You're the man with a guitar. You can start tonight."

The kitchen door swung open and Celeste Florin walked in. She was an attractive brunette with a slim figure. After waving hello to Gene, she glided up to Chet and gave him a friendly hug. "I know how you hate being kissed by pretty young women." Then she planted a wet one on his cheek.

He smiled and shooed her away. "You're enough to give a man a heart attack."

Celeste grinned and stepped behind the bar. After tying an apron around her waist, she grabbed the rag Gene had been using to wipe down the bar and started on the tabletops.

Chet's face grew somber. He slipped his red-and-black checkered cap off his head and ran a hand over his balding pate. To Gene, he said, "You heard about what happened?"

Gene shook his head. "Nope. Been here all day."

"You remember Denny Cain's son, Jimmy? He was found dead up

near the campgrounds." Chet took a deep pull of his drink. "Heard it was an animal attack. He was all chewed up."

Gene couldn't remember ever meeting Jimmy, but his father was another regular at the Lula. "That's terrible."

"Yeah, I guess it was pretty gruesome." He swirled the ice around in his glass. "Sometimes you see this kind of thing during hunting season. Some idiot with too much beer and too few deer gets lost in the woods. Ends up as bear bait." He put his cap back on. "But those two were on a hiking trail and should've been fine."

Gene frowned. "He wasn't alone?"

"Nope." Chet downed the rest of his drink and pushed the empty glass toward Gene. "Natalie Morris was with him. I guess they went to a dance together and then headed up to the campgrounds for a little fun."

"Fun?" Gene said, still frowning. He picked up a clean glass and dumped some ice into it. "On a hiking trail, in the dark?"

"Ain't saying I understand kids these days."

"What does Natalie have to say about it?"

"She ain't saying nuthin'. She's missing."

Gene stopped pouring the bourbon. "Missing?"

Chet nodded. "If she don't show up, there's gonna be a big search tomorrow. Izzy's trying to get a bunch of people to help." He looked sharply at Gene. "Say, ain't you—?"

"Natalie's godfather," Gene finished.

"Aw shit, I'm sorry," said Chet, his weathered face pink with embarrassment. "I shoulda told you right away."

"And this was last night?" asked Gene.

"Yeah," Chet said. "They been looking for her all morning."

An uneasy feeling grew in Gene. Why hadn't Stanley or Izzy called? He would have dropped everything to help. "Well, I'm sure they've found her by now."

"Yeah," Chet repeated, though he sounded doubtful. "I'm sure you're right."

Gene noticed that Owens' glass was empty. Tapping the bar, he asked, "Get you another one, Mr. Owens?"

"Huh?" Owens said, startled. "Oh, no thanks."

Gene gave him a curious look. "You okay?"

"Just hungry, I guess. Is your cook any good?"

"Best in the Upper, if you ask me."

"You think he'd be willing to whip up something special? I haven't had a good meal in a while."

Gene shrugged. "Sure. Any preferences?"

"Not really," Owens said with a shake of his head. "I can't boil water without burning it, so anything would be a treat."

Gene turned to Celeste. "Tell Sam that a guy out here wants to see what kind of magic he can conjure up."

As Celeste breezed through the door into the kitchen, Owens said, "One more thing. Do you know where I could find a place to stay? Nothing fancy, just somewhere to put my things and get some sleep?"

"That depends on how far you want to drive."

"It has to be nearby," Owens said. "I don't have a car."

"How'd you get here?"

"Took a bus," the man said. "Then walked the rest of the way."

"You walked all the way here from, what, Newberry?"

Owens slid his empty glass toward Gene. "There's not much of a taxi service up here."

"No," Gene said warily, taking the glass. "I guess not." He thought for a moment. "There's a small place about a mile away. You can try there. But we're talking more than a hundred a week."

"I'll check it out after I eat," said Owens. "What time do you want me to start?"

Gene got the message: mind your own business, barkeep. "Nine okay with you?"

Owens nodded. "Nine's fine."

Celeste came out from the kitchen and set a meal in front of Owens. "Sam says enjoy."

Bart Owens thanked her. Then he attacked his meal with such ferocity that Gene wondered when the man had eaten last.

CHAPTER
5

The sun slid slowly, inexorably toward the horizon.

The encroaching darkness had made it impossible to continue the search for Natalie; the deadfalls and the uneven ground were too treacherous to navigate without sunlight. Izzy was desperate, but she wouldn't risk the lives of her colleagues. So, reluctantly, she'd told everyone to go home.

She, of course, had intended to stay and continue searching. Flashlight in hand, she'd planned to scour the ground until she uncovered some evidence of where her daughter had gone. But when Sten had learned of her plan, he'd protested strongly that she was making a bad situation worse by putting herself in danger. They had gone back and forth, neither giving ground, until Sten had pulled his trump card: he'd told the others about her intentions. After that, no one would leave if she didn't agree to suspend her search for the night.

She'd been furious, mostly because she knew they were right. And she'd had little choice but to agree. So she had stowed her equipment in the trunk of the car and left the campgrounds, driving absently through town, relying on instinct to guide her.

When her cell buzzed, she looked idly at the screen. She'd gotten an email from the lab. Heart pounding, she pulled over. It contained test results. The blood found at the scene was type A negative. The same as Natalie's. Her baby was hurt.

With her mind reeling and her heart aching, she barely remembered pulling back onto the road. Now, as she turned into her driveway, the car's headlights washing across the façade of red bricks, Izzy noticed that the house was completely dark. All the lights were out, even the outside lights at each doorway and the two on the garage.

The neighbors on either side had their lights on, so power wasn't an issue.

Which meant either the lights had been purposefully turned off—or something had happened to interrupt the power *in* the house.

Stanley was supposed to be home. And if that was the case, why hadn't—

Her stomach clenching, she hurried up the walkway. The front door was locked. She fumbled for the correct key on her keychain, unlocked the door, then shouldered it open. Her hand went to the wall on her right. Her fingers scratched along the surface until she felt the toggle switch. She pressed the lower half, turning on the overhead foyer light.

Nothing. The house remained dark. Thin blades of yellow light penetrated through the living room blinds, providing some meager illumination, though not enough to see by.

Her hand went automatically for her gun, but she wasn't wearing it; she'd left the Glock locked in a metal box sitting on the top shelf of her bedroom closet. And the Maglite was back in the trunk of her car.

Shit.

"Stanley!" she called out. No reply. "Damn it, answer me!"

She strained to hear a voice, a scrape, a rattle—anything that would tell her that she wasn't alone in the house.

Silence. Silence…and darkness.

She kept a flashlight in the nightstand drawer next to her bed, so she decided to make for the bedroom. With her hands held out in front of her, she made her way through the dark heart of the house.

She turned left into the living room, taking small, careful steps, all the time listening. After a few feet, her knee bumped into something soft. The leather recliner. Okay. Shift right. Another step, and her fingers grazed what felt like stiff fabric: the shade for the lamp next to the sofa. Carefully, she slid her hand under the shade and felt for the little plastic knob. Finding it, she gave a twist; the sharp click sounded loud in the dead silence of the house. She wasn't surprised when nothing happened. Then, on impulse, she lifted her hand…and *was* surprised to discover the bulb missing.

Had someone—had *Stanley?*—removed all the light bulbs in the house? What possible reason could he have had for doing something so absurd?

Just off to her right were two hallways. One led to the bedrooms and the bathroom, the other to the kitchen and the dining room. She felt along the wall until she found the hallway leading to the bedrooms. She needed the flashlight, and her gun.

With one hand stretched out in front of her and the other running lightly against the right-hand wall, Izzy moved down the hallway. The darkness felt oppressive; it was like wading through a black sea. Her heart galloped in her chest.

After several steps, her right hand bumped up against a line of wood molding, and then the wall disappeared. The doorway to Natalie's room. Her and Stanley's bedroom was about ten feet further down the hallway.

Almost there.

She was about to take another step when she heard something. A noise of some kind. Like a whisper—or a whimper.

"Hello," she said, still wishing she had the security of her gun. "Stanley?"

Another sound. This time the rustling of cloth—movement.

It came from Natalie's room.

Izzy turned toward the doorway. "Stanley? This isn't funny. Are you in there?"

When she didn't get a reply, she stepped cautiously into the room. Then anoth—

POP!

Startled, she jerked her foot back. A light came on.

In the retreating darkness, Izzy saw her husband lying on Natalie's bed, his hand moving away from a small lamp on the nightstand. He had the comforter pulled up around his shoulders. A wet line of snot ran from his nose and down his whiskery cheek. He had obviously been crying.

And there, scattered on the carpet between the door and the bed like tiny land mines, were a dozen or so light bulbs. As far as Izzy could tell, Stanley had removed all of them—all except the one he'd left in Natalie's lamp. He had even removed the small colored bulbs she used in the hallway nightlights. There was a shattered bulb just inside the doorway. The noise she had heard was her foot breaking it.

She lifted her eyes. "Stanley, what's with the light bulbs?"

His eyes twitched to meet hers. "I can smell her, you know."

"You can what?"

"Smell her," he said, and his voice raised the hairs on her arms. It sounded desolate, like a man who had woken from a nightmare, only to find out he wasn't dreaming. "I can smell her. On this pillow, in the sheets. Her scent is everywhere."

"My God, what's happened to you?"

"God?" Stanley said. "God's got nothing to do with this. God would've brought my little girl home. Which is more than I can say for you, isn't it?"

"That's not fair." Stepping around the field of glass, Izzy approached the bed. "I've spent the entire day looking for her."

"Tell me, how did that go for you? Are there any leads? Are you 'hot on the trail'?"

Izzy sat down on the edge of the bed, Stanley's bent knees resting near her. Gesturing to the light bulbs, she said, "This isn't helping. We've both got to keep it together. If you start losing it...." She scrubbed her face with her hands. She was exhausted and didn't need this right now. "Look, there's going to be a search tomorrow morning. Lots of people have agreed to help. Something's going turn up."

"You're a day late and a dollar short, Iz. The search should've been done *today*."

"These things take time. I've done my best to pull everything together. And even if Natalie's hurt, we still have enough time to find her before—"

"She's not hurt. She's dead. I can tell." He knuckled his chest with a fist. "In here."

"It's only been a day," she said with a hint of irritation. "We need to stay positive."

"It's that feeling you get," Stanley went on as if he hadn't heard her. "You know, after your child is born. That connection, like some kind of psychic tether, that tells you she's all right. I've felt it every day—every *single* day—since Natalie was born. I felt her here, in my heart, and I knew she was okay. I don't feel that anymore. I don't feel anything."

"No," she said, her voice tight with anger. "You're not doing this. You're *not* giving up. Natalie needs you, now more than ever. You're her father. Start acting like one."

"I'm not giving up," Stanley said, his red-rimmed eyes narrowing. "I'm facing the facts. She never came out of those woods. She never found her way to a road or the trail. She didn't follow the shoreline to the campgrounds. She didn't do any of those things." He pulled the blanket up to his chin. "She didn't do any of those things, because she's dead."

She turned to face him, anger flaring within her. This self-centered apathy was what had driven a wedge between them. "I refuse to believe that. I refuse to even *consider* it. Our daughter is alive, damn it! And we're going to keep looking for her—both of us—and we aren't going to stop until we find her."

"Yes," he agreed. "We'll keep looking, but for different reasons." He sighed, and closed his eyes.

She returned to her earlier question. "Are you going to tell me what's with the light bulbs?"

"I don't know," he whispered. "The darkness made me feel safe. It hid anything that might remind me of Natalie. By taking away the light, it took away some of the pain." He gave an almost imperceptible shrug. "Guess I went a little overboard."

"Couldn't you have just turned them off?"

"It wouldn't have been the same." His voice was so low she had to lean in to hear him. "Don't ask me why, but it wouldn't have been the same."

"Okay, then why are they on the floor?"

"I was afraid."

"Afraid of what?"

"Natalie," he said. "I was afraid that she would come back—a dead, shuffling, shambling *thing*—and that she would accuse me, the man who was supposed to keep her safe, to protect her, of failing. I was afraid she would take me away and make me suffer for letting her die." He shivered. "The light bulbs were there to warn me.

"Now, go away and leave me alone."

Then he buried his face into the pillow.

Izzy wanted to tell him that Natalie wasn't coming for him, that it was his own misplaced guilt that stalked him, but decided that it would be heaping cruelty upon his own self-inflicted punishment.

She got up and started picking up the light bulbs. It wouldn't take her long to replace them.

There was already enough darkness in her life. She wasn't going to live in it.

* * *

Eugene Vincent prided himself on being pretty laid back. He wasn't surprised by much of anything. But now he stood behind his bar, a look of astonishment on his face.

Owens had plugged in his guitar—an expensive-looking Martin acoustic with custom pickups—into the amp. The Music Man wasn't intended for an acoustic guitar, but Owens had fiddled with the knobs along the front casing until he was satisfied. After tuning up the guitar, he'd started to play. And the man played well. Very well.

He'd opened with Fats Domino's "Ain't That a Shame." But instead of the usual upbeat, swing rhythm, he'd slowed it down, added breaks that weren't in the original, and gave it a bluesy feel.

The next five songs were also classic oldies hits. Again, they were transformed by the fingers and voice of Bart Owens into something deeper, more emotional.

Then the man shifted to rock songs. He changed the tuning on his guitar and slid into a slow, soulful rendition of Led Zeppelin's "The Rain Song." After a Stones' and a Beatles' tune, he launched into a jumping, rockabilly version of J.J. Cale's "After Midnight."

When he finished the song, Owens took a sip of water from a bottle sitting on the amp. He talked to the crowd for the first time that night.

"Thank you all for being here tonight. Hope you're enjoying the music. I'm going to take a brief break. Be right back."

He walked off the stage and headed for the restroom.

"Well, I'll be damned," Gene said, mostly to himself.

"Can't you get some real music in here?" came an unexpected reply.

Gene looked down at the end of the bar. Denny Cain glared back at him.

Denny had wandered into the Lula early that evening. Gene had wondered why the man was here and not home with his wife but figured it was none of his business. He'd given Denny two drinks and all the food the man had wanted, on the house. But Denny—having found his drinking buddy Chet Boardman—had downed one scotch after another, matched by Chet's bourbon and cola. Feeling sorry for the guy, Gene had let the drinking go on longer than he should have; after all, the man had just lost his only child. But both were now pretty plowed and he'd cut them off.

Gene walked down to Denny and Chet. He stopped in front of

them and put his elbows on the bar top. Leaning in close, he asked, "You got a problem, Denny?"

Denny blinked slowly. Grief and alcohol had etched red lines into the whites of his eyes. He hadn't shaved, and the stubble gave his face a haggard, sunken look.

"Problem?" Denny replied. "Yeah, Gene, I gotta problem. You see, my son's dead, all ripped to shreds and lying in a morgue. I ain't never gonna see him again. So hell yeah, I gotta *huge* fucking problem."

"Fuckin' problem," Chet chimed in drunkenly.

Other customers looked over at them. Gene said, "Keep your voices down, okay? Now, can I get you guys something else to eat? Some coffee, maybe."

"Don't want nothing," complained Denny. He glanced over to the stage. "But you can tell *him* to stop squawking."

Gene frowned. "Who, Owens? Come on, the guy's good. Easily the best musician I've had in here. Not my fault if you don't like the music."

"It ain't the music," clarified Denny somewhat blearily. "It's him."

"I'm not following," said Gene. "What's your beef with Owens?"

Denny glared at Gene. "You saw that mark near his eye. That teardrop thing. I ain't stupid, Gene. I seen stuff like that on television, on those cop shows. That's a prison tattoo. The guy's been locked up."

"You don't know that," countered Gene, though he'd had similar thoughts earlier in the day. "And even if it's true, that has nothing to do with him working here. As long as he minds his own business, I've got no problem with him."

"I knew he was trouble," said Chet, "from the moment I saw him."

"And you," Gene said, jabbing a finger at Chet, "can quit stirring the pot."

Chet sat quietly, sliding his empty glass back and forth across the bar, first to one hand, then to the other. Back and forth. Back and forth. His eyes followed the glass. "I thought you wanted a real musician. I didn't think you was gonna bring in one of them."

So that was it, Gene thought. And I thought I'd left that garbage behind in Chicago. "Chet, you don't need to go there."

Then Denny Cain finished it. "You brought in a nigger."

"My kid's dead and what does that asshole do? He throws *me* out!" Denny shoved one hand down his jacket pocket, fumbled around, and came up empty. His other hand was no more successful than the first. "Where the fuck are my car keys?"

"Gene took 'em," Chet replied. "Yours and mine, remember? We're walkin' tonight."

Denny didn't remember. Truth be told, after he'd gone to see his boy, he didn't remember much of anything. His day in hell had started late this morning with the visit from Chief Morris. The woman had broken the news about Jimmy's death. Then things got worse. Maddie, after learning that her boy was dead, had taken down every dish, plate, saucer, glass, knife, fork and spoon from the cupboards and washed them—every single damn one of them. And when she was done with them, she'd piled that crap on the floor and proceeded to wipe down all the cupboards and counters. Then Denny had gotten the call: could someone come over to the hospital and positively identify the deceased's remains? He'd asked Maddie if she wanted to go. At the time, she was scrubbing the ceiling with a brush and a bucket of undiluted Pine-Sol. With a flick of her wrist, she'd nailed him point blank on the top of his head with the brush. Well, having gotten his answer, Denny drove alone to the hospital. And when the doctor pulled back the sheet, when Denny saw what had been done to his son, he ran to the nearest sink and threw up until he got the dry heaves. After that, the rest of the day was a smudge of memory.

But now, in the cold clarity of the night, Denny's alcohol-hazed brain *pushed*, a thought advanced—and the smudge was gone as completely as if it had been scrubbed away by Maddie's mad brush.

He knew who'd killed his boy. It had to be. *Goddammit*, it was so simple. Why hadn't anyone else figured it out?

"He did it."

"Who did it?" Chet asked as he continued to lead Denny out of the parking lot. "I mean, who did what?"

"That guy. Owens. He did it. He killed my boy."

Chet Boardman stopped walking. He let go of Denny's arm. "You ain't serious."

"That damn nigger killed him."

"Come on, Denny. That's crazy. The man looks like trouble, sure, but—"

"He's an ex-con," Denny said, his voice hot enough to raise blisters on asphalt. "He came into town, killed Jimmy, and now he's in there singing." He gestured toward the Lula. "Like nothing happened. How fucking arrogant can you get?"

"Christ, you've lost your mind. Seriously, who'd kill someone and then hang around, in public, while the cops are investigatin'? It don't make no sense."

"Excuse me, fellas," said a new voice.

Denny turned. A Chevy Silverado sat in the entrance to the Lula's parking lot, blocking any potential traffic. Under the harsh glow of a nearby streetlamp, the truck looked colorless; it could've been white or silver, or perhaps even light blue. A man sat in the cab. His left arm hung outside the window, a cigarette dangling casually from between his fingers. Shadows concealed his face.

"Sorry to bother you," the stranger continued, "but I thought you fellas might need a lift. Especially you." The man flicked cigarette ashes in Denny's direction. "You look like shit." He brought the cigarette to his lips and drew in deeply, then blew smoke out from a wide smile that Denny could barely see from within the cab's shadows.

"How'd you know we were walking?" asked Denny.

"Good ears," replied the stranger. "So, you guys up for it?"

"No thanks," Chet said hastily. "We're fine."

Denny was about to agree—who took rides from strangers anymore?—when the man stuck his other hand out the window. He was holding an unopened bottle of Johnnie Walker Gold. It was the good stuff, the *expensive* stuff. The stuff Denny couldn't afford on his wages.

"Hold on," he told Chet, placing a restraining hand on his friend's shoulder. "The man's just being polite. Maybe we should catch a ride home. After all, the night's gettin' cold."

"Are you outta your mind?" Chet said, almost shouting. "You don't need more trouble tonight. I'm telling you, let's just walk."

"Fellas," the stranger said. "This is a limited time offer. Either partake now or forever hold your regrets."

Denny found himself walking toward the truck. Chet tagged along behind him, continuing to jabber on about how this was a bad idea.

Denny spun around. "Look, I've had a real shitty day. Worst goddamn day of my life. I just want to drink a little more and forget. Is that such a bad thing?"

"No," Chet said, his expression softening. "It's not. So let's go drink, but not with *him*. I mean, who drives up in the middle of the night and offers two strangers a ride and that kind of booze? Doesn't that set off any warning bells?"

Under other circumstances, it may have. But Denny's warning bells had been rung earlier in the day, rung hard, rung until his damn ears almost bled. He was deaf to anything else. All he could think of now was getting so bombed that the image of his dead son faded from memory.

"I'm going with him," Denny said flatly. "Either come along or shut up."

Chet looked like he was about to say something, to argue his point further. Then he threw his hands up in the air. "Fine. Have it your way. At least it'll be two against one if he tries anything...queer."

The stranger looked pleased. "Good to see you boys have reached an accord. Hop on in."

Together, they walked over to the SUV and climbed in.

The Silverado pulled out of the parking lot, turned smoothly onto the road leading back into town, and was eventually swallowed by the night.

CHAPTER
6

Sunday

The October morning was overcast. Slate-and-ash-colored clouds had rolled in and chased away the morning sunshine. Along the hiking trail, trees defined and limited the terrain—they huddled closely together, arm in arm, conspiring to keep the ground soft and muddy. The decaying leaves gave the air a musty, wet smell that wasn't entirely unpleasant.

Crying softly, Katie Bethel stepped between two trees. She was only dimly aware of the other volunteers scouring the area where Jimmy's body had been found. So far, they had searched either side of the trail, starting at the campground's parking lot and ending here, where the tragedy had taken place—without success. They had moved quietly through the woods, treading solemnly, eyes downcast, as if they were praying for a miracle.

Perhaps they were.

"Excuse me," said a voice next to her.

Katie's head snapped up. A man stood there. One of the volunteers—along with Sgt. Talbert, Mr. Vincent and several high school friends assigned to search this part of the woods. She wiped her tears with muddy hands.

"I'm sorry—who are you?" she asked nervously.

The man gave her a peculiar little bow. "Bart Owens. I work at the Lula. Mr. Vincent brought me along to help." He gestured to her tears. "I saw you were crying. Are you okay? Do you need me to get somebody?"

"I'm fine, thank you," she said, taking a cautious step away from the man.

"This kind of thing is never easy," Mr. Owens continued, nodding to the searchers milling about. "You hope to find something, but you're also afraid of what you might find."

Frowning, her tears momentarily forgotten, she studied the man more carefully. He was taller than she, perhaps in his late fifties or early sixties. He wore jeans and a heavy nylon jacket that he had zipped up to ward against the brisk morning air. His face seemed pleasant enough, with high cheekbones and an angular jaw. His dark skin was smooth, perhaps a little too smooth for someone his age, and she wondered briefly if he was yet another citizen of the Botox nation. And then there were his eyes: so blue, like the sky on a hot August day. His only disturbing feature was a small teardrop he'd had tattooed under his left eye; it seemed out of place to her, almost as if he were purposefully drawing attention to it.

"You've done this before?" she asked.

Mr. Owens nodded, then reached into his pocket and pulling out a handkerchief. He offered it to her. "You have a little mud on your face."

Katie gazed down at her mud-stained hands. Horrified, she grabbed the handkerchief and scrubbed at her cheeks. By the time she had finished, the white cloth was streaked with brown dirt. She held it out with a trembling hand. "All I seem to do today is cry."

"'To weep is to make less the depth of grief.'" Mr. Owens took back his handkerchief. "Everyone should know a little Shakespeare. And luckily, I knew it'd be muddy out here. I came prepared." He pulled out another handkerchief and handed it to her. "I take it you know the girl we're looking for?"

"Natalie was—*is*—my best friend. We were at a dance together. The other night. She was supposed to come over to my house after it was done, but she ended up here with Jimmy."

"So you weren't with her when…?"

"No. J.J. and I went back to my house instead."

"J.J.?"

"My boyfriend. Jack Sallinen, Jr."

Mr. Owens eyes searched the crowd of volunteers. "Which one of these young men is your boyfriend?"

"He isn't here," she said. "His dad wouldn't let him help."

"Isn't that a little odd?"

"Not if you knew his father. Mr. Sallinen can be controlling. And, occasionally, pretty mean."

"That's unfortunate. His mother didn't have a say?"

Katie shook her head. "Divorced. His mom lives down state, in Grand Rapids. Because of the distance, he only sees her every few months." She grimaced. "I think it's more because she doesn't want to see her ex."

"Another shame," he said. "It must be hard for the young man, having only him and his father. This J.J.'s lucky to have you."

"Oh, he's not alone," Katie replied. "J.J. has a brother. He's only eight, but he's real sweet. Has some rare form of autism. Von...something."

"Kliner's?" Mr. Owens supplied.

"Yeah," Katie said, her eyebrows drawing together. "Von Kliner's syndrome. But how...?"

The man shrugged. "I must have read about it somewhere, and the name stuck. You have to admit, it's pretty unusual."

"That'd be an awfully strange coincidence." She was feeling cold now, in the pit of her stomach, and she didn't think it was due to the weather. "No, I think there's more to it. The way you came up with that name. It was fast—almost like you were expecting to hear it."

Mr. Owens was quiet for a moment. Then: "Sounds like you're the one stretching coincidence."

Katie brushed a strand of hair from her face. Here was a stranger, someone who came out to help search for a girl he'd never met, and he also happened to know about an obscure autistic illness. That cold feeling was spreading to her knees, making her feel weak. "You know, I think I should get back to the search."

"Wait," Mr. Owens said, his hands held up, his palms out. "Look, I'm sorry. I didn't mean to upset you. Also...I have to apologize. I'm afraid I wasn't completely honest with you. A friend of mine, someone dear to me, had von Kliner's syndrome." His shoulders dropped, and he stuffed his hands in his pockets. "That's how I knew the name."

"Right," she said and started to back away. "And the dog ate my homework. Now, if you don't mind—"

"Please," Mr. Owens said. "I'm telling the truth."

Katie paused. "All right, then why lie about it? Why not tell me about him from the start?"

"*Her* name was Jesse. And talking about her is painful."

"Was? You mean—she's dead?"

Mr. Owens nodded. "Some years ago."

"Did she die young?"

"When you get to be my age, everyone seems young. But yes, she died far too soon. It was tragic."

She could hear the sorrow in his voice and was inclined to believe him. Then a thought occurred to her. "It's Jesse, isn't it? She's the reason you're here."

Mr. Owens eyes widened slightly, as if her question had surprised him. "What do you mean?"

Katie tried to pull her thoughts together. "Maybe Natalie's situation is similar to this Jesse's—enough that it brought out some feelings in you." Enough that he wanted to help with the search. "By helping now, you're helping your friend—or her memory, I guess." She made a vague, frustrated gesture with her hands. "Oh, I don't know what I mean."

The man's smile returned. "You're a remarkable girl, Katie."

Katie could feel her face grow warm at the compliment. "Not really. All it takes is a little thought."

"A little thought is a rare thing nowadays," he said. "But, I think you're right. We should continue with the search." He gestured to the handkerchief. "You can keep that, if you like."

She looked down at the white cloth gripped tightly in her fists. She forced her fingers to relax and stuffed the handkerchief into her pocket.

"Thank you," Katie replied. "And thank you for helping today."

Mr. Owens raised his hand as if he were tipping an invisible hat, a gesture Katie found curiously out-of-date.

"My pleasure," he said. "Now, let's go find your friend."

It wasn't until Mr. Owens had walked away that she realized, despite their long conversation, she still knew next to nothing about him.

He had avoided answering most of her questions.

CHAPTER
7

Izzy Morris zipped up her black police jacket, closing it against the chill breeze from the northwest. Still, she shivered as she watched the wind carry an oak leaf along the ground, a tiny, fragile hand tumbling, spinning, cartwheeling, waving goodbye.

I refuse to say goodbye, she thought. Even if I have to cut down every tree between here and Black Pine Lake, I will not lose you, Natalie. I promise.

But God, it was so hard.

Several yards down the trail, Gene Vincent emerged from the woods, brushing leaves and pine needles from his pant legs. He made his way over to her, his limp more pronounced than earlier. Instead of showing his usual lopsided grin, his face was drawn tight with worry.

"Any luck?" he asked, giving her a quick hug.

Izzy shook her head. "It doesn't make sense. There has to be *some* sign of where she went. I mean, she sure as hell didn't fly away."

"No, she didn't," he said. "Which means something will turn up. Give it enough time. Let these people finish their search."

"You're not hearing me, Gene." She lowered her voice, forcing him to lean toward her. "We found Natalie's blood on a tree branch, and there was some on the ground under it. But the blood, it's just...there. We can't find any trace of it leading off in any direction. How is that possible? How can a person be bleeding and not leave a *goddamn blood trail?*"

"Calm down," Gene said, not unkindly. "I don't have an answer. Besides, you're the cop, not me."

"A lot of good that's done me," she replied. Nat had been missing for almost thirty-six hours now, and she still had no idea what had happened or where her daughter was.

"Don't start second guessing yourself. You're an excellent cop, Izzy. Keep doing your job and you'll find her."

"I wish I had your confidence in me."

"Stop it," he said. "You're starting to sound like the old Izzy."

The old Izzy. By which, Gene meant the young Izzy—the teenager who had been consumed with doubts about herself, always feeling inadequate, inferior. Those feelings had pushed her to excel at everything she did, with little regard given to the feelings of others. That kind of attitude had quickly alienated the other kids, except for two: the thin, somewhat nerdy brainiac who would later become her husband, and the larger, more athletic boy with the funny rock-'n'-roll name.

"I'll keep that in mind." She nodded toward the black man who'd been talking with Katie Bethel. "Who is that guy?"

Gene turned and saw Bart Owens stepping over a small deadfall. "He's the musician I hired to play at the Lula." He filled her in on what little he knew about Owens.

"So what's he doing *here*?" Izzy asked.

"Said he wanted to help with the search." He paused. "Why? Did I do something wrong?"

"No," Izzy said, staring at Owens. "You did the right thing." The man had gotten her attention because she knew some criminals liked to revisit their crime scenes. They got off on watching the police trying to catch them. But to the best of her knowledge, none had ever been this bold about it.

"By the way," Gene said, interrupting her thoughts. "I had some trouble with Denny and Chet last night." He told her about what had happened and about Denny's racial slur.

Izzy's eyes drifted over to Denny Cain, who was crouched behind the tree where they had found Nat's blood, his hands carefully sweeping aside leaves and sticks. Stanley's assistant manager and the father of the late Jimmy Cain had been given bereavement time from work. In fact, she had been surprised when he'd shown up this morning to help with the search.

Izzy looked back at Gene. "He really said that, huh?"

"Yup, though I shouldn't have been too surprised. We don't have much pepper mixed in with the salt up here."

"You grew up here," she said. "You know how people in these rural Upper towns are."

Gene shrugged. "Doesn't make it right. Anyway, after he said it, I gave him and Chet the boot."

"You didn't let them drive, did you?"

He gave her a flat look. "You know me better than that. Denny came by the Lula early this morning for his keys. Apologized for being a jerk. As far as I'm concerned, we're good. Hell, he even helped clean the place up while I went to make the morning deposit." Gene frowned. "I never thought to ask him how he got home. Or back to the Lula."

"What about Chet? He ever come by for his keys?"

"Not that I know of."

Izzy thought for a moment, then gave a mental shrug. Right now, she had bigger problems to deal with than Denny and Chet. "I want to get back to Mr. Owens for a moment. You say he's from Nashville?"

"So the man told me."

"Do you know for a fact that he came from Nashville?"

Gene frowned, as if the question had caught him off guard.

Izzy didn't wait for an answer. "And do you know *when* he got into town?"

"Well," Gene said. "He walked into the Lula around three yesterday. I kind of assumed...."

"So you really don't know where he's from or when he got here?"

"No," he admitted, a bit sheepishly. "I guess not."

She pulled out a small notepad and began jotting down notes.

"Wait a minute," Gene said, putting a hand on her arm. "You think Owens might have something to do with this?"

Glancing up from her notepad, she said, "Can you prove to me he doesn't?"

"Well...no, of course not. But I heard Jimmy was torn open, his ribcage ripped out. Owens doesn't look big enough to do that kind of damage."

"No, he doesn't. But he *is* new in town. That alone means he gets a closer look."

There was a commotion, some raised voices. And then Detective Sten Billick came storming out from behind a copse of alders. He was dragging Stanley Morris by the arm.

Red faced, Stanley yelled, "Get your fucking hand off me, you fuck!"

Sten kept his rock-like grip on Stanley's arm, half-dragging him along the trail until they'd reached Izzy and Gene. Then Sten released Izzy's husband, but not until after he'd given the pharmacist a shove that almost sent him tumbling to the ground.

Izzy rushed forward and caught Stanley before he fell.

"Give it back!" Stanley shouted as he struggled to get around her and charge at Sten. "Give it back, asshole!"

Izzy got both hands on her husband's chest. Gene stepped up and grabbed one of Stanley's arms. Denny had come to stand near them, his face pulled into a curious frown. Bob Talbert was hurrying up the trail, drawn by the noise.

"*Give it back!*" Stanley shouted, spittle flying from his lips.

"Stanley!" she shouted back. "Stop it! That's enough!"

Her husband let out a hiccupping cough, which evolved into a rattling breath. "He stole it from me." He was pointing at Sten. "Make him give it back."

She kept a restraining hand on Stanley's chest and turned to face Sten. "What's he talking about?"

Sten reached under his jacket and removed a gun from his waistband, a nickel-plated .38 Smith & Wesson with sandalwood grips.

"He was carrying this," Sten said, lifting the revolver. "I noticed the bulge in his jacket pocket."

Izzy stared at the gun, not sure if she should believe what she was seeing. But there was no denying it.

Turning back to her husband, she said, "You took one of my guns?"

Stanley glared at Sten, then shifted his attention to her. "After what happened, do you think I'd set foot in these woods unarmed?"

"We have *kids* out here," she said, stunned at his lack of forethought. "What if you had mistaken one for an animal and opened fire?"

Stanley's mouth twisted, his face turning scarlet. "I know the difference between a bear and a person. I'm not an idiot."

Izzy gaped at him. He'd been a hunter for years, knew damn well how many people were killed in shooting accidents.

Before she could tell him exactly that, Katie Bethel called out her name.

"Chief Morris! Over here! I think I found something."

The girl stood near the tree where Natalie's blood had been found.

"We'll deal with this later," Izzy told Stanley and Sten.

Sten placed the gun in his pocket. "You'll get this back, Dr. Morris. *After* the search is finished."

Stanley looked like he was going to protest again. He opened his mouth.

Before he could speak, Izzy said, "You heard him. After the search."

Fury smoldered in her husband's eyes. She'd essentially pulled rank on him, and he hated it. She tensed, ready for another verbal assault. But then, with a final, resentful glare, Stanley shut his mouth. Rubbing absently at his chest, he mumbled, "Sure. Whatever."

Izzy let out a sigh, and Gene let go of his friend's arm. Stanley pushed past them and started walking toward Katie Bethel. Izzy hurried after him, followed by the others.

"Whatever it is," Izzy called out, "don't touch it."

Katie nodded, pointing to something on the ground. Izzy crouched down. There, nestled among the leaves and twigs, was a piece of dark plastic a little larger than the tip of her thumb. Roughly triangular, it looked thicker at the base, and there were corrugated marks like crosshatches along the wider bottom. Izzy could see swirls of light brown within the black plastic; it looked like creamer being stirred into coffee.

"Bob, get some pictures of this," Izzy said to Sgt. Talbert, her heart racing.

Bob Talbert set down an orange evidence marker and then snapped several photos from various angles. After he was finished, Izzy donned a pair of latex gloves and picked up the piece of plastic.

She asked, "Anyone have an idea what this is?"

"That's a plectrum, Chief Morris. A guitar pick."

Izzy turned. Bart Owens standing behind her, his brown face devoid of emotion.

"And I'm afraid it's one of mine," he finished.

* * *

"Can you explain this, Mr. Owens?" Izzy asked, holding up the pick in her gloved hand. She was careful to keep her roiling emotions from spilling into her voice.

Owens shook his head. "I don't know how it got here."

"Where do you usually keep them?"

He reached into his pocket, pulled out one identical to the one in her hand. "I have more sitting on the amp back at the Lula."

Izzy paused. Too many people had access to the picks. Finding one out here wasn't enough to arrest the man, let alone bring him in for questioning. But he was now her prime suspect.

"Do you know anything about what happened up here? Do you know where my daughter is?"

"I'm sorry," Owens replied, and she heard the first hint of emotion in his voice. It sounded like regret. "I don't."

Everyone was quiet for a moment. Then Stanley pushed past her to stand in front of Owens.

"Goddamnit, where is she?" he rasped. "Where's Natalie?"

Owens took a half-step back. "I'm telling you, I had nothing to do with this. I'm just here to he—"

"That's not what I hear," Stanley said matter-of-factly.

Izzy threw her husband a puzzled glance. Then Gene caught her eye and nodded at something behind her. She turned. Not two feet away, Denny Cain was devouring the exchange between Stanley and Owens with an expression of black hunger on his face. Worse yet, when he caught her staring, he looked away—a sure sign he felt guilty about something.

He and Stanley were friends. Had Denny said something to her husband?

More shouting drew her focus back to the conflict. Stepping up to stand beside Stanley, she said in a low voice, "Please, let me handle this."

Stanley's bloodshot gaze lit on her. "And do what? Read him his rights? 'You have the right to keep your mouth shut'? 'You have the right to take our daughter and hide behind a lawyer'? I swear, you're useless."

Izzy stiffened. "Don't do this. Not here."

He would not be deterred. "What comes first with you? Mother, wife, or cop?"

Stanley bared his teeth in a grin so uncharacteristically fierce that Izzy wondered where her husband had gone. This wasn't the man she'd married or the one who had taught Natalie to ride a bike and drive a car. Nor was this the man who had attended every Fourth-of-July town picnic wearing the same flip-flops with white socks and those ridiculous red-white-and-blue framed sunglasses, laughing and cheering as he helped run the kids holiday baseball game. And this certainly wasn't the man who had at one time quietly discounted the cost of medications for the town's poor and uninsured, absorbing the difference from his profits. No, that Stanley was gone and maybe had been for some time. But this Stanley...well, he looked crazed. Crazed and broken.

"I'm supposed step aside and let you do your job?" Stanley shook his head. "No, not this time. You may be Police Chief first, but I know what it means to be a father." He pointed a finger at Owens. "*He* took Natalie, Iz. He took our baby!"

Denny Cain stepped out from the crowd gathered around them. He thrust his chin at Owens. "Look under his eye. See that teardrop thing? That's one of them prison tattoos. This guy's an ex-con." He jabbed a finger into Stanley's shoulder. "Wouldn't surprise me if he knows where your kid is—or did her in himself."

There was a flurry of activity, all at one time. Gene turned and grabbed a fistful of Denny's jacket, while Sten snatched his arm. As both men began dragging the protesting Denny Cain back from the crowd, Stanley threw an arm up and crashed violently into Izzy, knocking her to the ground. Then he launched himself at Owens. Bob Talbert, apparently surprised by the pharmacist's transformation, hesitated only a moment before starting after his boss's husband.

The rest of the search party took a startled step back.

Stanley threw a wild, roundhouse swing at Owens' head. The other man easily ducked beneath the blow, straightened, and lifted his hands, putting them defensively in front of him. He'd clearly been in a fight or two.

Snarling, Stanley tried a quick left, but Owens bobbed his head back, and Stanley's jab hit nothing but air. Stanley followed with another right, this one coming in high over his shoulder. Owens shifted to his right, and Stanley's fist passed harmlessly through the space where the other man had just been standing.

Stunned by her husband's attack, Izzy scrambled up from the ground. A dozen or so yards away, Denny shouted insults at Owens until Sten clamped his other hand over the man's mouth.

Stanley, his eyes shining with rage, drew his right fist back—and Bob Talbert grabbed his arm.

"That's enough, Dr. Morris," Sgt. Talbert said. "It's over."

Without hesitating, Stanley snapped his left fist up like a piston, slamming it hard into Talbert's jaw. The cop grunted as blood spilled down his chin. He released Stanley, his hands coming up to his face.

"My fucking tongue!" Only it came out *my fuhin on!*

Stanley slid his hand down to Talbert's belt, found his gun, and yanked it free of the holster. He stepped back, brought the big Glock up until it pointed at Owens. Shaking, he gripped the pistol with both hands.

Izzy shouted, "Stanley, no!"

"He killed Natalie." Stanley racked the slide, chambering a round. "He has to pay."

Bob Talbert, his lower face coated with blood, took an angry step toward Stanley.

"No," Izzy told her officer. "Let me handle this."

Glaring at Stanley, Talbert backed off.

Speaking calmly, Izzy said, "Put the gun down, Stanley."

"I won't let him get away with this!" Tears were running down his cheeks.

Owens, his hands still held protectively in front of him, said, "You don't want to shoot me, Dr. Morris. Or you would have already pulled that trigger."

"Shut up!" screamed Stanley.

Izzy said, "Mr. Owens—"

Owens shook his head. "I'm the one with the gun aimed at my head, so I suppose that gives me the right to speak." His attention shifted to Stanley. "I'll make you a deal, Dr. Morris. You put the gun down, and I'll willingly go down to the police station. Your wife can question me all she likes." He took a deep breath, then lowered his hands. "I have nothing to hide. I didn't take or hurt your daughter. For all anyone knows, she might still be alive."

Stanley slowly lowered the pistol. Izzy thought Owens had gotten to him, but what he said next puzzled her.

"Heavy," he panted, his face coated with sweat. "Why's it so heavy?" He jerked his arms up, but the weapon only moved fractionally.

Izzy took another small step near her husband. "Let me take him in," she said. "See if he knows anything."

"No no no," Stanley cried, sounding like a little boy whose favorite toy had been taken from him, broken, and then returned. "I can't let him live, not after what he did!"

With an effort that made his arms shake, Stanley wrenched the gun up and fired. The crack of the gunshot shattered the chill air, echoing loudly across Black Pine Lake. Mud flew up from the ground inches away from Owens' feet. One of the girls in the crowd screamed.

Bob Talbert shot forward and made a grab for the gun, but Stanley twisted, heaved the Glock around until it was pointed at the officer. Talbert's eyes grew wide, and he threw his body to the side. Another shot. Behind Talbert, the trunk of a gnarled oak exploded, sending pieces of wood hurtling through the air. There were more screams, and people scattered.

When Stanley started to turn back toward Owens, Izzy placed herself between the two men. She saw Sten let go of Denny, reach for his gun, and start running toward them.

"Stanley!" she yelled, her ears ringing from the gunfire. Her own gun was in the paddle holster at her waist. She left it there. She refused to draw down on her husband. "Stanley, look at me!"

He turned until he faced her. The barrel of the Glock was leveled at her chest, but Stanley seemed to be having a hard time holding the gun up. He was panting, his arms trembling. Again, his hands started to drift down.

"Get out of the way, Iz," he said evenly.

"I'm not going to let you do this," she said. Sten was now a few feet away, his pistol aimed at Stanley. And behind her, she could almost feel Owens' tense presence. "Not to that man, not to yourself, not to us."

"Don't make me shoot you."

"Drop the gun," she said.

"He killed Natalie!"

"Drop the gun."

"He needs to pay for what he did!"

"He will, but not this way."

"Move, damn it!"

"No," she replied, swallowing hard. "I won't. I guess you'll have to shoot me"

Stanley's eyes flared with rage. His lips peeled back into a terrifying grimace. With a scream, he tried to jerk the gun up, but his hands wouldn't move.

Izzy felt hands grab her from behind and throw her aside. She hit the ground hard, rolled onto her back. Owens sprang forward. He grabbed Stanley by the wrists and wrenched his arms upward. They wrestled for several seconds, the gun pointed at the sky. Another shot split the air. Then Stanley threw his head back and shuddered. Owens yanked the gun free and tossed it to Sten, who easily caught it.

Gasping for breath, Stanley went rigid. His complexion paled, his skin taking on the color of congealed bacon fat. His knees buckled. Owens eased him to the ground.

Izzy scrambled over to her husband.

"Iz," he whispered. His eyes closed. "Hurts…oh, God."

"Bob," Izzy called out. "Get an ambulance up here!"

Stanley's eyes fluttered open. His mouth opened. In a breathy voice, he said, "Pain…worse than before."

"Don't talk," Izzy said, tears running down her cheeks. "Save your strength."

"I…I'm…." His eyes opened wide. "Oh my—" Then he shuddered. His head slumped to one side.

"Stanley!" Izzy shouted and shook him. When he didn't respond, she checked for a pulse. "No!"

She saw a flash of movement. Someone dropped to the ground across from her. Dark hands, one atop the other, fingers locked together, found a spot on her husband's chest, just above the base of his sternum. Izzy looked up. Owens' blue eyes met hers.

"Breathe for him," he said.

Izzy stared numbly at the man, then she shifted to Stanley's head and opened his airway. As she bent down to blow life back into her husband's lungs, Owens began the chest compressions.

It seemed like ages before she heard the wailing siren of the approaching ambulance.

CHAPTER
8

Sounds floated in the air like big red balloons, bouncing off one another in lazy collisions that sent shimmering sparks raining down around Kevin Sallinen. He giggled, the echo of his own laughter making him happy. He felt the same way when his dad gave him chocolate milk with his Pop-Tart.

"Smart tart milk fart," Kevin said, breaking out into gales of laughter. He fell onto his back and bumped his head on the thick carpet of his bedroom floor.

Flipping onto his stomach, he sprawled out, his laughter draining out of him in little sighs and hiccups. With his left cheek resting against the carpet, he flicked his finger at the thick fibers. Each scrape of his nail sent little plumes of dust billowing up like clouds rising into the sky. He blinked slowly as a tiny mote traveled across the long divide of his reach, sailing on crystal blue currents of air, to dance before him.

"Who who who, Lindy Sue?"

Kevin pursed his lips and carefully blew a ribbon of air at his little Whoville, sending the small world flying off to other adventures.

Drawing his legs under his body, he pushed up into a kneeling position. From this height, he could see the stuffed animals lying on his bed—Sponge Bob, a furry sheepdog, a white monkey with long arms and one gray foot—as well as his desk cluttered with piles of drawing paper and several boxes of crayons. A folding chair sat in front of the desk.

Kevin's narrow face lit with excitement. He knee-walked over to his desk, his tongue poking out of his mouth as he tried to keep his feet from touching the ground, his skinny arms flapping to help keep his balance.

When one toe touched the carpet, he jerked both feet up hard. His heels dug into his butt. His tummy bowed out, and his head had little choice but to follow. With his hands still busy trying to keep the balance he'd already lost, his upper body slid forward and his forehead smacked hard into the edge of his desk. Pain shot over the top and around the sides of his head.

"Ayiee ahh!" Kevin cried as his hands finally grabbed the desk. With his eyes watering, he pulled himself up and sat on the chair. He stared at his reflection in the mirror that hung on the wall opposite him. There was a red mark on his forehead. He rubbed it with one hand, then brought up the other and jammed his thumbs in his ears. Wiggled his fingers. Stuck out his tongue. A giggle escaped from his lips. He blew air into his cheeks and crossed his eyes. Laughter overtook the giggles. He laughed so hard that his face turned red.

While Kevin gasped to regain his breath, a *clearness* spread inside him. It was as if someone had opened a dirty window and let the outside world stream in.

The outside world, and more.

Thoughts that were normally blocked or shunted off to meaningless areas of his brain found their correct paths. Connections, that since his birth had been so misaligned, nudged a little closer to true. He looked at the boy in the mirror, the one with rosy cheeks and tousled hair, the one who kept him company in his room.

"That's me," said Kevin.

He quickly snatched a sheet of paper and spilled a box of crayons. The clearness wouldn't last long. Kevin closed his eyes.

Trees and mud surrounded him. He stood before a wide glade. Across the field of grass rose a low hill with a dark hole on its face like an open mouth screaming into the forest. A cave? He sensed that something lay inside, something that was here but shouldn't be. And through it, he sensed another.

Thin fingers skimmed over the rainbow of wax sticks until he found the ones he needed. As he put crayon to paper, a name flashed through his mind.

Natalie.

CHAPTER
9

Patrolman Carlton Manick pulled his police cruiser into the drive-thru lane and ordered two breakfast burritos with extra hot sauce and a large black coffee. When he fished out his wallet, he found four singles. That was it. Payday had been two days ago, and he'd set aside two hundred, enough to get him through until his next check. But after his little run-in with Morris yesterday morning, he'd felt agitated, out of sorts. He'd needed some release. So he'd gone out last night and hit the casinos. Hit them pretty hard. Now he'd be scrimping for the next couple weeks.

Pulling up to the pick-up window, he tried a wink and a smile on the girl taking the money. Maybe he'd get a little cop courtesy and she'd give him his breakfast for free.

"That'll be $3.06," the girl said with a roll of her eyes.

Sighing, Carlton handed over the last of his cash. Damn kids didn't appreciate authority anymore.

"Thanks," he said sourly as he got his change. "I'll remember this."

He parked in an empty space near the exit, set his coffee in the console cup holder, and attacked the first burrito.

It had been a bitch of a morning.

Painfully hung-over, he'd snored through the alarm and had to shower and dress quickly for work. Outside his apartment, he found his motorcycle sitting in Mrs. Burkowski's space with a terse note from his neighbor taped to the windscreen. He stuffed the note into his pocket, wondering—not for the first time, either—what he was doing to himself.

He'd raced to the police station and parked his 2004 Harley-Davison Springer Softail near the back entrance. Knowing he had only a minute or two to spare, he'd bolted for the door, dropping his keys, grabbed them, found the one that unlocked the back entrance, hurried to the time clock, and jammed his timecard in the slot after it had ticked forward to 7:01 am.

Shit shit shit! Morris had already warned him about his job

performance and being late again wasn't going to help. He slid the timecard back into its slot. Oh well, maybe he'd get lucky, pull over some guy, and find her kid stuffed in the trunk. Maybe that'd get the bitch off his back.

Carlton finished his first burrito in three huge bites. He was reaching into the bag for the other one when a white Chevy Silverado blew by the McDonalds.

"Aw, damn it," he muttered. Now his burrito was going to get cold.

Flipping on the overhead bar lights and siren, he took off after the SUV.

About two blocks ahead of him, the truck turned right on Newman, fishtailing before the driver regained control.

Carlton reached for his mic. "Base, seven. In pursuit of a white Chevy Silverado traveling east on Newman. Haven't seen the plate yet."

"Ten four, seven," replied Aggie Ripley, the shift dispatcher. "Let me know if you need assistance."

He clicked his mic twice to acknowledge he'd heard her.

Right on Newman. The Silverado ran ahead of him. He stomped on the gas and closed in. Jersey plate. He called it in.

"Seven," Aggie came back. "The plate belongs to a white Silverado. Registered to a Darryl Webber."

The vehicle finally pulled over, the driver's window rolling smoothly down.

Carlton parked behind the SUV. The Silverado's windows were darkened. No way to tell how many were inside.

"Any wants or warrants?"

Aggie replied, "He's clean."

"Roger. I'll stay in touch."

Carlton got out of the car. He approached cautiously, his hand on his sidearm. In the side view mirror, a wedge of a man's face—a slice of cheek and one green eye—followed his steps.

Carlton stopped at the rear edge of the window. The driver looked to be in his mid-forties. Long pale hair down to his shoulders. Jaw that came to a squared-off point like some shitkicker's boot. About three days' worth of beard. A jagged scar from his ear down his jaw line.

The smell of cigarette smoke, Old Spice, and something he couldn't quite identify—something unpleasant, like a mixture of pine tar and spoiled meat—wafted through the open window. There was some death-metal crap blaring from the radio. Other than butts in the ashtray, the inside of the cab was clean. Carlton looked in the back of the cab. No Natalie. Damn.

"Please turn off the radio," Carlton yelled.

The man dialed down the sound but didn't turn it off.

Carlton sighed. Another one with no respect for the law. "Driver's license and registration, please."

The driver produced a battered leather wallet from his back pocket, removed two pieces of paper, stuck his hand out the window. His green eyes never left Carlton's.

After a quick scan of the papers, Carlton said, "Darryl Webber?"

"That's me..." Webber glanced at Carlton's nametag. "Officer Manick."

"Do you know why I pulled you over?"

Webber looked up and flashed him a smile. The man's grin spread, stretching wider and wider, until his skin tore apart, separating in bloody, ropey tendrils. The ghastly smile continued like a zipper being opened, ripping through Webber's skull, until Carlton thought the top half of the guy's head was going to slide off and plop onto the floor.

Carlton closed his eyes, shook his head, opened them. The man's smile was normal.

Christ, this was one mother of a hangover.

"You look funny," Webber said. "Like you seen a ghost or something?"

Carlton took a few moments to gather himself, then said, "Do you know how fast you were going?"

Webber raised a hand to his mouth and removed the cigarette. Blue smoke drifted from the window. "Sorry, Chief. No idea."

"Sir, you were doing at least twenty over the speed limit."

"That much?" Webber took another drag on his cigarette. "Guess I wasn't paying attention. My ass is still fried from losing my money last night at one of your lovely casinos. Damned things are everywhere up here."

Carlton paused. He was about to say something, but the thought slipped away.

The cell phone clipped to Webber's belt went off. Carlton heard the thin strains of Soundgarden's "Black Hole Sun."

The man glanced down at the display, then looked back up at Carlton. "I walked into one last night, about an hour out of town, my wallet fat and happy with dead presidents. A few hours at the blackjack table and I was broke. And they don't even give you free drinks, like in Vegas. I tell you, Chief, it just ain't right."

Carlton frowned. There was only one casino near Kinsey, and he'd been there last night playing blackjack. He didn't remember seeing this guy hanging around. Then again, after pounding a few Buds, he didn't remember much of anything.

"You're looking a little green around the gills," Webber said. "You sure you're feelin' all right?"

"Yup, fine," Carlton mumbled.

"I'd say you're about as fuzzy as a daylily with a pickle in its mouth." Webber laughed, but Carlton didn't get the joke. "You know what you need, Chief? A little hair of the dog, that's what."

Carlton again had the feeling he should be doing something, but it was now only a faint tickle at the periphery of his mind. And he *had* been wondering about the beer. He was pretty much broke, and the old fridge was as bare as that Hubbard bitch's cupboard.

"That one's not in the cards," Carlton said, amused at his own attempt at humor.

Webber tapped his cigarette ash out the window. "Tell you what. You seem like a good enough joe. How 'bout we meet up later? Tip a few. My treat."

On some primitive level, the one where instinct trumped logic and tried to take control, Carlton Manick understood that danger lay ahead. There was a question here, an important one, but his hung-over mind couldn't quite grasp what it was; thinking had become hard, like trying to pull water out of a river with a fishing net. And when you got down to what *really* curled your short-hairs, payday was almost two weeks away, and that was a long time to go cold turkey.

"Sure. I get off at three. I'll meet you at the Lula. It's down on Asher."

"Ah…no, not there," Webber said quickly. "I'm not much for plain old bars. Why don't we meet in front of that Kwik-N-Go party store I saw back there on the main drag?"

"I know the place."

"I thought you might." Webber took another pull on his cigarette, held it, and then let wispy threads of smoke drifted out from his nostrils.

For some reason, the sight unsettled Carlton; he knew it shouldn't have, but it did.

And that fuzzy, hung-over feeling was back. His head felt thick, like it was filled with molasses. He tried to push through the stickiness, to clear his thoughts, but the effort only made him feel worse. His eyes started to burn, his lids grew heavy, and Carlton wondered if he was going to pass out.

"Need you to do me a favor, Chief." Webber's voice, though he spoke softly, cut through the fuzzy-sticky mass of his hangover. "A show of faith, let's say. For all the beer I'll be buying."

Carlton tried to blink, but his eyelids had grown so goddamn *heavy*. Jesus, what was wrong with him?

"Fuzzy as a daylily," he mumbled.

"I bet you are, Chief," Webber said. "I bet you are. Now, come a little closer. Let me tell you what I want you to do."

And Carlton, who was thinking of that "hair of the dog" and getting rid of this hangover, listened with interest.

*   *   *

Gene watched Bart Owens ease himself into the back of the police cruiser. As Bob Talbert walked around to get into the driver's seat, Owens stared at him through the window. He briefly shook his head. The message was clear: I didn't do this.

Owens and Izzy had managed to keep Stanley alive until the EMTs could stabilize him by using a small defibrillator to shock his heart back into beating. Before she'd left in the ambulance with her husband, Izzy had approached Owens.

"Thank you," she'd said, her face flushed from exertion and emotion. "For helping save him. I know you didn't have to, not after what he tried to do."

Owens had simply nodded in reply.

Then she'd asked him if he was willing to go down to the station and answer a few questions.

"I don't have many answers," the man had said. "But I'll hear your questions."

That had been enough for Izzy.

The cruiser pulled away with Owens in the back seat.

A handful of spaces over from his Jeep, Gene noticed Denny Cain pull out a cell phone. Turning his back to everyone, the man put the phone to one ear, his finger in the other. He began talking.

Gene strode over to Denny, the wind masking his footsteps. Just as Denny shoved the phone back in his pocket, Gene tapped him on the shoulder and said, "Hey there."

Denny spun around. "Jesus, Gene! You scared the hell outta me."

"Have you lost your damn mind? What were you thinking back there?"

"Sorry," Denny replied, looking down and away. "Don't know what you mean."

"You know *exactly* what I mean. You provoked Stanley into that attack."

"Look, I got stuff to do. And besides, I'm not much interested in your conspiracy theories."

Gene poked a finger in Denny's chest. Hard. Construction work had sheathed his arms in thick muscles, and rehab had only added to his strength. Denny winced and took a step back.

"We all heard you. And in his state of mind, Stanley would've listened to anything." Gene took a step closer. "So you whispered in his ear—nudged him in the right direction—and he attacked Owens. I've known that man since we were in third grade. He's never been violent in his life."

"Where's your proof, Gene?" Denny looked around, made sure everyone else was out of earshot. In a harsh whisper, he added, "That jig bastard killed my son. I'm gonna make sure he gets what he deserves."

Gene shook his head in disbelief. "You don't know what happened any more than I do. Stanley's been your friend for years, and you almost got him killed. Hell, he might still die."

"You'd like that, wouldn't you?" Denny said. "Oh, yeah. We know about you. How you've had the hots for Izzy. Some even figure that's why you left Kinsey." Denny's lips curled into a smug grin. "The way I see it, I did you a favor. Her old man kicks off, and you can move in. Maybe finally tap some of that."

Gene caught hold of Denny's shirt with both hands and jerked him forward. His back cried out in protest, but he was too angry to care.

"Listen to me," Gene said. "You so much as set foot in the Lula again and I'll—"

"You're on the wrong side of this one," Denny spluttered as he struggled to free himself. "You'd best start looking out for yourself."

"I don't have a clue what you're talking about." He shoved the man away. This time his back practically screamed. "Beat it, Denny. Get the hell out of here."

Denny stumbled off, glaring at Gene. He never lost that smug, knowing look.

Gene worked at his back with his fingers. He was angry at Denny, but he was more dismayed by what the man had said. How people had come to the truth of why he'd left town.

And why he had returned.

CHAPTER
10

"J.J., stop it!"

Katie Bethel stood in middle of the Sallinen's living room. After the search for Natalie had been called off, Katie planned on catching a ride home with Brittany Parsons. Then she realized that she really didn't want to go home. Her mother would likely be awake by then, hung-over and feeling miserably depressed. Not about the drinking, of course; it was *never* about the drinking. No, her mother would be depressed about letting Katie down. Again.

Yesterday afternoon, her mother had said she wanted to help with the search. But this morning, when Katie had shaken her repeatedly, her mother couldn't be roused. She lay there, snoring loudly, her breath sour from old alcohol. There was an empty fifth of vodka lying on the floor next to her bed, and Katie knew her mother had purchased it yesterday afternoon.

Dealing with another litany of her mother's empty apologies was more than Katie could handle right now, so she'd asked Brittany to drive her over to J.J.'s house.

"Stop what?" replied Jack Sallinen, Jr., as he danced around the living room, skirting the leather sofa and hopping over a marble coffee table. He held a box of crayons high above his head.

His brother Kevin chased after him. The boy's knees banged against the furniture, and his skinny arms grabbed and slapped at his older brother. He made incoherent sounds as he tried to get his crayons back.

"Stop teasing him!" Katie yelled.

"C'mon, Katie. It's just a little game of 'Keep Away'." J.J. laughed harder when Kevin tripped over a reclining chair and skinned his elbows on the carpet.

"Look," she said. "Now he's crying."

J.J. stopped moving and shot her an angry glare. "He's not *your* brother, so butt out."

Kevin bounded up from the floor and hustled across the room. Clearly furious, the boy clenched his slender hand into a fist and drew back as far as it would go. Once he'd reached his brother, Kevin threw his fist forward and punched J.J. square in the crotch.

J.J. collapsed soundlessly to the floor, the box tumbling from his hand. Kevin dove for it, but J.J., red-faced and sweating and looking pissed, managed to scramble between his brother and the crayon box. He snatched Kevin's arms and hauled him to his feet.

"Little retard," muttered J.J. and got Kevin in a head-lock. He spun him around, let him go, and then shoved him hard to the ground, where the younger boy curled up into a ball and howled like a wounded animal.

Katie marched up to J.J.. She slapped him as hard as she could; despite putting some heat into it, the blow barely moved J.J.'s head. "Kevin's your brother. He's got a disability. And still you treat him like this? What's your next act, J.J.? Stuff someone's cat in a microwave?"

J.J. looked at her with pain in his eyes. The slap had left a red mark on his left cheek. "Don't lecture me. You don't know what it's like living here." He pointed to his wailing brother. "This whole damn house revolves around him. My dad is constantly with him, making sure he's not playing with the stove or that he's eating all his food or that he's wiped his ass completely. And me? I barely talk to my dad anymore, and I'm lucky if my mom calls more than once a month." He made frustrated little gestures with his hands. "I float around here like I'm some goddamn ghost."

"It's not his fault," Katie returned. Her previous anger had burned itself out. Now she felt a mixture of sadness and pity. This was a side of her boyfriend she hadn't seen before, and she wasn't sure if she should be relieved or concerned. "He didn't ask to be born like this."

J.J. glanced down at Kevin, then back at her. "I know. Look, I'm sorry. He caught me off guard with that punch. I'll make it up to him." J.J. bent down and put a hand on his brother's shoulder. "Hey, Kev. I'm sorry. Let me help you get your crayons."

Kevin curled up tighter and sobbed into his crossed arms.

J.J. grabbed the green and yellow box. He shook it to make some noise. "Hey, bro. Here they are." He rubbed Kevin's shoulder. "Come on, I gave you your stuff back."

Kevin ignored him.

"Fine," J.J. said, dropping the box. "Go ahead and cry." He walked over to one of the recliners and plopped himself down in it. Frustration darkened his features.

Katie picked up the box of crayons. She walked over to J.J. and held it out to him. "You started it, you finish it. Try again or I'm leaving."

He refused to look at her for several seconds. Then, with a small grunt, he took the box and got up. "Have it your way."

J.J. went over and sat cross-legged in front of his brother. He looked around, spotted a box of Kleenex on the coffee table. Pulling one out, he used it to tickle Kevin's ear.

Nothing happened at first. Then—one of Kevin's hands swiped at the air. J.J. had been expecting this and yanked the tissue away in time. Again he tickled Kevin, and this time Kevin turned his head enough to peek out of the crook of his elbow; it looked comically like the eye-gazing-out-of-a-keyhole shot in old *Three Stooges* reruns.

J.J. lifted the crayon box and placed it near Kevin's head. "Go on. Take it."

Kevin's sobbing had fizzled into sniffles. First, he grabbed the Kleenex from J.J. and carelessly wiped his face, missing most of the snot and tears. Next he snatched up the crayon box. He ran for his room.

J.J. looked sullenly at Katie as he walked back to the chair and sat down. "There. Happy now?"

Katie got up and approached J.J.. She sat on the edge of the recliner, an arm draped over his shoulder. "I know it's hard, but you've got to remember, he's just a kid. He didn't ask for any of this. I mean, can you imagine what his life's going to be like? No job. No wife. No kids. Always needing someone to take care of him. How happy can he ever really be?"

J.J. stared hard at the carpet. "But what about me? I try so hard to make my dad proud. I made varsity football my sophomore year. I'll probably get to play freshman ball at Ann Arbor. Hell, as much as money means to him, I thought he'd be impressed that I may get a full ride at college. But neither he nor my mom ever says anything. It's all about Kevin."

"Life's full of hard times." She knew this fact better than most.

Had experienced it first-hand. "You might as well get used to it."

J.J. opened his mouth to say something but simply shrugged. "Enough about Kevin. How'd it go today? You guys find anything?"

"Yes and no," she said as she told him the day's events.

"No shit. Nat's dad really shot somebody?"

"He didn't hit anyone. And he had a heart attack. They had to do CPR on him."

J.J. gave a wistful sigh. "I miss all the cool stuff."

Katie punched his arm. "Nat's dad could've died, you idiot. He still could. Now when she's found, she'll have to deal with that, too."

She felt J.J. squirm under her arm.

"What?" Katie asked.

"Nothing," he said. "I just...I don't want you to get your hopes up. It's been two days. The chances of finding her are pretty slim."

"Don't be so sure. There's something strange going on around here. And besides, I don't think Mr. Owens did it."

"The black guy?" J.J. shook his head. "He's toast."

Katie sat up straighter, took her arm off his shoulder. "What happened to 'innocent until proved guilty'?"

"Come on, be realistic. He's a stranger. He just got into town. And something of his was found at the scene. Don't *you* think that's a little odd?"

"I know it doesn't look good. But there's something about that guy. He doesn't seem like the kind of person who could kill someone."

"The cops'll figure it out," J.J. said confidently. "Anyway, enough of all this depressing talk. I think my dad might have a new bottle of scotch in his office. I wouldn't mind trying a sip. Come on."

He started walking away, but Katie stayed where she was. It took him several steps to realize he was alone. He turned and gave her a puzzled look.

"What *now*?"

"The scotch," Katie said, her arms crossed under her breasts. "You know how I feel about drinking."

J.J.'s shook his head and sighed. "Look, I know you don't drink. And I'm not asking you to. But that doesn't mean I can't." He held out his hand to her. "Only a sip, I promise. If I took any more, my dad would notice and raise holy hell."

"It starts with a sip," Katie said as she got up, but she refused to take J.J.'s hand. "Remember, my dad thought he could keep it to a sip.

Look at what happened to him."

"Katie, please. I'm not your father. What he did was horrible. But I'm not like that."

"How do I know? How do you even know? We never know what we're capable of until it's too late."

"Come on, settle down. You're getting worked up over nothing. Really." He cupped her face in one hand. "Hey, I tell you what, how about we go see him tomorrow? Your dad? You haven't been there in a while."

"No," said Katie, her voice hitching with emotion. "I'm tired of pretending. Pretending for you; pretending for my mom. His body may be there, underneath all that cold dirt, but I know he can't hear me. Not anymore. Not where he is now. My dad ended up where I can't follow."

Uncrossing her arms, she pushed J.J.'s hand from her face. "Suicides burn in Hell."

Katie sat in an antique Regency Carver mahogany chair in Mr. Sallinen's office. She knew it was an "antique Regency Carver mahogany chair" because J.J.'s dad had made a point of telling her several times. Truthfully, it looked like one of those cheap pieces of furniture you could get at SecondHand Rose's Resale Repository for around ten bucks.

She'd been in this room a handful of times before, and, in spite of the disappointment at the chair, she'd been impressed each time. The lower half of the walls was encased in dark walnut paneling, while the upper half was painted dark amber, like the color of overripe pumpkins. Thick carpeting muffled their footsteps. The antique chair she occupied and its twin sat in front of a large wooden desk. Various community awards hung on the wall behind the desk, as well as some photographs of Mr. Sallinen with people she didn't recognize. The air in the room was stale, as if no one ever opened a window to let in the outside world.

J.J. sat in a comfortable leather chair behind the desk. He'd rummaged through the desk, found a locked drawer, and used a letter opener to jimmy the lock. Inside, he'd found a rectangular gray metal box, also locked. He was now using the letter opener to try to pry it open.

Katie got up and moved to a painting on the wall across from the desk. It depicted a woman lying asleep on a sofa, her arms dangling over her head and her neck exposed. A creature—a demon of some sort—sat on her chest and looked out at the viewer. The head of a black horse, its eyes painted bright yellow against the darker colors surrounding it, emerged from a part in the curtains that made up the background. It was a disturbing image. Katie had asked Mr. Sallinen about it once. "It's called *The Nightmare,* by a man named Henry Fuseli," he'd said. "It represents the relationship between sleeping and the dreams we have. How our darker side surfaces in the night. It's really quite beautiful."

She hadn't thought so then, and she didn't think so now. It was still a creepy painting.

J.J. blurted, "Hey! I got it op—"

Katie turned. J.J. stood with his back to her. His arms were bent, his head tilted down, looking at something he held in his hands.

"Did you find your precious scotch bottle?" she asked.

J.J. stuffed whatever it was into his pocket and spun to face her. His face was pale.

"Um…it's nothing. Just, you know, some old junk of my dad's."

"Don't keep me waiting," Katie said. "Show me what you found."

"Really, it's nothing." He ran a hand over his face. "Look, I think you should go. I don't want to push my luck. If my dad catches us in here…."

Katie started toward the desk.

"No! No, don't come over here. I'm sorry, but you need to leave. Please? I'll call you later."

Katie frowned. "I—well, sure. I guess."

"Thanks," he said, sounding relieved. "Maybe we'll go see a movie or something tonight."

She stopped at the office door. "You sure you're all right?"

J.J. nodded. "Yeah, I'm fine. Later, okay?"

"Later," she replied and walked out of the office.

Well, that was interesting, she thought once she was outside.

Her walk home took about half an hour, and during that time, she grew more curious what J.J. had been hiding from her.

CHAPTER
11

Jack Sallinen, Sr., felt his cell phone vibrate against his hip. "Excuse me," he said to the man sitting across from him and thumbed the answer button.

"Sallinen."

"Hey, Dad," his son J.J. chirped into his ear. "Got a minute?"

"No, actually, I don't."

"Well, you better make time, because what I've got to say is important."

Jack paused. Assertiveness was something new for J.J.. Typically, the boy showed as much initiative as a tree sloth. Unless, of course, he was conniving with his bitch of a mother. Jack had lost a lot of his wealth in the divorce, in part due to his son's interfering and ill-timed comments.

"All right," Jack said, his chair creaking as he settled back into it. "This had better be good."

"Oh, it's good, Pops. Headline news stuff." There was a pause. "Natalie Morris. I know you're involved with what happened to her."

Jack felt the skin tighten along the back of his neck. "That's ridiculous."

"I found photos of her in your desk," J.J. said. "And she looked dead."

The words made Jack grow cold inside. His grip on the cell tightened until his knuckles blazed white.

"What's the matter?" J.J. said. "For once, you've got nothing to say?"

Jack pulled in a deep breath, giving himself a chance to think. J.J. wasn't the sharpest knife in the drawer. He *did* call here first and not the cops. Or did he?

"Who else have you talked to about this?" he asked, realizing there was no sense denying it now.

"Not the cops, if that's what you're thinking."

"Good," said Jack, then reluctantly added, "thank you." The words burned like acid on his tongue.

"Jesus—you *did* kill her!" J.J.'s words spilled out in a stunned rush. "And Jimmy."

Jack lifted his eyes to the man sitting across the table from him. Darryl Webber met his gaze with a grin and a wink.

"I haven't killed anyone." Jack sneezed once, twice. He grabbed a Kleenex and wiped at his nose.

"Bless you, father, for you have sinned," J.J. said with a nervous laugh. "So, tell me. What're you doing with photos of a dead girl—someone the whole town is looking for?"

"I'm not explaining myself to you," snapped Jack. "Especially not over the phone. And why couldn't this wait until I got home?"

"Isn't it obvious? If you have these photos, then you know where she's buried. I figured that's worth something."

The idiot didn't even understand the question. How could he have fathered such a complete turd?

"Fine," Jack said. "What do you want?"

There was silence on the other end. Jack thought J.J. would finally fold. But his son surprised him.

"I want in. Whatever you're doing, I want to be a part of it. I want to help."

Great, *now* he gets ambitious. "I don't need a partner."

"Either you let me help, or I go to the cops with the photos. Not even *you* will be able to get yourself out of that one."

The little shit was blackmailing him? He wanted to reach through the phone, grab a fistful neck, and choke the life out of him. But he couldn't, not yet. J.J. had the photos. Or he'd seen them. But had anyone else?

"When I get home, we can talk. For now, let's keep this between you and me."

"Well…that's another thing. Katie was here when I found them. I freaked a little, but I think I hid it. Then I made up an excuse to get her out of here."

Jack exploded. "You went into a room where you're not allowed, forced your way into a locked drawer, got into a locked box, and you didn't have the presence of mind to do it alone? Jesus H. Christ, boy!"

Webber's shoulders shook with silent laughter

"Oh sure," J.J. said. "As if I knew what I'd find. Who thinks their dad's a serial killer who keeps photos of his victims in a drawer?"

"I'm not—" Jack clamped down hard on his rising temper. "Never mind. This makes the girl a problem. I can't count on her believing you, or keeping her mouth shut."

"No," said J.J.. "I won't let you hurt her. That's part of the deal. To keep *my* mouth shut."

"Something will have to be done."

"I don't want her hurt," J.J. repeated.

"Fine. She won't be touched."

J.J. hesitated. "Promise me."

"What!" Jack shouted into the phone.

"Promise or go to jail."

From across the table, Webber made a little "get on with it" gesture with his hand.

Gritting his teeth, Jack said. "I promise."

"Great," J.J. replied. "We can talk more when you get home."

"Whatever," Jack said, hanging up without saying goodbye. He threw the cell down on his desk in disgust and looked at Webber. "I suppose you pieced that together?"

Webber tapped his cigarette, and ashes floated like toxic snow onto the carpet. "You insisted on having those photos," he said evenly. "You wanted proof that I could do what I said. But I'm starting to wonder if a little pud-puller like you had other reasons. Let me guess—your subscription to *Playboy* ran out?" He stubbed out his cigarette on Jack's desktop, mere inches from an ashtray.

Jack's face grew warm. Webber's comment had hit a little too close to the mark. "Don't worry. I'll get rid of them."

"I told you to destroy them *immediately* after you'd seen them."

"They won't cause any more problems."

Webber shot him a look that made the hairs on the back of Jack's neck stand straight. "I've put too much work into this little endeavor to have you screw it up. Do it again and you'll find yourself cut out of our little deal." His lip curled in one corner. "Or worse."

Jack tried to swallow, but all he managed was a dry click. "I know you're supposed to be some kind of von Kliner's expert, but I don't see how any of this helps Kevin."

"It may not affect him," Webber said. "But it does involve him."

When Webber didn't elaborate, Jack said, "Okay, you want to tell me how?"

Webber pursed his lips, then shrugged. "I'm here to prevent a man from doing a bad thing. This guy—name's Bartholomew Owens—he's a nasty character. Comes across as some kind of harmless old guy. He's as harmless as a towel head with a truck full of nukes." He paused to light another cigarette. "Owens is here to cause trouble, and I'm here to stop him."

"So...this guy's got something to do with Kevin?"

Nodding, Webber said, "I'm just waiting for word that he's locked up in a jail cell. Then I'll deal with him."

"But you still haven't told me—?"

"Later," Webber said firmly.

Jack started to protest, but then felt something burn deep in his lungs. He broke into a series of violent, hacking coughs, brought up a thick gob of phlegm, and spat it into a tissue.

Webber peered at him. "You look rough."

"I think it's just a cold. I should be better in a couple days." Though, honestly, he did feel pretty crappy: aches and pains, shivers, night sweats. After his lungs had settled down, Jack said, "The Morris girl. Does she have anything to do with Owens?" Is that why Webber had grabbed her? To keep her away from him?

Webber shook his head but said nothing.

Jack decided to push a little harder. He had a suspicion, brought on by the condition of the Cain boy's body and the full moon. It was a bizarre thought, but bizarre was an excellent word to describe Darryl Webber. "The Cain boy wasn't killed by an animal, was he? At least, not a *natural* animal."

Webber gave him a flat, unfriendly stare and continued his silence.

"Fine," Jack said, exasperated. "Have it your way. But if this doesn't have anything to do with Kevin directly, why did you involve me?"

Webber leaned back in his chair. "I can't finish this *without* you. You're the most important man in Kinsey. You've got power, influence. Once I deal with Owens, you'll be indispensable." This time he tapped his cigarette ashes into the ashtray. "I assume you enjoyed the money I sent you?"

"Sure," Jack answered. Ten grand was hard to pass up when you worked in a small burg like Kinsey. "But that's a lot of money for information you could've gotten off the internet."

"A piece never knows it is part of a puzzle until it's put in its place."

"Run that by me again. In English this time."

Webber shrugged. "Help me finish what I need to do and, like I promised, your life will change in ways you can't imagine."

"It'd better," Jack said, scowling. "I'm risking a lot on just your word."

The man smiled. It looked false—a paper smile, like it had been fastened to his face with pins and tape. "Trust me."

Jack thought back to the call from his son. "I can handle J.J.. But what about the girl? I promised she wouldn't be hurt."

"Don't worry," Webber said. "I'll take care of her. Soon she'll be too busy to wonder about anything. Besides, I think your chief needs another crisis to help keep her from looking our way."

Jack peered closely at Webber. "What have you got in mind?"

Gently lifting himself out of his chair, Webber leaned in close to Jack, bracing himself on the desktop with his arms. He pushed his face close, so close that Jack could feel the scrape of the other man's whiskers against his cheek, so close that Jack thought Webber might kiss him.

"That's on a 'need to know' basis, Jack. And you don't need to know."

* * *

Izzy Morris sat at her desk, staring out her office window, trying to gather her thoughts. People strolled along the tree-shaded sidewalks of Asher Street, enjoying the cool fall weather and doing a little window shopping. Mrs. Lee had once again stopped to consider the clothes on display at Rose Dwight's resale shop. A widow whose husband had died in the first Gulf War, Olivia Lee had never recovered from her loss. She constantly sought the perfect dress to wear when her long dead husband finally returned from Iraq. As the woman entered SecondHand Rose's Resale Repository, Izzy finally understood Liv's pain. And the shallow comfort of her denial.

Stanley had been admitted to the hospital in critical condition.

While his heart had stabilized, he remained unconscious. The doctors were running tests and monitoring his condition. They were still uncertain as to what had happened or if it could happen again.

She had considered staying with him, but there wasn't anything she could do there. She had a missing daughter and a person of interest in the case, so she'd decided to come back to the station. Finding Natalie was the best thing she could do for Stanley—and for herself.

Izzy picked up the file containing what little information she had on Bart Owens and scanned Sten Billick's preliminary report.

With Owens' consent, Sten had run the man's fingerprints through the FBI's National Crime Information Center. The search had come up empty. The man had no criminal record.

When asked for ID, Owens had produced an expired Tennessee driver's license. A call to that state had also been a bust. Except for possibly driving without a valid license, Owens was clean in Tennessee. Then again, their DMV had also said that Owens didn't have a car registered in their state. In fact, looking as far back as their on-line records go, he hadn't ever registered a car there. She'd known people who had a driver's license but no car, except they usually lived in crowded cities like New York, Chicago, LA. But Nashville? She'd been there twice for police conferences. Everything was spaced well apart. That meant expensive taxi rides or a lot of walking.

Just to be thorough, Sten had searched Michigan's LEIN system. Izzy wasn't surprised when that came back negative, too.

She wanted a work history on this guy, but that would take more time. For now, she would use what was available.

Izzy didn't like to follow instinct. She trusted routine, methodical police procedures. But she'd also be a fool if she didn't trust her gut once in a while. This Owens guy was strange, and her gut told her that he was involved somehow.

It was time to talk to him. But first, she needed to do one thing. It might destroy her case against Owens, should there ever be one. But with Natalie missing, she was willing to take the chance.

She picked up the phone and contacted her dispatcher. "Aggie, who's out on the road right now?"

Izzy Morris opened the gunmetal gray door and stepped inside the interview room. It was a small, pale yellow cinder-block enclosure with a two-way window in one wall. Twin fluorescent fixtures spilled harsh light from the ceiling. To Izzy, the stale air smelled of old guilt and denial.

Bart Owens sat in one of two metal folding chairs, his hands together on the scratched surface of a long wood table. He'd shed the jacket he had worn during the search. Now he was dressed in a Nashville Predators sweatshirt, his head bowed, his short, crinkly hair almost glinting under the room's light.

His eyes were closed. Was he meditating? Praying? Sleeping?

On the far side of the table, Detective Sten Billick occupied the other chair. The tap-tapping of his pencil on a yellow legal pad meant that something was bothering him. Izzy could list five things off the top of her head that bothered her about this case. At least she wasn't alone.

At one end of the table sat a cassette tape recorder, its wheels slowly spinning.

She moved to stand next to Sten. "Mind if we talk, Mr. Owens?"

Owens opened his eyes. "I'm sorry about your husband. Is he going to be okay?"

Izzy waved aside his question. "Let's talk about you. Detective Billick tells me you're being evasive. That you're not answering his questions."

"I'm not trying to be difficult," Owens said, one finger tracing vague patterns on the table top. "I simply don't have the answers you want."

Izzy said, "And you maintain that you had nothing to do with my daughter's disappearance? Or Jimmy Cain's death?"

"I don't know where she is," Owens said. "And I believe the boy was killed by an animal. That would rule me out, wouldn't it?"

Sten cut smoothly into the interrogation. "For the sake of completeness, let's go over the basics again. When did you arrive in town?"

Owens turned to Sten. "Friday evening."

Picking up his notebook, Sten reviewed what he'd written. "You say you left Nashville early last Thursday. Arrived in Newberry on Friday afternoon by bus. However, you didn't show up at the Lula until *Saturday* afternoon. Where were you between Friday afternoon and Saturday afternoon?"

"I walked to Kinsey. By the time I'd arrived, it was dark."

"You walked all that way?" Sten said. "Why not take a taxi?"

"I needed the exercise," Owens replied calmly.

"And where'd you spend Friday night?"

"I don't remember."

"Bullshit," said Sten. "Where'd you stay?"

"It was a hotel. I don't remember the name."

"The same one you're staying at now?"

"No."

"How'd you pay for your room?"

"Cash."

"Why didn't you just charge it?" asked Sten.

"No credit card," said Owens, gesturing to the reports sitting on the table. "But you already know that, Detective."

Sten raised an eyebrow. From a stack of papers, he pulled out the credit report on Owens. No credit cards. No loans. No mortgages. No history of anything. He placed the paper in front of Owens.

"This isn't possible," Sten said, tapping the report with a finger.

Owens picked up the report, his eyes scanning it. "Everything looks correct to me."

"I couldn't even find a checking account. How do you pay your bills?"

Owens' gaze shifted to Izzy. "I don't see how any of this will help find your daughter."

Izzy pointed to the report in his hands. "Just answer the question."

"I like to pay cash," Owens replied, sliding the paper across the table. "I'm quite sure that's not illegal."

"Mr. Owens," Izzy said. "I know you're not under arrest. That you're here voluntarily. But look at it from our side. You're new in town. You have an unusual history, which in this case means no history at all. And we found something of yours at the crime scene. You have to admit, it would make any cop suspicious."

"I am who I am. All your reports are correct. And none of them points to me being a criminal."

"No, not directly," admitted Izzy. She was going to continue, but the door banged open. Aggie Ripley hurried into the room. She looked frazzled as she handed Izzy a piece of paper.

"Sorry to interrupt," the dispatcher said. "But I thought you'd want to see this." Then she left, closing the door behind her.

Izzy read the paper. The message told her all she needed to know.

Bart Owens had been lying the entire time.

She handed the paper to Sten. Then she leaned over and turned off the cassette recorder. Looking back at Owens, she said, "Before I came here, I sent a couple patrol cars over to the hotel where you're staying. I know the manager, and she let Officers Hamilton and Manick into your room."

Wariness bled into the man's features. His eyes darted to the paper in Sten's hand.

"That's right," Izzy said. "Now, they didn't find anything during their look around the room—you're obviously too clever to leave anything out in the open. So I also left orders for them to go through your possessions."

Owens' eyebrows rose in surprise. "Without a search warrant?"

"My daughter's missing," Izzy said evenly. "I don't give a damn about a warrant."

Owens stared at her for a moment, then nodded heavily. "You may as well tell me what they found."

"Why don't *you* tell us what they found," interjected Sten.

"I don't know," answered Owens. "Because I had nothing to do with this."

Izzy snatched the paper from Sten's hands and shook it at Owens. "They found my daughter's necklace, you lying bastard! It was hidden in the bottom of your duffel bag!"

Owens laid his hands flat on the tabletop. "That necklace wasn't in there when I left this morning. I promise you."

Sten placed a restraining hand on Izzy's arm. Then he turned his attention to Owens. "I doubt that'll score you any points with a judge, Mr. Owens. But for now"—he turned the recorder back on—"I'm placing you under arrest." He read Owens his Miranda Rights. "Do you understand these rights as I have read them to you?"

"Listen to me," Owens said, his hands closing into fists. "This is the worst thing you could do right now."

"Do you understand your rights?" repeated Sten.

"I can't be locked up," insisted Owens.

Izzy threw the paper onto the table. "Then tell me where my daughter is!"

Owens raised his voice for the first time. "I don't know where she is."

Sten got up and placed his muscular body between Izzy and Owens. "All right. We're done for now. Come on, Owens. You need to be processed. Looks like you're going to be our guest for a while."

Izzy was about to protest—this man knew where her daughter was!—when Sten turned to her.

"This back and forth is useless, Chief. For now, let me dig a little deeper into his past. See what I can find. Then I'll come back and talk to him." He lowered his voice. "We're not giving up on your daughter."

Izzy's mouth worked silently as she struggled with her emotions. She knew Sten was right. He needed time to do his job properly. And that didn't mean she was giving up on her daughter.

But why did she feel like she was?

CHAPTER
12

Chet Boardman arrived early at Memorial Park. Picnic basket in hand, he strolled toward the large gazebo that sat at the western edge of the park; past the rusty swings and monkey bars and slides that made up the playground; past picnic tables and little steel barbecue units crusted black from years of grilling burgers and franks; past the Little League field where Stanley Morris had organized the children's Fourth of July baseball games. Behind the gazebo, the land gave way to a sandy beach and the dark water of Black Pine Lake gently lapping at the shoreline. The sun was a smear of vermilion clinging to the horizon, the sky a broad brushstroke of crimson clouds.

"Red sky at night, sailors delight," said Chet, reciting an old fisherman's rhyme he'd learned from his father when, as a boy, he'd helped his dad pull fish from Lake Superior. Fishing was a hard life. It'd taken his old man with pneumonia at the age of thirty-seven. Chet, then only seventeen and the oldest of three boys, had become the man of the house. He hadn't even been laid yet, but he was expected to work daily and provide for the family and help his mom raise his two brothers. So he'd dropped out of school—no great shakes since he'd never done well anyway—got all the necessary licenses and permits, and began his life as a fisherman.

Forty years on the water hadn't been easy on him either. His hands were like granite slabs, thick with calluses. His fingers were gnarled—they'd been broken countless times and set using Popsicle sticks and duct tape because Big Blue wouldn't insure him without taking every last dime he pulled out of the lake. Clothes hung loosely on his thin frame. People often mistook him for a pushover, the skinny kid in those Charles Atlas ads he'd seen in the comics long ago. But pulling in loads of fish day after day wasn't easy, and Chet was wiry strong, the veteran of many bar fights. Wearing his faded red-and-black checked cap and rumpled blue shirt, he looked like an extra from *Jaws*.

He arrived at the gazebo and climbed the risers. The wood boards creaked with each step. As he set foot on the floor of the structure, the sun dipped below the horizon and winked out. Chet set his wicker basket on the picnic table in the center of the gazebo. Thankful for the lack of wind, he pulled out two thick, white candles and placed them at either end of the table. He used his Zippo—the only thing his old man had left him—to light the wicks. Next out of the basket came dinner plates, silverware, and a platter of fried chicken covered with plastic wrap. Then two bowls, one filled with coleslaw, the other with corn. Last out were two bottles of wine—red, which a guy at the Kwik-N-Go said you were supposed to serve with meat—and plastic cups. After uncorking the wine—this was something else the guy had told him, though Chet wondered how could wine *breathe?*—he sat on the table's bench seat, listened to the chorus of frogs singing from the woods lining the northern edge of the park, and looked out into the darkness. The park was empty. Perfect, he thought with a smile.

His date should be here soon.

It wasn't long before a pair of headlights appeared at the park entrance. A car crawled across the blacktop and pulled alongside his old Ford F-150. Chet winced when the front of the car came too close to his and the grating sound of metal kissing metal cut through the air. It silenced the frogs, allowing the sound of branches breaking far in the woods to filter through. Chet shook his head. Damn deer were everywhere this year.

A car door slammed shut. A figure started walking toward the gazebo. Darkness seemed to gather around the person. It wasn't until she'd reached the pavilion's steps that he could make out her features. The flickering candlelight made her skin look sallow, transformed the dark circles under her eyes into angry bruises. Her light brown hair looked like it had been worked with a curling iron, and a small blue bow had been clipped to her hair at either temple. She wore a pale blue dress with frilly white lace at the hem and shoulders. Another bow with wide loops and dangling tails decorated the front of the dress at her waist. Chet, who may not have done well in school but had his own measure of smarts, wondered if she realized all the bows made her look like a present waiting to be opened.

"Hi, Chet," she said with a smile. Her teeth were perfectly straight. It was her smile that Chet had always found attractive.

"Why Jenny Bethel, don't you look wonderful tonight," was his reply.

"Thank you, Chet," said Jenny after they'd finished the candlelight dinner. "You're a marvelous cook."

"Welcome," he returned with a nod of his head.

"You caught me off guard when you called." Jenny refilled her glass with wine. One empty bottle already lay in the picnic basket. The other was half gone as Jenny worked her way through the wine. Chet had had only one glass—the last twenty-four hours had dried him out more than he would've expected—and he found he'd lost most of his taste for alcohol. Some strange shit had gone on, enough to give him the creeps. And a bit of perspective.

"Why?" he asked. "We've seen each other before."

She sipped her wine. "It was always you sneaking over to my place after Katie went to bed. We'd have a few drinks, fuck around a little, and you'd be gone before she woke up. But a date? A *real* date with candles and food? And look at the place you picked." She waved her glass around in a wobbly arc, sloshing a little wine on the table. "It's beautiful here. The full moon and the sounds of the lake. If I didn't know better, I'd say you were up to something."

He brought the cup to his lips, but then set it down before taking a drink. Jenny sat opposite him with slightly unfocused hope in her eyes, wearing what must be an old bridesmaid dress, their knees touching, her hand resting inches from his. And that smile. Bright and inviting in the darkness that surrounded them. He opened his mouth to say something, paused, and then did take a drink of his wine. After wiping his mouth with his sleeve, he pushed on.

"I ain't up to nothin'," he said. "I just...I wanted to get together. You know, not just mess around. I'm tired of just messing around." He swirled wine in his cup. "I never had much of a life. No wife. No kids. Been all by myself. I'm tired of having no one and nothin' to look forward to." His eyes lit up. "Like a boat that's broken its anchor line, I've been drifting all these years with nothing to hold me steady." He grinned, impressed with himself. That's about the most romantic thing he'd ever said.

Jenny stared at him. One bushy eyebrow crept up like an inchworm. "Did you just call me an anchor? A big, fat piece of metal?"

Chet's grin crumbled as his jaw fell open. He blinked, unsure of what to say. Had he gone and screwed it up, after all?

Jenny laughed and clapped her hands, which, wearing that dress, made her seem more a child than a widow in her mid-fifties. "Relax, Chet. I was just kidding! Seriously, men have no sense of humor." She placed her hand back on the table, but this time it covered his. "I appreciate what you did tonight. It's been a while, long before Adam died, that anyone went to so much trouble. But what I really want to know is, why? Why do you want something more now?"

He turned his hand to hold hers, his thumb caressing her skin. "I've had an odd couple days. Seen some of the uglier side of people I thought was my friends. Denny and me, we met this guy. He wants us to help him do something here in town, help him stop some…colored guy Gene's got playin' at the Lula. Said this Owens fella wants to cause trouble, hurt a few people, maybe kill someone. He thought the guy might even have Izzy's daughter."

"Wait a minute," Jenny said with a befuddled frown. "You think this guy knows something about Natalie? Have you told Izzy?"

"I don't know if he's telling the truth, Jenny. I mean, something ain't right about this Webber, the guy Denny and me met. He…when you're around him, you feel funny. See things that don't sit right. I suppose that could be the shakes. Hell, I had 'em before when I stopped drinking." He looked up at her. "But I feel fine. This wine? Tastes like water. I really don't want to finish it. And I don't even want a smoke. But that's a good thing, ain't it?

"What I'm trying to say is, I want to make a change, while I still have time. I want to make a difference. For you *and* me. This Webber fella? Denny drank his Kool Aid and is with him all the way. But me? I'm scared, Jenny. I gotta get away from all this. Try to live right for however many years I got left. And I don't want to be alone anymore." He tried to put all the sincerity in his voice that he felt inside. "I want you to come along for the ride."

She pulled her hands from his and looked down at her cup of wine. When she spoke, her voice was soft and sad. "You know me, Chet. I drink too much. Way too much. I've tried to stop, but that damn vodka bottle keeps calling to me from the freezer. I can't help myself." She looked back at him. "I'm damaged goods. If you really what a 'happily ever after' ending for your life, find a better person."

A coyote howled from the woods, giving voice to Chet's dismay. "Please, Jenny. It's not too late. At least, not too late to try." He lowered his voice. "Look at me. I don't got a lot of money. I certainly ain't no George Clooney." He slowly brought her hand to his lips and kissed it. "But deep inside I think I'm a good man, a *deserving* man. More so, I'm hoping you feel the same about yourself."

She looked at him for a while, silently regarding him or his words. Her grip on the cup tightened enough to crease the red plastic. She blinked several times, licked her lips. "I'm sorry, Chet. But I'm not like you. I'm not that strong." The hope fled from her eyes. "Adam used to say the same thing. That we could stop our drinking and be better parents for Katie. It didn't work out then, and it won't now. You *do* deserve a better life, just not with me. I'd only bring you back down. I couldn't live with myself if I did that to another person." She shuddered. "Once was enough."

The old Chet, hidden somewhere deep but still alive, screamed from the pain of another rejection, and the faint desire for a bourbon and cola swept through him for the first time in a day. The new Chet, still at the helm and steering the ship, ignored his old habits and smiled.

"How about this? We have another date. No fooling around. You and me have dinner again. We take it a day at a time. No promises, no commitments. Whadda ya think?"

Setting her cup of wine aside, Jenny sighed. "You know you're setting yourself up, right? You'll end up getting hurt, or worse."

"I figure my pain's my own business. I can risk it if I want to."

The coyote howled again. Only this time it was *much* closer, and maybe it wasn't a coyote. It sounded off. Funny.

Jenny threw a nervous glance toward the woods. "They don't usually get this close, do they?"

"It's probably just the chicken bones." Chet scooped up the scraps and dumped them into a bag. "Damn animals can smell food a mile away."

"But what if—?"

A shape emerged from the tree line. In the pale moonlight, it was a dark mass set against the darker backdrop of the trees. Larger than any coyote he'd ever seen. Larger than a bear....

"Chet," Jenny said worriedly.

He grabbed her arm. "Get behind me."

As he pulled her around the table, the animal broke into a loping run. It covered the distance with surprising speed and halted near the gazebo's steps. A growl issued from its throat, a thrumming, two-toned sound, as if it were using different sets of vocal chords. Chet could make out sleek fur, but it looked uneven, patchy. Twin flickering points of red flame danced in the darkness: the candlelight reflected in the eyes of whatever it was.

Chet stepped around the table. Got between the creature and Jenny.

Flapping his hands, he shouted, "Go on now! Get! Get outta here!"

The creature dug its front paws into the dirt and stretched, just like a damned cat. When it rose, its large head—that part looked faintly wolfish—scented the air. And maybe it was the dark playing tricks on him, but dear God, he thought he saw the creature *nod*, as if satisfied!

"*Ohmygodwhatisthatthing!*" Jenny shrieked and began crying.

Okay, it wasn't a trick of the dark. Jenny had seen the same incredible nod. Fear swept through him, old and primal, like a sailor's fear of being caught on the water with a summer thunderstorm rolling hard and fast over the lake. That kind of fear.

He didn't take his eyes off the creature. With one hand, he reached back. Groped along the top of the picnic table until he felt something thick and metallic. Brought his hand forward.

Great. He was now armed with a dinner knife. Against something *that* big.

"Jenny," he shouted. "Jenny! Listen to me!" She quieted down. "Stay behind me. If you get a chance, run for your car. Bring back help."

She didn't answer. He turned to see if she'd heard him. There was a rustling sound. Chet snapped his head around—and the creature was gone.

He whipped his head left, right, spun around to look behind him. Damn, where'd it go? He hadn't heard any twigs snapping, no leaves crackling, no sound at all.

It had to be nearby, but where?

Chet slowly looked up. The roof? Couldn't be, not up there—nothing can jump that high. And besides, he'd have heard it land. Still….

Slowly, silently, he slid one foot sideways, shifted his weight, drew the other foot in, edging back toward Jenny. Focus on the roof, he told himself. Wait for some sign that it was hiding up there. He slid again. Again. Now he was at the end of the table, no more than two feet from her. She had clamped her hands over her mouth, but she still made little whimpering noises. One of the bows had fallen out of her hair and landed on top of some leftover coleslaw.

"Jenny," he whispered, extending a hand.

Before she could lift a hand, the floor erupted in a storm of shattered boards and flying nails. The explosion launched the picnic table into the air. It flipped, collided with the gazebo's roof, and crashed to the floor, then skidded down the stairs and wedged between the wood handrails, blocking the exit.

With the candles snuffed out, darkness collapsed in on them, leaving behind the faint, crystalline glow of moonlight.

It took Chet a few seconds for his eyes to adjust. A broad swath of midnight climbed out of the hole in the floor. He laughed, brief, shrill. A panicked laugh.

Jenny backed away from the thing, muttering incoherently. She stopped when she hit the gazebo's railing.

Once out of the hole, the thing turned toward her.

"No!" Chet cried, slashing at the creature with his knife. The blade slid harmlessly across its thick hide. Twisting, he landed a solid blow with his left fist, and the creature grunted. So it *could* be hurt. He shifted his grip on the knife so the blade pointed down. With the creature snarling, its jaws snapping at him, he drew his arm back. Then, like a pitcher throwing a fastball, he launched a hard, overhand blow at the creature's back. Tears ran freely down his leathered cheeks as he drove years of frustration and rage into that one massive blow. He felt the blade skitter off something hard, and then sink in. The damned thing bellowed, turned...and stood up on its hind legs. Stunned, Chet didn't have time react. The creature hit him with a backhand blow to the chest. The impact drove the air from his lungs, and suddenly he was flying backward, twisting in the air, the inky black surface of the lake sliding across his vision. His hips lifted, gained altitude, and forced his head down. He tried to throw his arms out to catch himself, but he wasn't fast enough. He crashed hard into the picnic table, a thick board almost gutting him. The impact doubled him over. His head smacked solidly into more wood. The dark night turned a brilliant silvery-white, then back to black. He slid-rolled off the table and onto floor. The knife fell from his limp grasp. It clattered down the steps into the dirt below.

As Chet's body hung half in the gazebo, half on the steps, the creature turned and advanced on Jenny. Still upright, its head grazed the boards forming the gazebo's roof. Jenny, her eyes wide, stood transfixed as it reached with long, taloned fingers and grabbed her arms. Silhouetted against the moon-lit surface of Black Pine Lake, Chet saw the creature's shoulders bunch, saw muscles cord under fur and...and *scales*? Jenny's mouth split open into a soundless scream as the thing began to squeeze.

Chet tried to get up, desperately wanted to. He had to save Jenny. But the world had turned greasy from the pain wracking his body. He couldn't get his legs to work—they slipped, slid, folded under him. He cried out in frustration.

With her arms pinned to her side, Jenny finally found her voice. She screamed and screamed. Oh God, how she screamed. That sound, that horrid, pitiful, helpless *wailing*, filled Chet with coppery waves of terror.

The thing was killing her!

Adrenaline surged through his body like an electrical charge. His heart racing, Chet scrambled over the upturned picnic table, threw a hand out, fingers clutching for the gazebo's guardrail, banged clumsily against it, lost his balance and spilled forward. As he hit the floor face-first, something sharp ripped across his cheek. He brought his hand up, felt blood flowing from the wound; his trembling fingers pulled at the bent nail that had lodged itself into the meaty part of his jaw. The sour stench of urine filled the air, and he began crying when he realized he'd pissed himself.

All the while, Jenny's screams filled his ears until he thought they would burst.

The creature's jaws snapped at Jenny's face. Her hands flapped uselessly as her elbows were driven into her ribcage. Then, like a man playing an accordion, the creature brought its large hands together. Jenny crumpled like a used napkin. Her screams were cut off as gouts of blood flew from her mouth and nose, from her eyes and ears. Her hands spasmed into fists; her feet drummed against the floor.

The creature lifted her. Shook her. Threw her into the night. She landed on the beach, some thirty feet away.

She wasn't moving.

"No, no, God no," rasped Chet through his tears. "I'm sorry, Jenny."

The thing turned, dropped back on all fours. It issued a harsh, barking sound, almost like a hyena's. Almost like laughter.

"What are you waiting for? I'm not afraid of you!"

The creature skirted the hole in the floor. It stopped before Chet.

"Come on!" he screamed. "Come and get me!"

And it did.

CHAPTER
13

Monday

Izzy was back in the interview room with Sten and her suspect. Bart Owens' case file was tucked under her arm. A large cardboard box sat on the floor next to Sten Billick.

She plopped the file on the table, then rubbed absently at her eyes. They felt gritty from lack of sleep. Last night, she'd stopped at the hospital. Stanley's condition remained unchanged, and, if anything, the doctors were increasingly concerned that he hadn't regained consciousness. She'd stood by his bedside, listening to the cadence of his heart monitor and the brooding hiss of his oxygen feed. His eyes were motionless beneath their lids. She wondered briefly if he could dream. Perhaps not—*hopefully* not. At least that way he would be free, however temporarily, of whatever demons haunted him.

After several minutes of watching his still form, she'd murmured a few words of comfort, brushed a stray hair or two from his forehead, and given him a quick kiss on the cheek. Then she went home to a meal of cold leftovers and not enough sleep.

The morning news had brought more bad news: a massive snow storm was rushing their way. The area could expect drastically colder temperatures and potentially several inches of snow.

Twenty years ago, when Izzy was still driving a patrol car, a blizzard had hit the area around Halloween. The states west of Michigan had been slammed the hardest. Still, Kinsey had received almost a foot of snow. The storm had paralyzed the town for almost two days. Four people had died from exposure.

She had to find Natalie, and quickly.

"Mr. Owens," Izzy said, making sure the recorder was turned on.

"I understand you've waived your right to an attorney. Is that correct?"

Owens nodded. "Only the guilty need a lawyer."

She pulled out the affidavit she'd brought with her, pushed it across the table, and handed him a pen. "Could you please sign this? It states that you've waived your right."

Owens signed it in one fluid motion and pushed it back. "There, now we're official."

"Thank you," she said, sliding the form into a file folder. "Sten?"

The detective sat down. "Mr. Owens, we have evidence linking you to the disappearance of Natalie Morris. Right now, you're looking at a variety of charges, all of them serious. And if she"—he glanced uncomfortably at Izzy—"if she turns up dead, you'll be charged with murder. That'll mean jail for the rest of your life. But we're willing to make a deal. Cooperate, tell us where to find Natalie, and we'll talk to the judge. Maybe work out some kind of arrangement."

Owens said, "And if she *is* dead, Detective? What then?"

Izzy grew cold. "This is your only shot at a deal, Owens. I'd take it if I were you."

Owens shifted his attention from Sten to Izzy. Those blue eyes threaded into her. "I'm not a stupid man, Chief Morris. My initial arraignment has to be held before tomorrow afternoon. At which time, I'm going to ask the judge if I could see the search warrant that allowed your officers to search my personal property and find that necklace. When he discovers there wasn't one, the evidence will be ruled inadmissible. Your case will be dismissed, and I will walk away a free man." He turned back to Sten. "So let's not confuse the issue with talk of reduced sentences and leniency."

Sten's expression didn't change. Izzy simply nodded. She had expected something like this, especially after Owens had mentioned the search warrant yesterday. Their offer of cooperation had been a long shot, but one worth taking.

She reached into the cardboard box next to Sten and withdrew a clear plastic evidence bag. Inside it was a small silver necklace—two interlocking hearts attached to a thin chain. She tossed the bag onto the table. "Look familiar?"

Owens studied the necklace. "I assume it's your daughter's."

"It was found at the bottom of this." She retrieved his duffel bag from the box and laid it beside the necklace.

"It was *found* in my kit bag," said Owens. "That doesn't mean I *put* it there."

A moment of silence, then Sten: "Seriously? You're telling us it was a plant?"

"You should at least consider it," replied Owens, picking up the plastic bag containing the necklace. "This wasn't in my room when I left yesterday, which means one of the officers searching my room had it." He turned to Izzy. "That person *does* know something about your daughter."

Sten shook his head. "'The cops framed me' is the oldest excuse in the world, Mr. Owens."

"No, that would be 'my neighbor did it.'" Owens set the evidence bag back on the table. "Find who planted this and you'll be closer to finding the girl."

Izzy and Sten exchanged glances. They had both read the chain of custody documentation. The signature of the officer who'd found the necklace had been very clear.

Carlton Manick.

But he had an alibi for Friday night. He'd been on patrol, and she had a whole night's worth of call logs to verify it.

"All right," Sten said. "This is getting us nowhere. We're going to start from the beginning. And this time, no more talk about planted evidence."

"Hold on," Izzy said. She had seen something, a splash of color against the drab green of Owens' duffel. She turned it over and pointed to the design stitched into the material. "What is that?"

Owens ran his finger lightly over the worn threads. "That's the insignia of the 761st Tank Battalion. From back in the second World War."

Sten cocked an eyebrow. "So this is some kind of family heirloom? Your grandfather fought in the war?"

Owens smiled ruefully. "No, afraid not."

"Then how'd you get it?" Sten asked.

"I collect old war memorabilia."

Izzy said, "Kit bag."

Owens frowned up at her. "I'm sorry?"

"Kit bag," she repeated. "You called your duffel a 'kit bag.' I've met plenty of military over the years. That's pretty much an Army term." She smiled. "So, where'd you serve? Nam? Gulf War?"

Owens stared at her for a moment. Then he scooted back his chair and stood.

"I've been cooperative up to now, Chief Morris. You know my arrest was based on evidence found in an illegal search. I demand to be released."

Sten shot to his feet, and Izzy moved to block Owens' access to the door.

"Sit down," she said sharply, pointing to the chair. "I have you for another day, and I plan on using it. You *will* tell me where my daughter is."

Owens remained standing, his body tense. For a moment, Izzy thought he might actually make a run for it. Then he relaxed and slowly folded himself back into the chair. He scrubbed his face with his hands. When he was done, he looked expectantly at Sten.

"May I have some coffee, please?"

Sten frowned. "Now?"

"Please," he repeated. "After that, we'll talk. I promise."

"Get the man his coffee," Izzy said tiredly. "We could use a break."

But could Natalie?

Sten returned with three large, steaming mugs, two black and one with cream and sugar for Izzy. She held hers cupped in her hands, grateful for the warmth flowing into her fingers. Sten slid Owens' mug across the table, and the other man drank two large gulps.

Izzy blew into her mug, took a sip and burned her lips. She jerked the mug back, spilling more onto her hand.

"Damn," she muttered, then looked curiously at Owens as he swallowed another mouthful.

He caught her staring at him, smiled, and lifted his mug. "Good coffee."

The room was quiet as the three of them finished their drinks. Owens set his empty mug off to one side. He folded his hands and rested them on the table. Looking first at Sten, then at Izzy, he said, "Can you please turn the tape recorder off?"

Izzy said, "Why? Are you afraid you may say something to incriminate yourself?"

"Either the recorder gets turned off, or we sit here looking at one another all morning."

Sten was shaking his head, but Izzy overruled him by hitting the recorder's off button.

"Satisfied?" she asked.

Owens nodded. "As I've already told you, I did not kill that boy. Nor did I kidnap or in any way harm your daughter. And before you ask, I don't know where she is, either."

Izzy opened her mouth to protest, but Owens quickly raised a hand.

"I know," he said. "We've already been over this. Please, let me finish."

"Fine," she replied. "But denials and conspiracy theories aren't going to keep you out of jail."

"Chief Morris," Owens said. "You're familiar with the name Sallinen."

Sten leaned forward, as if he hadn't heard Owens correctly. "Come again?"

"Yeah," said Izzy, equally confused. "What's Jack Sallinen got to do with this?"

"Not him," Owens said, "as much as his son."

"J.J.?" Sten laughed. "Now you're going to try and pin this on *him*?"

Owens shook his head. "I didn't even know he existed until yesterday, when that girl, Katie, mentioned him." He picked up his empty coffee mug and rolled it back and forth between his palms. "No, I'm talking about his *other* son."

She thought back to the young boy in his too-small pajamas and his Picassoesque drawings. "You mean Kevin."

Owens sucked his lower lip in between his teeth and nodded. "He's the reason I'm here."

While Sten stared disbelievingly at Owens, Izzy stumbled over what to say next. Owens was talking about an eight-year-old, harmless autistic child. From her notebook, she pulled out the drawing Kevin had given her. A basic crayon scribble of an animal standing in the rain and lightning, nothing more sophisticated than what a four-year-old could do. How could this poor kid be involved in anything dangerous?

"He's just a sweet kid with autism," she said, showing Owens the drawing. "I don't understand what he's got to do with this?"

Owens looked uncomfortably at the picture. "That's the complicated part."

"Sure," snorted Sten. "Because it's total bullshit."

Even though she tended to agree, she laid a restraining hand on Sten's shoulder. "He brought it up. Let him answer the question."

Sten hesitated only a moment. "You're the boss."

She gave his shoulder a reassuring squeeze. "Well," she said to Owens. "Let's hear it."

Owens' nostrils flared as he drew in a deep breath. When he spoke, his voice echoed in the small room. "What's happening in your town—the taking of your daughter, the death of her boyfriend—is being done intentionally. They're distractions, meant to keep you preoccupied. Looking elsewhere while plans are put in place to take the Sallinen boy. Before you know it, he will quietly disappear. And if that happens, you'll never see him again."

Izzy said, "What does this have to do with you?"

"I'm here to keep that from happening," Owens replied with complete seriousness.

"I see." She was beginning to wonder if perhaps Owens was mentally ill. Paranoid delusions about kidnapping plots? Grandiose self-image as the hero who stops the bad guys? If that was the case, Kevin *could* be in danger—from Owens. "How'd you learn about this plot against Kevin?"

"I know it's hard to believe without thinking I'm crazy—"

"You got that right," said Sten.

"—but the boy is in serious danger."

"Answer my question," Izzy insisted. "How'd you learn about this 'danger' to Kevin?"

"We don't have time—"

"Answer the question."

"You wouldn't—"

The door abruptly opened and Sgt. Talbot stuck his head in the room.

"Chief, we just got a call. There's another dead body. Memorial Park, near the gazebo."

Izzy felt her stomach drop. "Any idea who it is?"

Bob Talbot nodded. "Jenny Bethel."

CHAPTER
14

Almost four hours later, the activity at Memorial Park had died down. Under a cold, cloudless sky, Al Hamilton and Carlton Manick had strung up yellow police tape around the crime scene. It restricted access to the two cars in the parking lot—one was Jenny Bethel's, the other Chet Boardman's—and the destroyed gazebo. More tape cordoned off the area of the beach where Jenny's body had been found. Pictures had been taken; evidence tagged, bagged, and sent off for processing. All that was left was for Izzy to try to piece together what had happened.

The ME had finished examining Jenny's body and had sent her remains ahead to await an autopsy. This was the second body from Kinsey in less than three days. The look on his face as he walked toward her spoke volumes about his concern.

Dr. William Buzynski, MD, had been the county's medical examiner for the last thirty-two years. Big and burly, with a head of thick, white hair, a commanding presence, and a no-nonsense attitude, he could easily have made it as a cop. But she'd known him for years, and the gruff exterior was all show. Inside that man was the kindest soul she'd ever met.

"I'm sorry to hear about Stanley," he said, offering her a hug. "I'm sure he'll be fine. And Natalie. Have you made any progress finding her?"

Izzy gratefully accepted the hug. "We've got one suspect in custody, but he's being difficult. I had to break off the questioning to come here."

"You'll find her, Elizabeth. You're the best."

"I hope you're right." She gestured for Sten Billick to join them. "But for now, we've got another dead body. What can you tell us?"

The ME shoved his hands deep into the pockets of his jacket. "Time of death was somewhere between eight yesterday evening and midnight. Looks like someone beat her in the back of the head with a blunt object— that part of her skull was a mess. But that's not what killed her." He paused, the breeze ruffling his white hair. "She was crushed to death. I wouldn't be surprised to find multiple rib fractures, bones ground together and lacerating just about every internal organ that poor woman had. Whoever did this—he had to have been incredibly strong. Dying that way…hell, if I hadn't seen it with my own eyes, I would've thought it impossible."

"You don't think Chet Boardman could've done this?" asked Izzy.

"I don't know the man," replied the ME. "But I don't see how two or three people working together could've done something like that. So, no. I doubt it was him alone."

Sten said, "There was a lot of blood on the gazebo's floor. My guess is most of it is Jenny's. We'll have to wait on the lab results for confirmation. But this is what I don't understand: her body was found all the way on the beach. Correct me if I'm wrong, doc, but after bleeding that much, walking or running would be out of the question."

"That'd be my opinion," Dr. Buzynski said.

"And," Sten continued, "there were no tracks leading from the gazebo to her body, and nothing to suggest she was dragged."

"So, what do you think?" asked Izzy.

Sten's eyebrows drew together. "I think she was thrown there."

Thrown? Izzy thought. From the gazebo? But that was at least thirty feet. No one had that kind of strength. There had to be another explanation.

"Then there's the damage to the gazebo," Sten said. "The way the boards are shattered, I'd swear someone busted up through the floor. Hard enough to toss the picnic table down the steps. Again, how big would you have to be to do that?"

"Let me add a little flavor to this discussion," the ME said. "I dictated the Cain boy's autopsy report yesterday. I'll give you the condensed version. The edges of his abdominal wound were jagged, irregular, and there were eight puncture marks along the midline, between the sternum and umbilicus." He smiled. "That's the belly button. Anyway, in my opinion, this boy wasn't cut open with a knife—he was *torn* open, like someone had stuck his fingers into his guts and ripped him apart. And then there's his ribcage. If you tried to rip one out, all you'd do is lift the body off the ground. Give it a sharp, strong jerk and *maybe* you'd break a rib or two. But his was torn completely off his body, every rib broken. Again, we're talking about an incredibly strong man."

"Then you're ruling out any kind of animal attack?" asked Sten.

The ME nodded. "Doesn't fit the evidence."

"All right," said Sten, gesturing to the gazebo. "It looks like Chet and Jenny had dinner in there. And whatever happened took place *after* they'd eaten. There was a knife in the grass, just off the steps, with blood on it. Did Chet use it to protect Jenny, or kill her?"

"I'll check for any sign of knife wounds," offered the ME.

Izzy said, "We need to find Chet. His car's still here, so where'd he go?" And when did he get his keys back from Gene?

"Speaking of going," said the ME. "I've got this woman's body waiting for me." He gave Izzy a hug, shook Sten's hand. "I'll let you know what I find."

As the ME walked toward his car, Izzy looked around the crime scene. She thought back to the interview with Owens.

"What's happening in your town," he'd said, *"is being done intentionally. They're a distraction, meant to keep you preoccupied, looking elsewhere."*

Already, four hours had gone by since he had said it.

"Jimmy was buried today," she said to Sten. "I'll head over to the wake. Denny'll be there. Maybe he knows where Chet is. Katie will probably be there, too. I need to tell her about her mother." Christ, how did you tell someone she was an orphan?

"What about Owens?"

"Go back and start working him."

"And Natalie?"

"If Owens is right, all this is connected. We keep working the case, we eventually find her."

"And if he's lying?"

Izzy grimaced. "Let's hope he's not."

Jimmy Cain's burial had been an expedited event. The coroner's office had released the body late Saturday morning. Surprisingly—or maybe not—Denny and Maddie Cain had arranged for a closed-casket service yesterday, with a burial this morning. Izzy didn't understand their haste, but she had also never buried a child.

At least, not yet.

The reception hall holding Jimmy's wake was located a block and a half from the funeral home. Once a VFW hall, an ill-advised second mortgage encouraged by Jack Sallinen had ultimately been beyond the veteran's ability to pay. Jack's bank had quickly foreclosed on the property. He had then sold it to Del Crest, his buddy and the owner of the funeral home. When Del didn't need it for funeral business, he rented it back to the veterans for their fish fries. Probably at an exorbitant rate.

Neither Jack nor Del had put their lives on the line for their country, and Izzy was sure neither had lost a minute's sleep over how they'd screwed the vets. To them, money was the be all and end all.

She stood in the doorway to the hall, reluctant to enter a place of mourning with news of more death. The air was thick with the aroma of fried chicken and coffee. Most people sat at long folding tables, eating or chatting quietly with one another, their murmurs broken by the rustle of paper plates and the dull scrape of plastic cutlery. Several individuals had gathered at the far wall, where a big screen television displayed a picture of Jimmy in his football uniform. That picture slowly dissolved into one of Jimmy as a baby at his christening.

Izzy spotted Jimmy's parents in the throng of people at the back of the hall. She made her way over to them.

Maddie Cain sat on a chair in front of the television. She wore a plain black dress with white trim along the collar and a small pillbox hat with a dark veil. Her hand clutched a wad of tissues, which she would occasionally slip under her veil to wipe away her tears. Denny stood next to her, also in black. When he saw Izzy approaching, he whispered something to his wife and moved off toward the bar.

When Izzy had reached Maddie's side, she crouched down so the other woman wouldn't be forced to look up at her. Grief brought all low and should be shared that way.

"I'm so sorry," Izzy said to Jimmy's mother. "So very, very sorry."

Maddie dabbed at her eyes once more. She wore no makeup, had made no attempt to hide her pain under a patina of blush or mascara.

"Denny tells me you have the man who killed Jimmy," Maddie said, her voice distant, emotionless.

"We have a suspect in custody, but there's still work to be done."

"And your daughter?" Maddie whispered. "What about Natalie?"

Izzy opened her mouth to say something, but the words stuck in her throat. All she could manage was a shake of her head.

Maddie smiled weakly. "I understand. I'll pray for you, Izzy. For you and Stanley. I'll pray you get your daughter back. I'll pray, because that's all I've got left."

Izzy grasped the woman's hand. Blinking back tears, she said, "I'll figure this out, Maddie. I promise."

At that point, Jack Sallinen walked up with Denny Cain trailing him like a baby duck following its mother. Jack was the only mourner not wearing black; he'd decided on a cream-colored three-piece suit. He even had a Bluetooth in his ear.

"You'll get through this," Izzy said to Maddie, and then stood. "My condolences, Denny."

Denny opened his mouth to say something, but Jack stepped smoothly in front of him, cutting the man off.

"Chief Morris," Jack said with an easy smile. "I heard about your husband. What a terrible thing to happen. I hope he's doing well?"

"He's fine, thank you." Izzy tried to step around Jack's bulk. "Denny, have you seen Chet?"

Jack side-stepped, keeping his body in front of her. "You know, now that you mention it, I don't recall seeing him. Surprising, really, since he and Denny are friends."

"Thank you, Jack," Izzy said dryly. She'd hit so many roadblocks today, and Jack was becoming another one. "But I don't remember asking you the question. In fact, I don't remember asking you anything. So why don't you be a good boy and go eat some chicken or something and stop interfering."

Jack's smile melted like wax under a hot flame. "I didn't know I was *interfering* with anything."

A small crowd had gathered around her and Jack. She saw Gene Vincent, and behind him, J.J. Sallinen. She still needed to speak with Jack's son.

And then she saw Katie. Her insides knotted up. The girl was alone in the world, and she didn't even know it yet. But that news was for later. And in private.

She raised her voice. "Excuse me? Has *anyone* seen Chet Boardman? Either this morning at the church or later at the funeral?"

"I was at the both services," Gene volunteered. "I don't remember seeing him at either."

"What are *you* doing here?" Jack said, frowning at Gene. "You can't actually consider yourself a friend. Not after you threw Denny out of your bar—for no reason, I may add. And the very next day, you assault him! What's it going to be today? Knife fight in the parking lot?"

"You're a real ass, Sallinen," Gene said. Then to Denny: "If you want me to leave, just say so. I don't want to cause you or your wife any more pain."

Denny's mouth twisted into a scowl. His wet eyes roamed the crowd around him, finally settling on his wife. She gave an almost imperceptible shake of her head.

"Naw," he said quietly. "It's okay. Stay if you want."

Jack's face grew bright red, and for a moment Izzy thought the man might actually explode. She smirked as she imagined bloody bits of him flying out in wet arcs, splattering everyone around him. She would even offer to help clean up the mess and flush him down the nearest toilet.

"Something funny, Chief Morris?" Jack asked, having caught her grin.

"No, Jack," she said, losing her smile. "Nothing about this is funny. Now, has anyone seen Chet at all in the last couple days?"

Blank looks and silence. Then, softly, "He was at our house."

Izzy looked down at Maddie Cain.

"You saw Chet?" Izzy asked her.

Denny stepped up to his wife. "Stay outta this, Maddie."

Izzy held up a warning finger at Denny. Then to Maddie, she said, "When did you last see him?"

"Yesterday morning," Maddie replied. "He and Denny, they were arguing about something. And then that strange man showed up."

"Chief Morris," Jack cut in. "Really, I don't see the purpose in this. These two people buried their son today. Haven't they suffered enough without having to answer your questions?"

She rounded on Jack. "Let me make myself clear. Unless I ask you a direct question, you're to keep your mouth shut and let me do my job. Think you can handle that?"

Jack opened his mouth, the heat of his words telegraphed by the anger glinting in his eyes.

Before he could speak, Izzy got right up into his personal space. He smelled of sweat and avarice. "You're close to an obstruction charge, Jack. Keep it up and you'll find yourself in a jail cell."

The entire reception hall was watching the exchange. Jack had the weaker hand, and he had to know it. Izzy could almost see him weighing his options and the resulting outcomes. Sweat beaded on his forehead, and he absently wiped at it with his sleeve. Gradually, the anger in his eyes dimmed, then went out.

"Of course," Jack said, taking a hesitant step back. "You're just trying to do your job. My apologies."

Izzy nodded, turned her attention back to Jimmy's mother. "Tell me about the stranger."

"I don't know his name. He's a new friend of Denny's."

"What does he look like?"

"Tall. Sandy hair. A beard. Except for a scar here." Maddie traced a line along her left jaw with a trembling finger.

"What happened when he showed up?"

"He took Denny and Chet into the back room and closed the door."

"How long were they back there?"

"Well," Maddie said. "Chet came out a few minutes later, looking relieved. And a little happy. He left. I haven't seen him since."

"And the stranger?"

"What about him?"

"Did he stay?"

"For a little while. Then he left, too."

"I'm sorry to interrupt," Jack frowned, "but this sounds like an interrogation. I thought you had your man locked up in jail?"

"Okay," Izzy said, exasperated. "Let's go, Jack. I'm going to call someone to take you into custody."

"No." This came from Vickie Milkins, who worked at the IGA store. The tall redhead stood off to the left with her husband, Walt. "He's got a point, Izzy. I thought you made an arrest. That you caught the guy responsible for this."

"Yes," Izzy said. "We do have somebody in custody."

"Then why aren't you talking to *him*?" Vickie continued.

A murmur of agreement ran through the crowd.

"Please, Vickie." Izzy raised her voice slightly. "Everyone. Just because we have a suspect doesn't mean we stop an investigation. We're going to be as thorough as possible. That's part of the job."

"I can't believe Chet Boardman would be involved in this." The statement came from Celeste Florin, Gene's waitress from the Lula. "I've known him for years. He seems so harmless."

"I can't talk about an ongoing investigation," said Izzy. "When I know something concrete, I'll be sure to let everyone know."

"You're going to pin this on Chet, aren't you?" Denny said bitterly. "That's why you're looking for him. You got that damn nigger in jail, but you're going to let him go and blame Chet for my son's death."

Izzy didn't like where this was headed. "Okay, this is going to stop right now. I cannot—I *will* not—discuss the details of this investigation with any of you."

"So Chet Boardman *is* a suspect," Jack said, smiling again. He'd clearly sensed the shifting mood of the crowd, and it had made him bolder.

"No, Owens is...our...." Her words trailed off as she recalled Owens' warning about Kevin Sallinen. "Jack, where's Kevin?"

Jack frowned. "Kevin? You mean my son?"

"Yes, your son. Where is he?"

"At home, with a neighbor." His small eyes grew wary. "Why?"

She didn't want to say anything more until she understood better what kind of threat Owens posed. "Just do me a favor. Keep an eye on him."

"Why?" he repeated, then his eyebrows climbed in alarm. "Is it that Owens guy? Has he been talking about Kevin?"

Izzy blinked, amazed that he made the connection so quickly.

The surprise must have registered on her face, because Jack exploded. "You keep him away! Do your goddamn job for a change and keep him away from my boy!"

"Wait a minute," Izzy said. "I never said anything about Owens. Don't go jumping to conclu—"

"Keep him away!" Jack shouted, the veins in his neck pulsing in synch with his words. "Or I'll kill him myself!"

"Jack, seriously," Izzy said, puzzled at the man's vehemence. "Owens is sitting in a jail cell. He's no threat to anyone. Please, calm down."

"You better hope he stays locked up." Jack was practically snarling now. "Because if anything happens to Kevin, I'll hold you personally responsible."

He turned and stormed out of the hall.

"Chief Morris?"

She turned and saw J.J. Sallinen standing behind her with Katie at his side. His face was pale. "*Is* my brother in some kind of danger?"

"I'm sorry," she said. "I didn't mean to upset you. Or your father. No, Kevin's not in any danger. It's just…I don't know, a precaution."

"A precaution against what?" he asked.

She had to get out of this before she dug herself in further. "Look, I've some business to take care of. All I'm asking is that you keep your eyes open, okay?"

"Sure," he said, clearly still confused. "If you say so."

Izzy's eyes found Katie. "Can I talk to you for a moment?"

"Sure," Katie said. "What about?"

"Privately?"

It only took Katie a few seconds. "It's my mom, isn't she? She's drunk again. Where'd you find her this time? Passed out in her car?"

"J.J., could you give us a moment, please?"

The boy nodded, kissed Katie on the cheek. "I'll meet you outside."

"How bad is it?" Katie asked after J.J. had left. When Izzy didn't answer, Katie said, "Oh God, don't tell me she was driving and hurt someone."

Izzy quietly led the girl out of the reception hall, ushered her into an empty office, and gently shut the door on the rest of the world.

CHAPTER
15

Anger seethed through Jack Sallinen. Morris had embarrassed him. Worse, she'd done it in front of everybody. Who was she, the little Be Nothing bitch, to talk to him like that? To get up in his face and *threaten* him?

He pushed hard against the hall's glass door and strode outside. Cool air dampened the flames of his displeasure as he made his way to the parking lot. Cars filled the empty spaces, their windshields glinting in the bright October sun. Heat rose from the tarmac and softened the bite from the chilled air. The warmth pleased him. While never one to mind cold weather, he'd recently found the thought of spending another winter here, buried for months under several feet of snow, repellent. If there were anyone he could trust to run the bank in his absence, he would lounge away the winter in sunnier climates. But the risks were too great: buried deep on his hard drive, hidden under layers of passwords, was his *other* set of books, the accurate ones, the ones which showed the profitability of the bank was greater than he reported. While the bank examiners wouldn't be likely to find them, a good businessman knew which risks paid off, and which didn't. For now, he'd have to be content with keeping his offices warm. Quite warm, in fact. Eighty was ideal.

He'd passed the first row of cars when he heard his son's voice calling out.

J.J. trailed after him, jogging to catch up. There was no sign of his girlfriend. Webber said he'd make sure Katie was pushed out of the picture, but he didn't say exactly what he'd had planned. Perhaps Morris's appearance had something to do with it? Jack grunted. He'd certainly enjoy one less nuisance in his life.

"Hey," J.J. said when he'd reached Jack. He wore a shit-eating grin on his face.

"Whatever you want," Jack snapped. "It can wait until I get

home."

J.J.'s smile crumbled into a petulant frown. He looked so much like his mother, Jack wanted to slap him.

"We had a deal," his son said. "You were going to make me a part of your plans. Well, I think now's a good time." He gave Jack a flat stare. "Don't forget, I've seen those photos. I'm sure Chief Morris would love to see them, too. You think you could survive prison?"

"Keep your voice down," Jack hissed, glancing around. "Yes, I haven't forgotten. But right now, there's nothing for you to do. You're going to have to be a little more patient."

"What about Kevin?" J.J. asked. "I suppose *he* has something to do with this?"

"No," Jack said with barely restrained patience. "Your brother isn't involved. Morris was just trying to cause trouble."

J.J. stared at him. "I know you had Jimmy killed. And Natalie. Somehow, you benefited from their death. You wouldn't risk so much unless you came out on top. Big time." He pointed to the VFW hall. "But Natalie's mom? She isn't going to give up. That means what you're getting is worth the risk." J.J.'s lips curled up at the corners. "So I want to know. What're you up to?"

Jack scowled. "Not *now*, and especially not *here*." A flash of sunlight caught his eye. He saw a white Silverado turning into the parking lot. "Look, I've got to go. You want to help? Keep an eye on that little girlfriend of yours. If anything out of the ordinary happens, call me on my cell. Now get back inside before you're missed."

"She's busy talking with Chief Morris," replied J.J.. "Does that have anything to do with what you're up to?"

Two quick blasts of a horn got Jack's attention. Webber had parked near the back of the lot. One arm hung lazily out the window and made that same little "hurry up" gesture.

Jack stepped close to J.J.. He jabbed a thick finger into his son's chest—and was surprised when J.J., who topped the scales at 210 lbs, took an unbalanced step back.

"I don't know why Morris is here," he said. "That's the truth. But if it does have something to do with your girly-friend, remember that whatever happened is your fault. You brought her into this." Jack snorted. "You think you're a man? That you can blackmail me? That you can fuck me over the way you did with your mother? Well, there are consequences to everything, though I doubt you have the brains to figure that out. Now get the hell out of here. I'm tired of looking at you."

J.J.'s face flushed red. "You're the one who messed it up with mom. I didn't have anything to do with it. And what happened in the end? Kevin and I ended up paying the price." Some of the color drained from his face. "I'll keep an eye on Katie. But we're not done here. I expect you to follow through with your part." He turned and headed back toward the hall.

Finished with his son, Jack turned his attention to the Silverado. His nerves danced an edgy jitterbug as he crossed the parking lot. His lips pressed into a thin line. Blood rushed in his ears.

Webber's arm folded into the cab. Jack saw a flash of light, and the man's arm emerged with a cigarette wedged between two yellow-stained fingers, the end glowing a soft red, smoke rising in thin wisps until it was caught by the breeze and whisked away.

"Hello there," Webber said, grinning. "Don't you love it when a boy and his dad have one of those tender moments? I don't know about you, but it makes me feel all warm and fuzzy inside."

Jacked grabbed the cigarette from Webber's hand, dropped it, and ground it out with his shoe. "Bad habit you have there. Don't you know those things can kill you?"

"That may be," Webber said evenly, withdrawing another cigarette and lighting it. "Care to tell me why you're in such a foul mood?"

"Chet Boardman. Morris is in the hall asking about him."

"I'm sure she is." When Jack raised an eyebrow in an unspoken question, Webber added, "Look, Chet came to me yesterday. Said he'd had second thoughts and wanted out. Said he couldn't get past this 'uncomfortable' feeling he got around me. But see, I worked hard at gathering together our little group. I wasn't going to let him simply walk away. And I certainly wasn't going to risk him talking about our plans. So, Mr. Boardman is no longer an issue."

"What'd you do? Kill him, too?"

"Who said he was dead? Besides, killing is a baser impulse of the human condition which I avoid whenever possible."

"But didn't you...?" Jack looked meaningfully back at the hall where the mourners were gathered.

"You think *I* did the kid in?" Webber asked, frowning.

It was Jack's turn to frown. "Well, with the full moon, and the way he was torn up, I kind of assumed—"

"What, that I was a *werewolf*?" Webber laughed. "You've been watching too many movies."

"Then...?"

"What's been causing the ruckus? That's above your pay grade for now. When I think the time is right, maybe I'll introduce you to my friend." After taking another pull on his cigarette, Webber continued. "This is why I do the thinking, Jack. All you need to do is follow my orders. Nothing more."

"I don't follow anyone's orders." Jack was angry. Angry at being laughed at, at being wrong, at being humiliated. In a moment of déjà vu, he grabbed the cigarette from Webber's hand and ground it out. "You're the one who needs me, not the other way around. How about you come find me when you can show a little more respect?" He turned to leave.

"We're not done yet," Webber said.

Jack gave him the finger.

"Don't make me teach you a lesson."

"Go to hell."

"No," Webber said. "I think maybe you should."

Jack had gone two steps when the world suddenly *thinned*. It was as if reality had become two-dimensional: the hall, the cars, the sky and the trees had all flattened, lost their depth. While his eyes told him he was being drawn forcibly into that gap between perceptions, his stomach said otherwise, and the conflicting signals made him nauseous. He stretched out a hand, expecting to hit a solid wall of existence. His fingers felt nothing. Then, like a painting left out in the rain, everything around him began to wash away.

Reality melted and ran in wide, raw streams. Blue sky and green trees and yellow sun and pale concrete and black asphalt mixed into a foul sludge that hardened into the ground beneath his feet. A darkly red world of stone and shadow began to emerge. Gone was the disturbing, two-dimensional reality he'd just experienced. What had lain hidden behind the landscape of his ordinary world horrified him.

He stood in a long corridor where walls of sharp rock, craggy and broken, stretched high into the shadows above. The corridor ran before him as far as he could see, lit by a blood-red glow rising from numerous cracks in the stone floor. It was hot here. He was immediately drenched in sweat.

But it was the smell that hit him like a physical blow. It was the stench of rotting flesh: hot, wet, oily. It filled his nostrils with a putridity so loathsome that his stomach threatened to rebel and empty its contents onto the ground.

And there was a sound, faint at first, but growing. It was a scuttling, like beetles crawling over old bones. As the noise grew, he could feel them, hideous insects entering him—through his mouth, his nose, his ears, his anus, the tip of his penis—filling him, digging deep under his skin, into his body, biting, chewing....

The nacreous red glow flared. Jack, hugging his writhing abdomen, could now make out creatures perched among the rocky crags that made up the tunnel's walls.

Black among the dark shadows of this hell, numerous shapes—or perhaps *misshapes* would be a better word—made the nightmare complete. One creature had a hairless, spherical body of suppurating flesh; three arms extending from its midsection, two of which gripped the ledge where it stood while the third pulled at a decaying carcass and stuffed what it could gather into a wide mouth on top of its body. Another resembled a giant starfish clinging to the stone, except where the tentacles met at its central point, a woman's wretched face—mouth working silently while insane eyes shed tears of blood—had replaced its body. Farther down, two others were locked in a struggle to either kill or mate: one humanoid creature stabbed repeatedly with a long appendage growing from the center of its chest, while the other, which looked like a diseased flower attached to a snake's body, accepted the demanding thrusts into its floral mouth while sharp teeth rent the flesh from the intruding phallus.

Jack turned to look behind him. The tunnel continued in the other direction as far as he could see. He wanted to run, to escape from this place. He wanted to—

The tunnel abruptly disappeared. He was back in the parking lot, under a dome of blue sky. There was no melting this time, just the jarring snap back into his world.

Jack's mind reeled. His hands flew to his gut, felt around for some sign that the insects were still inside him. There was nothing—no movement, no gnawing, no *scuttling*.

"Jack"

He spun around, his heart pounding at the top of his throat. Webber sat slumped in his cab, breathing heavily, a slight sheen of sweat on his brow. He looked exhausted, as if he'd tried to move a mountain by pushing it with his hands.

"Jack," Webber repeated. His voice was weak, but it was enough to anchor Jack's mind and keep it from sliding into the abyss. "Come here."

Numbly, Jack stumbled over to Webber's SUV, the harsh scrape of blacktop beneath his shoes oddly reassuring. He stopped next to the cab.

"Reach into my shirt pocket," Webber said. "Get a cigarette and put it in my mouth."

Jack did.

"Lighter's in the same pocket."

Jack reached in and removed it. His hand trembled as he spun the striking wheel; it took three tries before the sparks caught. He held the flame under the business end of the cigarette.

"I can put you there again if I want to," Webber said, drawing deeply on the cigarette. "And I can leave you there if I need to. Fuck with me again and I'll do just that. *Capisce*?"

"Yeah," Jack said, his mind wailing at the possibility of being marooned in that place. "I *capisce*."

"Good. Now, besides having a bug up your ass about Chet, did you learn anything else from your Chief of Police?"

"She knows about you now," Jack said, summarizing the events from the wake.

"That was inevitable, though I would've preferred another day or two of anonymity," Webber said. "Anything else?"

"Owens. It sounds like he's been asking about Kevin."

"There we are," Webber said, his words frustratingly nonchalant. "I think it's your son. He's the one this has been about."

"But I don't understand." Jack struggled with the next words. "Kevin, all he does is draw pictures. He can't even talk...." His shoulders sagged. "I wanted so much more for him. God knows, I tried."

Several months before, Jack had brought Kevin to Dr. Ron Westwood, an autism specialist, to definitively diagnose his son's condition. That final meeting had been one of the worst days in Jack's life.

He and Kevin had been ushered into the doctor's office by the man's secretary, Ms. Li. After sitting down with Kevin in his lap, he'd received the bad news.

"What you're telling me," Jack had said, "is that Kevin has something more than autism? Von...something?"

"Von Kliner's Syndrome," Dr. Westwood answered. "It's a rare subset of autism and even less understood. So much so that we don't have defined treatment protocols." The man paused before continuing. "I know this is hard to hear, Mr. Sallinen. Your son is going to need significant assistance throughout his life: special education, behavioral therapy, psychotropic medications. Maybe even placement in a group home as an adult."

"Group home?" Jack said, tears standing in his eyes. He hugged Kevin tighter. "You know money's not an issue. I'll pay for any treatment that will help cure him."

"Mr. Sallinen, if you're going to be the best support for your son, there's something you have to understand, right here and now: *there is no cure.* Sure, you can afford the best help available, and that's a wonderful asset for both you and Kevin. But as long as you continue to search for a cure and not focus on his care, you'll be allowing him to fall even farther behind developmentally." His expression had grown somber. "I doubt he'll ever be able to hold a job. Or even get married."

The news rocked Jack to his core. What the doctor had just described...it wasn't a life. It was purgatory; a living hell. To be hidden beneath layers of autism—no, his son deserved better.

Wiping at his eyes, Jack said, "I understand. But I want you to know that I will do anything to help Kevin. No matter the cost. Anything."

Westwood held his gaze for a moment. Reaching into his desk drawer, he pulled out a business card and handed it to Jack. "I have an associate. He knows more about von Kliner's than most. Has had considerable firsthand experience. He knows the dangers, the risks, of the condition. You may want to get in contact with him at some point. He may be able to help."

Jack had looked at the card. It was white with embossed black letters, but it provided no title. "This Darryl Webber," he said, lifting his eyes to Westwood. "Is he a doctor?"

"No, more of a behavioral specialist. But a good one." The man had smiled for the first time. "I think you'll like him."

Jack had slipped the card into his wallet. Afterward, he would pull it out. Agonize over it. He'd refused to accept that there was no cure, that he had to turn to "behavioral" solutions. Finally, weeks later and increasingly desperate to help his son, he'd pulled it out.

Sometimes he wondered if he'd made a mistake.

"Listen, Jack," Webber said, his voice surprisingly friendly. "You did the right thing by calling me. I may be the only person standing between your son and the old man."

"Owens is locked up. He can't get to Kevin."

"Don't get too comfortable with that thought. I doubt Owens' stint as public enemy number one is going to last. That old man's crafty. He can spin lies better than a D.C. politician. Pretty soon he'll have Morris convinced he's the savior of the world. Once he's set free, our job becomes decidedly more complicated. We need to make sure that doesn't happen."

"And how're we supposed to do that?"

"First we go get your son, then we take out Owens." He said this casually, as if he were ordering burgers and fries at the drive-thru.

"You mean kill him?" Jack said incredulously. Owens was locked in a jail cell, in the middle of a police station, surrounded by cops, and Webber thought he was going to waltz in and put a couple bullets into him? "That's your big plan?"

"Yeah, I know," Webber said, nodding. "Sounds almost impossible, given where he is. But that's why I worked so hard to put him there." His fingers tapped the steering wheel. "The whole shebang hinges on Carlton Manick. He has to get you, me, and your kid into that cell for a minute or two. That's all I'll need. Owens will have nowhere to hide. It'll be like fish in a barrel, Jack. Fish in a barrel."

Jack could see about half a dozen flaws with Webber's plan. Like how they were going to get out after killing Owens. But, given what he'd witnessed of the man's strange powers, he was willing to discount most of them. One, however, wasn't going to fly with him.

"We're not taking Kevin in there. It's too dangerous."

Webber squinted, his eyes flashing darkly, like chips of obsidian in the sunlight. "Are you giving me shit *again*?"

Jack swallowed hard. "When it comes to Kevin, yes, I am. He's all

I have in this world, and I'm not going to risk his life for you or anyone else."

"He is, huh?" Webber drew on his cigarette. "What about your other boy?"

"Fuck him. Kevin's the only one that matters."

"Now I know why reality TV is so popular," Webber said with a roll of his eyes. "You're a real douche, Sallinen."

"Fuck you very much," replied Jack succinctly. "Are we all square on this? You and Dirty Harry can go do the deed, but Kevin stays out of danger?"

"Sorry, but after Owens is finally dead, we can't waste time going back for the kid. So, like it or not, he's going in with us." His voice grew sharp, lethal. "Or if you prefer, I can send your fat ass back where you were. Leave you there and just take your boy. Now, are we all square on *that*?"

"Yes, sir," Jack said, his voice dripping with sarcasm. "But explain this one to me. If we get to Kevin first, why even bother with Owens? By the time Morris lets him go, we could be long gone. That old man wouldn't stand a chance of finding us."

Webber's face grew hard. "Because 'that old man' has been a problem for a long time, and I want to be the one who gets rid of him. Besides, he and I have a score to settle." Webber pointed to the puckered scar that ran along his jaw. "Owens gave me that."

Jack stared at the scar for a moment, then met Webber's eyes. "Who is he, anyway?"

"He's one of the most dangerous men in the world," Webber said with complete aplomb. He pointed to the hall. "After this little party is done, round up Denny and Carlton. We need to move quickly."

Jack nodded. "I'll let them know. Should we meet back at the hotel?"

"That'll work." Webber dropped his half-smoked cigarette at Jack's feet. "One more thing."

"Yes."

"Tell them to bring guns."

Two rows down and four spaces over, J.J. Sallinen crouched behind a truck. He listened to his father and the stranger talking.

Tears streamed down his face. He watched his father head back into the hall. The stranger gunned his truck and pulled out of the parking lot.

Fuck him. Kevin's the only one that matters.

J.J. wiped away his tears as he headed for his car.

Two can play at that game, Dad.

CHAPTER
16

Izzy Morris pulled her cruiser into the space reserved for the Chief of Police. In the rear-view mirror she could see Katie Bethel sitting in the back seat, a blanket from the trunk wrapped around her shoulders. Her eyes were red from crying. For now, though, her tears had given way to a depressed silence. She'd taken the news of her mother's death hard; despite the woman's many problems, Jennie Bethel had been the only person left in Katie's life.

"Ready?" Izzy asked the passenger seated next to her.

"You sure this is a good idea?" replied Gene Vincent.

"Well, Katie doesn't have anywhere else to go. Besides, both of you have spoken to Owens. It may help to have different opinions. This guy...."

"He's a little different, isn't he?"

"More than a little. He's the key to all of this. I can feel it. I just need him to explain how." She paused. "Are you sure *you* want to do this?"

"Natalie's my goddaughter," Gene said. "I know it's only a ceremonial thing, but it still means something to me. And Nat does, too. So, yes, I'm very sure."

"Thank you," said Izzy, touched by his words. She turned to face Katie. "Come on, honey. We're going inside."

Katie nodded without answering, joining the other two as they entered the police station.

Izzy led them down a long hallway with two doors on the right and one on the left. She stopped at the second right-hand door and poked her head in. Sten Billick sat at his desk. He was going over some notes.

"Bring Owens to the interview room." She turned to leave but stopped. "Wait, make it my office. And no cuffs."

"Not a good idea, Chief," Sten said as he closed the file.

"I've gotten nowhere with him. If I'm going to find Natalie, I need to try something different."

Izzy saw Sten's eyes shift to Gene and Katie standing behind her.

"You're bringing *them*?"

"Do you have a better idea?"

"Not bringing in civilians, for starters."

"It's not your daughter's life on the line, Sten," she said quietly.

"Yeah," he said, checking and holstering his gun. "It's not. Be there in a few."

While Sten went to retrieve Owens, Izzy and Gene brought in two chairs from her office and set them along the wall with the window overlooking Asher Street. Gene and Katie sat while Izzy slid into the chair behind her desk. Together they waited for Bart Owens to arrive.

Less than a minute later he walked in, followed by Detective Billick.

"Have a seat," Izzy said, indicating the chair opposite hers.

The old man's eyes traveled from her, to Gene, then to Katie, where his gaze lingered for a few moments, and then back to Izzy. "Thank you." He sat down across from her.

Sten moved to stand behind Owens.

Izzy said, "I've brought in a couple of people you know. They're going to sit here and listen for now. Is that okay with you?"

Owens shrugged. "It's a little odd, but I have no objections."

"We're going to do this differently," Izzy said. "Maybe something a little less confrontational will help the cause. You up for it?"

"As much as I can be."

"Is that a yes or no?"

"I'll do my best," Owens replied.

"It'd help if you stopped being so damn cryptic."

"A lot will depend on your questions," Owens said. He crossed his leg, folding his hands on his knee. His long, brown fingers were unadorned with rings.

"Let's start with an easy one," Izzy said. "Are you married?"

Owens shook his head. "No, not currently."

"So, you were married at one time?"

"Yes," he said. "It was a long time ago. She's passed on."

"I'm sorry to hear that."

"Thank you."

"See how easy that was. Next question: how old are you?"

Owens hesitated for a fraction of a second: "Fifty-four."

"And we were doing so well," Izzy said, sighing. "Now you're lying."

"Check my driver's license. I'm telling the truth."

"I thought we were going to cut through the bullshit?"

Owens moved his hands from his knee to fold them across his chest, a classic defensive posture for a person with something to hide. He must have realized this, because he unfolded his arms and placed them on the arms of the chair.

"Age is a sensitive topic for me," he said. "I will tell you this much: I'm a little older than fifty-four."

"How much older?"

"Next question," Owens said with a shake of his head.

"Goddammit, how hard can it be to tell me your age?"

Owens expression hardened. "Please don't do that."

"What?" Izzy asked.

"Blaspheme."

"You're a musician *and* a priest?"

"I had a very religious upbringing."

"And where was that?"

"Sorry," Owens said with another shake of his head.

"So your past is off limits?"

"I'd like it to be, yes."

Frustrated at getting nowhere again, Izzy paused to collect her thoughts. She did a quick mental run-through of this morning's questioning.

"Earlier you said you were here to protect Kevin Sallinen. Protect him from what?"

"There's a man who's also come to your town, like me. He's after the boy."

Izzy shook her head. "I'll need more than that."

"His name is Darryl Webber," said Owens. "Mid-thirties. Light-colored hair. Has a scar running right about here." Owens used a finger to trace a line along his left jaw.

"That sounds like the stranger who showed up at Maddie Cain's house." Izzy described her visit to Jimmy's wake.

"So you know him?" This question came from Sten.

"I should." Owens said. "I'm the one who gave him the scar."

Izzy asked, "How did you know this Webber was here in the first place?"

"A friend of mine, a colleague of sorts, had been keeping an eye on him. When Webber left New Jersey, my friend tracked him here."

"Why isn't this friend here helping you?"

"Different people, different specialties. He observes."

"And your specialty?" she asked.

"I protect."

"All by yourself?" Sten said, his mouth twisted in disbelief. "You must be tougher than you look. I searched you when you were arrested. You had no weapons. No body armor. No cell phone to call for backup. What are you, Special Forces? SEAL? Or do you beat the bad guys off with your guitar?"

"Trust me," Owens said. "I'm capable enough—"

"What's the matter with you people?" said Katie Bethel. She wiped at fresh tears with the edge of the blanket. "Don't you understand that my mother is dead. Somebody *killed* her. Now, why don't you cut the crap before somebody else dies?" She wrapped the blanket tighter, then addressed Bart Owens. "It's obvious you know more than *we* do, sir. So rather than play guessing games, why not just tell us? Okay?"

Gene Vincent gave a low whistle of admiration. Sten Billick actually cracked a smile, however briefly. Izzy didn't know if she wanted to jump up and hug Katie or have her leave to spare her any further pain.

Bart Owens turned slightly in his chair so he faced Katie. In a voice heavy with regret, he said, "I don't understand why your mother was killed. As far as I can tell, she didn't have anything to do with this. And if I'd been there, I might have been able to save her. But I've made mistakes. Now you're paying the price. I hope you can forgive me."

"Help us," Katie said flatly. "Then I'll forgive you."

"Jenny wasn't alone in that park," said Izzy. "Chet Boardman was with her. He's missing."

"My mom and Mr. Boardman had a history together," added Katie, blushing. "Dating and...things."

Owens shifts his attention to Gene. "Wasn't he one of the men thrown out of the Lula that night?"

Gene nodded. "That's him. The other guy was Denny Cain, the dead boy's father."

"Okay, let's try and put some pieces together." Izzy picked up her pencil, started making notes. "We know for sure that Webber's here. He's been seen with Denny and Chet, so it'd be a good guess that they're involved somehow. If those two are involved, then...." Her voice trailed off as a realization hit her.

"Izzy," Gene said, inching forward on his chair. "What is it?"

"That son of a bitch." Izzy threw her pencil on the desk. "I bet he knew what was going on all along."

"*Who?*" said Sten, Gene, and Katie in unison.

"Jack Sallinen."

Izzy called a break at that point. She had someone bring coffee and sodas into her office. The tension in the room had slowly built as they had discovered some of what had been going on underneath their noses.

"Okay," Izzy said after everyone had settled down. "I need to get this straight in my head. Simply put, Webber's here to get Kevin, and you're here to stop him." The last part was directed at Bart Owens.

"Yes."

"Does he plan on killing the boy?"

"No, I don't believe so," Owens said. "Not unless...."

"No more secrets. We're talking about a boy's life here."

Owens sipped at his coffee. "Not unless Webber believes I'll get to him first. Then he may kill the boy rather than let me have him."

"What do you mean 'have him'?" Izzy protested. "Neither of you is taking him. And what's so special about him, anyway?"

The old man's eyes dropped to his coffee. "I'm not exactly sure."

"Stop it," Izzy said, irritated. "Stop jerking us around. What is so special about an eight-year-old, autistic boy?"

"Do you have that drawing the boy made?" asked Owens.

Izzy pulled her notebook out of a desk drawer. She slid the drawing out and laid it in front of Owens.

"See the lightning bolts? Webber had a nickname, a while ago. Lightning. And the raindrops aren't raindrops, they're tears." Owens touched the mark under his left eye. "I'm in the picture, too."

"Okay," Gene said, joining the discussion. "Kevin Sallinen drew a picture of you and Webber. But since he's never met you—and we can assume he's never met Webber or he'd be gone, right?—he drew representations of both of you. How could he possibly know anything about you or Webber? None of this makes sense."

"Yes, I know," said Owens. "I'm afraid I don't have all the answers."

Sten Billick leaned over Owens' shoulder and pointed to the animal. "What's that thing?"

"I'm not sure, Detective," said Owens. "But I have a suspicion."

Sten looked on expectantly.

"I think," Owens said, "that's what's been doing the killing."

There was a moment of quiet, then Izzy said, "What is it?"

"I honestly don't know," said Owens. "But you've seen what it can do. You're going to need help, Chief Morris."

"And you're the one to help us."

"I'd like to, but can't while I'm locked up."

Sten snorted. "We should just release you? Let you walk free?"

"It'll happen anyway," replied Owens. "At my arraignment. By that time, though, it may be too late."

Sten shifted his attention to Izzy. "I'm sorry, Chief. But this is so much bull. He's telling stories, and then wants us to trust him and let him go? This stinks from every angle."

Izzy glanced at Sten. The decision was hers. People were dying. Her daughter was missing. And this mystery man, her only suspect, was asking to be set free so he could "help." It went against every tenet of police work she'd ever learned. Plus the public would be howling for her badge. The risks were too great.

Nevertheless, she had to do something to save her daughter.

"Okay," she said. "I'll release you."

Sten gave a resigned shake of his head. Owens looked relieved.

"He's right," she said to Sten. "The judge is going to order his release anyway. And I've gotten nowhere. Every hour that passes means less of a chance of finding Natalie."

Sten spread his hands wide. "Innocent is as innocent does."

"Okay, Owens," she said. "You're a free man. What do you recommend we do first?"

"I'm here to help," Owens said. "You're still in charge. It's your call."

Izzy thought for a moment. "Looks like we go get Kevin."

"What about your authority to *take* Kevin," Sten interjected. "How are you going to explain that?"

"I'll worry about it later," answered Izzy. "If this helps me find

Natalie, I'll gladly turn in my badge." She turned her attention to Gene and Katie. "You two stay here until we get back."

"In for a penny, in for a pound," said Gene, then smiled at Sten. "You think you're the only one who can be witty."

"Me, too," Katie added quickly.

"No," Izzy said to the girl. "Absolutely not. I'm not putting you in danger."

"My mom *died* because of this," Katie countered. "I have a right to be part of it. I am coming along, even if I have to steal a police car to do it."

"You're staying here," Izzy said. "End of discussion."

"He'll be with us, right?" Katie pointed at Bart Owens. "He's a protector. So let him protect."

"I'll keep an eye on her," Bart said.

"Oh, no." Izzy shook her head. "No way. I don't even know you. I'm not putting her life into your hands."

"You may not have a choice." Owens nodded at Katie. "I believe she would actually try to follow us."

"Damn right I would," said Katie, her eyes bright with determination.

Izzy wanted to argue the point, but she was running out of time. If Webber and Jack beat her to Kevin, then all this was pointless.

"Fine." Izzy sighed. "But stay near Owens." To him, she said, "Any sign of trouble, you get her out."

Owens nodded.

Izzy turned to Sten. "You're good with this?"

"No," he said. "Not at all. But I've been outvoted."

From her desk drawer, Izzy removed her Glock P24. Then she pulled another clip from her desk drawer and stuffed it into her pocket.

"All right, let's go get that little boy."

* * *

The ride to the Sallinen house was tense. Next to Izzy, Gene shifted uncomfortably in his seat, pulling on his safety restraint as he tried to ease the pressure on his back. Seated behind him, Katie appeared smaller, burdened by her grieving. Sitting beside the girl, Bart's brown face was serene, his eyes closed, as if facing such perils were as mundane as breathing.

Izzy rolled down her car window and let the crisp autumn air wash over her face. She'd hoped the cool breeze would help clear her head; instead, it made her feel brittle. Her cell phone vibrated and she answered it.

"I'm in place," said Sten. She'd sent the burly detective ahead in an unmarked car. He should be a few houses east of the Sallinen residence.

"See anything?" Izzy asked.

"Nope," he answered. "No activity at the house. No cars out front. Street's quiet."

"Start making your way to the back of the house."

"I might be seen."

"I know. Be careful."

Several seconds passed before Sten spoke again. "Chief, there's still time to do this right. Get some backup. Secure the area. And I don't like that we're risking civilians."

"Understood," Izzy said. She wanted to explain herself to her friend, but her doubts were too numerous to contemplate right now. "Make your way around and cover the rear of the house. I'll be there soon and take the front."

She could hear his sigh over the phone. "All right. See you in a few."

Izzy hung up. She turned east on Ryanwood. A gust of wind sent a patch of crimson leaves swirling around the car like a warning.

About a hundred feet west of Jack Sallinen's house, she pulled to the curb and killed the engine. She had taken the other unmarked car. No sense advertising what they were doing.

Sten's car sat three blocks down, looking inconspicuous with a scattering of dead leaves dusting the Buick's hood. He must have tossed a handful of them over it, making it look like it'd been there a while. The man liked to be thorough.

He was right: the street was quiet. No cars coming from the east, and a glance in her side view mirror revealed more of the same to the west. Maybe she'd finally caught a break.

Unbuckling her seat belt, Izzy turned to face the others. Gene regarded her with quiet confidence, his face still hinting at the pain in his back. Katie's wounded look made her want to wince. But neither one shied away from her steady gaze.

Bart Owens had opened his eyes; the certitude she saw in them left her conflicted. The man was an enigma and therefore shouldn't be trusted, yet every instinct told her to believe in him. She hoped he would measure up to the task.

"Okay," Izzy said, "here's how we're going to run this. You three stay here until Sten and I have had a chance to check out the house. Once we've secured the area, I'll call you in. Until then, you're not to leave this car for any reason. Understood?"

All three nodded in agreement.

"Good," she continued. "Gene, once I leave I want you to move into the driver's seat. If you hear any gunfire, or if you think the situation's getting out of hand, I want you to go. Take the others and go back to the station. Same goes for anyone pulling up at the house. Just leave."

Gene nodded. "I won't let anyone get hurt."

Izzy got out of the car. With her eyes locked on Jack's house, she hurried across the street. The cold whipped around her, biting at her exposed hands and face, lifting the dry, moldy scent of dead leaves to her nose. The air tasted stale.

No movement.

Not at the house.

Not on the street.

Nothing.

When she reached the other side of Ryanwood, she stopped. She eased the Glock from its holster. Bravado may get people killed, but so did plain stupidity, like walking unarmed into a potentially dangerous situation. Holding the weapon near her cheek, the barrel pointed toward the sky like a benediction, she slowly approached the Sallinen house.

Weather had stripped most of the foliage from the two oaks guarding the front of Jack's property. The remaining leaves fluttered like tattered bits of cloth on a pair of scarecrows. Early morning frost had started to kill off the delicate tea roses lining the front of the colonial, their pink and amber petals curling to a pulpy brown around the edges. The blinds on the lower level windows had been drawn. Her eyes rose to the second floor. White lace curtains could be seen behind two sets of double-hung windows. She paused for a few moments but nothing stirred behind them.

Izzy began to wonder if anyone was home.

Step by step, she eased her way up the walkway to the front door. Her heart hammered hard against her breastbone. Adrenaline raced through her, charging her nerves, sharpening her hearing.

She listened at the door. Nothing.

Izzy grasped the brass doorknob. The cold metal stung her skin. Slowly, *slowly*, she turned her hand. Expecting to meet resistance, she was surprised when the door cracked open.

A man like Jack Sallinen would have expensive tastes. A house full of treasures. The door wouldn't be unlocked unless someone was home.

Damn.

She was committed now. Izzy pushed the door open and stepped inside. No alarm went off, though there was a security keypad on the wall next to the door.

Someone *had* to be here.

In the dim, grainy light seeping through the shades, Izzy saw an empty living room on her left. A half-full glass of milk and a paper plate sat on the coffee table in front of a leather sofa. Above the fireplace on the southern wall hung a large screen television; it played some children's cartoon show, the volume turned all the way down. A scattering of crayons and drawing paper littered the carpet.

A narrow hallway with hardwood floors led further into the home. A stairway beckoned her to the second floor. The kids' rooms were likely up there. To her right was a set of closed French doors with frosted glass panes. Through the glass's opacity she saw more blinds. The handle had a locking mechanism and dead bolt. The room practically screamed "private."

Jack's office?

Her phone vibrated. She ignored it. Likely it was Sten wanting to know where she was. She advanced a few more steps down the hallway, the heels of her flats clicking loudly against the parquet wood inlays. She passed the stairway and glanced up, expecting to see Jack's angry face glaring down at her from the second story hallway.

Nothing.

She moved far enough to look into the kitchen at the end of the hall, then the dining room adjacent to Jack's office. Both were empty.

A shadow passed behind her.

The creak of a floorboard.

Shit—

Izzy spun, the Glock whipping around as she aimed at the dark shape silhouetted by the light coming from the open front door.

"Chief, it's me."

Sten Billick.

Izzy removed her finger from the trigger and brought the gun back up near her face. "Damn it, Sten. I could've shot you!"

He stepped toward her. His blue nylon jacket was open at the neck, and she could see the edges of his Kevlar vest. "Anything?"

Izzy shook her head. "The door was unlocked and the alarm wasn't set. The television is on. Somebody must be here."

"But you haven't heard anything?"

"Not a whisper."

"Might as well get this over with," Sten said. In a louder voice: "Police! Anybody home?"

The silence was complete.

"Okay," Izzy said. "Go check the upstairs."

She stayed downstairs while Sten explored the second floor.

"Nobody's here," he said as he came down the stairs. "But I found Kevin's room. His dresser drawers are open. And his closet. Looks like he might be missing a few clothes. And there was a scuffle as well. A chair's knocked over. Some of his drawings ripped up."

Izzy's shoulders sagged as she holstered her gun.

"We're too late," she said. "They've got Kevin."

They'd gathered in the Sallinen's living room. Izzy stood by the fireplace, her hopes battered again. Gene hovered nearby, arms crossed, as if he dared Izzy to blame herself for what had happened. Katie, the only one familiar with the home, had turned off the television, taken the milk glass and paper plate into the kitchen, and returned to sit on the sofa, where she'd fallen silent. Owens had placed himself midway between Katie and Gene, one hand stuffed into the pocket of his jeans, the other rubbing absently at something under his Predators sweatshirt. Next to the old man, Sten Billick wrote with precise lines in his notebook, facts—or perhaps facts as he *wanted* to remember them—which would be used later in his report.

"Don't do this," Gene said to Izzy. "Don't blame yourself for everything that's happened. It's unfair to you, and it's unfair to the people counting on you."

Izzy turned to him. "I've been playing catch-up since this whole thing started. Natalie's still missing. I've still got some twisted killer running loose. And now Kevin's gone." Frustration burned in her stomach like acid. "I've gotten exactly nowhere."

Gene said, "What more could you have done? You learned about Webber *and* Jack's involvement. Then there's Denny and Chet and whatever role they're playing. And with his help"—he pointed to Owens—"you've started putting the pieces together. It's only a matter of time before you figure this out."

"You don't understand," said Izzy angrily. "You're not a parent. Natalie's out there, and I don't even know if she's alive or dead. Kevin might've been able to help, but I was too late—again." She turned her back on him, and repeated, "I've gotten exactly nowhere."

"Maybe this is too much for you," Owens said with unexpected bluntness.

She rounded on the black man. "You know this Webber. Do *you* have any idea where he took Kevin?"

Owens shook his head. "No. Besides, isn't that your job?"

Her anger rising, she strode past Gene and up to Owens. His placid expression, which she'd envied minutes ago, now seemed arrogant, the teardrop-shaped mark on his cheek full of false empathy.

"You're part of this," she said furiously. "You and Webber. Ever since the two of you got here, people have either gone missing or died. I know you could've easily told me what was going on, but you had to play games instead. Now the only link to finding my daughter is gone. You really are a son of a bitch, you know that."

Bart Owens' stony demeanor hadn't changed. "You're looking for the easy answers, Chief Morris, and in life there aren't any. The world's bigger and far more dangerous than you know. It's a place where innocents die and the guilty go free just as often as the other way around. There's no changing that." His gaze intensified. "You want some honesty? How about this: if you ever want a chance at finding daughter, you'd better grow up fast. Feeling sorry for yourself won't do it."

Stung by his rebuke, she did something that surprised even her—she slapped him. And when she did, pain flared up her arm, setting her nerves on fire. She bit back a scream and pulled her arm to her chest, cradling it like she would an injured child. But the unexpected agony had shocked the rage out of her. She watched as Owens nodded, an affirmation that she was back in control.

"Don't worry," Bart said. "I've had worse than a slap in the face before. More to the point, are you okay?"

"You did that on purpose," said Gene, pointing an accusing finger at Owens. "You goaded her. She's already under enough stress, and you added to it."

"No," said Izzy as she rubbed the pain from her arm. "It's okay. He did the right thing. I—I needed to get that out."

Gene peered at her for a moment, then mumbled, "I still don't have to like it."

"So what do we do now?" asked Katie.

"Find Kevin," said Sten Billick. "We don't have any other leads."

"Wait a minute," interrupted Katie from her spot on the sofa. Her brow was furrowed in concentration. "I just remembered something."

"What?" Izzy asked the girl.

"Yesterday," she replied. "When I was here with J.J.." She rose and began to walk, her fingers lightly touching the furniture as she passed by. "We snuck into his dad's office." Words started to spill out of her in an excited rush. "He broke into one of his dad's desk drawers, thinking he'd find booze. But he found something else instead. I don't know what." She headed for the French doors Izzy had seen earlier. "In here," she said, placing the palm of her hand against the frame. "J.J. found something that scared him." She turned to the others. "I wonder if it's still in there."

Izzy, Gene, Katie and Bart stood at Jack's massive oak desk. Sten Billick, who'd made quick work of the lock and deadbolt, hovered near the office's open door.

"I was over there," Katie said with a gesture, "standing near that creepy painting. J.J. said he'd gotten the drawer open. Then he just freaked. Wouldn't tell me what he found. Then he practically ran me out of the house."

Izzy ran her finger along the damaged top edge of a drawer. "This one's been forced open." She grabbed the burnished metal handle and slowly pulled the drawer open.

Empty.

"Damn," she said, and began opening the other drawers. Inside the lower right one, she discovered a small, gray metal box with a steel lock fasten to the hasp. She pulled it out and set it on the top of the desk. The metal on the box was covered with scratches, as if someone had been working at it with something sharp. The lock looked new.

Gene batted at the lock with a finger. "Anyone here love a good mystery?"

They were all focused on the metal box to the exclusion of anything else, which explained their slow reactions when they heard the front door open and Jack Sallinen's voice came booming from the other room.

"We'll just get Kevin and—hey, what the hell are *you* doing in my house?"

For a moment no one moved, then Izzy saw Sten turn, his hand going for his gun. But his movements were too slow and too late.

The thunderous blast of a single gunshot roared through the house.

Sten Billick's body spun around, blood spraying in a wet pattern along the office wall. The detective continued to twist as he fell, landing heavily on the carpet, his left arm trapped under his body.

He wasn't moving.

Izzy reached for her own gun. Next to her, Gene tried to slide in front of Katie, to put himself between her and the gun fire, but his foot caught on the corner of the desk and sent him sprawling onto the floor behind the desk. He managed to swing his hands out in front of him, cushioning the fall, but the impact must have jarred his back. He rolled over, his face pale and bathed in sweat.

Seeing Gene go down, Owens stepped in front of Katie.

Izzy freed her Glock. She watched as a man eased into the open doorway with a Sig P226 held out in front of him. Stunned, she took in the dark blue uniform, the leather gun belt with its handcuffs and empty holster, the Kinsey Police Department badge. His hard eyes and cruel grin.

Carlton Manick.

Izzy pointed her gun at the patrolman's chest. "Don't move," she said coldly. "Or so help me God, I'll shoot you where you stand."

Carlton's eyes darted from her to Bart to Katie and then back to her. Without taking his eyes off Izzy, he said, "Three people. Morris. The Bethel kid. And the black guy."

"You said he was in jail," said a voice heavy with fatigue.

Owens surprised her by speaking. "You sound tired, Darryl. Don't tell me you were showing off again. I thought she taught you better than that?"

The other French door swung open. Denny Cain stood there, holding a hunting rifle. Behind him stood Jack Sallinen and a man who must have been Darryl Webber.

Denny swung his rifle around to cover Owens.

Jack held a small .38 pointed in the general vicinity of the floor

Darryl Webber appeared unarmed. But Owens was right: the man looked exhausted.

"You're outgunned, old man," Webber said. His eyes widened when he saw the gray metal box. "God damn it, Jack! I told you to get rid of that thing!" Snarling, he said, "Manick, kill the cop."

"Go ahead," Izzy told her patrolman. "Give me a reason to blow your ass away."

"Where's my son?" Jack shouted from behind Denny. He still wore that awful cream-colored suit from earlier that day. "Where's Kevin! What'd you do with him?"

Izzy frowned. "What? We—"

"—thought it'd be better if *we* watched him for a while," Owens finished for her. He gave Izzy a hard look. "Gene Vincent's already got the boy miles from here. You'll never catch him."

"*No!*" Jack howled, the cry evolving into an odd thrumming that Izzy could feel as well as hear. The effect made the hairs on her arm stand on end.

Webber grabbed Jack by the collar and yanked him back. "I said kill her!" he shouted, then both men fled.

Carlton Manick tensed as he prepared to fire.

Izzy didn't hesitate. She pulled the trigger. There was a loud explosion, and the stench of burnt gunpowder filled the room. Her round slammed into Carlton, staggering the big man backwards. She fired again. The second round furrowed through his right shoulder and sailed on to shatter the big screen television in the living room. The third bullet caught him in the throat. Blood and bone and tissue exploded from the back of Carlton Manick's neck. With a look of shocked disbelief on his face, he crumpled to the floor.

Denny Cain drew a bead on Izzy. There was a flurry of movement on the floor as Sten rolled onto his back, raised his gun and fired. But he'd been injured. His aim was imperfect. The bullet impacted with the Remington's wood stock near the barrel and tore the rifle from Denny's grip. It crashed in a broken heap on the floor under the Fuseli painting.

When Bart Owens advanced on Denny, the man fled.

Izzy hurried over to Sten. The detective lay panting on the floor, blood flowing from the wound in his shoulder. Sweat had slicked his white hair flat against his scalp. Squinting up at Izzy, he asked, "Do you know how hard it was not to move while that *prick* stood there above me? Too bad I wasn't the one who shot him."

"Your vest?" asked Izzy.

"Bullet nicked it," Sten replied thinly. "Lucky for me. My shoulder would've been trashed worse than it is."

"I'll radio for an ambulance," said Izzy. "Just lay still."

Over by the desk, Gene hauled himself off the floor. He walked gingerly over to Owens and Katie, one hand holding his back. "Thanks for the excuse to stay down," he said to Owens. "I think I'll leave the hero stuff to you." Then to Katie, who was crying softly and still had her hands over her ears, he said, "Katie? It's over. It's okay now."

Katie pulled her hands from her ears and used them to wipe at her tears. "People are dying, Mr. Vincent. Tell me how that's okay."

Gene opened his mouth to say something, but simply nodded in agreement.

After calling an ambulance for Sten, Izzy joined the others.

"He should be okay," she informed them. "His shoulder's pretty torn up. I can't believe he got that shot off." She looked at Owens. "That was quick thinking on your part. Now they think we have Kevin. That should tie their hands a bit as they figure out what to do next."

"But if *they* don't have Kevin," Gene said, "and *we* don't have him?"

"That's the question," she said. "Where is Kevin Sallinen?"

PART TWO

OF MONSTERS
AND
MADMEN

The line of M4 Sherman tanks lumbered over the grassy terrain outside Morville-les-Vic, France, their thick treads throwing up big, wet chunks of mud. Heavy rains fell from a bruised sky, cutting visibility down to almost nothing. Mortar rounds exploded around them like small earthquakes.

Crouched in the upper turret seat of his tank, Sgt. Bartholomew Owens, commander of the 761st Tank Battalion B-Company, shouted over the grinding howl of the R975 engine that pushed them closer to war.

"Bucky! Anything?"

"Ditches, Sarge!" PFC Robert "Bucky" Hatton shouted back from the driver's seat. He jammed the controls forward and the tank surged ahead. "They everywhere. Gonna be a real bitch getting past them."

"Just keep rolling," Bart yelled. He wiped the sweat running down his grease-stained face. Despite the cold November air, it was hot as a blast furnace inside the tank. "Dex! Al!"

"Got us one in the chamber," answered PFC Dexter Grant, the tank's loader.

Wedged beneath the big gun assembly, his gunner, Cpl. Allan Richmond yelled, "Nazi bastards are dug in like ticks." Bart couldn't see his friend from where he sat, but he knew Al was grinning, his white teeth bright against the sooty darkness of the tank's interior. He was the only man Bart knew who wore his helmet everywhere, even in the tank. "Must have been holed up for a good long time. We're in for a rough one."

Bart grunted. Rough one, indeed. The brass at 26th Division had had their eye on Morville-les-Vic since the start of the war. If it could be taken, the town's bridges would provide a more direct route to the German border. They might even catch Hitler off guard. But Army Intel had found out that the town was full of German soldiers. Patton had simply chosen to pass it by—he knew trying to go through would only slow him down. However, if the infantry following the general were able to use the bridges, they could catch up with him later and bust through into Germany.

So B-Company had been ordered to spearhead the advance on Morville-les-Vic.

Bart wasn't stupid: his division's inaugural mission was a suicide run. They wanted to send in the 761st, America's first all-Negro tank unit, and let the Germans use up their ammo cutting down his men like a scythe through tall grass. Then the infantry—the *white* infantry—could sweep in and finish the job.

But this was the Army. Orders were orders, and B-Company had rolled. However, contrary to his captain's intentions, Bart had his own reason for getting into that town.

"Bucky!" he shouted. "Find a way past those ditches."

The twenty-year-old from Arkansas laughed. "Sure, Sarge. You want I should keep rolling right through to Berlin? Drive this thing down Hitler's throat?" But the man's laughter died as mortar fire blasted the ground next to the tank. "Shit!" he cried, jerking the tank to the left. Bart pitched forward but managed to catch himself on the periscope. Cpl. Richmond clung to the gun's housing. PFC Grant fell on his ass.

Al didn't wait for the order. The recoil from the big 75mm gun rocked the tank.

"Dex!" Bart roared. His loader popped up and shoved a heavy M48 round into the gun's chamber.

"Hit it!" Dex cried, and Al fired again.

More enemy shells exploded near the tank, buffeting it back and forth.

"Ten degrees right," Bart ordered from above.

While Al rotated the gun turret, Dex loaded another round. "Go, go!"

Al fired. This time the gunner whooped, "Got 'em!"

Before Bart could say anything else, Bucky screamed, "Ditch! Ditch!" and pulled hard on the controls—but he was too late. The tank's front end collapsed into an anti-tank ditch, throwing everyone forward. Bart twisted, taking most of the impact on his shoulder. Bucky Hatton flung his arms out in front of his face, bounced off the smaller machine gun assembly and slumped back in his seat. Al's helmet ended up saving his life: the gunner's head flew forward and collided with one of the thick metal gun supports. The crease it put in his helmet was as long as his little finger.

PFC Dexter Grant wasn't so lucky. When the tank abruptly stopped, he'd been reaching for another round. With his body bent in half, he'd had no time or leverage to protect himself. He was tossed around like a rag doll. When he crashed to the floor, his neck was twisted and bent at an unnatural angle. Blood seeped from his wide nostril and the corner of his mouth. His dead eyes stared blankly up.

Bart stared back. Around his neck he wore a chain with a small piece of wood attached. He lifted his hand, felt for it through the cloth of his shirt. When he found it, he closed his eyes and silently said a quick prayer. Dex Grant had only been nineteen.

Mortar fire brought him back to the present. He pushed open the turret hatch and yelled to his two remaining men. "Out! Out! Get out!"

Bart gripped the metal sides of the hatch and pulled himself out of the tank. Al Richmond's helmeted head followed soon after.

After the humid, oily interior of the tank, the cold wind felt like a slap in the face. Rain lashed at them. There was the familiar, high-pitched scream of mortar fire, and the ground twenty feet to their right exploded.

"Check on Bucky," said Al as he struggled through the hatch. "I don't think he's moving."

Bart spun around and scrambled over the slippery surface to the front of the tank. At the driver's hatch, he began tugging at the metal door. It wouldn't budge.

"Bucky!" yelled Bart. His fists pounded on the door. "Open the door! Bucky!"

The hatch's handle slowly rotated. Bart jerked the door open.

Bucky Hatton's brown face was streaked with blood from a cut on his forehead. His eyes looked glassy, and Bart wondered briefly if the man had a concussion. The driver reached out with a trembling hand. Bart helped him out of the wrecked tank. As the man emerged from the hatch, Bart noticed his other hand gripped a canvas duffel.

They hurried around to the rear of the tank. Everyone ducked when a German mortar blasted a hole in the ground where they had just been standing.

Protected behind the now-useless hunk of metal, Bart turned to Bucky Hatton. "I ordered you out of that tank, Private!"

"I ain't gonna apologize, Sarge. Not this time." Bucky held out the duffel. It was Dexter Grant's kit bag. "He was so proud of this," Bucky went on. "Carried it with him everywhere. Even used it as a pillow. Says to everyone how it make him feel like a real man.

"Dex, he looked up to you, Sarge. Say you like a poppa to him. Say he would follow you to the end of his days...and I guess he did." He held out the bag. "It yours now, seein' as you don't got one. I think Dex would a wanted it like that. Maybe even make him feel kind a proud."

Bart nodded and grabbed the duffel. It wasn't very heavy. Dexter Grant had come from rural Mississippi. Bart knew from the many times he'd seen it opened that all it contained were Dex's clothes and a Bible.

"Thank you," he said, hitching the kit bag high on his shoulder. He blinked the rain out of his eyes, squinted at the water-soaked battlefield. "Come on. We're not done yet. We need to get into that town."

CHAPTER
17

Izzy stood on the lawn of the Sallinen home. In the northwest, dark clouds built towers high into the sky. The wind had picked up, bringing in chillier air. Snow was coming.

The ambulance had just pulled away with Sten Billick secured in the back. The coroner was due to arrive soon for Carleton Manick's body.

She could sense Owens and Katie standing behind her, waiting for her to do something. At the old man's urging, Gene had stayed inside and out of sight. "You never know who's watching," he had said. "If Darryl and his friends want to think Gene's far, far away, let them. We'll need every advantage we can get."

Izzy had shaken her head in wonder. Musician, my ass.

She turned and nodded toward the door. The gesture was clear: *Let's go inside.*

In Jack's office, they found Gene standing at the desk. Owens took a position at the living room window, watching the street. Katie came to stand next to Izzy.

Gene held up a long-bladed screwdriver with a large yellow-and-red striped plastic handle. "I found it in a kitchen drawer. Figured we could use it to bust open the lock on this." He tapped the gray metal box with the tip of the screwdriver.

"Why not?" Izzy said. "The State Police are going to be involved soon, so we may as well find out what we can, while we can."

Nodding, Gene took the screwdriver and jammed the flat tip between the lock's hasp and the body of the box. Then he struck the end of the screwdriver with his hand. The metal barrel shot down through the hasp, snapping it free of the lock.

Izzy turned the metal box around to face her. "Let's see what had Webber so annoyed."

She grabbed the lid and flipped it open. It took her a moment to fully comprehend what she was seeing. Then it hit her—

She started to collapse. Katie grabbed her arm and yelled her name. She felt Gene catch hold of her other arm. She tried to stand, but she couldn't seem to feel her legs, couldn't seem to feel anything. There was nothing left for her to feel.

Inside the box were photos of Natalie.

"*Oh my God*," Izzy whispered, and then she started to cry

In the one picture Izzy could see, Natalie was splayed out on the ground, dirt underneath her as if she were in an old-fashioned fruit cellar. It must've been dark where she was—the photo had that too-bright, grainy quality of cheap flash photography. Natalie was wearing the change of clothes she'd brought to the homecoming dance: jeans and a white designer blouse that Izzy had gotten her for Christmas last year. But the shirt wasn't white anymore. Dirt had left ugly brown smudges on the fabric. And there was blood staining it, spreading out from her abdomen. Her daughter had been bleeding. Dear God, she *was* hurt.

Izzy's gaze shifted fractionally. She took in her daughter's pale face. There were five small wounds gouged into her flesh near the hairline. Lines of dried blood, so dark they looked almost black against her alabaster skin, drew ghastly patterns on her cheeks and neck. Her beautiful auburn hair was tangled and knotted, with leaves and twigs caught in it. Her eyes were closed. She looked dead.

No! Tears filled Izzy's eyes, blurred the edges of her vision. *She can't be dead! She can't be!*

Izzy felt new hands, strong hands, replace the others. She was lifted. Turned. A face swam into view, brown, intense. Blue eyes bore into her, commanded her attention, pulled her back from the place where she'd been falling.

Bart Owens. He was speaking to her, but she couldn't hear him. Didn't want to hear him. Her life was over.

Her baby was dead.

Through her dismay, she began to hear Owens' voice, deep, compelling. A singer's voice. He shouted her name, but his voice sounded distant, as if he were talking from another place, another time.

"Chief Morris!" Owens yelled. "Izzy!"

She found the strength to say, "Not dead. Can't be dead."

"Izzy!" Owens again. "Listen to me! You haven't seen all the photos. Look at what Gene found."

Gene thrust a photo in front of her face.

Reluctantly, Izzy looked. It was another photo of Natalie. She didn't understand what he meant. Then she saw it. She snatched the photo from Gene and brought it close to her face.

Natalie's eyes were open. They were open. She had been alive at the time. Maybe she was still alive.

Still alive.

Owens released her. She found she could stand on her own. She snatched the other photos from the box and rifled through them. Of the six snapshots, only one other showed Natalie with her eyes open. The blood stain on her daughter's shirt made Izzy want to vomit. Whatever that injury was, it had happened three days ago. If Natalie had been bleeding all this time....

She ran a finger lightly over one photo. "Be alive. Please be alive. I'm coming for you, honey. *Be alive.*"

Katie came into the room carrying a glass of water. Izzy hadn't seen the girl leave. She accepted the glass and drank it down completely.

Gene took the empty glass from her hand. "Better?"

Izzy nodded. "Thank you. Thank you all."

"Do you want more water?" asked Katie.

"No, sweetheart," Izzy replied. "That was fine. Right now, I need to think." She turned away from the photos; they were too upsetting. "Those were taken at most three days ago. Natalie was bleeding. She's likely in shock, and she could have an infection. If she hasn't been getting any water, then she'll become dehydrated. On top of all that, it's getting cold at night. If she's in someone's basement or cellar that may not matter as much, but if she's outside.... I don't think she'll survive through to tomorrow night at the latest." Her insides felt heavy, as if her guts had melted and settled at the bottom of her pelvis. "I have a little over a day to find her. If she's still alive."

Owens moved to stand in front of her. He used one hand to gently lift her chin so that her eyes met his. "Listen to me. I believe your daughter is alive. It's only a feeling I have, but it's a strong one. And I agree that we don't have much time—we need to find her, and soon. The key is Darryl Webber. He's the one who'll know where she's hidden. Now, what we need to do is find him."

"And Kevin," added Katie. She shook her head, frowning. "I—there's something I'm missing here."

Gene cut into the conversation. "I don't think finding either one is going to be easy."

"True," Owens agreed, then turned to Katie. "I'm afraid finding Darryl is going to have to come first. We have to keep him away from the boy."

Katie shook her head again. "I don't agree. If we find Kevin first, then this Webber guy will eventually come to us. Wouldn't that give us the advantage?"

Owens pursed his lips. "Not bad. But let's think this through. First, your suggestion turns this into a race. Can you guarantee that we'll be the first ones to find to the boy?"

"But we—" Katie began, then stopped. She pulled her lower lip in between her teeth. "I suppose not."

"And if we *are* the first to find him," Owens went on, "Darryl could very well be right behind us. That places Kevin in the middle of a possible—no, a *probable* gunfight. Do you think that's going to keep him safe?"

Katie began shifting from foot to foot, a scowl on her face. "Okay, I get it. Bad idea."

"No, there are no bad ideas," Owens countered. "Only incomplete reasoning. And complete reasoning, of course, comes with experience."

Katie stared at the man for a moment, her expression unreadable. Then she relaxed and allowed herself a small smile. "At least I tried."

"Yes," Owens said, returning her smile. "You did."

"Okay," said Izzy. For some reason, the interaction between the old man and Katie had made her uncomfortable. Owens was a stranger, no matter how helpful he might appear. His easiness, his sense of familiarity with Katie, almost bordered on inappropriate. "Where do we start looking for Webber and Jack?"

Owens gave Katie a final nod of encouragement, then turned his attention to Izzy. "You know, Darryl has to be staying somewhere. I can't see him sleeping in his SUV all this time."

"That poses its own problems," Izzy said. "Finding where he's holed up could take hours, if not longer. There are dozens of motels within thirty miles, not to mention the campgrounds or the small places he could hide if he has a trailer. We just don't have that kind of time."

Owens said, "I may be able to help with this one." He walked behind the desk and picked up Jack's phone. With his back turned to Izzy, he punched several buttons. He turned, holding the receiver to his ear. After a few seconds, he spoke into the phone. "Hey, Phil. It's me. Got a quick question, if you have a moment? When you trailed Darryl here—yeah, I'm in Kinsey now. Look, when he got here, was he towing anything? Trailer? Camper? Boat?" He frowned at Izzy and shook his head. "Nothing but the truck. Great. Thanks for the help." He paused to listen. "No, it's not been my best work, but I'm getting there. I'll let you know when I'm done. Bye." Then he hung up the phone. "It looks like you can stick with the hotels in the area."

"Who was that?" Izzy asked.

"An old friend of mine."

Izzy looked at the phone. "That call will be traced, you know. After all this." She gestured vaguely at the destruction in Jack's office.

Owens seemed unconcerned. "It's for an empty office building in Colorado whose ownership is, shall we say, muddled. But before it got there, the call was routed through several switches. Someone might get as far as Lithuania. After that, forget it."

While Gene and Katie looked at Owens in frank amazement, Izzy absorbed the man's words. Only a federal agency could manage what he claimed he had just done. Which of those would have an interest in an eight-year-old boy? "Are you FBI? CIA? NSA?"

"I'll let you work that out for yourself," Owens said. "But for now, we have to get moving." His gaze found Gene. "We can't afford to let Darryl see you. Is there a place where you can hide out?"

"Oh, I know a few spots that would work," Gene replied, his hand lightly rubbing his back. "But I won't be using them. I'm coming with you."

"Not a good idea," said Owens. "If Darryl discovers that you're still in town, things will get busy fast. Busy and dangerous."

"All the same," Gene said, standing a little straighter. "We're in this together. 'All for one and one for all'."

Owens crossed his arms over his chest. "I'm sure Dumas is rolling in his grave somewhere."

Gene crossed his arms. "And I'm not hiding while you guys risk your necks!"

Izzy stepped between the two men. "We don't have time for this."

Then she took Gene by the arm and led him away from the others. "You know he's right," she said. "The best way you can help is by staying out of sight." She gave his arm a gentle squeeze. "This is about Natalie's life, as well Kevin's. I need you to do this."

With extraordinary care, he removed her hand. Then he took her shoulders in his large hands and drew her close. He was peering at her with such intensity that her pulse quickened. An unexpected warmth spread through her. Or perhaps, she thought with a pang of guilt, it wasn't so unexpected.

"It's always been the three of us," Gene began. "You, me, and Stanley, ever since we were kids. Always together, always watching each other's backs." He paused, his eyes searching hers. "I've still got your back. And that means I'm coming along. I can't imagine doing anything else. And don't forget, Natalie's important to me, too."

That warm feeling grew, and with it, her sense of guilt. She shouldn't be feeling this way—at least, not anymore. Brushing his hands from her shoulders, she said, "All right. You win. I guess it couldn't hurt to have a friend with me."

Gene opened his mouth, as if he was going to say something. There was a look in his eyes that she couldn't quite read. But then he gave her that lop-sided smile. "Besides, you wouldn't deprive me a chance to save the day."

Izzy rolled her eyes. "Come on, hero. Let's go."

CHAPTER
18

After leaving his home, Jack Sallinen, with Denny Cain crouched in the back seat and Darryl Webber driving, had driven to a motel east of Kinsey. At the door to the room, Webber had ordered Denny Cain to stay outside and watch for anyone driving up to the motel. He crumpled a twenty, tossed it at Denny and pointed to the party store across the street. "Go get yourself some beer. At least you won't look like a complete idiot while you're sitting there." Denny, who was nursing a sore hand from his rifle having been torn from his grip, glared at Webber. Jack thought Denny was going to say something, maybe tell Webber to go fuck himself, but the man simply picked up the money and skulked away.

When Denny left, they went into the room, and Webber began unloading on Jack.

"What's the matter with you, Jack? That box on your desk. That's where you hid those photos, isn't it?"

Jack's eyes tracked the man pacing in front of him. "What's the big deal? So Morris has them. It's not like she can find her brat from looking at them."

"I wanted her preoccupied with her kid, you jackass. Now she knows you're involved."

"She just saw us together. She doesn't need the photos to figure that out." Jack's tone sharpened. "Anyway, let her come after me. That'd be perfect. She knows where my son is. I'll choke the information out of her."

Webber shook his head. "She's got Owens with her now. You stand as much a chance of getting through him as you do walking through this." He slapped his hand against the room's cracked wall.

"He's only one man." Jack reached into his pocket and withdrew the handgun. "A couple shots and we'll be rid of him."

Webber snatched the .38 from Jack's hand. "Give me that before you hurt yourself. I swear you couldn't hit the ground if you were aiming at it."

Jack was growing tired of Webber's insults. "And what about you and your brilliant plan? Remember, we're supposed to be helping Kevin. So where is he? Oh, wait! A *bartender* has him! Shows how goddamn smart you are."

Quicker than Jack could've expected, Webber pressed the barrel of the .38 hard against Jack's forehead. The cold metal dug painfully into his skin.

"Shall I cancel our agreement right now?" Webber said evenly.

A growl escaped from Jack's throat.

Webber's grip on the pistol tightened. "Rein it in, Jack, or I'll splatter your fucking brains all over that bed."

Jack's lips peeled back from his teeth. His nostrils flared, and he could suddenly smell Webber. Knew the man had eaten a burger with onions earlier that day. And there was that awful *noise*—like loud static, except he thought he could hear voices hidden within the sounds. It filled his ears until they almost hurt.

His muscles tensed. If he was fast enough, he could grab the gun. Jam it into Webber's mouth and pull the trigger. Watch the man's face fly apart in gobbets of red meat….

Webber jabbed him in the forehead with the barrel. The pain brought Jack back to his senses.

"Not yet," said Webber. "Not *just* yet. We have other things to finish first." He eased the barrel from Jack's forehead. "Now, you back with us?"

Jack nodded.

"Are we clear on who is the boss?"

He nodded again, his expression carefully neutral. "You are."

Webber set the pistol on the nightstand. "You're a good man, but you need to learn your place, especially if you're going to run in my circle. Not all my friends are as patient as I am."

Jack glared at Webber. One day he would have his moment with the man. He'd have his retribution. One day…but not today.

"We need to find Kevin," Jack said. "Vincent's got him, and they could be headed anywhere by now."

"Maybe. Maybe not. Don't forget, Owens is the one who wants Kevin. As long as the old man sticks around, Vincent will eventually bring your boy back."

"Then what? We still have to get him back, and from what you said, I don't think Owens is just going to hand him over."

Webber's eyes widened in surprise. Then he smiled.

"You know, there's hope for you yet."

Izzy Morris sat at her desk. She and her group had just arrived at the police station. Her computer screen already displayed the results of an internet search for hotels near Kinsey. The station's Yellow Pages directory lay open to the Hotel-Motel section. She was reaching for the phone to start calling when it rang, startling her.

She answered the phone. It was her dispatcher, Aggie Ripley.

"Phone call for you, Chief."

"Now's not the best time. Tell whoever it is to call back."

Then Aggie told her who it was. Izzy sat up and snapped her fingers. Owens, Gene and Katie looked up at her.

"Put him through," she told her dispatcher.

"Good afternoon, Chief Morris. Did you like my pictures?" Jack Sallinen sounded so close she could have reached out and choked him.

"Where's my daughter, you son of a bitch?"

Jack laughed. "Not so civil now, are you?"

"Where is she?"

"Where you'll never find her. Is Owens with you?"

"Yes."

"Put me on speakerphone," Jack said. "I want to talk to him."

"Like hell. You're dealing with me. Now tell me where my daughter is."

She could almost hear the shrug over the phone. "Have it your way. You can bury your brat after I've mailed her back, piece by piece."

"You're bluffing. You're a mean-spirited bastard, but you're not crazy."

"Think about it," Jack said. "What have I got to lose? Those pictures mark my end. I might as well make it worthwhile."

Izzy thought for a moment. "Listen to me. Tell me where Natalie is, and I'll work with the district attorney. Give her back to me—alive—and I'll fight for a reduced charge. Work with me, Jack." *Tell me where my daughter is, damn you.*

"It's insulting, you know. Thinking I'm stupid enough to believe you'd give me a break."

"I just want my daughter back. Give her to me and I'll help you. I promise."

There was silence, enough that Izzy began to wonder if Jack had hung up. Then he said again, "Put me on speakerphone. I want Owens in on this."

She took a deep breath. "Don't hang up." She put Jack on hold, hit the speakerphone button, then reconnected his line. "You still there?"

"Present and accounted for. Can you hear me, Owens?"

Bart looked to Izzy, who nodded for him to go ahead.

"I'm here," he said. "Something I can do for you?"

"Yes, there is. I want my son back."

"And I want an early retirement," Owens replied. "Looks like we're both out of luck."

Izzy heard a tinny laugh that didn't belong to Jack. Where ever they were, Jack's phone had a speaker function. Probably his cell, which would make it harder to trace.

The new voice said, "Early retirement? Now *that's* funny!"

Darryl Webber.

"Let's stick with our deal, Jack," Izzy said. "Will you tell me where Natalie is in exchange for my help with the prosecutor?"

"And I just told you, you dumb-bunny bitch," Jack answered. "I want my son back."

Izzy stifled a groan. The stubborn bastard was going to—

"You still there, Morris?"

"Yeah, I'm here. Look, why did you call? You must want something."

"About time you got to the point," said Jack. "We're at what people call an impasse. I want my son. You want your daughter." He paused for a moment. "I'm proposing a trade."

Izzy's hopes soared. If they wanted to trade, then Natalie was still alive.

Still alive.

She was finally going to get her daughter back!

But Owens' next words brought her crashing down. With a shake of his head, he said, "There'll be no deal."

"*What?*" Izzy and Jack said at the same time.

"You heard me. No trade." The old man was scribbling furiously on a piece of paper. When he was done, he pushed it to Izzy. WE DON'T HAVE KEVIN! "Now let me talk to Darryl."

The answer seemed to have pushed Jack over the edge. He was screaming: "Give me Kevin or I'll kill the girl! I'll fucking kill her! You'll never see her again, Morris!"

Owens raised his voice. "Darryl, if you don't take the phone from this gentleman, I'm going to hang up. Then you'll never see the boy again."

Izzy started to protest—*you're going to get my daughter killed*—but Owens raised a hand to silence her. She glared at him. He nodded that he understood her concern, then mouthed *trust me*.

Through the phone she heard a struggle going on. Jack kept repeating that it was his phone. The other man said something low that Izzy couldn't make out. Then Webber was on the phone.

"Why do you have to be so difficult, Bartholomew?"

"I'm just being practical," Owens replied.

"Seriously," Webber said. "What's your beef with the trade?"

"Because you're in a worse situation than I am."

"How so?" There was a note of caution in Webber's voice.

"You know perfectly well what I mean. We both came here for the boy, and I'm the one who has him. I'd hate to be you when this blows up in your face."

"Not funny," Webber said, his voice thin with anger. "I will kill the girl. Jack here may not be a slicer and dicer, but you know perfectly well what I'm capable of. I'll send her home in tiny little bits. First her fingers, then her toes, then her mouth, and then her nose." Webber gave a chilling laugh. "Keep the boy from me, old man, and you'll have to watch that woman put her daughter back together like a fucking jigsaw puzzle. Take the deal."

Izzy watched as Owens' gaze rose to meet hers. She saw the answer in his eyes. There was going to be no deal. There couldn't be. They didn't have Kevin.

Stall, she mouthed to Owens. *Take the deal. Please.*

His small, sad head shake was like a stab in her back.

Natalie was going to die.

"I'm sorry, Darryl," said Bart. "There'll be no deal. I've got him and I'm keeping him. Good luck with the rest of your short life."

When Webber's voice came back, it was pure venom. "This is going to fall on your head, Bartholomew. Everything that happens from this point forward will be your fault. Morris and her daughter. The bartender and that girl. They're all going to die while you watch. Their blood will be on your hands—as if there isn't enough of that already." Webber was breathing heavily, his rage palpable even from this distance. "Do you know who you're dealing with, Chief Morris? Has he even told you the truth? No? Oh this is rich! You're gonna love this one. Chief, you've partnered up with one of the Fo—"

"—Bye, Darryl," Owens said and quickly broke the connection.

Izzy shot to her feet. "Wait! What was he going to say? One of the what?"

Bart Owens sat back, crossed his legs, and calmly folded his hands on his knees. Then he looked down and drew in a deep breath. When he spoke, he was still avoiding her gaze.

"I'm sorry. I can't let anything distract us from finding Darryl. His stories would've done just that."

Izzy's anger had been growing inside her, first at Jack, then at Webber, and now at Owens. "You told me to trust you, but you just sacrificed my daughter to that madman! You could've stalled. Given us more time to find them. But you didn't. And now they're going to kill her! You owe me, Owens. I want an explanation. I want to know what Webber was going to say. I want to know who you really are."

Gene was scowling openly at Owens. Katie looked like she couldn't decide whether to be concerned for Izzy or curious about Owens.

Owens closed his eyes and drew in another deep breath. Then he opened them. His expression was as hard and unforgiving as granite, and as lonely. "I'm sorry," he apologized again. "I can't."

Gene leaned back into his chair and threw his hands up in the air. "You're a piece of work, you know that. A real piece of work."

Owens ignored Gene. He continued to hold Izzy's gaze.

She stared into his hard, blue eyes. She knew he wasn't going to look away this time. He was waiting for her to give answer to his refusal.

She set her jaw and leaned forward, placing her hands flat against the desktop. "Fine. Keep your damn secrets. I have two kids to find and they need to come first. But don't think for a minute I like this situation. Or that I like you. I'm going to focus on finding Natalie and Kevin. And when they're found—and I *will* find them—I want you gone. Go back to your covert life, hiding behind whatever agency you work for. But Kevin Sallinen stays here. With us. Got it?"

Owens nodded a slow assent. "I understand."

"You put these pieces into play," said Izzy to the old man. "What do we do next?"

"Webber has a temper, a bad one, if you can get under his skin. Plus, he's got to be feeling the pressure. Failure for him is not an option." Owens expression softened a bit. "Don't forget, your daughter isn't his focus. He has to get Kevin. I don't think he'll waste time with her until he has the boy. But if he does find Kevin first…." He left the implications hanging.

"So we're back to either finding Kevin first or finding Webber." Izzy sat down with a sigh. "I think Jack was using his cell phone. Let's see if I can locate the towers he connected to. That'll at least narrow down the area we have to search. This is going to take a few hours."

Izzy reached for the phone and got back to work.

CHAPTER
19

While Webber argued with Owens on the phone, Jack Sallinen managed to pull himself into some semblance of self-control. It hadn't been easy—in fact, it'd been damned hard—but he'd managed. The fact that it'd been so hard bothered him. It bothered him because it looked like the Be Nothings were finally getting to him.

And that worried him. Worried him and, truthfully, frightened him.

At that moment, Webber let out a string of expletives that would've made a seasoned fisherman like Chet Boardman blush three shades of red. He stood, lips pressed hard together in a thin, bloodless line, and tossed the phone on the dresser.

"You okay there?" Jack asked Webber, ignoring his phone for now.

Webber's breaths were coming in short, ragged gasps; his lips moved as he formed words Jack could barely make out.

"....Thinks he's got me beat, does he? Thinks he can outsmart me?" Webber scowled at Jack. "I know what he's up to, you know. He's trying to fuck with me. Wants to see if I'll screw up. He'd love for that to happen. He'd downright *love* it." Jack was stunned to see tears in the corners of Webber's eyes. "I won't let it happen, Jack. I *can't*. If I don't finish this job, if I don't come back with your son—" Webber roughly wiped at his eyes. "Owens is too confident. Too sure of himself. That's always been his problem. This time, I'll make sure it's his undoing." He gestured for Jack to get up. "Come on, we've got something to do."

"Wait, what do you mean, 'come back with my son'? What the hell's going on?"

Webber shouted, "Let's go!"

Jack took a cautious step back. "Fine, but where are we going?"

"I want to look at the trees," was Webber's response as he strode out the door.

Jack didn't have much choice. He followed the man outside.

To the right of the door, Denny Cain sat in a chair he'd dragged from the room. He'd zipped his jacket up to his chin to help ward off the cold. At his feet sat a brown paper bag. His hand held a wide, green beer bottle, the kind with the wide mouth that helped you drink faster. From the wet look in his eyes, Jack thought Denny had probably gone through a third of his case already.

"Where you off to?" Denny asked.

Webber stormed by without answering.

Jack shrugged. "He said he wants to see the trees."

The color left Denny's face, as if what Jack had said scared him.

Jack stopped walking and stared at the man. "What's the matter with you?"

"Be careful," replied Denny. "Watch yourself. And don't go *into* the woods, no matter what."

"Jack," Webber called out as he rounded the corner of the motel. "Move your ass."

Jack wanted to ask Denny what he meant, but he also didn't want to make Webber more upset than he already was. With a dismissive shake of his head, he left Denny to his drinking and hustled after Webber.

The ground behind the motel was thick with weeds and tall grasses. Jack moved several feet in and found a white-enameled sink that someone had been using as a fire pit, along with a handful of empty beer cans, some cigarette butts, and even what looked like two used condoms.

The Be Nothings had set up camp here.

They're everywhere, son.

Yes, Daddy, they certainly were.

Webber had stopped near the edge of the woods. Jack knew this part of the forest stretched far to the north, maybe far enough to reach Lake Superior. The trees here were old, their massive trunks covered with gray-green mosses. They grew so close to one another that Jack couldn't see more than a few yards into the forest. The wind hadn't stripped the leaves from the branches, and the treetops almost glowed with the fires of autumn.

Watch yourself, Denny had said.

"You wanted trees," said Jack, spreading his hands. "Well, there they are. Now can we go back? It's getting cold."

"Not so fast," Webber said. From his pocket, he withdrew a small knife that Jack hadn't seen before. The handle looked like it had been hand carved from some kind of dusky white material, maybe ivory or horn—or bone. There may have once been ridges running along the handle's surface, but they had been worn smooth until they resembled the veins under a dying man's skin. The blade was also white, the same white as the handle. Jack realized the entire knife had been carved from one piece of material.

Bone, his mind whispered to him. You know it's bone. But is it *human* bone?

Jack pointed to the knife. "What're you going to do with that?"

Webber began to lift his shirt. "Think for me, Jack. I want you to think. Think really hard." Then he grinned, and Jack thought he could see a hint of lunacy in the man's smile. "Think about Izzy Morris."

Jack frowned. "Why would I think...?"

His words fell away as Webber lifted his shirt up to his breastbone. The man's abdomen was a patchwork of puckered white scars. They weren't thin; he hadn't simply been cut. No, his scars were about half an inch wide and nearly two inches long, like the skin had been torn from him. There were at least a dozen of them, and all but two appeared old. Jack's mouth dropped open when he saw that the patchwork wasn't random. The scars roughly spelled out a word.

Bitch.

"Start thinking," warned Webber.

"At least tell me why—"

Webber's wrist flashed. Jack felt a hot line burning across his cheek. He raised his hand to his face, and it came away wet with blood.

"Hey! What the shit!"

"Think about her," Webber said, his voice trembling with fury. "Or I'll cut you to ribbons."

Jack stared at his bloody fingers for a moment, his own anger seething inside him. He didn't *want* to think about Morris. Her superior attitude or her Be Nothing ways. No, thinking about her would just make him angrier—

"That's it," Webber said, his face sweating despite the cold, his jaw set in a grimace of pain. "Yes, think of her. You hate her, don't you? Hate her. And hate is hungry work. Leaves you with that empty feeling in your guts. An emptiness that hurts. We can't have that. Here, have a little something to hold you over."

Jack watched Webber lift a hand, felt the man push something small past his lips. His teeth closed reflexively. Whatever it was felt rubbery, chewy, like steak fat but with no taste. He frowned. His tongue caressed it, flipped it over. More chewing. Hints of…blood and gristle?

"Swallow," whispered Webber. "This is my body, which shall be given up for you. Swallow—and think of Morris."

Jack gagged. Webber clamped a hand over his mouth. He didn't want to swallow, oh God he didn't, but swallow he did. He wanted to retch, wanted to vomit up the bit of flesh that Webber had fed to him, but it slid too easily down his gullet and was gone.

Watch yourself.

Jack began to sense a presence, an intruder prowling at the outskirts of his mind. Somebody whispered Morris' name. He was no longer sure if it was Webber or himself—or the intruder. He thought he could feel the bit of Webber's flesh moving around inside him, working its way deeper and deeper.

Morris

He could hear something. A noise, like the static you used to get when a television station signed off for the night. Or when you'd tune into an AM radio channel that had no station broadcasting. It was getting louder by the moment, filling his ears, making his skin itch. And there were voices in the noise, wordless but human, cries of pain and suffering. He thought he had heard it earlier, when Webber had sent him to that hellish place.

Jack started to tremble. Why do I keep hearing that noise? What's happening to me?

Morris

Stop saying her name, he wanted to scream. I don't want to think about her!

Morris

Images began to flash through his mind. Earlier today at the wake. Izzy Morris up in his face, so close he could feel her warm breath on his skin, smell her perfume; and days ago on his front porch, her clothes clinging to her sweaty skin, strands of her hair caressing the sides of her face, hazel eyes glaring at him, resenting the power he had over her, wishing she had the same power, wishing she had *him*—

Stop it! he protested silently. Get out of my mind!

—Izzy Morris at the summer picnic, shorts hugging the curves of her hips, her ass, and her long legs, shapely legs, legs which should be wrapped around him; legs that flexed smoothly as she walked by, her full breasts pushing at the thin cotton blouse she wore, that perfume again, dizzying, pulling at him, making him want her, desire her—

No! Not true!

That horrific noise—that god-forsaken *screaming*—surrounded him. It was loud now. Loud enough to hurt. It filled him until there wasn't room for anything else.

The intruder was here. Jack could sense something moving back and forth in the forest, pacing restlessly, just beyond his sight.

Don't go into *the woods.*

"What did you do to me?" panted Jack. "What the fuck did you just do to me?"

Webber laughed. He'd put away his knife. There was a thin red line forming on the fabric of his shirt. He caught Jack staring and zipped up his jacket.

"Unpleasant," the man said, "but necessary. I had to reach out and touch someone, as the saying goes. Or in this case, some*thing*."

Then Jack hadn't been imagining things. The intruder was real. He began backing away from the woods. "What is it?"

Webber studied Jack for a moment, then shrugged. "I've been using it to help me get the job done."

"You're some kind of monster," Jack said warily. "Some devil or demon or something."

"Wrong again," replied Webber. "I'm as human as you. And just because I go to extremes doesn't mean I'm evil. I'm simply thorough. I like the odds stacked heavily in my favor, and my pet is my ace in the hole."

Jack pointed a trembling hand at the forest. "That thing killed—?"

Webber nodded. "But let's keep that between you and me. I want Denny to keep thinking Owens killed his boy."

"Why is it here now?"

Webber made a quick gesture with his hand and the presence started to retreat. The noise in his head faded until it was gone. "It has another job to do."

"What?"

"It's going to kill Izzy Morris."

* * *

J.J. Sallinen stood on the front porch, knocking on the door and shivering from the icy wind that sliced through his clothes.

"Come on, answer the damn door." He changed from rapping smartly on the door with his knuckles to pounding loudly with his fist. "Katie! Mrs. Bethel!"

A half-minute of hammering yielded the same result.

He tested the handle.

Locked.

Another wave of shivers ran through him. He rubbed his arms to warm them. The unexpected turn in the weather had caught him by surprise. His varsity jacket didn't provide nearly enough protection.

He threw a quick, worried look back at his car. His dad was the reason he was standing there freezing his nuts off. *All you had to do was give me a little respect,* he thought. *Was that too much to ask?*

Fuck 'em. Kevin's the only one that matters.

Guess so.

J.J. found a little ceramic frog nestled off to the side of the porch. He grabbed hold of its warty back and lifted. The figurine came apart. Inside he found a key and used it to unlock the front door. Then he put the key back where he found it and went inside.

"Hello," he called out. "Anyone home?"

Nada.

He gave the house a quick walk-through. Finding it empty, he hurried back out to his car and opened the passenger door.

J.J. extended a hand to his passenger. "Come on, Kev. Let's go inside."

It had taken J.J. the promise of something sweet—a candy bar he'd brought with him—to get his brother out of the car and into Katie's house. The little booger was still upset over being hauled away while he'd been busy with his cookies and milk and cartoons. He'd actually bolted upstairs, tried to hide in his closet. There'd been a minor tussle when J.J. had to carry Kevin out of his room and downstairs—one of Kevin's flailing legs had kicked over a chair, while his hands had raked across his desk, scattering his drawings.

After he'd wrestled a jacket and some shoes onto his brother, J.J.

had grabbed a couple chocolate chip cookies (and the candy bar, of course) and dragged Kevin by the arm out to his car. He'd pushed him into the passenger's seat, tossed the cookies onto the kid's lap, and then slid behind the wheel. The cookies had kept Kevin quiet during the drive to Katie's.

He watched as Kevin, now huddled on Mrs. Bethel's couch with a blanket draped over his thin shoulders, munched on a Kit-Kat and watched more of his stupid cartoons. J.J. had come across the word "imbecile" while reading *Of Mice and Men* for English class. His brother was the poster child for the word. He also worried that Kevin was destined to play Lennie to his George.

He shook his head. "I may be stuck taking care of you for the rest of my life. It isn't fair."

Kevin showed no reaction to what J.J. had said; he remained unreachable, oblivious within his cocoon of autism.

J.J. turned his attention to the empty house. The wake had ended hours ago. He thought he'd find Katie here. Or at the very least, Mrs. Bethel would've shown up by now. Katie had told him about her mother's date last night, about how the woman hadn't bothered to come home. Either she was sleeping off a massive hangover or she was still going at it with her date. J.J. made a face at the latter thought. Old people sex. Gross.

He wandered into the kitchen. Fruit-shaped magnets hung on the fridge's door. Each one held up a coupon or recipe that'd been clipped out of a magazine, but there were no notes from Katie or her mother. Yesterday's paper and Saturday's mail still sat on the kitchen table. It was past 8 pm and no one had brought in today's mail? It looked like no one had been home since he and Katie had left this morning.

His curiosity piqued, J.J. turned to head to the back of the house and Katie's bedroom. That's when he saw the answering machine sitting on the countertop near the fridge. The little red display light blinked insistently. There were eight new messages.

He'd never known Katie or her mom to have more than a message or two, most of which were from him. He walked back to the fridge and hit the PLAY button.

The first one was from Katie's friend, Brittany Parsons. In a breathless, tearful voice, she said how sorry she was to hear that Katie's mom had died.

Stunned, he thought, No way. I must not have heard her right.

Brittany went on to tell Katie to call if she needed anything. Four more of Katie's friends had called to offer their condolences; Brittany had called back twice.

Mrs. B's dead? The thought left J.J. cold.

Where was Katie? Had Brittany ever gotten hold of her? Did she even know? He'd left the wake without talking to her. It was stupid, he knew, and rude. But after listening to his father—

Hold on. His phone call the other day—he'd told his dad about finding those photos of Natalie. His dad knew Katie had been there, had said he wanted to do something to keep her mouth shut.

I won't let you hurt her, J.J. had said. *That's part of the deal. To keep my mouth shut.*

Okay, fine, his dad had responded. *Something will need to be done, but I promise she won't be hurt.*

Was his dad involved in Mrs. B's death? Is this what he considered not hurting Katie? He pulled his cell phone out of his pocket and hit speed dial. He got his dad's voicemail.

"Hey, it's me. Some weird stuff's going on, and I think we need to talk. Someplace private. Call me back." Then he remembered his dad's tendency to ignore him, so just before he hung up, he added, "Oh, by the way, I've got something you may want."

J.J. stuffed the cell phone back into his pocket. He wished he could call Katie, but she didn't have a cell phone. She and her mom— well, now just Katie—barely made do with the proceeds from her dad's life insurance policy. They couldn't afford the luxury of a cell phone.

While he waited for his dad to call back, J.J. walked into the living room and sat down next to Kevin. His brother was sitting motionless on the couch, his eyes dancing across the television screen as the cartoons played.

"I need to find someplace safe to hide you," J.J. sighed. "You're the only bargaining chip I've got. I'm not about to let Dad have you without getting something back first."

He threw a blanket over them both. Kevin snuggled up close to him.

Then J.J. waited, and, eventually, he slept.

CHAPTER
20

It moved silently, gliding past tall brown columns, hard, close, comforting. It hated open spaces, hated especially the vast emptiness that stretched above it.

Sky. It remembered the emptiness was called sky.

Thick muscles bunched as it leapt over barriers; sharp claws dug wounds into the earth; lungs pulled air in through its nostrils. The bitter cold gouged furrows of pain through its skull. It hated the cold.

It hated this place, and the man who kept it here.

Something exploded from beneath it, thrumming loudly into the air.

Animal. No—bird.

It ignored the flying thing. Images of the female flashed through its mind. It felt a need to shift direction, angle slightly left.

The female.

She haunted its thoughts.

* * *

The two men passed the Be Nothing camp on their way back to the motel room. Jack Sallinen was still shaken from what he'd witnessed. Darryl Webber strode silently beside him.

The first flakes of snow began to fall. They drifted gently through the air, spinning lazily until they came to rest on the ground.

The snowflakes continued to drop as Jack and Webber rounded the end of the motel. At first there hadn't been many, what Jack's mother used to call a *little bitch of snow*. But the numbers had grown. Now they were walking through heavy swirls of white. He wondered if it was going to turn into a *big bitch of snow*.

The curtain of white flakes parted, and Jack found himself standing under the awning that ran above the motel's walkway. He could see that Denny Cain—the everyman's alcoholic—was gone. The straight-backed wood chair from the room was there, as was the brown paper bag into which Denny had stored his treasure of beer. But the man himself was nowhere to be seen.

"There better be a damned good reason for this," muttered Webber.

"The truck's still there," Jack said, pointing to the Silverado. "Maybe he's inside—"

From the far end of the motel, the office door creaked open. Denny emerged, his face ruddy from the cold and the beer. He saw Jack and Webber, nodded a greeting, and hurried over to them.

When he got close enough that he didn't have to shout, Denny said, "Dammit, guys. You locked me out. I had to use the office restroom to take a piss."

Webber stepped up close to Denny, so close that their noses almost touched. Jack wondered how Webber could put up with Denny's beer breath. To him, Denny smelled as sour as a cheap brewery.

"Hold it next time," Webber told Denny in a low, menacing voice. "We're not playing a game here. Wander away again, and you won't have to worry about Owens or Morris. I'll kill you myself. Understand?"

Jack waited for Denny to back down. The old Denny, the one Jack knew only a week ago, wouldn't have been so meek. The old Denny would've had a few words for Webber, would've shown a little in-your-face attitude of his own. Jack supposed Jimmy's death had eviscerated the man; he'd been hollowed out as easily as someone scooped out the insides of an overripe honeydew, leaving nothing behind but a useless shell. Jack marveled at how far some people could fall when confronted with a little unpleasantness.

Look who's talking, the devil on his shoulder whispered into his ear. Does the word *cannibal* mean anything to you?

Jack mentally flinched. His stomach rolled a little at the thought of what had happened back at the tree line. Swallowing hard, he shoved aside his own bit of unpleasantness with brutal efficiency. He didn't have time for distractions.

But Denny surprised him. The man gave Webber a little push back.

"Kill me, huh?" He and Webber were still nose to nose. "I buried my son today, Mr. Webber. He's lying cold in the ground. My wife's at home right now, probably scrubbing the house clean again, like maybe she could scrub away the memory of his death. I should be there with her, *for* her, but I'm not. I'm here, trying to help you get back at the guy who killed my boy." Denny took a step forward, forcing Webber to move back a step. "Kill me? Be my fucking guest. I got nothing left to lose."

Webber's hands curled into fists. He drew in a deep breath, his nostrils flaring wide. He held the air in for a few moments, then let it seep out. His hands unclenched.

"You're right," Webber said to Denny. "I keep forgetting what you've been through. Look, you don't need to stay with us. Jack and I can finish things from here on out." Webber picked up the paper bag and placed it in Denny's hands. "Go home to the little woman. We'll let you know when Owens is dead."

Denny's mouth dropped open. His jaw started working soundlessly up and down. To Jack, he looked like a big fish who'd just been yanked from his small pond and cast onto shore.

"Wait—no! That's not what I meant." This time it was Denny who took a step back. "I'm here, and I mean to stay until Owens is finished. I owe Jimmy at least that much. It's just…it's been a long day. And I don't take kindly to threats." He placed the bag back on the ground. "I've done everything you've asked. What if I'd've got caught planting that pick? And I almost got killed by that damn detective. No, I think I've done good by you, but I draw the line at asking for permission to take a piss."

Webber's lips curled into a smile. "Right again, Denny. You've done well. I shouldn't have been so short with you. Chalk it up to nerves." He put his hand on the chair. "You mind still keeping watch?"

Denny shook his head. "I got no problem with it, but it's gettin' late. Where am I gonna sleep?"

Webber's smile slipped a little. "Unless you want to spoon with Jack here, I suggest you take the truck. Maybe the cold will help sober you up by morning."

Denny gave Webber another hateful glare. He sat down, pulling a beer out of the bag and opening it. After taking a long pull, he said, "I'll let you know if I see anything."

"You do that," Jack muttered as removed the room key from his pocket and inserted into the lock.

Once inside the room, Jack tossed the room key onto the desk. Turning to Webber, he said, "How long will it take for that thing to do its job?"

Webber shrugged. "I should know something within a few hours."

"I'll finally be rid of Morris," Jack said, gloating at the thought.

"Don't get too happy," warned Webber, moving over to a bed and lying down. "We still have to find your son."

Jack took the other bed. He yawned and said, "Killing Morris will bring the bartender back. And my son."

Jack looked over at Webber. The man's eyes were already closed. His eyes were also getting heavy. He thought momentarily about getting his cell phone, but he was too tired to get up. Anyway, he'd hear if anyone called.

* * *

The noise surrounded it, filled it, soothed it—made it remember the darkness, the pain, so much pain.

Home.

The female: her image burned hot, a crimson flame.

Ahead, under the emptiness, away from the closeness of the tall, gray, rough....

Sticks?

No, wrong—trees.

It burst past the trees, loping low, fast. White was falling from the emptiness, covering the ground. Good. It could hide, even if the cold hurt.

It crouched, muscles tensed. Leaping high, it landed, skidded. Claws dug in, found purchase. Slower. Careful. It jumped higher, from place to place. Clear open spaces.

The female. Nearby now.

It dropped down to the ground, hidden by the white, hidden by all that clutters this world. It hurried. A stone wall. Scale it. On the other side, creatures, black and white. One left, lights flashing, red and blue. It waited until the other creature was gone.

Through the white it moved, silently. In front of it, a barrier, like a wall within a wall.

The female.

She was on the other side.

CHAPTER
21

Izzy Morris sat in her office, weary from calling motels and getting nowhere. They hadn't been able to narrow their search; the call from Jack had been unexpected, and tracing it had proved impossible. It had been another setback, another delay. She needed to catch a break soon, or she was afraid her daughter would die.

"It's getting late," said Gene. He sat between Owens and Katie, a cup of hot coffee in his hands. "We're going to need some rest."

"I know," Izzy said. "But that poses its own problems. I've put off the State guys until tomorrow. In the morning, they're going to want to talk to me about Carlton Manick." She picked up her own coffee and took a sip. "I'll be tied up with them for who knows how long."

"Not if they can't find you," said Gene. "Screw the calling. Let's go and check out the motels ourselves."

Izzy shook her head. "I should've listened to Sten. He was right all along. I think it's time to bring in the cavalry. We're not going to be able to do this alone."

Katie leaned forward. "And how long will that take?"

"Well, nothing can happen tonight. In the morning—"

A thundering bang startled her into silence.

For a few seconds, everyone stared silently at one another.

Katie said nervously, "What was that?"

Gene got to his feet. "Sounded like someone ran into something."

Izzy pushed back her chair and stood up. "Yeah, it did. And other than Aggie, I think we're the only ones here." Izzy walked toward her door. "Everyone stay put."

There was another explosive bang, this time forceful enough for Izzy to feel vibrations through the floor. She stepped back and drew her gun. The weight felt reassuring in her hand.

Owens stood. He was fingering whatever hung by a chain under his Predators sweatshirt. What Izzy saw in his face sent a shiver through her.

The normally unflappable Bart Owens looked worried.

"We need to leave," he said. "Right now."

"I agree," said Izzy. "New plan. Follow me."

She edged quietly up to the door. Listened. Nothing. She eased the door open.

Her office was at the junction of two hallways. One stretched before her for sixty feet and ended in a thick, steel door that opened to the parking lot. The shorter one went left and led to the dispatcher's office, the lobby, and the entrance to a small resource room.

Both hallways were empty.

Nodding for the others to follow, she crept forward. The long hallway was empty, she could *see* it was, but it didn't *feel* empty. Whatever was going on, it was that way. Another step. Something was down there, lurking, waiting. She heard a scrape, saw movement to her left. She brought the Glock around hard and fast. There was a terrified yelp, and Izzy recognized the frightened face of Aggie Ripley. The poor woman had agreed to work a second shift, and Izzy had just drawn down on her.

"Shit." Izzy lowered the gun, her heart racing.

"Chief," said Aggie. "What's going on? Who's making that racket?"

"Aggie, go," urged Izzy. "Get—"

At the end of the long hallway, something crashed into the metal door. Thick steel buckled in one corner, the top hinge snapping free of the metal frame with a sound like a firecracker exploding. Another blow and the upper half folded in like it was some kind of cardboard movie prop. Two arms reached through the opening, longer than a man's, thickly muscled and covered with coarse, black hair. Claw-like hands gripped the door and pulled. There was a loud screech as the remaining metal hinge tore free. The door was thrown into the dark night.

A creature advanced through the opening.

Izzy's first thought was wolf, but much, much larger, with a long muzzle and narrow ears folded flat against a broad head. But parts of it didn't make sense. Black hair covered most of the chest and body, but then it thinned in places, disappeared, where it looked like it had—

No way. Not possible. Were those...*scales*?

Izzy said, "Quickly, everybody out the front—"

The creature lifted its head and throated an eerie, thrumming howl. Then it started charging down the hallway on all fours, claws digging into the carpet, sharp teeth snapping at the air.

"Go!" Izzy shouted. In one smooth motion, she brought the gun around and fired. The creature surprised her—it leapt high and to the side, colliding hard with the wall, and slid to the ground. The bullet plowed uselessly into the floor where the thing should have been.

"The door on the right!" It was Bart Owens. He'd grabbed Katie and Aggie each by an arm and practically threw them down the shorter hall. Gene ran after them. "Into that room!"

The creature dragged itself off the floor. Then it was rushing at her again, its claws ripping the carpet. Izzy sped around the corner of the hallway, tried to reach the room. She wasn't quick enough. The creature rounded the corner, panting, growling, close enough she could smell it, making her eyes water—the stench was acidic, like pine tar, but mixed with something foul, rotting.

From the doorway, Owens yelled, "Hit it! Slow it down!"

She spun, leveled the Glock at the thing's head, and fired. She knew to expect some kind of evasion and let the recoil bring her gun up. The creature leapt high and she fired again, the bullet slamming into its chest, spinning it in midair. Momentum carried it forward, and it collapsed onto the floor at her feet.

"Yes!" Izzy gave a small fist pump.

Owens grabbed her arm, propelled her toward the room. "It's not dead."

"Bullshit. I killed it." Izzy tried to pull her arm free but couldn't. "It's over."

When they were at the doorway, Bart released her arm and pointed back down the hallway. "Look."

Izzy turned. What she saw couldn't be real. I'm dreaming, she thought. This is some kind of nightmare.

The creature, the *monster*, was slowly pushing itself off the ground, blood trickling from a wound that should have killed it. Now that it was close, she could see its eyes: they were a bilious green-yellow and far too expressive for an animal. As it glared malevolently at her, those eyes looked almost human. Then it screamed a sound that chilled her—she thought she could hear two voices, both wailing in pain.

Swearing under her breath, Izzy ran into the room and slammed the thin wood door. She pushed her shoulder against it, then realized how futile that was: the creature had just busted through steel like it was paper. She looked around. The resource room was small, with a door opposite her and another one to her right. There was a conference table, four chairs, a wire rack holding informational pamphlets, a distilled water dispenser, and a four-foot-tall file cabinet full of extra pamphlets. Not much to defend themselves with.

Owens raced toward the cabinet. "We need to block the door."

As Gene rushed over to help the old man, Izzy noticed Aggie Ripley crouched in the far corner of the room, her hands knotted in her hair, her face strangely slack. Katie was kneeling beside the dispatcher, shaking the older woman's shoulder.

Izzy holstered her gun and ran over to Gene. "No, let me."

Gene's back was flat against the cabinet, and he was pushing with his legs. Through a grimace of pain, he said, "I got this."

"Gene, please. If your back gives out, we won't be able to save you *and* ourselves. You'll get us all killed." He shot her a wounded look. She'd hurt him, hurt his pride, but there was no time. She would apologize later, if they were still alive. "Go see what's up with Aggie. She doesn't look right. Please."

For a moment, she thought he was going to refuse. Then he stood without saying a word and stalked off across the room. He never lost the hurt look.

Izzy put a shoulder to the cabinet. She pushed as Owens pulled. With a final effort, they wedged the cabinet against the door just as the monster crashed into the other side. The door bucked, and they threw their weight against the cabinet.

"Where to now?" Owens asked as they strained to hold the thing back.

Izzy quickly scanned the room. "That door" —she nodded to the door opposite them—"leads to an observation room. No way out. The other goes into a break room. We can get back into the hallway from there. There are some guns stored in the room across the hall."

The monster slammed into the door again, throwing them forward. They scrambled back against the cabinet, their feet digging into the carpet. Izzy could hear claws raking the door.

"Take the others and go," said Owens. "I'll meet you in the hallway. What's the biggest gun you have?"

"Remington 700P assault rifle."

"Good. It might be enough. Get it."

The door bucked again. This time a crack formed along the middle.

Izzy shook her head. "I'm not leaving you here."

"Go!" he yelled. "And be ready when I come running." He squatted and pushed hard against the cabinet.

She stared at him for a moment, then muttered, "Crazy old man," and ran for the other side of the room, where Gene crouched in front of Aggie.

When Izzy got there, Gene looked up. "We got a problem."

"We got a lot of problems," Izzy replied. "That thing's coming through the door."

"I don't get it," said Katie, her face tight with worry. "She won't move. Just sits there, staring."

Aggie leaned against the wall, her eyes staring blankly out into space, her mouth moving but not making any sound. "Grab her. We're going that way." She pointed at the door to the break room.

Gene grabbed one arm, Izzy the other—

—and that's when Aggie Ripley went wild.

"No!" she screamed, and began thrashing and slapping and kicking. "I didn't mean it! Don't put me in there!"

Izzy tried grabbing Aggie's wrists, but the woman was fighting like a terrified child. One hand lashed out and smacked Izzy hard across the face. Gene let out a grunt when her foot connected with his knee. All the while, Aggie kept yelling, "Don't put me in there! I'm sorry!"

"Aggie, listen to me!" Izzy was still trying to grab the woman's arms, but it was impossible. The dispatcher's knee came up and slammed into her chest. "Damn it, stop!"

A sharp crack rent the air, and Katie yelled, "Oh God!"

Izzy spun around. The upper door had broken apart and exploded inward. Jagged pieces of wood lay on the floor. Owens had hunched down further, sweat running down his face, his legs shaking as he pushed against the metal cabinet.

One hideous arm reached in through the opening, clawing the top of the cabinet, while the other pushed through, stretching, rearing back and smashing into the side of the cabinet, collapsing the metal.

"Look out!" Izzy shouted, drawing her gun

A claw ripped through the air. Owens turned his head, but he was too slow. It caught his cheek and neck, tore jagged gashes into his skin. Bright red blood erupted down his face. Then his legs gave out and he slid to the floor.

Without Owens holding the door, the thing shoved it open, charged into the room, leapt at Izzy. She dove under the conference table, scrambled to get to the other side. The creature landed, snarling, and with a sinuous turn it sped around the table after her. She rolled back under the table, aimed and fired *BANG BANG*, the bullets thundering through the air, grazing the thing's leg, blood flying. It howled in pain, then grabbed the table and flung it into the far wall. And now the creature was over her, its stench overpowering. She flipped onto her back, brought her gun up, but it was so fast, too fast, and it swiped at her wrist, tearing open her skin, sending the gun sailing away, landing across the room, and its black lips peeled back into an ugly grin as it raised a deadly claw, *oh God NO—*

"Hey!" Gene Vincent shouted. When the creature paused, he launched himself across the room and hammered into it, wrapping his arms around its middle like a pro linebacker. Both tumbled to the ground.

But the monster was too strong for him. It shrugged out of his grip as if he were a child and rose. Gene cried out in pain as one massive claw clamped down on his chest, pinning him to the floor. Then it lifted the other claw high, ready to deliver the deadly blow.

Izzy scrambled for her gun, but she was too far away. She'd never make it in time.

A chair came crashing down from behind the creature, knocking it away from Gene. Snarling in rage, it turned to face this new threat.

Bart Owens was back on his feet. He stepped away from the thing, his sweatshirt wet with the blood flowing from his wounds, his steady gaze locked on the creature. When he spoke, his voice was hard as steel.

"I never did like your kind."

The creature snorted, blowing fetid air from its nostrils, then it turned and charged after Izzy. Panicked, she sprinted across the room toward Owens, barely missing another attack. The monster followed, and in two quick, loping strides, it had crossed the space between them, its head raised, jaws stretched wide.

Owens stepped up and threw his shoulder into its chest. The heavier creature knocked him back into the broken cabinet, but the block gave Izzy enough time to retreat back across the room. The monster turned, claws scrabbling for purchase. It shot across the floor after her, this time coming in low.

With a quickness that defied his age, Owens dove onto the thing's back. He clamped his arms around it before it could reach Izzy. His hands locked together.

And then he squeezed.

The creature convulsed, dropping to the ground, dragging Owens down with it. It began shrieking—a cry of pain so horrible Izzy hoped she'd never hear anything like it again. With claws raking the air, it rolled and rolled, howling in agony, smashing Owens repeatedly against the ground, trying desperately to dislodge him. The old man grunted when his head smacked hard against the floor. And when a claw laid open his arm down to the bone, he let out his own cry of pain and tightened his grip. The thing screamed—dear God how it *screamed!* Frantic to escape, it spun, fast. Owens suddenly found himself facing it, its jaws snapping at his face. He angled his head back, away from the teeth. Claws dug into him, shredding his sweatshirt, carving deep, lethal wounds into his chest, his stomach. Owens sagged, released his grip, and shoved the creature away.

Once released, the monster fled out the broken door, down the hallway, and was gone.

Bart Owens, blood flowing from too many injuries, lay on the floor. He wasn't moving.

Izzy tossed her cell at Katie. "Call for an ambulance!" As the girl put the phone to her ear, Izzy scrambled over to Owens. She watched his wounded chest rise and fall in thin, rapid breathes. When she grasped his hand, he opened his eyes. His gaze found hers. She smiled, squeezed his hand, and she felt him squeeze back.

"The ambulance," she told him. "It'll be on its way soon. Try to keep still."

"Where's Gene?"

"Right here," Gene answered, crawling over to them, a hand clutching his chest. "I feel like someone kicked the shit out of me, but, thanks to you, I'm still alive." He picked up a broken piece of door and held it up. "What was that thing?"

Owens coughed, and a thin stream of blood trickled out of one corner of his mouth.

Katie snapped the phone shut. "This whole town's messed up. I keep calling 911 and no one answers."

Izzy cursed herself for her stupidity. Emergency calls were routed through the police, and her dispatcher was currently sitting in a corner with the mental acuity of a scrambled egg. She was about to tell Katie to call the fire department directly when Owens stopped her with another squeeze of his hand

"Don't bother."

Izzy shook her head. "I'm not going to let you die."

The old man gently lifted the tattered fabric of his sweatshirt, exposing his abdomen. He angled his head to examine his injuries. Gene winced. Katie covered her mouth and turned away. His flesh was a mass of torn muscle, exposed bone, and red gore. With a sigh, Owens said, "What could they do?"

Izzy was stunned. The damage was worse than she had expected. How much blood had he lost? There were only trickles of it seeping from his wounds. And the pain he must be in—she couldn't understand how he was lying there, like *that*, and not be either screaming in agony or passed out from the pain. "I'm still going to try," she said.

Owens gripped her hand until it hurt. "Let me do this with dignity. Not surrounded by a bunch of strangers."

That made Izzy pause. She stared at the old man. His skin already seemed lighter. Given his wounds, she supposed his request wasn't all that outlandish.

"Katie," Izzy said. "Go get a blanket. There's one in the room across the hall." At least they could keep him warm.

Katie's face flushed. "What—you're not giving up, are you?"

Izzy put her head close to Katie's. "You saw the wounds," she whispered. "There's nothing—"

Turning to Owens, Katie said, "So you're not even going to try? You're going to let yourself die? Take something precious and throw it away?" The grief in her next words was immeasurable. "You're no different than my father."

Izzy felt herself go cold. "Oh, honey, no. This isn't the same thing."

Gene gave Izzy a puzzled look. Owens managed to turn his head to look at Katie, who continued to glare defiantly at him.

"Her father," Izzy said. "He...well, he had a history of depression. Let's just say she has a reason to be sensitive about this."

Gene muttered something unintelligible and looked away.

Owens continued to stare at the girl, his expression unreadable. Finally, he called her name. When she didn't respond, he said it more forcefully. After a few silent moments, she asked what he wanted.

"What I'm doing...you have to trust me."

Katie shook her head; she had progressed beyond mad to furious. "Don't tell me that. Don't lie to me. What you're doing—it's no better than what my dad did. It's just another form of cowardice."

Bart let out a wheezing breath. "Don't expect you to...understand."

"Fine." Katie spat out the word like it was poison. "It's your life. Throw it away if you want. I'll go get the blanket." She stormed out of the room.

After Katie had left, Izzy said to Owens, "She's had so many losses. I can't blame her for how she feels."

"Me either," said the old man.

"I really don't want to leave you here alone."

He managed to nudge his head toward Aggie. "Go help that poor woman. She needs you."

Gene touched Bart's shoulder. "It doesn't have to be this way. You know we'll stay with you until...."

Bart closed his eyes. "Must I beg?"

"No, of course not." Gene's voice was tinged with sorrow. "You're a strange man, but I like you. Thank you for saving my life." He patted the old man's shoulder, then went over to help Aggie.

Katie came in with a gray wool blanket and hastily draped it over the old man. "There. Now you'll stay warm while you die."

"So angry," Owens whispered. He opened his eyes. "I have…a deal for you." A breath. "Katie, you can stay. But your father…you have to tell me about him." Another. "Not his death, but his life…the good things you remember about him. Deal?"

"Wait a minute," said Izzy, worried about where the conversation was headed. "She doesn't need to see another—"

"No," Katie said, sitting down next to him. "I'll do it. But you have to give me something in return. You have to tell me why you're doing this. Why you're letting yourself die. So there. Deal?"

Owens nodded. "I'll try."

Izzy didn't like this recent turn of events, but short of dragging Katie out of the room, she didn't have a choice. "Have it your way," she said. "If you change your mind, we'll be in my office."

She left the two of them alone, hoping this wasn't another one of her mistakes.

* * *

Tuesday

Jack Sallinen was dreaming. Running—he was running, through the woods, past buildings. And there was pain, unimaginable pain ripping through his flesh. And then…and then….

And then he woke. At first, he felt disoriented. He was confined, restricted. It took him a few seconds to realize that sometime during the night, he had crawled under the covers of his bed; they were knotted around him, binding his arms, and his pillow had ended up on the floor.

As he extricated himself, he heard Webber snoring softly in the bed next to him. There was a faint pink glow coming through the window. With his arms free, he squinted at his watch. A little past six. He smiled.

Morris would be dead by now.

He reached for his cell phone—he wanted to see if her death had made the news—but found the nightstand empty. Then he remembered. Webber had set it onto the dresser last night.

Rolling out of bed, Jack walked across the room and snatched up the phone. That's when he saw the little red light flashing. He had a message.

He hit the call log, and then swore when the password screen opened.

He thumbed in the code. J.J. had called him. Last night, before Jack had gone to bed. J.J. had probably learned that his little girly-friend's mother was dead.

He pressed the 1 button and connected to his voicemail. As he listened to the message, his euphoria seeped out of him like helium from three-day-old balloon.

J.J. Sallinen was dreaming. He was lying in a hammock on a beach, but there were no trees, and he could see that the hammock wasn't tied to anything. He seemed to be floating in air. He wondered briefly where Katie was, why she wasn't here with him. The hammock started swaying. Then it started jerking back and forth. In the distance, he could hear someone calling his name. It didn't sound like Katie. It didn't sound like anyone he knew.

"J.J.! Wake up!"

"Go 'way," he mumbled.

"You got to wake up NOW!"

Pain, like he'd been punched in the arm. J.J. cracked his eyes open. Kevin stood over him, his young face anxious.

"They're here," Kevin cried, shaking his shoulder. "I can feel them. Somewhere nearby."

"What do you mean? Who're you talking about?" J.J. tried to shrink back from his brother, but Kevin's grip on him was surprisingly firm. Then he realized who he was talking to. Saw the awareness in Kevin's expression. The sense of being there that he'd never seen before. "Holy shit, you—you're—"

Kevin was trembling. "A man. A man and...and a woman. And...a *thing.*"

"What going on?" said J.J., wide awake now. "I mean, you're talking. I can even understand you."

"Listen to me! The man, he's closest. Closer than the woman. But the thing...it scares me, J.J.. Scares me bad."

"Wait a minute." J.J.'s brows drew together in an angry knot. "You've been able to talk all along, and you've been hiding it?"

"No," panted Kevin. "No, it...won't last. I can...." He screwed his eyes shut. "It's bad, J.J.. Really...wheelly...rad...no, *BAD*! Baddity bad." Kevin gritted his teeth. "Not yet!" Kevin opened his eyes, and J.J. saw that they were twitching, as if he were going through a seizure or something. Kevin suddenly drew a hand back and slapped his own face—hard. The twitching stopped. Kevin looked straight at J.J. and said, "Please, help me. I'm scared." Then Kevin lost whatever battle he'd been fighting. The awareness faded from his expression, replaced with the familiar dullness of his autism. He turned from J.J., his attention drawn once again to the cartoon images flitting across the television screen.

J.J. gently shook his brother's shoulder. "Hey, you in there?"

Kevin shrugged his shoulder away, frowned, and began picking his nose.

He sighed. His brother was gone—or back, depending on how you looked at it.

Man, woman and thing? He wondered what that meant.

J.J.'s cell phone began vibrating in his pocket. He pulled it out. His dad was calling him.

What was he supposed to do now? He was going to use Kevin as a bargaining chip, but after what he'd just witnessed—

His phone buzzed insistently in his hand. Answer, or let it go to voicemail?

His brother sat there, still rooting around his nasal cavity, oblivious to everything around him. Or was he really? J.J. wasn't so sure now.

The phone continued to vibrate, his father's name on the display screen.

He had to think fast. How was he supposed to choose between an asshole father and a dumb-shit brother who may not be so much of a dumb-shit? Too bad there wasn't a third choice.

Wait a minute. His eyes widened. Maybe there was.

J.J. thumbed the answer button and said, "Hi, Dad. Just the guy I wanted to talk to."

Jack Sallinen sat on the motel bed, his cell phone pressed tightly to his ear, and waited for his older son to answer. The phone kept ringing. He was getting ready to hang up when he heard J.J.'s voice.

"Hi, Dad. Just the guy I wanted to talk to."

"Yeah, sure," Jack said. "And you're the bright spot of my morning, too."

A brief pause, then, "Couldn't you to at least pretend you like me?"

"I'm severely lacking in 'warm and fuzzy' at the moment. Get to the point. You said you had something I wanted."

"You're a real jerk, you know that."

"Tell me what this is about or I'm hanging up. I don't have time for games."

"What, you and Silverado Man busy getting all buddy-buddy?"

Jack's eyes slid over to Webber. Silverado Man was currently sitting in a chair, eyes closed, his hands held protectively over his abdomen. After waking, he'd changed out of the blood-stained shirt. He now wore a black pullover.

"Been sticking your nose in where it doesn't belong, huh?"

"Who is he, Dad? Why's he so interested in Kevin?"

Oh, great. Like I need another complication. "I'm still not hearing what you want."

"Answer the question. What's so special about Kevin?"

Jack thought for a moment. Maybe a little truth could work to his advantage about now. "All right, I'll tell you. Your brother's been kidnapped. That colored guy in town, Owens? He took him. Silverado Man and I are trying to get him back."

"Oh, man, this is great." J.J. was chuckling. "You don't have a freaking clue, do you?"

"About what?"

"About Kevin." J.J. paused before going on. "No one took him. I have him."

Jack shot to his feet. "You what?"

Webber looked up at him, curious.

"Yeah," J.J. said. "He's sitting right next to me."

"Who's there with you?"

"Nobody. Just me and Kevin. Why?"

Jack was speechless. Morris had been playing him, lying to him about Kevin. She and Owens both. And he'd fallen for it. He'd let a couple of Be Nothings stick it to him. Anger burned through him. How could he have been so goddamned *stupid*?

"Okay," Jack said, pulling himself together. "Give me a second here. So you have Kevin." Across from Jack, Webber sat up straight in his chair, his expression eager, almost hungry. "Good. At least he's safe. Now, tell me where you are. Even with the snow, it shouldn't take me long to get there."

"There's something different about Kevin. I mean, more than just his autism."

Jack frowned. That hadn't sounded like a question; it was more like a statement of fact. "What are you talking about? Did something happen? Is Kevin okay?"

"So you really don't know."

"Know what? For Christ's sake, spit it out."

"No," said J.J.. "I think I'll keep this one to myself. It's nice to have the upper hand for a change. But I do want to talk to you. Face-to-face."

"Why is it always a game with you?" snapped Jack. "Just tell me where you are and—"

"Don't talk to me about games," J.J. yelled back. "You're the one playing the games. 'Kevin's the only one who matters. Fuck the rest of them'. What kind of game is *that*?"

Jack bit the inside of his cheek. "I see. And just how long were you listening in on that conversation?"

"Long enough."

Jack closed his eyes. What a pain in the ass this kid was turning out to be. God, he hated making nice, but if he was going to get Kevin back.... "Look, I'm sorry about that. Not one of my better moments. Forget I said it." He opened his eyes. "I do love you. You're my son, after all."

With tears in his voice, J.J. asked, "Was that so hard to say?"

"Let me come get you. Then we can talk."

"I don't think so. I'll meet you back at the house—"

"No," Jack interjected. "I don't want to draw any attention to our home." At least, no more than there already was.

"Okay, where?"

Jack thought for a moment. "My office?"

"Sorry, no one gets home field advantage. Pick a neutral spot."

"There are no neutral spots in town. I don't know why—" Jack stopped. Old age was getting to him. The answer was simple. "How about somewhere away from town? There's a place about ten miles east of here, down 28 on the north side. The Hiawatha Trails Motel. I'll meet you in the parking lot. And don't forget your brother."

"Fine, give me an hour or two."

"Why so long?"

"Because I said so," his son replied, then hung up before Jack could get another word in.

From his chair, Webber said, "So your boys were together the whole time."

"Yeah," said Jack. "Looks like we'll get Kevin, and we've eliminated Izzy Morris." He smiled at Webber. "Not bad."

Webber twirled a finger in the air. "Whoop-de-fucking-doo."

After hanging up on his father, J.J. checked through his cell's directory, then hit the call button. When Katie's best friend, Brittany Parsons, answered, he said, "Hey, it's me. I'm sorry to call so early, but I need a favor and I can't find Katie. Can you come over to her house and watch my brother for me? It's kind of an emergency. I shouldn't be more than a few hours. You can? Thanks. I appreciate it. See you in a few."

He tucked his cell phone into his back pocket and turned to Kevin.

His brother sat there, seemingly oblivious to everything around him.

"Man," J.J. said. "I hope you're worth it."

CHAPTER
22

Izzy woke to the sound of her office door opening. She blinked, and then noticed Gene perched in a chair across from her, fast asleep.

"Gene," she whispered, and his eyes snapped open.

The door finished swinging open, and Katie stepped into the office. Her pale face was wet with tears, and her clothes were rumpled. She held a wad of tissues in her fist.

"Katie," Izzy said, yawning. "What time—?" She glanced at her desk clock. "Oh, honey. You didn't have to stay in there all night by yourself."

"It's okay," replied Katie. "It was…different."

Gene sat up, wincing from the abrupt movement. "We were waiting for you. Figured you would come get us after, well, you know…." He rubbed at his eyes. "Figured we'd continue the search for Jack, but we ended up falling asleep sometime after midnight."

"I have to call the coroner again," said Izzy, dropping her head in her hands. It would be another delay. More time spent not looking for her daughter.

"You might want to hold off on that," Katie said. "There's something you want to see first."

Izzy and Gene exchanged puzzled glances.

"Just follow me," Katie added mysteriously and left the room, leaving the other two with no choice but to follow.

In the resource room, they found Bart Owens's body lying amid pieces of the shattered door, the broken remains of the filing cabinet, and the long conference table, which now leaned against the wall like an upended coffin. Under the glow of fluorescent light, Katie sat down cross-legged beside his body.

"They're here," she said.

Izzy was about to ask Katie who she was talking to when Owens spoke.

"Thank you," he said weakly. Then he added, "Could you two come over here? I don't want to hurt my neck twisting it."

Gene's jaw dropped open. "No fucking way."

Izzy ran over to the old man. No one could've survived the wounds he'd sustained. The blood loss alone was fatal. Yet his eyes shone with a clarity that told her he might still live.

"Katie," Izzy said harshly. "You should've said something. Gene, we're going to need that ambulance."

Owens lifted a hand in the air, stopping her. "I'll be all right. That woman. Aggie? How is she?"

Izzy paused for a moment, wondering if she should get an ambulance anyway. Owens looked strong, remarkably strong. But still, he would need—

"The woman," the old man repeated. "Is she all right?"

"Her husband came for her," Izzy replied, and thought of Aggie's near catatonic state. "He took her to the hospital."

Owens pulled air in through his nose, his wide nostrils flaring. "What have you told your officers?"

"Not a whole lot yet," said Izzy. "We were lucky this happened during the night shift. But keeping 'the current event' under wraps is going to get harder. I need to come up with a good explanation for all this."

"Hopefully we'll be done soon and I'll be gone." Owens took another deep breath. "Gene, do you need an engraved invitation?"

"Right. Sorry." Gene crossed the room. Careful not to aggravate his injured back, he eased himself down across from Katie. He looked at Owens with a mixture of awe and relief. "You should be dead, you know."

Owens managed a smile. "Good to see you, too."

"Don't turn this into a joke," Izzy snapped. "It's not funny. We were *attacked*." She pointed to Owens. "And Gene's right. You should be dead. Those wounds—" She gripped the blanket covering the man and yanked it down around his waist. When she lifted the shreds of his Predators sweatshirt, she received another shock.

Owens's wounds, the deep lacerations that had torn his flesh apart, were knitted shut. All that remained of his injuries were pink-brown lines of healing skin and blotches of dried blood.

"Oh, man," breathed Gene. "You sure the FBI doesn't have an X-Files division."

Dropping the blood-soaked cloth, Izzy's voice shook as she said, "You're healed. That's impossible. No one can do that. "

Katie brushed a strand of hair from her face. "I don't know how he did it. It just—happened."

Owens asked, "Could someone find me some food and water, please?

The more the better. This kind of thing always wears me out."

Katie got up and left the room. Gene's eyes were looking a little wild as he stared at Owens.

Izzy's mind was spinning with questions. "Who—no, *what* are you?"

"I'm a living, breathing person. Same as you."

"Hardly. I can't heal myself the way you did."

A hint of bitterness crept into Owens's voice. "It's not something you'd want."

That gave Izzy pause. "Most people would consider it a miracle."

"Most people haven't had to be me," Owens replied.

Katie returned with an arm full of snacks and several bottles of water. She set them down next to Owens. He thanked her, opened one of the bottles, and drank until it was empty. He ripped open a bag of cookies. Fig Newtons began disappearing into his mouth, one after another.

Between bites, Owens said, "I don't know what to tell you about the healing. I've been able to do it for as long as I can remember."

"You mean you were born with it?" Izzy asked.

"Well, I can't remember quite *that* far back," Owens said. "But yes, that would be a fair assessment."

"Then why hasn't anyone ever heard of you? I mean, you're a medical miracle. Entire text books would have been written about you."

"Yeah," added Gene, grinning. "You should've at least made the cover of the *Enquirer*."

"I'd rather avoid that kind of exposure," said Owens, opening another water and taking a long drink.

Izzy wanted to pin him down, try to force a better answer from him, but another thought had occurred to her. One that left her feeling cold. "This healing, does it only work when you're hurt?"

Owens's hand stopped midway to his mouth. Izzy thought she saw a hint of caution in his blue eyes. "What do you mean?"

"I mean," Izzy said, "does it cure colds? Stop heart disease? Beat cancer? Prevent *aging*?"

There was a moment when no one moved. Then, sighing, Owens plopped the Fig Newton into his mouth. He chewed slowly, deliberately, like a man in need of time. After washing the cookie down with more water, he said, "I see where you're going with this. The man heals fast. Amazingly fast. So you have to run it to extremes. Now you think I don't get sick. Or age." He shook his head. "That's why I don't like involving others in my work. Too much rampant speculation."

"Not amazingly fast," Izzy countered. "*Impossibly* fast. And it's more than speculation. You *told* me you were older than you looked. I wouldn't be surprised if it had something to do with this healing."

Owens shrugged. "Believe what you will."

"The creature," Gene cut in. All eyes turned to him. "It's more than the healing. It's the creature, too. You'd said something, like you'd recognized it."

Owens regarded them for a moment, his expression shifting from cautious to concerned—maybe even a little irritated—all within the span of a heartbeat. Izzy suddenly realized they could be playing a dangerous game. Bart Owens was a man with no known past. No means of identification. A man who can heal himself and apparently has run-ins with monsters. If he were provoked enough, what else might he be capable of?

"You don't understand," Owens said. His words were clipped. "I'm trying to keep you alive. It's been a priority of mine since I arrived. These questions...all you're doing is running *toward* the danger. Why can't we focus on finding the missing kids? After that, I'll be on my way. And you three can go on living long and happy lives."

Izzy picked up a piece of broken door and brandished it like a contradiction. "How much closer to the danger can we get? We're not like you. If that thing had gotten to us, we'd be dead now."

"Yes, I know. But—"

Katie piped in. "A thick metal door didn't stop that thing. Mrs. Morris's gun didn't stop it either. But you did. Without a weapon or anything, you beat it. You *hurt* it. We all heard it screaming. And if it hadn't managed to get away, I think you might have killed it—killed it by doing nothing more than grabbing it." She left the obvious question unspoken, hanging in the air like a pall.

Owens lowered his eyes. Working his way into a sitting position, he opened his third water bottle and took a drink. He started fingering the folds of the blanket.

"I see you're not going to let this go." He kept his eyes downcast. "After what you've been through, I suppose I wouldn't, either. But what you're asking of me...." He finally raised his head. Izzy thought the color of his eyes had darkened; they now resembled the hard blue of a glacier. The bold lines of his face seemed to accentuate the starkness of his gaze.

"There are struggles going on around us," Owens continued. "Wars. Acts of terrorism. You see them every day on the news. But there's another battle being fought. One you don't see." He tore the top off a bag of chips and dug in. "I'm on one side of that fight. Darryl Webber's on the other."

"So we're back to the CIA theory?" said Izzy. "Black ops stuff. Spy versus spy."

Owens shook his head. "No, no governments. Nothing like that. But it's a war nonetheless. One I've been fighting for a long time."

Izzy heard an odd inflection in Owens's voice. Gene must have caught it too, because he asked, "How long?"

"Long enough that I've met some interesting people in my day." Owens hesitated, using the opportunity to stuff more chips into his mouth. When he was done chewing, he said, "The Beatles were nice, the one time I'd met them. What a jam session that was. George played guitar a lot better than people gave him credit for." Another handful of chips, this time followed by a mouthful of water. "The Second World War was rough. I was a tank commander back then."

Katie frowned. "But that was—what?—seventy years ago? You'd have to be over ninety by now."

Owens nodded. "If the Second World War was rough, the first one was ten times worse. That time I was a medic. When you're out there in the trenches, patching up people in the mud and the blood, there's no separation from the violence. No emotional distance, like the kind you get from sitting in a tank. The destruction's right here." He held his hand up, inches from his face. "Right in front of you." He lowered his hand. "I've lost a lot of friends over the years."

Nobody spoke for a moment, and then Gene started singing, "Da da da dum, da da da dum. Daaa—da da da dum!"

"You may not be that far off," she said, recognizing the theme from the *Twilight Zone*. "If he's not making this up, he's over a hundred years old." She rubbed at her temples. "I don't know what to think anymore."

Then Katie said, "I think it's amazing."

The words drew Izzy's attention. "What do you mean?"

"Look at him," Katie said, her voice full of wonder. "Look at what he's done. He has to be part of something big—bigger than us. I guess it kind of gives me hope." She looked away, as if she were embarrassed by her words. "Hope that there's something more to this world than misery."

Owens's gaze lingered on Katie for a moment. He opened his mouth, and Izzy thought he was going to say something to the girl. But he must have thought better of it. With a brief shake of his head, he returned his attention to Izzy.

"Let's not forget why we're here. We need to find Kevin. If Webber gets to the boy first, they'll disappear. We'll never see Kevin, or your daughter, again."

Izzy's stomach cramped at the mention of Natalie. How many hours had passed since she'd seen her daughter's photos? She grated at the delay, but there was still more she needed to understand before she could decide how to save her daughter.

"You say Webber's behind this," Izzy said. "That he's on the other side of this war you're fighting. Is he like you, then? Did he have something to do with the creature that attacked us?"

Owens nodded. "He sent it. He *must* have. Remember what I said about his temper? Well, you just saw how bad it can be." He began twisting the water bottle in his hands. "And, no. He's not 'like me.' But he's still a very dangerous man. I wouldn't underestimate him."

"Didn't you say you gave him the scar on his jaw?" asked Gene.

"Twice he's set traps for me," Owens said. "Twice he's failed. That scar was from our last meeting."

"And the creature?" Gene continued.

Owens blew air out his pursed lips. "Yes, the creature. Let's just say that Webber has access to certain—oh, call them allies—that he uses to fight for him. What attacked us was one of them. I'd never seen that particular one before."

"Come on," Gene persisted. "You can do better than that."

"Fine. You'll never see one on Animal Planet."

"Yeah, we got that already." Gene leaned forward. "Where did it come from?"

Owens ran a hand over the top of his head. The conflict within him could be seen in the set of his jaw, the tightness around his eyes. He went for another drink, but set the water bottle down before it reached his mouth. When he finally spoke, his voice was apologetic but firm. "Sorry, Gene. We're running out of time. And explaining that would take too long."

"But—"

"You want to risk those two kids' lives just to satisfy your curiosity? I've told you enough already. More than I should have." Owens slowly got to his feet. "We need to get moving."

"He's right on that point," Izzy said. "We've wasted too much time already. But there's one more thing I'm going to insist on knowing." She gave Owens a level look. "I want to know how you stopped that creature. I didn't see you doing any kind of damage, but still you drove it away. So, if I'm going to rely on you in a fight, I need to know what it is you can do."

"I don't think that's a good idea," Owens said, shaking his head. "If explaining the creature would take a while, explaining that would take a lot longer."

"Then you'd better start," Izzy said firmly.

"Seriously, I'd rather not—"

"And I'd rather not have had my daughter taken from me, or be attacked by a monster, or argue with a man older than my great-grandfather." With the shock of Owens's revelations wearing off, his evasiveness was getting to her—again. "I've been patient with you, but if Natalie's still alive, then Webber isn't going to let me simply walk in and take her. You have a way to help me. I need to know what that is."

"Don't go there," Owens said softly. "Please."

"Enough with the mystery man bullshit." Izzy voice cut through the air. "This could mean my daughter's life. Now *tell me!*"

Owens actually flinched. At his sides, his hands worked, opening and closing like a man groping for a reason to stay in control. Then his expression grew hard, even defiant.

"No," he said flatly.

'What?" Izzy wasn't sure she'd heard him right.

"No," Owens repeated. "I'll keep whatever secrets I want. I don't answer to you."

"But Natalie?" Her surprise at Owens's attitude gave way to a burgeoning anger. "She could die if—"

"Then she does." Owens tone was cold.

Katie gasped. Gene, his face flushed with anger, said, "What the hell do you think you're doing?"

Owens ignored them. His focus was on Izzy. "You want to ask questions? Fine, keep at it. But if your daughter dies, it will be your fault."

Gene tried to get between Izzy and the old man. "Stop it!"

Owens shifted away from Gene and continued his attack. "Face it, Izzy. If Natalie dies, it will be because of you." He paused. "You will have failed as a mother."

The old man's words had pushed her past her limits. She balled up her fist and punched him.

When she hit the man, her hand exploded in pain—a pain that was so acute she thought she'd broken every bone in it. She cried out and yanked her hand back, holding it close to her chest. Looking down, she flexed her fingers, expecting shards of broken bone to dig into her flesh. But, other than red knuckles, her hand appeared fine. In fact, the pain was fading rapidly.

Gene rounded on Owens. "What kind of shit was that?"

"She wanted to know," Owens said. "She wanted to know how I stopped that creature. I could've told her, but feeling is believing." His voice softened. "I know it hurt, Izzy. I apologize. You needed to be mad enough to hit me. I couldn't think of any other way."

Izzy gaped at her hand. The pain—it had been agony. "You *did* that?"

Gene and Katie said in unison, "Did what?"

"Pain," Izzy muttered. She still couldn't believe how it had hurt. "Like nothing I'd ever felt before. I thought I'd shattered my hand. Then it just stopped."

Gene glowered at Owens, obviously still upset. "I don't get it."

"Pain," Owens said plaintively. "When I grabbed the creature, it started to feel pain. As I kept hold of it, the pain intensified, building every second. If I'd held on long enough, it would likely have died."

Izzy peered up at Owens. "Do you—do you also feel that pain?"

Owens hesitated, then nodded.

"And as it grew?" she went on. "As you wrestled with that creature, the pain you felt—that I just felt—it multiplied?"

"Yes," Owens replied.

"My God" Izzy whispered. "This pain, is it always there?"

Owens finally looked away. "Not to such an extent, but, yes, it is."

Izzy heard Katie stifle a cry. Gene was shaking his head in horror.

"What happened to you," she asked him. "Why are you being punished like this?"

"There's more," Owens said. He still couldn't meet her gaze. "You're not putting it together."

"Then explain it to me."

Owens struggled for a moment. He swallowed hard. "Two days ago. We were in the forest, looking for signs of your daughter. You'd just found the guitar pick. Then—"

"Stanley," Gene said, interrupting Owens. "He attacked you. You two were wrestling with that gun. Then he collapsed."

"There was nothing I could do," Owens said. "The pain might have triggered his heart attack."

Realization hit Izzy like another punch to the gut. "You mean...."

Owens nodded. "If he dies, it will be my fault."

CHAPTER
23

J.J. Sallinen pulled into the parking lot of the Hiawatha Trails Motel, his windshield wipers slapping away big, fluffy snowflakes. He nosed his Dodge Charger into an empty parking spot near the office. His dad's Benz wasn't there, but he spotted the white Silverado parked near the end of the lot. An inch or two of snow covered it. No one was standing around waiting for him, so he decided to sit for a moment and let warm air from the car's heater wash over him. He cranked up the radio. The Stone Temple Pilots sang about digging a hole to China.

Before leaving Kevin in her care, he'd given Brittany Parsons some fast talk and slick half-truths about what had happened these last twenty-four hours. He'd told her if anyone were to call and ask, she should play dumb. No one, and that included his father, was to know that she had Kevin. He'd thanked her again and said he hoped to be back before evening. Bewildered, she'd simply nodded her head and went to sit with Kevin.

After shrugging into his varsity jacket, J.J. had stepped over to the couch. Kevin's vacant expression hadn't changed. J.J. had reached out and mussed up Kevin's hair. His brother shot him a quick smile. On an impulse, J.J. leaned down and kissed the top of his brother's head. This change in Kevin had brought to light an understanding about himself that he'd been conveniently ignoring: so long as Kevin had been blissfully unaware, it had been easy for J.J. to blame his brother for everything. But now he had seen something different. There was a scared little boy buried deep inside Kevin, a scared little boy who had claimed to know things, who had begged for help. Kevin had looked lost, confused, and desperately lonely.

Maybe he and his brother were more alike than he'd ever imagined.

J.J. saw movement outside the car. Turning, he saw his father's scowling face filling the window, snow dusting his head and shoulders, making it look like he had the world's worst case of dandruff. J.J. started to laugh—then stopped. He looked closer. There was an angry red line running down his dad's left cheek, like he'd been cut.

J.J. killed the ignition. He wasn't fully out of the car before his dad was in his face.

"Where's your brother?"

"I told you. This one's just between you and me." He pointed to the cut. "What happened to you?"

"Never mind that," his dad answered. "You were supposed to bring Kevin so we could keep him safe."

"That may have been *your* plan," said J.J.. "But it wasn't mine. Anyway, Kevin's fine. No one will get to him where he is."

His dad's scowl deepened. "I don't suppose you're ready to share that little bit of information?"

"If I told everyone who asked, he wouldn't stay safe, would he?"

"That's not funny. He's in danger."

"Yeah, I'm beginning to realize that. Only, I'm not too sure who's the bigger threat." A shiver ran through J.J.. "It's freezing out here. Can't we take this inside?"

"Fine. Follow me. Third room from the end. Number eight." His dad turned toward the motel.

He put a hand on his dad's arm. "Just you and me, remember." He nodded at the Silverado. "Your friend's not invited."

His dad shook his arm free. "He's not my friend. And don't forget, you wanted to be part of this. Well, welcome to my world." He strode off toward the room.

J.J. didn't like the idea of two against one, but what else could he do? Go back and think of a Plan B? If Kevin was in so much danger, maybe Chief Morris *would* be a better—

"Jack Junior," his dad shouted from ahead. "Move it, boy!"

"Coming," J.J. answered, thoughts of Chief Morris pushed from his mind as he hurried after his father.

The snow thinned as he approached the motel. J.J. could make out a figure sitting in a chair outside his dad's room. It resolved into Jimmy's dad, his jacket bundled around him. His eyes were half-closed, a vague frown on his ruddy face.

"Hey, Mr. C.," J.J. said when they'd reached the door. "How you holding up?"

Mr. Cain turned his wet gaze up to J.J.. There was a peculiar hollowness in his expression that J.J. found unsettling; it was like grief had eaten the man up from the inside until there was nothing left but some skin and a couple of marbles for eyes. Jimmy's dad drew a trembling hand across his mouth.

"He did it," Mr. Cain said, his voice weak. "I know it. I *feel* it. What I did, I did for Jimmy. I had to. I'm his dad. You understand that, don't you?"

"Understand what?" said J.J., puzzled by the man's words.

His dad opened the room's door and said, "Never mind him. He's just hung-over. Come on, let's get inside."

Before J.J. could move away, Mr. Cain reached out and gripped his hand. "Please. Tell me you understand. I need to know it's all right."

"It...it's okay. I understand." J.J. didn't know what else to say.

Mr. Cain released J.J.'s hand and took a swig of his beer. "Remember to stay out of the woods, boy."

"What does that—?"

"Inside," his dad snapped from the doorway. "Now."

J.J. left Mr. Cain alone with his beer and his grief. When he stepped through the doorway, he was greeted by a blast of hot air; it must have been near eighty in the room. He could hear the steady dripping of a leaky faucet coming from the bathroom on his left. Ahead of him, darkness grew at the edges of a shabby bedroom— someone had drawn shades, keeping the daylight out, and a solitary lamp threw off light so weak it died before reaching the yellowed walls. Two small end tables flanked twin beds covered with rumpled sheets. A long dresser, its wood veneer chipped in several places, squatted along one wall. A rifle rested ominously against it. Across the room sat an oval table; its veneer matched that of the dresser and was equally abused. There were two chairs set by the table. One was empty. In the other, a man wearing a black pullover and jeans looked at him and grinned. It was the creepiest smile J.J. had ever seen.

Silverado Man's gaze shifted to Jack. "Missing a son, aren't we?"

Jack removed his coat and laid it on the bed. Then he sat down next to it. "He didn't bring Kevin. Apparently, he thinks he can protect him better than we can."

J.J. stated to protest. Surprisingly, Silverado Man beat him to it.

"Ease up, Jack. The kid's only doing what he thinks is best." The man gestured to the empty chair. "Have a seat, J.J.. Take a load off, as we used to say." He held his hand out. "Darryl Webber. Pleased to finally meet you."

Walking slowly across the room, J.J. slid out of his varsity jacket and draped it over the back of the empty chair. Reluctantly, he shook Webber's hand and then sat down. "This was supposed to be between my dad and me, you know. Just the two of us—*alone.*"

Webber kept that creepy smile pointed at him. "Your dad tells me you're a football player. Pretty talented one, too. What position?"

"Corner," said J.J. tersely, wondering what this had to do with anything. "Sometimes free safety."

"Ahh, excellent. So you're used to reading your opponent, taking in the big picture pretty quickly?"

"Yeah, I guess. Look, do you think my dad and me could have a few minutes—?"

"Because I want to make sure you can see the big picture of what's happening now." Webber was still grinning, but now there was no humor in his voice. "Your brother's life may depend on it."

"That's what doesn't make any sense," J.J. said. "He's only a kid. What kind of threat could he be? Why would someone want to hurt him?"

Webber sat back in his chair. J.J. caught a slight wince run across the man's face. "Why did 9/11 happen? Or the British subway bombing? Or the killings in Jakarta? Those people died for what? They weren't a threat, but they're still dead. You never know for sure what people are thinking, or how they're going to distort the truth to fit their beliefs. The fact is, Bart Owens thinks your brother's a threat. Should we ignore that danger? Are you willing to risk your brother's life on it?"

J.J. nudged his chin at the Remington on the dresser. "Do you really think *that's* necessary?"

From his seat on the bed, his dad said, "What are we supposed to protect Kevin with, a butter knife and a can of Nigger-B-Gone?"

"Jesus, Dad. What is it with you?"

"Owens is trying to take my son," Jack replied flatly. "That puts him several notches below 'African-American'."

"The rifle is needed," said Webber, "because the other side has guns. Bart Owens has conned your Chief of Police into helping him.

That gives him a lot of leverage. She has the power of the law behind her." He leaned forward, his expression intense. "I'll give you an example: Yesterday, your dad and I went to your house to get Kevin. With Owens out of jail, we needed to move immediately. When we got there, we saw people moving around inside. So we called the cops. Figured that was the right thing to do. We were wrong. When we got inside, we found Owens and Morris. Her officers didn't react, of course. She's one of the 'good guys,' right?" Webber licked his lips. "Chief Morris opened fire on her own men. Blew one away and seriously messed up the other."

Stunned, J.J. turned to his dad. Jack nodded. "She killed Carlton Manick. Shot him right through the throat. That Detective? Billick? Took one in the shoulder. He was lying on the floor when we ran out of there."

"So, people are dead or dying," Webber continued. "And guess what? We're not done yet. Owens won't stop until he has your brother, and if Chief Morris is willing to fire on her own men, do you think she'd hesitate *one second* before unloading on us?" The man shrugged. "I don't know about you, but personally, I feel better having some firepower of our own."

Confused—and a little frightened—by what the two men were saying, J.J. hesitated. The steady *drip drip drip* of the leaky bathroom faucet seemed to keep time with his thinking.

"Mrs. Morris shooting her own cops," J.J. wondered aloud. He thought back to the times he'd met Nat's mom. Cold-blooded killer wasn't a phrase he'd use to describe her. "No, that's too...out there. I can't see her doing something like that."

His dad rolled his eyes and muttered, "I can't believe I've raised an idiot."

"Quit with the names," Webber snapped at Jack, and J.J. marveled when his dad closed his mouth. Then to J.J., Webber said, "Fair enough. Call the hospital. See if that detective's there. Use your cell."

J.J. had been thinking the same thing. Their story seemed so outrageous it could easily be a bluff. After a quick wireless search for the hospital's number, J.J. called. It only took a few seconds to confirm that the detective was still in the ER.

"Satisfied?" Webber asked, one eyebrow arched in a question.

"I—this all seems so crazy," replied J.J. as he struggled to make sense of this new information. "Only three days ago, everything was fine."

"Things changed," nodded Webber. "And not for the better. Br'er Rabbit's put a tar baby in the middle of your town, son. And the more anyone struggles with it, the more he's stuck to it. It's snared your Police Chief, that bartender fellow, Vincent—and your girlfriend."

"Katie? She's part of this?"

Webber nodded again. "Afraid so. That's why we want to move fast. If we can get Kevin out of here, then Owens will follow. Your girlfriend and the others will have lost their usefulness. He'll let them go, unharmed, and move on." He pulled a pack of cigarettes from his pocket, shook one out, and lit it. "Your brother's the key," he said, blowing smoke out the corner of his mouth. "We need him so we can end this."

"We're the ones who can protect Kevin," his dad said. "Us, not just you. So you need to get with the program and tell us where your brother is." He smiled. "You wanted to be part of this. Here's your chance."

J.J. rubbed his hands on his thighs. He was so confused. He'd come here wanting to prove to his dad that he meant something, that he mattered. He had Kevin. He knew things. About Kevin. About Natalie.

Wait a minute.

J.J. put his hands up. Focused his attention on his dad. "You're the one with photos of Natalie. They're in your desk, like—like some kind of treasure or something. I mean, that's *sick*. Yet you still want me to believe Kevin will be safer with you." He turned to Webber. "How stupid do you think I am?"

"Oh, for *fuck's* sake—" his dad began, but Webber quieted him with a look.

"I'm trying to be patient here," Webber said softly. "I know you want to protect your brother. I get that. I'm cool with it—I have a sister, myself. But the fact is Owens...." Webber's voice trailed off, his eyes growing unfocused, like he was no longer paying attention. After a few seconds, he blinked. His face grew hard. "I'll be right back. Don't leave. We're not through yet." He stood, grabbed a jacket and started across the room.

Jack said, "What's wrong?"

Webber left without answering.

J.J. shook his head. Then to his dad, he said, "What're you doing hanging with that guy? Can't you see there's something wrong with him? Jesus, the man's a walking ad for *America's Most Wanted.*"

"He's trying to do a job—an important one."

"Really? Was killing Jimmy and Natalie part of his 'important job'? And what about Katie? I guess killing her mom was part of the job, too?"

"I do what I have to. I don't expect you to understand. You're in way over your head as it is."

J.J. laughed bitterly. "Then *you* tell me where Kevin is. *You* tell me what's so special about him. Hell, why don't you tell me anything important? Because as far as I can see, Webber's the one in charge." He sighed. "You know what I think? I think you don't know shit. You're the one who's in over your head."

"Don't you dare talk to me like that, you—"

The door burst open. Webber stalked into the room, slamming the door shut behind him. He stood there a moment, shoulders hunched, fists clenched, melting snow dripping from his long, lank hair and the end of his sharp nose. The dim light cast angry shadows across his face, giving him a ghoulish appearance. Hard eyes searched the room. They briefly regarded Jack before sliding over to J.J.. Webber's brows slowly drew together, knotting his forehead. A sneer creased his face as he glared at J.J.. Whatever had happened, the man was seriously pissed. He crossed the room. When he was close enough, he grabbed two fists full of J.J.'s shirt and yanked the boy to his feet.

Shoving J.J. until his back slammed into a wall, Webber said, "I'm done fucking around, kid. This is your last chance. Where's that little shit brother of yours?"

"What the—!" yelled J.J. "Get your goddamn hands off me!"

Jack shot to his feet. "Hey, what're you doing?"

Webber slammed J.J. against the wall again. "Where's Kevin? Where is he? *Where the fuck is he?*"

"Figure it out yourself, asshole," J.J. said and threw a solid roundhouse punch at Webber's head. The man lifted a shoulder to block part of the blow. Still, J.J. felt some satisfaction when Webber's head snapped back. J.J. followed up with a jab to Webber's gut. The man grunted, letting go of J.J. and clutching at his stomach. J.J. took the opportunity to send a hard uppercut at Webber's head. Webber dodged at the last moment, but J.J.'s fist clipped Webber's ear and sent the man staggering back.

Then his dad was there, stepping in between them. "Stop it! That's enough." Then to Webber: "What the hell is going on?"

Hunched over, hands on his knees, Webber said, "Morris is still alive, you jackass! The Fek failed!" His words came out faster. "And it's been hurt. Owens. It had to be him. He's the only one who could've done it." Webber slowly stood, his face filled with rage. "And frankly, I'm tired of playing games with you people. I need to get this job done and get out of this shithole you call a town."

Jack gaped at Webber. "You've got a name for that *thing*?"

"Park your ass on that bed," Webber said coldly. "Or I'll send you back to your own private little Hell. Only this time, you'll stay forever."

J.J. watched as the blood drained from his father's face. His dad looked at him. Their eyes met, held for several seconds. Then his dad looked away and walked over to the bed. He sat down, head bent, eyes closed.

His dad was leaving him alone to deal with this madman.

Webber rubbed his sore jaw. "You got lucky just now. Trust me, it won't happen again. Tell me what I want to know and you might still get out of this alive."

J.J. made a rumbling sound deep in his throat and spat in Webber's face. He didn't want this man anywhere near Kevin. No way. "Piss off, motherfucker."

With a cry of fury, Webber charged, his clenched fist swinging wildly toward J.J.'s head. J.J. blocked the blow with his forearm. But Webber surprised him with a quick jab to the stomach, followed by a blistering right to J.J.'s chin. Blinking from the pain, J.J. brought his arms up to protect himself. Webber used the opening to pound J.J.'s back into the wall and knee him in the groin. J.J. collapsed to the floor. Webber knelt down, grabbed J.J.'s shoulders, and hammered his forehead into the boy's nose. Bone and cartilage shattered, a burst of phosphorescent pain exploding brightly behind his eyes. Blood ran freely down his chin and neck.

J.J. curled up, holding his broken nose.

Webber's face appeared close to J.J.'s again. His words were frighteningly quiet. "Where's your brother?

Blinking up at Webber, J.J. spat, "Kiss my ass!"

Webber reached out and grabbed one of J.J.'s wrists, yanking it from his bloody face. He forced J.J.'s hand open, gripping his index finger. "It'll be hard to intercept passes with broken fingers. Now, talk to me. Where'd you hide him?"

J.J. glared at the man. "Fuck off."

Calmly, almost clinically, Webber bent J.J.'s finger back until there was a loud pop and it broke at the knuckle. J.J. cried out, but when Webber gave the digit a vicious twist, ripping tendons and ligaments, his cry turned into a shriek. Black spots swam across his vision.

"I can do this nine more times," Webber said calmly as he reached for J.J.'s middle finger. "Then I'll have to start getting creative. You don't want to go there. Now—where's Kevin?"

J.J. tried to pull his hand away, but the pain had weakened him. Through his tears, he begged, "God, no, stop! Dad! Help me! Make him stop!"

Jack sat on the bed, his face expressionless. "I warned you. In over your head. Maybe next time you'll listen to me." He made no move to get up.

Webber slowly began extending the digit backward. "And this little piggy couldn't catch a football to save his fucking life."

J.J. could feel the skin tightening on his hand, the pressure mounting in his knuckle as his finger was bent backward. Already, the pain in his hand was hot, searing, as if he'd stuck it in a pile of hot coals. So much pain. It tore through him. No more. He couldn't take any more. He thought briefly of Kevin, of the sweet smile he'd given J.J. before he left, only hours ago.

I tried, Kevin. I'm sorry, but I tried. Please, forgive me.

Before another finger broke, J.J. cried out, "No! No! Stop! I'll tell you! I'll tell you!" Sobbing, he said, "Katie's. He's at Katie's house."

"You told your dad he can *do* stuff. What can he do?"

"I'm not sure. He—he talked normal, like his autism was gone. Said something about a man. And a woman. And a thing. I don't know what it means."

Webber's eyes widened with surprise, and J.J. felt the man ease up on his finger.

Fresh tears ran from his eyes. "Please stop. Don't hurt me anymore."

A sneer erased Webber's shocked expression. "See," he said, "you *can* be cooperative." Then he jerked J.J.'s finger back, the knuckle cracking apart, until the digit rested flat against the back of J.J.'s hand. After J.J.'s screaming, he said, "That's for making me work at it."

J.J. sent out a silent plea to his brother. *Run, Kevin! Hide!*
Then, like a cheap horror movie, the world faded to black.

CHAPTER
24

The white-and-brown Luce County Sheriff's car rolled into the Hiawatha Trails Motel parking lot, newly fallen snow crunching under its black tires. Inside, Patrolman Steve Campbell radioed his arrival and status as unavailable, responding to a call. He checked his gear, made sure his notepad and pen were in his shirt pocket, and got out of the cruiser. The snow was slippery. He was careful not to fall as he made his way to the manager's office. Missing the start of deer season with an injured back and doped up on painkillers wasn't his idea of fun.

Campbell pushed open the office door. A little brass bell attached to it jingled. Like most hole-in-the-wall dives, this motel's lobby was sheathed in pine boards which had been stained dark with age rather than varnish. Frayed red-and-white-checked drapes covered the window. There was no television turned to ESPN, no radio playing the music, not even a wire rack full of brochures highlighting the usual tourist traps.

He heard movement from the room behind the counter.

"Be right with you," a voice called out.

"It's just me, Deke," answered Campbell.

Deke Frenz emerged from the office. The motel's owner was in his mid-fifties. A fringe of gray hair ran in a semi-circle below the green John Deere cap perched on top of his head. His eyes were sunken. The laconic set of his jaw gave the impression that the man couldn't be surprised by anything short of the Apocalypse. He wore a flannel shirt that matched the drapes and a pair of old jeans with one of the belt loops missing.

"Afternoon, Stevie," Deke said as he withdrew a small red tin of chewing tobacco from beneath the counter. With a smooth, practiced motion, he wedged a wad between his cheek and gums, making him look like the world's most laid-back chipmunk. "Thanks for comin' by."

"Sure," replied Campbell. "Another disturbing the peace?"

Deke nodded. "Yep. Fella in room 7 complained about the noise comin' outta the room next to him. That'd be the south one. Room 8." He flipped open the register; computers hadn't quite made it to the Hiawatha Trails Motel. "Guy signed in as Jack Snow. Paid cash." Nicotine-stained fingers scratched at the stubble on his chin. "Seen three of 'em, though. Came in drivin' a Silverado. Anyway, I'd've checked it out myself, 'cept one of 'em gave me the creeps. So I called you."

"Gave *you* the creeps?"

Deke nodded, his eyes serious.

Campbell wandered back to the door and peered out. "I see a Charger, but no Silverado."

Deke shrugged. "Must've left. Same as that fella from 7. Do me a favor, Stevie. Check it out anyway." He tossed Campbell a key to the room. "Let me know if there's any damage."

"Sure," Campbell said, catching it easily. He smiled back at Deke. "You all baited?"

"Was out to my blind last night," said Deke. "There's some big-ass buck out there. The rubs are huge. I'll find 'em. Then I'll kill 'em."

"Do you ever miss?" Deke was an ex-Army Ranger and one of the best shots in the county.

"Not since you was in diapers."

Campbell chuckled. "I'll be right back."

Deke spit tobacco juice into an old coffee can. "Just be careful, Stevie."

Heading out the door, Campbell swung right and made his way down the walkway. He passed several rooms and came to a stop in front of number 8. He knocked on the door. When there was no answer, he knocked again. Then pounded.

"Police! Open up!"

He tried the door. Locked.

While bringing the key to the lock, Campbell heard a muffled thump come from inside Room 8. Quickly, he palmed the key into his other hand, drew his gun and swiveled away from the door, his back pressed firmly against the wall to the left. With a clenched fist, the plastic key fob digging into the flesh of his palm, he hammered on the door twice.

"Luce County Sheriff's Department! Open the door!"

He listened, ears straining, sweat trickling down the back of his neck despite the cold. All he could hear was the sound of the wind blowing ropy snakes of snow across the parking lot. Something didn't feel right here. In fact, it felt completely *not right*. He briefly considered calling for backup but decided against it. If this ended up being a bunch of guys jerking each other off, it'd mean months of ribbing from his fellow cops.

"Damn."

Reaching down, he slid the key into the lock. A sharp twist and it released. He eased the door open with the flat of his hand. The hinges screeched like an alarm. Hot air washed out from the room like the devil's breath.

"Hello! Anyone in there?"

Still no answer.

Lips pressed into a thin line, he gripped his weapon with both hands and spun into the room. Arms out straight, he peered over the barrel of his gun, swiveled left, then right. Bed. Table. One chair knocked over. Dresser. Small closet to his right. Bathroom to his left. Hit the light. No one.

The room was empty.

Had the sound come from somewhere else? Maybe another room? The person who owned the Charger, perhaps? He should have asked Deke if any of the other units were occupied.

Campbell crossed the room to put the chair back on four legs—and that was when he saw a damp stain on the carpet. He crouched down, careful not to touch anything. It looked like blood. Not so much as to suggest someone was shot or stabbed, but definitely more than a nosebleed. Looked like there'd been a fight, and someone had caught the worst of it.

He heard the thud again, this time not so muffled.

He rose and spun around. The noise had come from the small closet near the door.

Stepping quietly, he approached the closet. The doors were mirrored glass. They slid sideways rather than opening like a regular door. He tried to ease one of them open, but it was caught on something or broken and wouldn't budge. He pulled on the other one, and it gave slightly. Felt like something heavy was pressed up against it. He gave it a firm yank, the door skidded open, jumping loudly on its tracks, and a body spilled out onto the carpet.

"Shit!" cried Patrolman Campbell, jumping back.

It was a kid, and he was pretty messed up. His arms and legs had been duct taped together. A wide strip of silver tape had been placed across his mouth. His nose was mashed out of shape. Dark rings circled his closed eyes. Blood had drenched his shirt and jeans. His hands had been taped together like he'd been praying. Two of the fingers looked funny, and that was when Campbell realized they'd been broken. There was a Kinsey High School varsity jacket crumpled under him.

The boy's black-rimmed eyes cracked open and gazed dully at Campbell.

He reached for the mic clipped to his shirt. "19 to base. We need an ambulance at my 20 ASAP. Injured teenager." After he'd received acknowledgment of the call, he gently removed the tape from the boy's mouth. The kid drew in a thin, shallow breath. Whoever had done this was lucky the kid hadn't suffocated trying to breathe through that shattered nose.

Or maybe whoever did this had wanted the kid to die that way.

"It's okay," he said to the boy. "I've called for an ambulance."

The kid stared back at him with uncomprehending eyes. His mouth started to open, but his eyes lost their focus and closed. He'd passed out.

A quick search found a wallet and driver's license. He reached for the mic again.

"19 to base. Someone call Kinsey PD. We've got one of their kids. A Jack Sallinen, Jr. See if they can locate his parents. Tell them we'll be transporting him to Newberry Hospital."

Patrolman Campbell shook his head at the wrecked form lying on the carpet.

"Jesus, kid. What'd you get yourself into?"

CHAPTER
25

Izzy Morris sat behind her desk, chafing at a morning full of delays.

Her office door opened, and Gene walked in, followed by Katie and Bart Owens. The old man was now dressed in a plain gray sweatshirt and jeans that Gene had retrieved from the hotel room where Owens had been staying. His bloody garments had been conveniently and quietly disposed of.

"Are you feeling better now?" Izzy asked Owens after they had sat down. Despite his remarkable healing, he had required more rest. Izzy had placed him in Sten's office, covered him with a blanket, and let him sleep.

"I'm fine," he replied. He looked curiously at her. "And you and I? Are we okay?"

Izzy slowly pulled in a breath. After Owens's revelation that he might be responsible for her husband's heart attack, she had first felt stunned, and then angry—angry at the old man for telling her, angry at Webber and Jack Sallinen for starting this nightmare, and, ultimately, angry at Stanley for attacking Owens.

Ever since Natalie had disappeared, roadblocks had been thrown up that kept her from finding her daughter; three days later and she was no closer to finding her than she was when she started. Owens's admission had simply brought her closer to the snapping point. She suspected that he had seen her anger and had used his need for rest as an excuse to give her time to calm down.

"Yeah, we're good," she told him. "I guess I can't blame you for protecting yourself. But knowing that was another complication I didn't need right now."

"How's Stanley doing?" asked Gene.

"I called the hospital. There's been no change in his condition. They don't know why he won't wake up."

"And the State cops?" he added.

Izzy grunted. "I suppose that could've gone worse." The State Police investigator had been your typical hard-nosed bastard. He asked all the questions she'd expected, and some that she hadn't. Ultimately, it had come down to the photos found in Jack's office: they tipped the scales enough in her favor that she felt she would eventually be exonerated for shooting Carleton Manick. She just needed to bring Jack in to establish the connection between him and Manick. "I've still got a job for now."

"What about the search for Webber and Mr. Sallinen?" asked Katie. "Any luck with the hotels?"

Izzy shook her head. "I've only had an hour to try and find them." She looked at Katie and Gene. "Were you able to clean up the resource room?"

"There wasn't much we could do about the door," said Gene. "Or the file cabinet. But we picked up the debris and put the table back where it belonged." He gave her that familiar lop-sided grin. "You're going need the Extreme Makeover—Monster Edition crew to fix the place up."

"Very funny," she returned with a half-hearted smile. Then her attention turned to Owens. "You know Webber better than anyone. Can you tell me anything that would help me find him?"

Owens quietly regarded her. His blue eyes had lost none of their intensity, but the flesh under them was now darker than the rest of his skin.

"By now," Owens began, "Darryl will know that his attack failed. That will likely send him over the edge for a while, but when he calms down, he's going to redouble his efforts to find Kevin. That means he'll have to leave wherever he's staying."

Izzy nodded. "I'll put out an APB on his car." An All-Points-Bulletin would have every law enforcement agency in the area looking out for Webber's Silverado.

She picked up the phone. After she'd put out the APB, she asked Owens, "What if Webber gets to Kevin first? Where do you think he'll go? Where should I be prepared to look?"

"Well, he lives in New Jersey, but I doubt he'd go back there. It'd be too obvious." He glanced at Izzy and the others. "My guess is he'd head somewhere unexpected, so finding him would become very difficult."

"But then what?" Izzy said. "If Webber gets Kevin, what's he going to do with him? Is Kevin part of this war you talked about?"

"Obviously the boy's relevant," Owens said. "Otherwise, Darryl wouldn't have been sent here, and I wouldn't be trying to stop him."

"What do you mean 'sent'?" said Izzy, puzzled by the old man's words. "Sent by whom?"

Owens hesitated. He pressed his lips into a thin, tense line. Izzy thought he was going to refuse to answer yet another question, but then he said, "He was sent by someone who's been around for a *long time.*"

"There are two of you?" Izzy said, eyebrows rising in surprise. Gene and Katie gaped openly at Owens. "But I thought you were unique."

"She and I are nothing alike," Owens replied somewhat curtly. "True, we may share a certain predilection toward longevity, but that's where the similarities end."

"Who is she?" Gene asked. "Did she come here with Webber?"

Owens shook his head. "I doubt very much she's here. She doesn't like to get her hands dirty at this level. And it's much safer if you don't know her name. It will give her less of a reason to be focused on you."

"So Webber works for this woman," said Katie. And, like earlier this morning, there was a look on Katie's face—a sort of curious fascination—that bothered Izzy. "Who works for you?"

"I have a friend who helps out," said Owens, and Izzy remembered the phone call he'd made earlier to the mysterious Phil. "But *I* won't have others fight my battles. I won't risk getting anyone killed."

Izzy absently rubbed her hand, even though the pain from striking Owens had long since vanished. It was still hard to believe what the old man was saying. He was describing something that sounded less and less like a covert government operation, and more like...what? Some kind of ongoing conflict between two people who couldn't possibly exist? Between people who had apparently been alive for well over a hundred years. And that thought led to a question.

"Can you be killed?" she asked Owens.

"Certainly," he said. "Anyone can die."

"And besides the pain thing," she continued. "Is there anything else I should know? Anything else you can do?"

"Like what? In the past, I would've been asked if I could fly, or if I had X-ray vision. I suppose now it would be, can I change shapes? Am I a vampire or werewolf or some such nonsense." He shook his head. "Don't you think that if I could 'do' anything else, I would've done it during the attack? Rather than get mauled?"

Izzy felt her face grow warm with embarrassment. "I'm sorry. It's just that this is all so hard to believe." Her mind wandered back to her original question. "You never did say what was so special about Kevin—what makes him so important to you. And this woman?"

"Yes, the question of Kevin," Owens said, looking uncomfortable. "Well, you know that he's autistic. But it's his type of autism, von Kliner's syndrome, which makes him extraordinary."

"That's what I don't understand," Izzy said. "It's autism. A disability. The poor boy can barely function. And yet, you're telling me people are worth killing to get a hold of him."

"I know it doesn't make much sense to you," Owens said, "But—"

Before he could continue, Officer Al Hamilton popped his head into her office.

"We just got a call from Luce County," he said. "They brought J.J. Sallinen into Newberry Hospital. Found him at a motel outside of town. He's been beat up pretty badly."

Everyone exchanged startled glances. They had forgotten about J.J..

"Is he going to be okay?" Izzy asked.

"That's the thing," said Al. "The guy who found him? He thinks somebody tried to kill him."

Izzy was reaching for the phone before Al's words had time to fade away.

CHAPTER
26

Sten Billick paced restlessly across the small, curtained treatment room in the Newberry Hospital ER, waiting for the nurse to bring his discharge papers.

The searing pain in his shoulder had been reduced to a throbbing ache by painkillers. The ER doc had told him he'd been lucky. The bullet had ricocheted off a bone and exited cleanly out the top of his shoulder. Twenty-three stitches to close the entry and exit wounds. That's all. If his blood pressure hadn't unexpectedly spiked, he would have been discharged last night. But now that it was back under control, he was itching to be released.

He took three steps, spun around, took three more.

Back and forth. Back and forth.

He checked his watch. Rosie was on the way to pick him up. She had spent the evening with him, but he had insisted that she go home to sleep. Luckily, the kids were grown and out of the house. There was no need to call and upset them. He was going to be fine.

Three steps, spin, three more.

Where was the damn nurse?

Anger burned in his gut, an ache no narcotic could touch. He'd been shot by Carlton Manick. Of all people, it had been *that* idiot who'd tagged him. The most incompetent police officer he'd ever known had gotten the drop on him.

Izzy should've called for backup. She should've listened to him.

Three steps, spin, three more.

He knew it could've been worse. Someone who actually knew how to use a gun could've shot him. He could be lying in a refrigerated, stainless steel drawer in the morgue.

Carlton *fucking* Manick.

His shoulder—the bad one—caught on the room's white curtain, causing the coasters from which it hung to skitter along their tracks. The steely scrape of metal against metal pulled him out of his brooding. He stopped pacing and took in a lungful of antiseptic air. His stitches twinged in irritation at being stretched.

Where the hell was his nurse?

He yanked the curtain aside and made his way down the hallway to the nurse's station. As he drew closer to the long desk, he caught a few words from another treatment room that got his attention.

"...Have a seventeen-year-old male. Multiple contusions. Looks like a fractured nose. Jesus...his fingers. Who'd...?"

The voice belonged to his nurse. The rest of his words were drowned out by a cry from the poor kid they were working on.

A curtain three rooms down was drawn aside, and his nurse strode out. The man was tall and heavy, pushing nearly three hundred pounds. He wore wrinkled blue scrubs. A stethoscope hung around his neck.

When he saw Sten, he said, "Sorry, Mr. Billick. I'll get your paperwork as soon as I can." To the nurse behind the desk, he said, "Any word from that kid's parents? We need to treat him now."

The other nurse, a brunette with short hair and a sharp face, shook her head. "Luce County put in a call to Kinsey PD asking for help. No word yet."

His nurse shot Sten a questioning look. "Aren't you Kinsey PD?"

Sten nodded. "Who's the kid?"

"Hold on." The man reached over the desk and grabbed a clipboard. He quickly scanned it and looked up at Sten. "Jack Sallinen, Jr. Know him?"

"Yeah, I know him. I doubt you'll find his dad. Not sure where his mom is."

"Great," his nurse said, tossing the clipboard on the desk. "I'll check with the doc. This kid's going to need CT Scans, consults for his nose and hand, probably surgery. But right now he needs something for pain." When he turned to walk away, Sten stopped him.

"Can I talk to him?"

The nurse shrugged. "Be my guest. There's a guy in there now waiting to take a statement." Then the nurse hurried around a corner and disappeared. Sten wondered briefly how a man so big could be so light on his feet.

Sten walked into the room. J.J. lay on a large gurney, covered to his waist with a white sheet. An IV had been inserted into the back of his left hand; clear fluids dripped into a little reservoir, then into J.J. Wires attached to his chest led to a machine that beeped with reassuring precision. A clear plastic tube was looped loosely around J.J.'s face, with two small feeders pushing oxygen into his broken nose. His black-rimmed eyes were closed.

Whoever had done a number on him had been thorough.

Standing next to J.J. was a Luce County Sheriff's patrolman.

Sten stuck out his good hand. "Detective Sten Billick. Kinsey PD."

The man shook Sten's hand. "Steve Campbell." He took in Sten's sling and bandages. "Rough day?"

Sten gestured to J.J. "Not as bad as the one he's had."

"You know him?"

"His dad's a big-shot dirtbag back in Kinsey. Any chance you could fill me in on what happened?"

Officer Campbell recounted the events at the Hiawatha Trails Motel.

"Three guys," said Sten when Campbell had finished. "One calling himself Jack Snow and another who gave the owner the creeps."

Campbell pulled out his notebook. "Any idea who they might be?"

"Believe it or not, I think Jack Snow is Jack Sallinen, this kid's dad. Christ, he may have been involved with his son's beating." Sten gave Campbell the CliffsNotes version of events that had happened at the Sallinen home yesterday.

Officer Campbell's mouth twisted as he slowly closed his notebook. "What've you got going on in that town? And what kind of father does that" —he hooked his thumb at the unconscious J.J.— "to his own son?"

Sten shrugged, wincing as a sharp stab of pain cut through his wounded shoulder. "Damn that hurts," he muttered. "Anyway, I was being charitable when I called Jack Sr., a dirtbag. Douchebag would be more like it. Still, I never thought he'd sink so low as to beat his own son. Obviously the guy's more disturbed than I'd thought."

Officer Campbell opened his mouth to say something, but J.J. groaned loudly. Sten turned and found the boy had opened his eyes slightly. J.J. blinked slowly, his mouth working, his cracked lips starting to seep blood.

Stepping over to the gurney, Sten said, "Take it easy, J.J.. Try not to move."

J.J. blinked again. His eyes opened a little wider. "Where...oh *fuck*...hurts."

"You're at the hospital," explained Sten. "The nurse went to get you something for the pain."

J.J.'s face clenched. "Know...you. Cop."

"That's right. Detective Billick." He leaned in closer to J.J.. "Who did this to you? Who hurt you?"

"No," J.J. panted. "Katie...danger."

Sten gave J.J. a puzzled frown. Katie Bethel? The last Sten had seen of the girl, she'd been with Izzy, Owens and Gene.

"I think she's okay. She's with Chief Morris and —"

J.J. started to shake his head, then cried out in pain. "House," he said through fresh tears. "Katie's." The boy started to tremble. "Going there."

"What?" said Sten. "No. No, you can't go there. Not now."

J.J.'s agitation grew. His eyes were wide and wild. "Not me. They are. *They* are." Spittle flew from his lips. "Dad. Webber. Katie's house." His eyes found Sten's. "Stop them. You have to."

Sten heard a telephone ring shrilly outside the room. He turned to Officer Campbell. "Go get that nurse." As the man left, he turned back to J.J.. "Calm down, son. Please." He put a reassuring hand on the boy's shoulder. When J.J. had stilled some, he asked, "What do I have to stop? What's going to happen at Katie's house?"

"They'll get him," wheezed J.J.. "I hid him, but they'll find him." The bruises around his eyes darkened. "Oh my God. Brittany's there."

The male nurse entered the room. He was holding a syringe filled with amber-colored fluid.

"Who will they get? Who's there?"

"Give me a second, Detective," said the nurse. He uncapped the syringe, slid the needle into J.J.'s IV port, and pushed on the plunger. The drug rushed into J.J.'s system.

"J.J., who's at Katie's?"

With his eyes starting to glaze over, J.J. whispered, "Him. My...brother. Kevin. He's...he's...there...." Then J.J. was asleep, blissfully removed from his pain.

Oh shit, thought Sten.

"Excuse me," interrupted the nurse. "I wanted to tell you. There's a phone call from your Chief of Police. At the nurse's desk. She's looking for this kid. You want to talk to her?"

Sten Billick practically ran from the room.

CHAPTER
27

The pretty girl hummed, and the colors of her voice fascinated Kevin Sallinen. Tiny, shimmering specks of red and yellow and blue and green flew from her lips. They danced around him like fireflies, swirling and spinning and capering, beckoning to him. He reached out to touch one. It slid effortlessly from his fingers. He tried again, and the bright light eluded him again. He giggled. It was like trying to catch the stars in the night sky.

"What's so funny?" she asked him.

"Star bite, star right!" Kevin crowed. Then he clapped, a percussive sound that scattered the lights about him.

The pretty girl smiled. His heart sang. She was so nice.

"That's very good," she said. "Do you want to hear the whole rhyme?"

He brought his hands together like a thunderclap, sending little fireflies sailing around the room, tiny motes caught in a whirlwind.

Her smile widened. "You do? That's wonderful." Then she lowered her voice, and the colors she gave off faded to soft pastels. "Star light, star bright," she whispered. "The first star I see tonight. I wish I may, I wish I might, have the wish I wish tonight." She leaned forward and gave him a quick, friendly kiss on the top of his head.

"'Ite," Kevin tried repeating, his eyes fixed briefly on hers.

She reached out and gently tousled his hair. "Do you have any wishes, little man?"

He did have a wish. His face screwed up in concentration. "P-p-pop t-tart."

"You want a Pop Tart?" She got up from the couch. "Let me see if I can find one."

She had made it around the couch and half-way to the kitchen when the front door opened.

A man walked through. He was tall, skinny. He was smiling too, but Kevin didn't like his smile. It wasn't like the pretty girl's.

"That's what I love about you Midwestern folk," said the man. His voice was dark, shadowy, and it buzzed like a nest of angry bees. "You never lock your damn doors."

After a look of surprise, the pretty girl bolted for the kitchen. The man shot his arm out and grabbed her by the hair, yanking her back. When he'd hauled her flailing body next to him, he whipped a snow-covered arm firmly across her throat.

"Look what I got here," the man said. His voice stung the air with a hundred bee stings. He tightened his grip on her neck, and the pretty girl stopped struggling. "I don't know who you are, but you need to understand something right now. Do as I say, behave yourself, and things will be just great between us. Maybe we could even be friends. But cause trouble and, well...." Kevin watched as the man let go of her hair and pulled a black, metal thing from his waistband. Gripping the short end, he pushed the long end hard against side of the pretty girl's head. "Get my drift, missy?"

She nodded, her body trembling, tears running down her cheeks.

"Who else is here?"

"N-n-no one. Oh God, please don't hurt us."

The man dug the metal thing harder into her head. "I don't hurt anyone unless I have to. And I don't want to *have to* hurt you." He pushed his mouth close to the girl's ear. "So stop begging. It annoys the hell out of me."

The pretty girl cried harder. "Oh God, I'm sorry. I'm sorry."

The man eased the gun away from her head. "When I take my arm off your throat, I want you to go over to the couch and sit down next to Kevin. Don't do anything to piss me off, or I'll shoot you without a second thought. Are we on the same page here?"

She nodded through her tears.

The man let her go, and she moved to sit next to Kevin. She was shaking so badly he could feel her through the cushions.

Then the man focused his attention on him.

"Hello, my boy. Good to finally meet you." Over his shoulder, the man called out, "You can come in now."

When his dad slowly walked through the door, Kevin couldn't help but smile.

* * *

When Jack walked through the door and saw his son, he couldn't help but smile. It had only been a day since he'd last seen Kevin—

yesterday morning, in fact, before he'd gone to Jimmy Cain's funeral—but with everything that had happened, it felt like weeks.

Kevin's smile filled him with a certain happiness he rarely felt. He knew his boy was damaged: his von Kliner's syndrome was evident in every stray glace, every erratic movement. Because of that, his son would never ascend to the successes Jack had achieved. And yet, he knew that Kevin was special. He'd desperately wanted to believe that, ever since Kevin had been diagnosed. Webber's arrival had been like a dream come true. It had shown that Kevin was indeed special.

Jack looked past his son at the girl sitting beside him.

"I know you," he said. "Bridgette something?"

"Brittany," the girl answered quickly. "Brittany Parsons."

Jack nodded. "Right. I like Bridgette better. You can stay right there. Kevin, come here."

The Parsons girl wrapped her arms protectively around Kevin, pulling him close. Before Jack could tell her to let him go, Webber stepped between them. "No, Jack. I'd rather he stay there. What if Owens and his friends show up? What do you think will happen then? That Morris will read you your rights and ask you to come along quietly? Hell, no. They're going to come in with guns drawn. I don't want to risk your boy getting hurt. Better safe than sorry, right?"

"Don't be ridiculous," snapped Jack. "No one knows we're here. And even if someone does find out, we'll be long gone before anyone could get here. Now I want to see—"

"That's a bad habit you have there," Webber said, cutting him off. "Underestimating people. I mean, look what happened when I sent"—he shot a quick look at Bridgette—"my friend to visit Morris. Not only did she survive, they managed to hurt it. Trust me, that's no small thing. And with Owens in the mix, it's best to assume they're right behind you."

"What is it with you and that guy? I've never seen him carrying a gun. He can't be all that dangerous. Yet you make it sound like he's some kind of martial arts master."

"He's lethal one-on-one. And very resilient. But the thing he's got going for himself is experience. The man's been around for a long, long time. He knows his shit, Jack."

"Then *you* deal with him. Right now, I want to give my son a hug. I don't care what you say, he's not in any danger." His voice grew hard as he turned toward the couch. "Let him go, Bridgette."

The girl squeezed Kevin tighter. "I'm not going to let you hurt him."

"He's my son. My own flesh and blood. I would never hurt him. Now, take your damn hands off him."

Webber put a restraining hand on Jack's arm. "I already told you. I want him to stay—"

Jack rounded on Webber, pulling his arm free. "And I told you—!"

There was a phone sitting on an end table next to the sofa. It started ringing.

The Parsons girl released Kevin and grabbed for it.

Webber charged forward, gun raised. "Don't you *dare* answer that!"

Jack motioned to Kevin, and the boy got up and hurried over to him.

Picking up the phone, the girl hit the answer button and started yelling.

* * *

Izzy Morris rushed out of the police station. The others followed close behind. When she'd called the hospital, Sten had told her all she needed to know.

Kevin was at Katie's house. Webber and Jack were on their way there, and they had one hell of a lead. It was unlikely she'd get there before they grabbed the boy.

She tossed her keys to Gene. "You drive. I need to call Katie's house. Maybe I can warn Brittany before Webber gets there."

Gene caught them smoothly in one hand, but then slipped on a patch of snow. He fought to control his balance. He would have fallen had Owens not stepped up and grabbed him under both arms.

"Thanks," Gene told the old man.

"You're limping as it is. Hurt your back any more and you won't be able to help. I don't think you'd want that."

"Couldn't you just teach me how to, you know…?" Gene twirled a finger at Owens's healed abdomen.

Owens raised an eyebrow and cocked his head. The expression was unmistakable.

"Okay, okay," Gene muttered. "I was just asking."

Everyone climbed into the department's SUV, which would handle better in the snow than Izzy's vehicle. Izzy turned to Katie in the back seat and asked for her phone number. As Gene pulled out of the parking lot, she called the house. With the phone pressed so tightly to her ear she thought it would leave a permanent mark, she waited impatiently for the connection to go through. Someone picked up before the first ring was complete. A young woman—it had to be Brittany—began yelling into the phone.

"Oh God, help! There are two men here! One's got a gun! He's—!"

Izzy heard a muffled thud. The voice cut off.

"Brittany!" Izzy shouted. She gripped the cell until her knuckles turned white. "Brittany!"

No answer.

"Brittany! Answer me!"

Someone spoke, but it wasn't Brittany. When Izzy heard that languid yet menacing voice, her heart almost stopped.

"Chief Morris. How unfortunate. I didn't expect to hear from you so soon."

"What did you do to her, Webber? If you've hurt—"

"Save your breath, Chief. I haven't harmed the young lady. Well, that's not *completely* true. She may have a headache when she wakes up. Now, whether or not she wakes up at all, that's up to you."

"You don't need to involve her," Izzy said urgently. "She's got nothing to do with this. You want to deal with someone, deal with me."

"I've already tried to deal with you. Remember? Sadly, that didn't work out as well as I'd hoped. I assume the old man had a hand in that?"

"I managed to get a shot off. All that did was make the thing madder—whatever it was." Izzy made hurry-up motions to Gene. If she could keep Webber on the phone, they might have a chance. "But yes, Owens ended up saving us."

"Changed your worldview a bit, did it?"

Izzy turned to look at Owens. "That's putting it mildly."

Gene took a hard left. The Explorer fishtailed as its back tires broke free of the slick, snow-covered pavement. Gene turned into the slide and hit the accelerator. The transmission whined, a high-pitched tone that sliced through the cottony silence of the car's interior. Wet wheels fought for purchase, throwing up clumps of snow. The SUV's back end continued to swerve, gliding along the road's surface, until the treads bit, clawed, and the car shot forward. Izzy didn't realize she'd been holding her breath until she let out a jittery sigh.

"Sounds like you're having some trouble there," Webber laughed. "Anyway, back to the young lady. You called for a reason. I'm assuming Katie Bethel is still with you, so you didn't call to speak to her. And as much as it pains me to say this, I doubt you wanted to talk to *me*. That leaves the girl. Which means you were trying to warn her. Maybe you're even on your way here." Webber paused. "You play poker, Chief?"

"What?" Izzy said, puzzled at the sudden change in topic.

"Personally, I like a woman who knows how to gamble. How to play the odds." She heard the distinctive sound of a gun being racked, a round being chambered. "I've got a gun pointed at fair Brittany. If you don't turn around and go somewhere else, I'm going to have to blow her head off to express my disapproval. So, there's my opening bid. Now it's your turn. Ante up or fold."

"Webber, don't. You don't have to do this. She—"

"Ante up or fold. You've got ten seconds."

"You're just making things worse for yourself. If you—"

"Nine."

"Damn it, we can work something out. Killing her won't—"

"Eight."

Izzy's mind churned. She needed to get to Katie's house. Webber knew where her daughter was. And Kevin was there. But she couldn't risk Brittany's life in the process. And Webber's already shown he would kill to get what he wanted.

"Do you promise not to hurt her?"

"I make no promises. This is where you decide whether I'm bluffing or not. Now, have you turned around?"

Izzy hit on an idea. She gripped Gene's arm to get his attention. Shaking her head and motioning for him to continue on, she said, "Gene, turn the car around. Head back to the station." She waited a few moments, while Gene continued on to Katie's house. "There. You win this hand. But the game isn't over. As long as you have Natalie and Kevin, I won't stop looking for you. Eventually I'll find you. Then you'll answer for what you've done."

"Nice try, Chief. But you just made a novice mistake. You overplayed your hand. You should have lied and let it stand, but you trumped up your bluff. You tried to justify it. I call your bluff. You now have seven seconds."

"No! Wait! We turned around!"

"Six."

"Gene, pull over! Stop the car!" Gene eased the car to the side of the road.

"Five."

"Webber, don't! We've stopped. I'm not lying."

"Four three two one."

"What! No! No! Don't do it!"

"Looks like you had the weaker hand. I win, bitch."

When Izzy heard the sound of a gunshot rip through the phone, she turned to Gene.

"Hurry. Get to the house. I want that bastard."

CHAPTER
28

Jack Sallinen flinched when Webber fired the gun. In the confined space of the Bethel's living room, the shot sound like a cannon going off next to him. The smell of burnt gunpowder filled his nostrils and made his eyes water.

Standing in front of his father, Kevin clapped his hands over his ears, buried his head into Jack's abdomen, and began to cry.

Jack placed his arms around Kevin's trembling shoulders and hugged him close. He was grateful that his son's view was blocked by the couch—he didn't need to witness the girl's splattered head leaking blood and brains into the carpet.

He glared at Webber. "Can you give a guy a little warning next time?"

The other man grinned. "You snooze, you lose, Jack. Better stay sharp if you want to hang with the big boys."

"And the girl? You can be damn sure Morris will be after us now."

"She knows we have her daughter. She's not going to stop, no matter what I do. And again, you're making assumptions about what's going on."

Webber bent down. Grabbing one of Bridgette's arms, he dragged her out from behind the couch. Jack pressed Kevin more tightly into his stomach. But when the girl's head came into view, it was intact.

"What," said Webber in response to Jack's questioning look. "You thought I *liked* killing? Listen, this is about the bigger picture. The whole enchilada. There are stakes on either side of this little conflict we're involved in, and I'm just trying to play by the rules."

"More rules," Jack said, snorting derisively.

"Morris is on her way. We need to be gone before she gets here." Webber dropped the girl's arm and stuffed the gun into the waistband of his jeans. "You do want to get your son to safety, right?"

"Yeah," Jack said. Then he knelt down and placed a finger under Kevin's chin, gently raising his head. "Hey, buddy, you ready to go?"

Kevin's dark eyes met his—and they didn't turn away.

"Dad, what's going on?" Kevin's voice was high and light. "Where's J.J.?"

Jack's mouth dropped open.

"Hold on. I remember." Kevin looked around the room. "The girl? Where's the girl?" When he spotted Bridgette lying unconscious on the floor, he shied away. After a second, his gaze reached Webber. "Who are you?"

Webber eyed Kevin warily. "Um...name's Webber. Friend of your dad's."

"You—you can..." stammered Jack, dumbfounded.

Kevin frowned up at his dad. "Do you know him?"

Jack hesitated, then nodded. "Yes, he's my friend. *Our* friend. He's here to help us."

Kevin held his father's gaze for a few moments. Breaking eye contact, he turned and pointed a finger at Webber. It seemed such an insignificant gesture, but the blood drained from Webber's face. The man stepped around the unconscious girl's body, placed the couch between him and Kevin.

For the first time since Jack had known him, there was fear in the Webber's eyes.

Kevin kept his finger pointed at Webber. "Did you hurt her?"

"Jack," Webber said anxiously. "Talk to your son. Keep him there. Remember our deal. You help me with Kevin, I help you later."

Jack frowned, his eyes traveling between Kevin and Webber. What was going on here?

Kevin was panting now, his right hand clenched into a fist.

"You h-hurt her."

Webber put his hands up, palms out. "Hey, come on. That was an accident. She'll be fine. Really. Point is, I'm not going to hurt *you*. So why don't you be a good boy and stay right where you are?"

Kevin took a defiant step forward.

"There's s-something d-different about you. S-something I f-f-feel." He shook his head. "I d-don't think I like y-you."

"Jack," Webber called out. "What did I say? Keep him away from me."

"Kevin," Jack said, putting as much parental authority into his voice as he could. "Come here, son."

Kevin jerked his head around to look at his dad. He was blinking now. His right fist hammered his thigh over and over. "B-but you d-d-don't—"

"Yes," Jack said gently. "I do." Then he smiled and held out his arms.

Jack watched as Kevin's expression changed; his sense of *being there* faded like water into parched earth. A tremor ran through his son's body, hard enough to make his clothes flutter. Then Kevin's awareness returned. His son looked at him once more.

"I t-trust y-you, Dad. And l-l-love y-you. B-but...." Kevin paused, his brow coming together in a frown. Then his eyes widened in horror. He began to shake his head violently. "N-n-no, n-not you. N-n-not y-you!"

"Kevin? Son, what's the matter?"

"I-I-I-I-I—" Kevin spluttered. And he was gone.

Watching his son's efforts almost broke Jack's heart. He still had his arms out, and Kevin rushed into his embrace. His son's eyes roamed in the room, fixing on everything except the one thing Jack wanted them to.

Him.

Holding Kevin close to his chest, he stared at Webber. "What the hell was that?"

Webber shook his head. "It's not something I was expecting." He looked around the house, as if he was just now remembering where he was. "Shit, we gotta get out of here. Come on, Jack. We need to leave *now*."

Wrapping one arm under Kevin's thin legs, Jack lifted his son up into his arms. He walked over to the couch, grabbed his son's jacket, threw it over the boy. Looking down, he nodded toward Bridgette.

"What about the girl?"

Webber shook his head again. "Leave her. No time. We're out of here." He bolted for the door and threw it open.

Jack ran after him. Kevin squirmed in his arms, reached up with one hand and raced a finger lightly over Jack's chest. At some point known only to his son, the finger stopped and tapped on his breastbone.

"Fickle-fek," Kevin said in his silly, sing-song voice.

Hurrying after Webber, Jack shot a curious look at Kevin, wondering where the boy had ever heard the creature's name.

* * *

Izzy told Gene to turn right. He jerked the wheel around, but the Explorer was going too fast. Once again, its back end began to swerve, the tires spinning in the snow.

Muttering a curse under his breath, Gene struggled for a few moments, tapping the brakes and turning into the slide. When he'd finally pulled them out of it, he asked, "How much farther?"

"Just up ahead," answered Izzy.

"Third house on the left past the intersection," added Katie from the back seat.

About half a block from the intersection, Izzy saw the door to Katie's house open. Webber came hurrying out, followed by Jack Sallinen with Kevin in his arms. They were headed toward the Silverado parked in the driveway.

"There they are. Gene, once we get past the intersection, pull over. I'll deal with them. Everyone stays in the car. These guys are armed. I don't want anyone else getting hurt."

Owens and Katie voiced agreement. Gene nodded. Then his eyes darted left and he swore. Izzy leaned forward to look out the window.

An old, snow-covered Chevy Impala was rapidly approaching the intersection from the west. Someone had tried to scrape snow from the windshield, but the storm had thrown more at it. Its narrow wipers beat back-and-forth, attempting to make a clear spot so the driver could see.

"Too fast," Gene muttered. He gripped the steering wheel until his knuckles were white. "He's coming too fast."

Izzy didn't have a choice. She hit a switch on the Explorer's dashboard. Bar light on the roof came alive, flashing blue and red.

The Impala's brake lights lit, but it didn't stop. Rather, it began to coast forward on the slick pavement.

Farther down the road, Webber spun around. He stared at them for a moment, then climbed into the Silverado.

"Gene," Izzy said. "We can't lose them now." *I can't lose the only lead to my daughter.*

The Impala continued to glide into the intersection. The driver wasn't even trying to pump the brakes.

"Okay," Gene called out. "Everybody hang on." He hit the gas. The SUV surged ahead, the engine roaring as he tried to accelerate past the Impala. But the tires couldn't get enough traction in the loose snow. They weren't building up enough speed. They weren't going to get by in time.

Whatever the other driver was doing, it must have been every wrong thing they taught you to avoid in driver's education. The Impala's front wheels turned, and its back end started to swing around toward the Explorer.

Gene swore and mashed down on the accelerator, trying to pull past the oncoming car. And still the Impala came toward them, the gap between them closing rapidly.

The Impala's driver must have seen that it wasn't going to work. In a last-ditch effort to avoid a collision, he jerked the wheel around while simultaneously hitting the brakes. The Explorer slid in the same direction as the Impala. Like two boxers circling one another in a ring, the cars' momentum carried the SUV away from and around the approaching Impala. For a brief moment, Izzy's hopes soared as she thought Gene had done it, that he'd managed to avoid a collision.

Then the Impala hit them. Its back bumper slammed into the Explorer's front quarter panel in a crunch of plastic and metal. The impact shoved the SUV sideways. Izzy's seatbelt bit into her chest as she was thrown against the door. In the back, Katie slid into Bart; the old man managed to wrap his arms around her shoulders, keeping her from tumbling onto the floorboard. In addition to his seatbelt, Gene's grip on the steering wheel helped keep him from being jostled about. The SUV continued to spin until it hit a curb, where it finally jerked to a stop.

Izzy was out of the SUV within seconds. The Silverado was almost clear of the driveway. She drew her gun and aimed. She needed to stop them, but she had to be careful. Kevin was in the cab.

She fired. The bullet plowed into the truck's rear fender. Webber didn't slow down. The Silverado continued into the street.

She squeezed off another shot. Then another. The Glock bucked in her hands. The rounds slammed into truck's body, punching large holes into the metal.

That got Webber's attention. He stopped. A door opened and Denny Cain jumped out. He was holding the hunting rifle she'd seen yesterday. Izzy dove to one side as Denny took aim and fired. Snow erupted inches from where she'd been standing. She fired from the ground. The shot went wild. Again. The second ricocheted off the Silverado's roof next to Denny's head.

The man ducked. Then he brought the rifle up, his aim tracking away from Izzy—

—and toward the Explorer.

"No," Izzy shouted, firing. The shot went wide.

Denny paused for a moment, and then he fired. The rifle's report seemed to echo in Izzy's ears.

Because of the spin, the Explorer's back end was facing Denny. His shot blasted through the rear window. Right at where Katie and Owens were sitting.

Izzy scrambled to her feet as Denny jumped back into the Silverado. The truck sped off down the street.

They had gotten away.

Choking back her frustration, Izzy hurried over to the Explorer. She yanked the rear door open.

At first she thought Owens and Katie had both been hit. The old man covered the smaller girl. Then Owens stirred and sat up. Beneath him, Katie looked up at Izzy. She smiled weakly.

Izzy breathed a sigh of relief. "For a second there—"

"Izzy," Owens said. He was looking toward the driver's seat.

Turning, she saw Gene slumped to one side, his seat belt keeping him from falling over. From where she stood, he didn't look hurt. But he wasn't moving.

She opened his door. Reaching in, she grabbed his shoulders and pulled him upright.

Her hand came away wet with blood.

CHAPTER
29

Izzy ignored the blood on her hand and gently turned Gene's head.

The owner of the Lula had been very fortunate. Denny's shot had grazed the side of his head near his temple. Had the round hit just a bit lower, he'd have lost his ear; had it hit more directly, he'd be dead. As it was, the skin had been split, and he was bleeding down the side of his face.

"There's a first-aid kit in the trunk," she told Owens.

Gene began to stir as the passenger door opened, and Bart Owens slid in the seat with the first-aid kit in his hand.

"I'll take care of Gene," he said, opening up the kit and pulling out some gauze pads. "Someone should see to Katie's friend."

Katie started to get out of the car, but Izzy stopped her. "I'll go check on Brittany. But you can do something. Go see if the driver of the other car is all right. If he is, tell him it's okay to go. Right now, I've got more things to worry about than a bad driver."

Katie jumped out of the SUV and headed over to the Impala.

"I'll be right back," Izzy told Owens. Then she hurried to Katie's house.

In the living room, she found Brittany Parsons sitting on the floor, groggy, shaken, but alive. She had a nasty lump on the back of her head, but otherwise she appeared to be fine. After reassuring the girl that they would do everything to find Kevin, Izzy radioed in for a patrolman to come and take Brittany's statement, and then afterward, drive her home.

Back outside the house, she saw that the Impala had already left. Katie was making her way back to the Explorer. Izzy hurried to catch up.

Snow had piled up on the SUV already, covering the windows and blowing into the open space where the rear window used to be. It also began filling in the tracks she'd made walking over to Katie's house.

When she reached the Explorer, Izzy checked on Gene. Owens had finished wrapping a bandage around the dressing, covering Gene's wounds. She breathed a sigh of relief when Gene turned to look at her.

"And I thought my back hurt." He blinked hard and took a deep breath. "It feels like a bunch of kids played kick-the-can with my head."

Owens said, "The wound was shallow. Stitches would probably be a good idea, but other than his headache, I can't find anything else wrong with him." He gave Gene a wry smile. "You should be dead, you know."

Gene chuckled. Izzy remembered that Gene had said the exact same words to Owens only a few hours ago.

"So you're a doctor, too?" she asked Owens.

"Medic, remember? Couple of World Wars ago. I learned a lot."

Katie had slid into the back seat. "Brittany?"

"A little frazzled, that's all," Izzy replied. The news was met with looks of relief.

Gene sat up a little straighter. "What happened with Kevin?"

"They got away," said Izzy, spitting out the words like they were broken teeth. "But I don't intend on letting them get far. Gene, do you think you could move to the passenger's side?"

"Hell, yes," Gene said and exited the SUV. "Let's go get 'em."

Izzy's gaze slid over to Katie, then Owens. "I'm still worried—"

"I am *not* staying behind," Katie interjected. "These guys killed my mother. That gives me the right to be here."

"I'll keep my eye on her," Owens said. "They'll have to kill me to get to her."

Izzy wanted to argue the point, but she was running out of time. She climbed into the Explorer. Grabbing the mic hanging from the police radio, she updated the APB for Webber's Chevy Silverado: it had three bullet holes in the left rear body of the car. And they now had a hostage.

Next she had her dispatcher send out notices to Marquette's airport and the area bus terminals with the descriptions of all four individuals.

"Maybe we'll get lucky," she said as she hung up the mic. "Somebody might see them."

Izzy straightened out the SUV and headed in the direction the Silverado had gone. With the rear window missing, it was getting colder inside the Explorer. She kept the heat cranked up to high. The snow appeared to be easing up—the only thing going in their favor.

Traffic here had been minimal. She could see the Silverado's tracks turning left on Baker Street. She followed them. The next stop was Asher.

Now that they had Kevin, Webber and Jack would be headed out of town. A left on Asher would take them northwest toward the airport in Marquette and then on to Wisconsin. Right would lead southeast to the two bridges that provided ways out of the Upper.

She rolled to a stop. Being the main road through town, traffic here was heavier. And the road had been plowed.

She pounded the steering wheel with her fist. There were no tracks. She couldn't tell which way Webber had turned.

She had lost them.

* * *

The Lexus RX rolled east along M-28 toward Kinsey. The ride was smooth enough, the woman thought. But it couldn't compare to the feel of her favorite set of wheels, a fully-loaded Porsche 911 Carrera she'd picked up a few months ago. Driving that was like having a love affair with the road. Then again, spend over a quarter million dollars for a car and it had better drive like a dream.

No, she'd chosen the Lexus for practical reasons. The weather report had called for a snow storm to roll across this rural slice of Michigan's Upper Peninsula. So prior to leaving Dulles International Airport, she'd called ahead to the car rental counter at the airport in Marquette and arranged to have the SUV waiting for her when she arrived. Its wide tires and solid handling were perfect for traversing snowy roads. For now, function trumped form.

Just past a small town called Munising, the road banked left, following the shoreline of Lake Superior. The woman eased up on the accelerator. The Lexus's handling in the snow had been excellent, but there was no need to take chances. She would arrive in Kinsey in due time.

Working her way deeper into the heated seat, she pondered her current dilemma. Darryl Webber had disappointed her. She had sent him up here to collect the boy and bring him to her. That had been almost two weeks ago, and she still didn't have Kevin Sallinen.

One long, immaculately lacquered fingernail began tapping the leather-wrapped steering wheel. The current situation was unacceptable. She should have gone with her first instinct. Send Webber in and have him take the boy; the less complicated a plan, the better it worked. But she had allowed Webber to talk her into a more detailed operation. And, she had to admit, he'd had a point. She could secure the boy and rid herself of Bartholomew, all at the same time.

The operation hadn't been a disaster, but it certainly hadn't been a success, either.

She had last spoken to Webber thirty-six hours ago. Since then, she'd heard nothing.

There could be a couple reasons for that. Webber had noted that Kinsey's Chief of Police was more formidable than he'd expected. Not surprising, given that Darryl Webber was a misogynistic fool. Underestimating women was something she'd had to address with him in the past. It didn't look like the lesson had sunk in.

And then there was Bartholomew. While she had expected his involvement—had counted on it—he had the frustrating habit of throwing up all kinds of barriers. And he had twice beat Webber at his own game.

All in all, it was enough to irritate her.

She didn't fully trust Darryl with phone calls. In the past, he'd tried to explain away his failures, then go on doing what he was doing. So for this operation, she'd decided to delay her other obligations and stay close to the Midwest. Good thing she did. Once events in Kinsey had started going awry, she'd been able to come up here. Personally see to things. It wasn't something she liked to do. But if Kevin Sallinen had half the potential she suspected, it would be worth the inconvenience.

And if she could not secure the boy, she would make *damn* sure Bartholomew and his cadre didn't get him either.

Turning her attention to the GPS attached to the Lexus's dashboard, she saw it wouldn't be much longer.

Close enough? Probably.

She reached for her cell, but something made her pause.

Oh my, she thought, bringing her hand up to her face. Webber's antics must have upset me more that I'd believed.

Her perfectly manicured fingernails were gone.

She smiled at the hooked, razor-sharp claws that now extended from the tips of her fingers.

CHAPTER
30

Darryl Webber maneuvered his Silverado down the snow-slicked road. He checked the rear-view mirror. No sign of Morris.

Huddled in the back seat, Jack held his son; the gunfire had set the boy off on another crying jag. Denny Cain sat next to Webber, the rifle propped between his long legs. Adrenaline seemed to have burned away some of Denny's hangover. That, and the chance to take a shot at the man he thought had killed his son. Revenge was an excellent tonic for a tormented soul.

As they approached an intersection, he called out, "Jack. Directions."

"Left," replied Jack. "That'll take you out of town."

Denny looked over at Webber. "What do you mean, 'out of town'? I ain't leaving. Maddie's at home waiting for me."

"Seriously? You just shot at the Chief of Police. Blew out her car window. You think she's going to take kindly to that?"

Denny's face screwed into a frown. "But—but I don't wanna leave. What'll Maddie do without me?"

"Here," Webber offered, pulling the car over to the curb. "Let me drop you off. You can go back and apologize. Maybe Morris will understand."

"You know she ain't gonna do that."

"See what I mean?" Webber eased back out into what little traffic there was. "Buckle up, hoss. You're in it for the long haul."

"I—but—"

"No 'buts'."

Webber took the left. When his cell began playing "Black Hole Sun," he checked the display. He was tempted to ignore the call—he'd screwed up by not checking in. But he also knew he could stretch his luck only so far.

He clicked on and said, "It's me."

"Nice of you to pick up," came her voice over the phone, sounding uncomfortably close.

"Yeah, sorry about that. I've been kind of busy."

"Busy?" she said archly.

"I said I was sorry."

"Keep me out of the loop again and you will be."

"Understood." *Bitch.*

"Have you managed to get the boy yet?"

"Just now. I ran into a couple problems."

"Spare me your excuses." Her sarcasm was sharp enough to draw blood. "And Bartholomew?"

"He was one of the problems. We just managed to get away from him."

There was a pause on the other end. "You're saying Bartholomew got *that* close to the boy? Before everything was in place?"

"Yeah," he admitted. "Near the end."

"I gave you every advantage, and still he dogged your steps. Unbelievable. Makes me wonder."

"Yet I'm the one who ended up with the boy."

"More by luck," she replied. "What about my pet?"

Damn. He'd hoped not to go there. "Well, that's a different problem." Webber recounted his decision to send the creature after Morris. And how it had returned, injured, with Morris still alive.

The pause was longer this time. "How is that possible?"

"She got a shot off. It took a bullet in the chest."

"We both know it would take more than that."

"I told you she was resourceful. She—"

"What are you not telling me, Darryl?"

His mind churned as he tried to think of an effective lie.

"And don't try lying to me."

Webber let out a sigh. "Owens was with her at the time."

When she spoke next, her words were clipped and harsh. "You sent my favorite pet after someone protected by Bartholomew?"

"Yes," Webber said, thankful for the distance between here and Maryland.

"He saved her?"

"That's the theory."

"Don't be cute. It's annoying."

"Look," he said, desperate to change the subject. "I've *got* the boy. I did what you asked."

"I'll take that under consideration."

"One more thing."

"Now what?"

"The boy," Webber said. "He spoke to me."

"Spoke...how?"

"In complete sentences. *Coherently.*" He could almost hear her chewing on that one.

"You're sure about this?"

"He's not supposed to do that yet." Webber glanced at Kevin in the mirror. "What kind of danger am I in here?"

"No more than when he's speaking his gibberish."

"Wait a minute," Webber said, alarmed. "You didn't tell me that."

"Whatever made you think I'd tell you everything?"

"But my control over the Fek?"

"I'm still not sure about the extent of the boy's abilities, so I'd be careful if I were you."

Webber was stunned. "That would have been nice to know from the start."

"Life's full of little surprises," she said sweetly. "Now, where are you?"

Biting back his irritation, he replied, "I'm almost out of town. Give me a couple more days."

"Don't bother. I'm coming to you."

"You don't have to do that," Webber said in a panic. "Seriously, I've got everything under control."

"Yes, I do," she replied. "And no, you don't. Besides, I'm already here."

Oh, fuck. Not good. Not good at all. "Where?"

"About an hour or so from Kinsey."

He swallowed. "All right. I understand. What do you want me to do?"

"Where were you keeping my pet?"

"A cave outside of town." He gave her directions.

"Make your way there."

"Of course," he said stiffly. "I'm on my way."

"This had better work," she said. "I won't tolerate another failure." Then she hung up on him.

Webber shut his phone. It was amazing how fast things can go down the shitter.

Looking into the rear view mirror, he asked: "How's everyone feel about a walk in the woods?"

* * *

Deke Frenz picked his way through the woods. A hard wind blew the snow around, creating drifts and generally making the walk difficult. In one hand he carried a burlap bag filled with apples. The other rested on the strap of a rifle slung over his shoulder.

Earlier, after the ambulance had left with the kid found in Room 7, Deke had decided to flip on the NO VACANCY sign, close up shop and go check on his bait piles. There were no other customers, and he was unlikely to see more that day. Fishing season was winding down, and even though you could get some good steelies in the nearby trout streams, most people weren't willing to make the long drive just for that. Bow season for deer started next week. That might pull in a few people. But the major influx of customers started around November 15th. That was when firearm season opened. He already had enough reservations to fill the Hiawatha Trails for three weeks.

He stepped between two trees and approached his third and final bait pile. Despite the snow, he knew exactly where he was going. He'd lived his whole life up here, hunted from the age of fifteen. This was like his second home.

The last pile was in a shallow indentation in the ground marked by three trees, two large pines and a smaller aspen. He dropped the bag of apples and leaned his rifle against a tree trunk. Kneeling down, he began brushing away the snow. He frowned at what he saw.

Like the other two piles he had visited, the apples here were untouched.

He recalled the rubs he'd seen on the trees. The bark had been scraped away by the antlers of some huge buck. It had likely marked its territory, pissing all over the place and keeping the other deer away. But why hadn't it eaten the apples?

He thought he heard something moving in the woods. He stood and looked around, his ears straining against the crystalline stillness of the forest. The overcast sky had rendered the woods into a stark landscape of whites and dark grays. He didn't see anything. But still, there was something not...quite...right....

Sticks broke in another direction. He spun, eyes darting back and forth, his breath coming in shallow, quick gasps. Blood rushed through his veins, pounded loudly in his ears.

He wasn't one to panic in the woods. Nothing spooked him, really. But now he was afraid—unreasonably afraid.

He reached for the rifle. Before coming out here, he'd loaded the gun, chambered a round, and engaged the safety. He never wandered around the forest unarmed. It was a good thing, too.

Because he was certain something was out there.

And he got the feeling it was watching him.

* * *

Webber turned off the road and onto a small trail leading deep into the woods.

The drive had taken him back toward the Hiawatha Trails Motel. He would have preferred using less-traveled side roads—Morris had likely put the word out about them over the police band—but the cave was located near the motel, and M-28 was the only way he knew to get there. So he had sped along as fast as he could on the slick roads, keeping one eye out for the cops and the other for his turn-off.

Driving slower now, he continued down the trail for a few hundred feet, wanting to make sure the Silverado couldn't be seen from the main road. When he saw a beat-up, dark-green Ford pickup parked about thirty yards up ahead, he shook his head in disbelief.

"Who comes out here in a snowstorm?" he said.

"Baiting," replied Denny.

"What?"

"Deer baiting," Denny explained. "Someone's laying bait for deer season."

"That's just fucking peachy," snapped Webber. "Go see if that lunatic's in his truck. Jack, come on. We got some walking to do."

"What if he's there?" asked Denny while Jack bundled up Kevin. "In the truck?"

"Keep him distracted while we head out into the woods. Tell him—I don't know—tell him you're baiting too. So long as he doesn't follow us. Then catch up. We won't be that far ahead."

Everyone piled out of the truck. Denny slung his rifle over one shoulder and plodded toward the pickup. Webber, with Jack trailing close behind holding Kevin in his arms, left the trail and began hiking into the woods.

Deke Frenz stepped quietly to one side, his heavy boots crunching in the snow. One step. Another. A third. Once he'd cleared the trees, he brought his Remington .700 bolt-action up and placed the stock firmly against his shoulder. The rifle had been fitted with a Leupold Gold-Ring scope, which gave him excellent magnification up to two hundred yards. Squinting into the lens, he turned, letting the barrel skim the horizon.

Trees leapt into focus, only to dart back as he continued turning. The effect was unsettling, almost as if the forest were moving, creeping closer, hemming him in. He blinked the sweat from his eyes. Shook his head to clear his thoughts. Peered back down the scope.

Trees, trees and more trees. He had turned almost completely around without seeing anything unusual, when he heard a loud crack somewhere behind him.

He spun to face the other way. Something moved in the distance. Through the scope, the trees jumped at him, suddenly so close he could almost touch them. He searched, searched, but there was nothing. Nothing at—

No, wait.

There *was* something.

Just beyond a line of oaks. A flash of brown. He knew that the ground there gave way to swampland. And beyond that, the north branch of the Perry River. Maybe the snow had spooked the deer, driving them from swamp's warmth? Maybe it was his trophy buck?

No. The coloring had been too dark for a whitetail. It had been a deep brown. Brown like the chewing tobacco he'd left in his truck. Brown like a bear.

Another flash of movement through the trees.

Deke tried to track it, but it was traveling too fast. He'd never known a bear to move like that. Just when he thought he would lose sight of it, the animal stopped, and he could see it clearly.

It was big. Really big. With coarse, dark fur. Damned if that wasn't the biggest bear he'd ever—

Then the bear turned its head and looked directly at him.

Only it wasn't a bear.

Because bears didn't have scales. Or eyes that looked eerily human.

With that…that *thing* staring at him, Deke thumbed the rifle's safety forward to the off position. Then his finger slid onto the trigger. His heart was tripping harder now.

"Whatever the fuck you are," he whispered, "you ain't natural."

Almost as if it had heard him, the creature's lips curled back to reveal long, sharp teeth. Powerful jaws snapped at the air, and then it was gone.

Deke lowered the Remington. Fast as that thing moved, he knew he wasn't going to be able to follow it.

He turned and began running back to his truck, leaving the bag of apples forgotten on the ground. He had to get out of here, get back to the road, get a signal on his cell. He'd call the DNR—no, screw the DNR. He'd call the cops. Maybe the National Guard.

He was almost to the trail—he could see his pickup through the thinning trees—when he heard a different sound.

Voices. Human voices. Heading deeper into the woods, where that thing was.

He didn't even pause to think about what he was doing. He began running toward the voices and shouting.

"Hey! Hey! Stop! Don't go in there! Come back!"

Walking about ten yards in front of the others, Webber was so focused on getting to the cave that he didn't hear Jack calling his name until the man shouted.

"Webber! Hold on a second."

He stopped and turned. "What?"

"There's someone coming up behind us," Jack said. Kevin appeared to be asleep in his arms.

Webber listened. Sure enough, he could hear someone yelling for them to stop.

"Must be the guy from the pickup," said Denny. He'd found no one in the truck when he'd looked earlier.

Webber nodded. "And now he's sticking his nose where it doesn't belong." He paused, weighing his options. Time was running out. He didn't have any choice. "Denny, I don't want any witnesses. Go take care of him."

"What do you mean, 'take care of him'?"

Webber looked the man in the eye. "Kill him."

The attack caught Deke by surprise. He had gone behind a tree to avoid a deadfall, when he heard gunfire. The trunk near his head exploded. Surprised, he'd dropped to the ground, pressed his back hard against the rough bark.

Holy shit. Did someone just *shoot* at me?

A second shot rang out. The ground near his feet erupted in a cloud of snow and dirt.

"Hey!" he shouted. "What the hell are you doin'? I ain't no deer!"

The next shot hit the tree again. He could feel the impact through the wood.

Son of a bitch. He tightened his grip on the .700 and spun to his left. Using the deadfall as cover, he brought up the rifle, squeezed off two quick shots, dove forward, crawled along the ground, and came up behind another tree.

The return fire plowed into the deadfall, sending leaves and twigs flying through the air.

He dropped again. Keeping his gut tight against the ground, he used his elbows and knees to crawl farther from the deadfall. Sticks dug into his stomach. Bitterly cold snow melted and ran down the front of his jacket. He ignored it all and made his way to a large, dead oak that had fallen across a tree stump.

He had three rounds left in his Remington. He hadn't brought any spare ammo. The other guy had one, maybe two rounds left. Of course, he could have extra shells with him.

He reached the tree stump and brought himself up to a crouch. There was a small gap where the oak leaned at an angle against the stump. Easing the rifle barrel through the gap, he squinted into the scope. Time to find out who this asshole was.

It took him a few seconds to locate the guy. Deke watched as the man peered out from behind a tree trunk. He wore a heavy jacket with the hood up, casting his face in shadows. In his hands was a rifle.

Deke aimed slightly to the right and fired. Part of the tree next to the guy's head blew apart, sending shards of wood into the guy's face.

"I coulda killed you just now," he called out. "That was your one and only chance. You don't leave now, you don't leave at all."

The man popped out from behind the tree, brought the rifle up and fired. The dead oak broke apart. Deke bit back a cry as a piece of wood cut into his forehead.

Peering through his scope, Deke saw that the man's hood had fallen away, exposing his face. His eyes widened in surprise as he recognized the shooter. It was one of the guys from the motel, the ones the cops were looking for. The ones who had beat the crap out of that poor kid and left him to die. And now the guy was out here trying to kill him.

He didn't have time to think about the situation. The man was bringing up his rifle.

Deke had him dead center in his scope. Before the other guy could fire, he took the shot. It went a little high and nicked the guy in the shoulder. The other guy cried out in pain, but continued to bring up the rifle up.

"I warned you, motherfucker."

One round left. He took a half-breath, let it out slowly, and squeezed the trigger. The Remington recoiled against his shoulder. Through the scope, he watched the guy's chest explode in a spray of red blood. He fell to the ground.

Out of ammo, wound up on adrenaline and nauseous at the thought of having killed someone, Deke raced for his truck.

He definitely needed to call the cops.

CHAPTER
31

Izzy's police car sped east along M-28, bar lights flashing, siren wailing. Thanks to Luce County's efficient snow emergency crews, the road had been plowed and salted. The SUV was pushing eighty. The few cars traveling on the road pulled over to allow her to pass. Whether or not anyone noticed the missing rear windshield, she neither knew nor cared.

It had taken almost two hours, but her APB had worked. Webber's Silverado had been spotted.

She crested a small hill. The sun was low in the sky. In the increasing gloom, she saw a group of emergency vehicles clustered in the distance, their own lights flashing. Her face was grim as she raced ahead. The pulsing lights resolved into two Luce County Sheriff's cars and an ambulance. She pulled in behind one of the Sheriff's cars.

"This is a crime scene," she told the others. "Stay here until I speak to whoever's in charge."

Izzy climbed out of the SUV and headed toward the nearest officer, a solidly built man who looked to be in his late twenties. When he saw her approaching, he stepped up to meet her.

"Chief Morris?" he asked. When she nodded, he stuck out his hand. "Steven Campbell. Met one of yours earlier today. Detective Billick. Seems like a good man."

"He is," she answered, shaking the officer's hand. She nodded toward the trail leading into the woods. "Who's running the show?"

Officer Campbell suddenly looked uncomfortable. "That'd be Lt. de la Rosa."

Izzy had heard of him. Vincent de la Rosa was an ambitious man who wasn't known for playing well with others. Apparently he had his sights set on the County Executive's job, and that might only be a stepping stone to what he surely saw as greater glories.

"What have you got back there?" She indicated the trail.

"Two guys. One dead from a GSW to the chest. I know the other guy. He owns a motel down the road. Says he was out here laying down deer bait when the first guy started shooting. They exchanged gunfire, and Deke was forced to kill him."

"You believe him?"

"Deke? Sure, I've always found him to be a straight shooter, no pun intended."

"So you found no one else? No little boy?"

Campbell shook his head. "Not that I know of."

"Any ID on the body?"

"You'd have to check with the lieutenant."

"And he's back there?"

"Yes, ma'am."

"Then I'll have to go ask him, won't I?"

Campbell hesitated for a moment, clearly anxious about something. "I'm sorry, but I've been told to keep everyone out of the area."

"Everyone?"

He nodded. "Including you."

"We'll see about that," Izzy said and started to move past Officer Campbell.

He stopped her with a hand on her arm. "Do me a favor? At least tell him I tried to do my job."

Izzy smiled. "As far as I'm concerned, you gave me two tons of shit before I finally pulled rank on you."

"Thanks, Chief," he said.

She strode toward the trail. An ambulance was parked near the entrance to the woods, its red emergency lights flashing. Webber's Silverado sat about thirty yards up the trail, and in front of it, an older model Ford pickup. Both vehicles were cordoned off with yellow police tape.

A man sat at the back of the ambulance, a bandage covering part of his forehead. Campbell's friend Deke, no doubt. An EMT seemed to be arguing with him.

"Sir," the EMT was saying, "you really should be checked out. That head wound may not look like much, but you never can tell without a closer examination. It won't take—"

"No time a'tall," the man finished, "'cause I ain't going to the hospital. That jackass out there tried to kill me. If all I get out of it is a scrape on the head, I'll count myself lucky. Besides, I wanna stay and see if they can bring that damned creature out of the woods."

Creature? Izzy thought and veered over to the ambulance. "Excuse me?" she said to the EMT, flashing her badge. "Can I have a moment with this man?"

"May as well," he said, irritated by his stubborn patient. "Looks like I'm done here. I'll go to see if they need help with the body." He began walking down the trail.

When the EMT was gone, the injured man peered up at her. "Who're you?"

"Chief Morris. Kinsey PD."

"Deke Frenz. What can I do ya for?"

"You mentioned something about a creature?"

Deke turned to stare off into the woods. At first he didn't say anything, and Izzy thought he wasn't going to answer. But then he spoke, his voice subdued.

"Yeah, I saw something. Some kind of animal. Thought it was a bear at first, but...."

"But bears don't have scales," she finished for him.

His gaze never left the woods, but she could tell he was surprised by what she'd said. "Any idea what it is?"

"Not really," she said. "All I know is, it's fast and it's deadly."

"You've locked horns with that thing?"

"Last night. It attacked me and my friends."

Deke pulled out a tin of chewing tobacco and put a pinch between his cheek and gums. "So how is it you're still alive?" he asked around the chew.

"Had a little help. You?"

"Plain old luck, I guess," he said, shrugging.

"Can you tell me what happened back in the woods?"

Deke had just finished relating his side of the story when a tall, thin man came rushing down the trail toward them. He was dressed in a Luce County Sheriff uniform. His black hair was cut short, the temples graying. His long legs were chewing up the distance.

"Hold on one damn minute!" he began shouting. "Whoever you are, you need to leave now. This is a crime scene. No unauthorized personnel allowed!"

Izzy told Deke, "He's my next stop."

Deke nodded. "Do me a favor and give that little prick hell. Okay?"

"Sure," she answered, amused at how fast de la Rosa could make friends. "And thanks for the info." Then she began walking toward the trail.

"Not this way. The other—" He stopped, his narrow face pulling into a frown. "Chief Morris."

"Lieutenant de la Rosa."

He bristled at the emphasis on his rank. "Is there something I can do for you? I'm rather busy at the moment."

"First, you can call off your guard dog." She jabbed a finger at Officer Campbell. "That man gave me hell for trying to get this far. In case you've forgotten, we're all officers of the law. I don't expect to be treated like an outsider."

Lt. de la Rosa's dark eyes cut to Campbell. He gave the man a brief, satisfied nod. Then he turned his attention back to her. "Patrolman Campbell is simply doing his job. I'm sure you'll understand that this is a crime scene. I've sealed it off, and I can't have people walking through it. Evidence could be ruined."

"Really? You don't think I know how to handle myself around a crime scene?"

"Of course you do" he quipped. "I respect your knowledge. But I can't risk my investigation by allowing anyone back there until we're done."

"And how long will that take?"

"Several hours, at least. We need to determine what actually happened."

"But you have an eyewitness," she said. "Someone started shooting at Mr. Frenz, and he shot back. I'm sure ballistics will confirm that there wasn't a third shooter. This is a case of self-defense. No way would that take 'several hours'."

Lt. de la Rosa looked askance at Deke Frenz. In a hushed tone, he said, "Self-defense has not been established yet."

Izzy was amazed at the man's obtuseness. "You can't be serious. Remember the APB? The people in that Silverado are suspects in two murders, two kidnappings, and they just shot up my police car. And you think this guy is good for a random killing out in the woods?"

His face flushing red, Lt. de la Rosa took a step forward, crowding her. He was a good head taller and appeared to enjoy using his height to intimidate others.

"Don't tell me how to run my cases, Chief Morris. This isn't Kinsey. I don't answer to you."

Izzy lifted her face to meet de la Rosa's glare.

"Step back, Lieutenant," she said. "Now."

Vincent de la Rosa opened his mouth as if to say something, then noticed that everyone was watching them. Uncertainty robbed the color from his cheeks. He licked his lips, then took a step back.

"I have a job to do," he said curtly. "I'm not going to half-ass it by making assumptions or ignoring all the possibilities. Mr. Frenz is a suspect until proved otherwise."

"Use your head, de la Rosa," she returned. "Would he have called the cops if it hadn't been self-defense? He could just as easily have left the man in the woods. The body wouldn't be found for days out here. Weeks, even. So why call all this attention to the killing now?" Izzy shook her head. "Looking at Frenz for this is wrong, and you know it."

The red was back in de la Rosa's cheeks. "I've wasted enough time with you, Chief Morris. I'm going to do a thorough investigation. And no one is going into my crime scene until I'm done."

This wasn't going to work. She needed to try a different tactic. "Look, Lieutenant," she said. "Maybe we can help each other out. Have you ID'd the body yet?"

"Yes, but why should I tell you?"

"Trust me. Who's the DB?"

De la Rose pulled out a small notebook and flipped it open. "Driver's license says his name is Dennis Cain." He looked up. "Isn't he one of the guys from your APB?"

Izzy closed her eyes, pressed her mouth into a thin line. Prior to the events of the last few days, before his son's death had broken him, Denny Cain had been Stanley's employee, a decent man with a quick smile, and a family friend. Now, to come to this end, lying cold and dead in the woods. How was she going to tell Maddie that she'd lost her son and her husband, all within a handful of days?

"Yes," she said, opening her eyes. "Denny is—well, *was* one of the guys from the Silverado."

"And your daughter and the boy? You think they might be in there?" He gestured to the woods.

Izzy nodded. "Yes."

Lt. de la Rosa was silent for a moment; maybe she'd finally gotten through to the man. Then he gave her a smug smile. "Very well. When I'm done here, I'll send a couple of my officers into the woods. I'll call you if I find anything."

Izzy was stunned. "We're talking about my daughter!"

"You really want to find her? Then drive down the road and walk in from there." His smug smile widened. "Simply go around me."

"You know the woods are too thick near the road," she said. "I need this trail to get in. And with the sun setting, I'll never be able to pick up their trail in the dark."

"That's your problem, Chief Morris. Now get off my crime scene before I have you arrested."

"You want to arrest me," she said. "Okay, let me give you a reason." Her left hand shot out and clamped down hard on de la Rosa's right wrist. With her other hand, she removed her handcuffs. Before de la Rosa could react, she snapped one cuff around his wrist. Then she grabbed him by the upper arm and shoved him against the back of the ambulance, securing the other cuff around a thick yellow bar just inside its open doors. Finally, she reached inside his jacket and took his handgun.

"What the—!" shouted de la Rosa. "You can't do this! Uncuff me, *puta!*"

Stepping away from the infuriated lieutenant, she said, "You're under arrest. You have the right to remain silent. You have the—"

"Arrested? On what charge?"

"Playing games with my daughter's life," Izzy replied flatly.

Officer Campbell came running up to the ambulance.

"Arrest her," ordered de la Rosa as he struggled against the restraint.

Campbell looked between his boss and Izzy. The conflict was plain on his face, but Izzy knew what he had to do. He was too young to lose his job.

"Sorry, Chief," he said. "I can't let this continue. You'll have to release him."

"I'm sorry too, Officer Campbell. But I can't. I'm going after my daughter. And no one is going to stop me." Izzy pointed de la Rosa's gun right at Campbell's chest. "I want you to do as I say and cuff yourself to the ambulance."

"Don't let her do this!" yelled de la Rosa. "Don't let her leave!"

Izzy saw the uncertainty in Officer Campbell's eyes. "You

wouldn't really shoot me, would you, Chief?"

Lt. de la Rosa's gun was a revolver. Izzy thumbed the hammer back, cocking the gun. The barrel never moved from the patrolman's chest. "Try me."

What Officer Campbell was thinking, Izzy didn't know. Maybe about a wife or a girlfriend. Or maybe he had kids. Or maybe he simply didn't want to risk dying so young. Regardless of the reasons, when he removed his handcuffs and secured himself to the bar opposite de la Rosa, she breathed a sigh of relief. Shooting him had never really been an option.

"God damn it, Steve," said de la Rosa. "What are you doing?"

"Living," was his reply. Then he caught her eye—and gave her a half-smile that de la Rosa couldn't see. "Don't want any payback for the shit I gave her earlier."

Izzy lowered the gun and eased the hammer down. "Okay, take your handcuff key and toss it into the snow."

After Campbell had complied, she said, "Now your gun. Do the same thing. Toss it."

Campbell lifted his gun by two fingers and threw it into a snow drift.

Reaching into her pocket, Izzy removed her handcuff key. Without pausing she threw it into the distance, where it too disappeared in the snow. Next she approached both men and removed their phones and Campbell's mic from his uniform. Those also ended up in the snow.

"I'll see that you're fired for this," de la Rosa said as he struggled against the handcuff. "You're done, Morris."

Izzy thought back to the words Stanley had said to her: *What comes first for you? Cop? Wife? Or mother?*

"You may be right," she said. "But as long as I get my daughter back, I'll be happy doing anything where I don't have to deal with assholes like you."

That sent Lt. de la Rosa into another fit of spluttering expletives.

"Deke?" Izzy called out.

Deke Frenz had been watching silently from several paces away. "Ma'am?"

"Lt. de la Rosa is going to want you to release him. I don't want you to refuse, but I would appreciate it if it took you a while to find the keys."

Deke flashed a big smile. "Can't even remember where you threw 'em. Might take me a while to remember."

Izzy nodded, then gestured for her friends to join her. When she saw that Owens had grabbed the large, black Maglite she kept in the Explorer, she nodded at his resourcefulness. She ran to Campbell's patrol car and took his Maglite, then a handful of flares stored in the trunk. After all, what was a little theft after her string of felonies?

After slamming the trunk shut, she saw that her friends had gathered at the mouth of the trail. She hurried over to them.

"It's going to get dark soon," she said, handing each person a flare. "If something happens and we get separated, use the flare. It'll help the rest of us find you."

Each person silently accepted a flare.

"You're all good with this?" she asked. "No one has to follow me."

"I think you already know the answer to that one," said Gene.

Owens and Katie nodded their agreement.

She supposed she did. Giving them a grateful smile, she turned and walked up the trail.

It was time to find Webber for the last time.

PART THREE

ALL THAT
YOU
HOLD DEAR

Sgt. Bartholomew Owens pressed his back against the rough stone wall. The building protecting them was tall and broad, with a ceramic-tiled roof and a broken stub of a chimney. A wood slat gate, painted the same terracotta orange as the roof, had broken free of its latch, exposing the narrow Rue Principale that ran the length of Morville-les-Vic. A German half-track filled with Nazi soldiers rumbled down the road.

"They lied, you know," said Cpl. Allan Richmond. He hugged the wall next to Owens. Beside him, PFC Bucky Hatton crouched low, a Browning 1911 semiautomatic gripped tightly in his hand.

"Who?" asked Bart, glad to be out of the wind and rain, even if it was only for a short time.

"The assholes who said France was beautiful."

Bart grinned in spite of himself. The three had crawled through mud and rain and a constant barrage of shelling to reach the outskirts of the French town. Ironically, the storm had ended up helping them by cutting visibility down to a few dozen yards. After two hours, they were inside Morville-les-Vic, cold, slick with mud, and nearly exhausted.

"We need to move," said Bart. "Our targets are probably near the center of town, where they'll be the most heavily defended."

Bucky's eyes widened. "Just the three of us?"

Bart nodded. "The rest of the 761st will be in the town soon. That should keep the Germans busy. Let us slip in close without being seen."

"Then what?"

"Patton sent us to take the town, so we take it."

There was a pause before Al asked, "You really think they're here?"

"She is," Bart replied. "I'm not sure about Kölbe."

"Maybe this'll be my lucky day," Al said. "I'd love to get my hands on that sadistic little bastard."

"You've certainly messed up his plans often enough," said Bart. "In fact, I think he hates you more than me."

Bucky leaned in close. "Who you guys talkin' about?"

"Our mission objectives," said Al, then hooked a thumb at Bart.

"He'll handle the woman. You and I'll deal with Kölbe if we see him."

"You...*know* these people?" Bucky said, frowning.

"We've met," said Bart. "All right, let's go."

They hurried north and east, keeping the buildings between them and the road. Luckily, the town had a passion for those orange gates—they connected most of the structures running along Rue Principale and helped hide their movements.

The wind shifted. Rain spat at them, now mixed with sleet as evening approached and the temperature started to drop. When they passed a water barrel filled to overflowing, Bart ordered their canteens filled. It might take days to find their way back to Allied territory.

They'd passed two shorter fieldstone structures—one looked to be a grocer, the other a butcher, both with rear doors firmly locked—when they ran into their first problem: instead of consecutive buildings, a large grassy lot sat between them and their next cover. Tables and chairs had been moved into the space. Empty wine bottles were piled up in one corner. A large steel drum with a red swastika painted on it sat in the middle of the lot, pieces of scrap wood stacked next to it. There was no fire in the drum, not in this weather.

Two Germans officers sat at one of the tables with what looked like a map spread out between them. The taller one was tracing a line on it with his finger.

Beyond the lot stretched an open plaza with a large fountain in the center. At least five Panzer tanks sat on the cobblestones. Several half-tracks rolled by. Soldiers practically filled the square.

"There's one bright side to this," Al said in a low voice.

Bart gave him a questioning look.

Al grinned. "Look at all the friends we're about to make."

Bart watched as Bucky rolled his eyes, but the boy also visibly relaxed. That was one of the many gifts Allan Richmond brought to Bart's work: a sense of humor that Bart found so elusive in his own life. Too many miles and not enough smiles, the others would often joke with him. Maybe they were right.

"We need a diversion," Bart said, thinking aloud. "Something to pull those officers into the plaza. The longer we remain unseen, the less killing there will be."

"Sarge," whispered Bucky. "We in the middle of a war. We don't kill them, they gonna kill *us*."

"I know," said Bart. "Still, I'd like to avoid as many casualties—"

The back door of the butcher shop swung open. Out walked a German soldier, a stick of jerky in his hand. He couldn't have been more than sixteen, with blonde hair and guileless features. He was smiling as he chewed on his snack.

He must have felt secure this far into town; it took him a few seconds to register that he wasn't alone. When he noticed three Negros crouched near the corner of the building, a look of surprise slid across his face, and he swallowed.

"*Wie geht es Ihnen?*"

"*Wir wollen nicht, Sie zu verletzen,*" Bart replied, raising his hands.

Then the soldier saw their uniforms...and the pistol in Bucky's hand. He dropped the jerky and fumbled for his gun.

Bart shouted, "*Nicht!*" but he was too late. As the boy drew his weapon, Bucky Hatton closed the gap, shoved the barrel of his Browning into the kid's gut, and fired three times. The rounds blasted through the soldier, splattering blood across the stone wall behind him. The boy's eyes rolled back into his skull, and he crumpled to the ground.

Al said, "We got company."

Glancing over his shoulder, Bart saw the two German officers running toward them, weapons drawn.

"Into the store," Bart said. "Both of you. This needs to be quick and quiet, or we'll have the whole town after us." He slipped the kitbag off his shoulder and handed it to his friend. "You mind?"

Al took it and raced for the door. When he began dragging Bucky with him, the man tried to pull away. "What're you doing? He doesn't even have a gun!"

"He doesn't *need* one," Al said and threw the private through the open doorway. Then he darted inside and slammed the door shut.

The first officer rounded the corner. Bart punched him hard in the face. Stunned by the blow, the man jerked to a stop. Bart grabbed the gun and wrenched it up, breaking at least one of the man's fingers and freeing the pistol. He brought it close to his body, thumbed the release at the bottom of the grip, and the magazine dropped free. A quick rack of the slide and the remaining round flew from the chamber. He tossed the empty gun aside.

The other officer—the taller one, Bart saw—pushed past the first, his gun thrust out in front of him. Bart dropped and spun, driving the heel of his boot into the man's gut. The man grunted and doubled over. Bart shot to his feet and grabbed him. The first officer, having recovered from Bart's attack, joined the fight, swinging wildly with his fists.

Bart pivoted, yanking the gun-toting Nazi around with him. He clutched at the man's wrist, keeping the weapon pointed toward the sky. The unarmed officer pounded on Bart's back and head, but without the gun there was little real damage he could do.

As they grappled, Bart saw the other man's eyes grow wide, his nostrils flare. The pain he was feeling would only get worse.

"Lassen Sie das Gewehr fallen!" Bart yelled, ordering him to drop the gun.

The tall officer's lips peeled back, revealing uneven, yellowed teeth. *"Zur Hölle!"*

"Boy, have you got your directions mixed up," Bart muttered.

Pulling down on the gunman's hand, he stepped in with his left foot and swung his own body around until his back was firm against the man's chest. Still holding tight to the Nazi's wrist, Bart wrapped his left arm around until he held the man's arm between his right hand and left forearm. Then he brought his knee up, shattering the man's elbow. The gun fell from the officer's nerveless fingers.

Finally, the pain inflicted by Bart proved too much. The man issued another scream, collapsed to the ground, and lay still.

The other officer, seeing his buddy go down, turned to flee. Bart grabbed him from behind and bashed his head into the stone wall, knocking him out cold.

Pausing to catch his breath, Bart checked the plaza. No one seemed to have noticed their altercation. How much longer could his luck hold out?

He hurried over to the door. Locked. "Open up, Al," he said, pounding on the wood. "It's me."

When no one responded, Bart began to worry. He shouldered the door, then kicked it. Nothing. He'd had enough of this. Closing his eyes, he focused on the door, on the wood from which it was made. A seed of heaviness took root in his gut. He allowed it to grow until he thought the door was light enough. He kicked again. This time, the wood splintered around the lock and handle and the door swung open.

Inside, he found Bucky Hatton crumpled on the floor in front of a long serving counter. Blood oozed from a nasty head wound; more blood had pooled around him, mixing with the sawdust that covered the butcher shop's flooring. His eyes were closed, his breathing uneven.

There was no sign of Al Richmond.

Bart checked Bucky's pulse. Not good. He looked for something to staunch the blood flowing from the boy's head. Except for some scraps of jerky in a large glass jar—the label said it was horse, which explained why it'd been left behind—the store had been stripped of anything useful.

Bucky gasped, coughed, and fresh blood trickled from his mouth. His eyes fluttered open. When he saw his CO, his lips moved. Bart had to lean in to hear him.

"Soldiers, they was in here," he said, his voice wispy. "One took my gun. Another...hit me. They...they recognized the corporal. Took him." He coughed again. More blood, bright red. His young eyes grew shiny with tears. "My momma, she gonna be waiting for me...and when I don't...I don't—" His hand shot out and grabbed Bart's. "Oh no...!"

Bart held the boy's hand. "I'll find her," he said. "I'll find her, and I'll tell her. She'll know." Smiling through his own tears, he added, "You're a hero, son. Now close your eyes and rest. You've done enough."

The private's eyes slid shut. His chest rose, slow and shallow. And again, a few seconds later. Then, as he let slip his last breath in this world, he smiled faintly, almost sweetly, like a newborn held in the comfort of his mother's arms.

Robert "Bucky" Hatton had gone home.

Bart Owens allowed himself a few moments with the dead private. He would have to leave the boy here and hope someone from the 761st found him later. There wasn't time for anything else. He had to end this.

The Germans had recognized Al. Bart had to assume he'd also been identified. The word was out about them.

But why *capture* Al? Why not kill him outright? Or them both, for that matter? He could survive a lot, but some heavy shelling from those Panzers would blow him apart, and there was no recovering from that. It didn't make sense. She would want them both dead as quick as possible, wouldn't she? Unless—

Kölbe.

Bart's skin prickled. Kölbe despised Al, had ever since the incident in Prague's Jewish quarter years earlier. That encounter had left Al with a punctured lung, three fractured ribs, and a broken nose. Kölbe had barely made it out alive, not that he didn't deserve what he'd gotten. All those young boys, horribly disfigured by Kölbe but kept alive for days, sometimes weeks at a time so they could be the objects of his perverse desires.

But the greatest damage Al had done was to Kölbe's ego. Already a man of tenuous sanity, the humiliation he'd suffered at the hands of Al Richmond had cracked his mind. Since then, his focus had been on exacting his revenge on the man who had bested him.

Not good at all.

Bart rose to his feet. He gave Bucky Hatton a final look, then moved to the window.

Nothing had changed in the square, except now he could see a German officer striding toward the butcher shop. When the man got close enough, Bart opened the door.

The officer, a captain judging by the insignia on his jacket, came to a halt. He was older, perhaps in his late thirties, with dark hair and a face like a ferret. His nose even twitched as he leveled his gun at Bart.

"If you will come with me, please, *Herr* Owens," the officer said in passable English.

Bart hesitated. He could easily overpower the man and take his gun—but then what? Kill soldiers until he somehow found Al? No, they were just grunts following the orders of a paranoid madman and his cadre of the lunatics. Besides, if Kölbe wanted him so badly, who was he to disappoint?

"Very well," he said, gesturing with an open hand. "Lead the way."

"You will not cause trouble?"

Bart's lips spread into a humorless grin. "Not yet."

The Captain led him across the plaza, past the soldiers glancing curiously at them, and toward a cluster of buildings that Bart assumed housed the town's administrative offices. But before they got much closer, the man veered left into a narrow side street. Frowning, Bart followed.

There were no soldiers in this part of the city. Either someone felt this area was secure, or privacy was the chief consideration. Given the disturbing nature of Kölbe's activities, Bart was betting on the latter.

He was about to ask where they were going when the officer stopped and gestured with his gun.

Bart lifted his eyes. He stood in front a simple stone building, long and broad with two shorter structures flanking the far end. It had a gabled roof and tall arching windows. Behind it, he could see the tip of a bell tower rising over the rooftop. He recognized the design. Had seen it countless times throughout Europe.

He turned to the officer. "My friend's in there?"

The man nodded.

"And Kölbe?" Bart asked.

The officer blanched at the name but nodded again.

"Anyone else?"

This earned him a shrug, after which the man jabbed the gun into his ribs. "Inside."

"Ouch," Bart said, then drove an elbow into the Captain's chin, snapping his head back. He snatched the gun away and brought it down hard on the man's temple, knocking him to the ground, where he lay, unmoving, on the rain-slicked cobblestones. Bart removed the man's shoes, used the laces to bind the officer's hands behind his back. Next, he gagged the man with his own socks. Finally, he broke down the gun and threw the parts onto nearby rooftops.

He checked both ends of the street and didn't see anyone, but he did spot an alleyway. Grabbing the officer by the arms, he dragged him until they were deep in the gloom of the passage. He tossed a few scraps of garbage over the man, then made his way back to the mouth of the alleyway.

The street was still empty. He could hear voices, but they were off in the distance. And the sounds of battle were growing louder. Maybe the 761st was making progress. That brought a brief smile to his face. But now he needed to get Al, finish the mission, and get out.

Easing his way out of the alley, he hurried over to the church and slipped through the doors into the narthex. Here he expected to meet some resistance, but the small room was empty. There was another set of closed doors directly across from him, which he assumed led into the nave. He noticed that the stoups, the tiny basins set on either side of the entrance, which would normally contain holy water, were dry. Except the one on the left—it had a smear of crimson across the rough stone rim, as if someone had tried to dip bloody fingers into it.

Al was left-handed.

Bart stepped across to the closed doors. He couldn't hear any activity on the other side—no murmur of voices, no one milling about. Nothing. His gut tightened. He wanted more time to assess the situation, to know better what he was walking into, but he had been told Al was behind these doors. With Kölbe. Grasping the handle, fully expecting to walk into a platoon of German soldiers with their guns trained at him, he opened the door.

There were no soldiers. In fact, the pews had been removed and replaced with long tables, upon which sat stacks of paper, communication equipment, and several coffee cups, but no one manned the posts. Off to one side, a large map of France pinned to a corkboard showed the placement of the German forces, along with the supposed Allied locations.

But at the altar, where the crucifix would normally hang, there was an oversized portrait of Hitler, the frame draped with a German flag. And just below that—

Bart gasped. Oh dear Jesus, no!

The missing crucifix...it now stood before the altar, upside down, its upper end shoved into a broad metal stand, its base sharpened to a crude point. And Al Richmond, his friend and aide-de-camp, the man whose smile could put anyone at ease—Al had been impaled on the crucifix, his mouth stretched open by the pointed end of wood jutting up from his throat.

Although Al's eyes were open, bulging from their sockets and bloodshot from the unbelievable pressures generated by the shaft of wood going through his body, his friend was obviously, mercifully, dead.

A man stepped out from one of the chancel rooms next to the altar. Dressed in a black Gestapo uniform, the man had short brown hair and a hint of beard. He was smiling, though his eyes shone with hatred.

"Do you like my new sculpture?" Kölbe asked, his words heavy with a German accent. Gesturing to the grotesque display beside him, he said, "I'm thinking of calling it 'Ode to Futility.' No, wait. Maybe something shockingly simple, like 'Dead Negro.' Which one do you favor, Bartholomew?"

Bart ignored the man's taunts. The muscles of his jaw worked as he fought the urge to kill Kölbe where he stood. But he knew this wasn't over yet: Kölbe wouldn't risk facing him alone. There was a threat here he hadn't seen yet. And he knew who that threat would likely be.

"He was a good man," said Bart evenly. "Nothing you can say or do will change that."

Kölbe's grin faded. "I create an amazing piece of work, and you can't even say something nice about it?"

"A three-year-old with pencil and paper would be more artistic. You're just crazy."

"This is brilliant." Kölbe pointed a finger at Bart's dead friend. "Stakes and saints! Don't you get it?"

"The symbolism isn't lost on me," Bart replied and began walking up the nave toward Kölbe. He could now hear something, a faint hiss, but he couldn't make out where it was coming from. "It's crude. And cruel. And, truthfully, not very accurate."

Kölbe's pale cheeks flamed with anger. "Wait until the world sees what I do with *your* body, old man." His eyes flicked to a spot above Bart's head. "I will be heralded as the greatest artist who ever lived."

Bart stopped and spun around. There was a balcony! That was where she was hiding! Quickly, he searched the shadows above him, looking for a shape, some movement, but he could see nothing.

There was no one up there.

Turning to face Kölbe, he said, "I think you have a problem."

Kölbe blinked, then frowned. "That's not right." He glanced fearfully at Bart. "What did you—?"

"He didn't do anything," said a new voice. It sounded thin, tinny, as if the words were spoken from a distance. "I simply decided to leave."

Kölbe's eyes darted to a piece of equipment on a table in front of him. It took Bart a moment to recognize it as a short-wave radio.

"Hello, my dear Bartholomew," the woman continued. Bart recognized the voice. He hadn't heard her in a long time. "I expect Kölbe finally understands the danger he is in."

Bart saw that she was right. Kölbe gaped at the radio. The man was trembling, his eyes wide with fear.

"No, this isn't right! You promised! You said I would get to help you kill him!"

"You've lost your touch, Kölbe," her disembodied voice said through the hissing static of the radio. "I find myself having to fix more and more of your mistakes. I don't have time for that."

"But—but you—" Kölbe backed away from Bart. "I still have work to do!"

"I have to go now," she said. "He's all yours, Bartholomew. Do with him as you wish."

"No—wait!" Kölbe yelled, but he was too late. The static hiss was gone. And so was she.

Bart advanced on Kölbe.

"You can't do this!" Kölbe pleaded. "I know who you are! I know *what* you are! You're not allowed to kill!"

"I *prefer* not to," Bart said as he came up next to Kölbe. The other man had backed himself up against the altar. He had no room to maneuver. "But in some cases, it's unavoidable."

As Bart reached up and grasped his head, Kölbe flinched. "Won't you at least grant me absolution?"

"I think not," Bart said, then snapped Kölbe's neck quickly, cleanly. The man's lifeless body fell to the floor. "You will have to answer for what you have done. May God have mercy on your soul."

He paused. "And mine."

It was a bitter victory, one that left the taste of ashes in his mouth. He had been outmaneuvered, had acted as an assassin on *her* behalf. In the end, all she'd lost was her acolyte.

He had lost so much more.

His eyes strayed to the map of France. Maybe there *was* a way to end this on a positive note. He knew Divisional HQ would love to have the information on that map.

And then there was the communication equipment. A false order sent out to the Germans that the Allies were also attacking from the other end of the city, and the Axis forces would be split. The 761st would stand a chance.

Bart turned to the body of his friend. He wanted to say goodbye to Al Richmond, but the words escaped him. So he bowed his head, said a quick prayer—and noticed something lying under the altar.

Reaching down, he grabbed it.

It was Dexter Grant's kit bag.

Bartholomew Owens slung it over his shoulder, and set about changing the tide of a war.

CHAPTER
32

Roughly thirty minutes into the woods, Webber called for a brief rest.

Evening was gathering. In the growing twilight the forest began to lose its definition. The towering pines marshaling in the distance became indistinct, their trunks dissolving into a dark, impenetrable wall surrounding them. Ordinary scrub bushes turned ugly and misshapen and threatening. There was no wind racing through the branches above them, no sounds of animals roaming the woods under the safety of the encroaching night. It was as if the forest had ceased to exist beyond what they could see.

Jack shifted Kevin in his arms. Despite the chase and the trek through the woods, his son had fallen fast asleep. "What do we do about Denny?"

"You heard the gunshots," Webber replied. "Idiot probably got himself killed. I just hope he took out the other guy first."

"So it's you, me, and Kevin."

"Isn't that the way it should be?"

Jack nodded. "Who is this person we're meeting? The one you were talking to on the phone?"

Webber grinned. "You'll find out soon enough."

"Still keeping secrets?"

"Everybody's got 'em," Webber said. "Now, you ready to press on?"

Jack nodded. "I feel like I could keep going all night."

Webber gave him a knowing look. "Not bad for an out-of-shape banker, huh?"

"What can I say? I feel great. Better than I've felt in my life."

"What about that cold you had?"

"Gone," Jack said. "Like it was never there. Why?"

"You're on your way to a better life, Jack," Webber said, clapping a hand on his back. "Let's head out. We still have a long walk ahead of us." Then he began trudging through the snow.

Jack's mouth twisted into an irritated frown as he fell in behind Webber.

As they plunged deeper into the forest, the trees grew taller, their boughs broader, and the choking groundcover grew scarcer. Travel became easier, and they were able to put some precious distance between them and anyone who might be following.

By the time Jack stumbled into the small clearing, he was drenched in sweat.

It was almost fully dark. A bright wedge of moon barely crested the treetops, bathing the glade in a thin, sterile light. Jack could make out a steeply rising hill at the other end, the front concealed by shadows. He couldn't see any footsteps on the snow-covered ground.

"Good," Webber said. "Doesn't look like anyone's found this place. Come on, Jack."

They were halfway across the clearing when Webber stopped and turned to him. "See that wide crack in the hill? It goes back about ten feet into a small cave. I have some lanterns stored in there. You and Kevin go on. I'm going to stay out here and see if I can't keep anyone from following us."

Jack eyed the opening. "Is it safe in there? I don't want Kevin getting hurt."

"You may not like the view," Webber said, "but there's nothing in there that can hurt you."

"Where's your friend?"

Webber's eyes lost their focus. Then, abruptly, his focus returned and he glared at Kevin.

"I don't think...I can't—" Webber made helpless, agitated gestures with his hands. "Oh, just get in the damn cave," he finished, shoving Jack in the direction of the opening. "Shout if there's a problem."

Jack stumbled forward a few steps, then spun around, ready to confront Webber. But Kevin stirred and pulled the jacket more snugly around his small body. Swallowing his anger, Jack decided it was best to get his son out of the cold night air. He turned and started for the cave.

The entrance was an uneven break in the surface of the hill, more like a gaping wound than a natural occurrence, as if something big had torn a hole into the ground. Maybe a huge tree had toppled; the weight of the trunk would have ripped the large knot of roots out of the ground, along with an unbelievable amount of earth. Decades of weather could have washed away the dirt and rotted the tree down to dust, leaving behind nothing but the cave.

Jack shrugged. Whatever its origin, it offered shelter from the elements. Pulling Kevin tighter against his chest, he bent slightly and side-stepped his way into the opening.

Darkness engulfed them as they disappeared into the cave.

* * *

Nighttime had settled in. The sky above them was a deep black span dusted with stars. The moon, only three days past full, provided enough light to penetrate the darkness of the northern Michigan trees, limning them in a ghostly glow. As they followed Webber's trail, Izzy noticed that the forest was quiet—the only sounds she heard were their own crisp footfalls in the snow.

Bart Owens had taken the lead, as he'd evidently had some experience with tracking in his long past. Both Maglites were on, their bright beams cutting through the night, allowing them to see the trail.

Owens raised his hand and Izzy stopped. Katie and Gene, who had been following behind her, also halted. The old man stood still, his head cocked, as if he were listening for something. He remained that way for several seconds. Then he turned to regard her and the others.

"This is too easy," he said. "Darryl didn't even try to hide his tracks."

Izzy ran her light over the footprints. "Maybe he was hoping the snow would do the job for him."

"Possibly," Owens said. "But that leaves too much to chance."

"What choice did he have?" said Gene. "Unless he can fly, tracks were inevitable."

"I know. But my concern is that he didn't even try. Like he wasn't concerned with being followed."

"Speaking of pursuit" Izzy said with a glance behind her. "We need to push on. No telling when de la Rosa will start chasing us." She turned back to Owens. "So if he's not worried about being followed, either he plans to be away from this area quickly, or he has a way to stop anyone who might get past Denny."

"Or both," added Katie quietly.

Owens nodded. "Or both."

Izzy thought about that for a moment. "We don't have a choice either. We need to find Webber and hope we can handle whatever he throws at us. Since the path is obvious, I'll take the lead." She looked to Owens. "Stay near Katie and keep her safe."

"What's your plan for when we catch up with him?" asked Gene.

"My first priority is Kevin," Izzy said. "After that, I'd like to take Webber and Jack alive—one of them knows where Natalie is. But if it does come down to us or them, we take them out."

"Take them out with what?" Gene said. He held out his hand, one finger pointed forward, his thumb aimed at the stars. "My finger's out of bullets."

"Very funny," said Izzy. "There should only be the two of them. Webber's the dangerous one. Jack's just an asshole with delusions of grandeur. I don't think he even knows how to fire a gun. Owens and I will handle the situation." She looked at Gene. "Remember, you're a civilian. You shouldn't even be here. But after what you've both been through"— her eyes darted over to Katie—"I feel we need to finish this together. Don't make it harder for me by asking for a gun. That would make you dangerous *and* a target. You've already been shot once." Then she smiled and nodded to Owens. "Who do you think you are? Him?"

"Fine," said Gene. "Maybe I'll give them my best Chicago glare. It's been known to frighten very old ladies and make small dogs wet themselves." Then he screwed his face into a knot and brought up his hands to claw at the air.

Izzy stifled a laugh. "Okay, we need to get moving." She looked at Owens. "Is there anything else we need to know?"

"Just one thing," he said. "Don't believe everything you see. Darryl is a magician of sorts. He can create...let's call them hallucinations. They look very realistic and very frightening. I don't know if he'll try it, though. It would leave him physically weakened."

Gene lowered his hands, his expression having lost all its humor. "Well, that was certainly a mood-killer. I bet you're a riot at parties, too."

"Gene, please," said Izzy. To Owens, she asked, "Is there anything we can do about it?"

Owens shook his head. "I don't think so, but it won't work on me. So if I see any of you freeze up, I'll try to break his concentration."

"This is too bizarre for words," said Izzy. "If there's nothing else?"

"I think we've got it covered," said Owens.

Izzy tightened her grip on the Maglite.

"Okay, let's go."

They had followed Webber and Jack's trail for about two hundred feet when Owens shouted, "Get down!"

Izzy spun around. In the Maglite's beam, she glimpsed Owens toss Katie to one side and drop to the ground. Gene backed away from the old man, tripped, and fell hard. Above his prone body, a shape burst from the darkness, charging the spot where Katie had been. Owens shifted and drove his right fist up hard and fast.

A piercing howl—the creature, the one that had attacked them earlier! How had it gotten so close without her hearing it?

"No one move," Izzy called out as she scrambled to find the creature, the barrel of her gun following the Maglite's narrow beam as it searched the darkness.

Owens also searched for the thing, his flashlight slicing through the night.

"Where is it?" she yelled. "I can't—"

She heard movement behind her. Twisting, she brought her gun up and fired. The creature cried out in pain. In the muzzle's flash, she glimpsed its broad head just before it slammed into her shoulder, sending her flying backward into the snow. She managed to hold onto the gun, but her flashlight went spinning into the night and landed in a snowdrift, its light smothered as completely as if someone had blown out a candle.

Owens was at her side in an instant, his flashlight trained on the creature.

Izzy fired again, hitting it near the top of its right rear flank. The creature crumpled to the ground. Struggled to its feet. Lurched after Katie.

Izzy tried to rise but cried out when pain tore through her ankle.

"Damn it," she swore. "I can't—hurry, go! Don't let it get her."

Owens didn't pause to answer. He bolted after Katie, his legs pumping as he dodged trees with agility that belied his age. Izzy heard him calling after Katie, telling her to keep moving.

Soon he disappeared behind a copse of trees, and his flashlight winked out of sight.

* * *

Katie bolted through the woods, her heart hammering against her chest wall.

The creature was behind her. She could hear its heavy footfalls, the shattering branches as it broke through small trees, the thud of its body slamming into larger ones. It was closing in; she could almost feel its hot breath on her neck. But she couldn't run any faster. The trees were too close. They leapt at her from the darkness.

More distant still, she could hear Mr. Owens calling to her. He wanted to save her, but he sounded too far away. He would never make it in time.

She was going to die.

A large tree materialized before her, blocking her way. She barely avoided a collision, cut right, hoping a change in direction might create more distance between her and the creature.

No, she thought angrily. She wasn't going to die out here in the woods. She wasn't going to give up. Allow herself be killed. She wasn't like her father.

She dodged right again, leapt over a fallen pine. Now she was heading back the way she'd come. Toward Mr. Owens. She heard him calling to her.

"Here!" she shouted. "I'm right here!"

Another tree punched up from the darkness. She dodged left, but a thick, low-hanging branch clipped the side of her head. Platinum streaks of pain flashed behind her eyes, and she fell to the ground.

Through the black night, the creature charged relentlessly toward her. She flipped onto her back and began scrambling backward.

"No," she cried. "Oh God, no."

The creature was almost upon her now. She could make out its shape rushing at her, blotting out what little of the forest she could see. Its snarls scraped at her nerves.

"I'm sorry," she whispered, though she wasn't sure who she was apologizing to. Maybe it was to her parents for failing to be better than them; or maybe to herself, for simply failing.

She heard footsteps behind her. A bright light flashed into the creature's eyes. It howled in pain and vanished, escaping into the relative safety of the darkness.

Bart Owens stepped between her and the monster. He searched for the creature with his Maglite.

"I don't see it," he said.

"We should be able to hear it," Katie said. "It made enough noise chasing me."

Bart held a hand out to help her up. "Come on, let's get back to Izzy and Gene. Maybe it went back for them."

Grateful to be alive, she reached for his hand.

Something exploded from the darkness and slammed into Mr. Owens. The flashlight flew from his hand, hurtling through the air to smash against a tree. The glass shattered, the bulb broke.

They were plunged back into darkness.

CHAPTER
33

In the faint glow of the moon, Katie saw two indistinct shapes flailing about on a carpet of snow. Then she heard the odd howl of the creature as it struggled with Mr. Owens.

She scrambled to her feet. Her hand closed on something waxy and cylindrical and picked it up. Standing in the darkness with the sounds of fighting going on nearby, desperate to do something to help the old man, she ran her hands over what she'd found.

The flare Izzy had given her. It must have fallen out of her pocket.

"Katie!" he yelled from the ground. "Get out of here!"

She yanked the flare's cap off. Gripping it tightly in her hand, she ran it across the flare's striking surface.

Nothing.

The creature started whimpering like a wounded animal.

She heard a muffled groan, and Mr. Owens called out, "What are you doing? Run!"

No, she thought. Not this time.

She rubbed the cap hard across the top of the flare and was rewarded with a small shower of sparks, but it didn't ignite.

"Come on," she muttered.

She grated the cap across the surface. More sparks—that quickly died out.

"Katie!" Mr. Owens pleaded, then fell silent as the sounds of fighting intensified.

Again she struck the cap against the surface, and again. White sparks shot into the night.

"Light," she said, scraping the cap as hard as she could across the top of the flare.

Nothing.

"Light, damn you!" she yelled and tried again.

Sparks flashed and then faded.

With tears streaming down her cheeks, she screamed, "Light, you useless piece of SHIT!" and slammed her hand down onto the top of the flare. Sparks flew, sputtered, then burst into bright red light as the flare ignited.

Katie spun around. The flare bathed the area in a crimson glow.

Mr. Owens was on the ground with the creature struggling atop him. He had one arm braced across the thing's throat, keeping its cruel teeth away from his face. The other hand gripped the coarse fur at the back of its neck. His legs were wrapped around its body.

The creature's face was a snarling mask of pain and saliva. Its razor-sharp claws had dug deep grooves into the ground on either side of the old man—he was holding the creature so close it couldn't get a clean swipe at him.

The scene pierced Kate's mind. In the space between one heartbeat and the next, she saw her mother lying on the ground, not the old man, with that hideous monster raking her flesh away in bloody strips, robbing Katie of her mother, leaving her alone in the world, and destroying the last hope she'd held of redeeming the woman who had, deep down, truly loved her.

And in that moment, Katie Bethel changed. She could almost imagine a switch flipping inside her.

Raising the flare high, she shouted, "Burn, you ugly son of a bitch!"

She charged the creature. It swiveled its head toward her, extending its neck to snap at her.

But Katie was faster. With a cry of rage, she plunged the lit end of the flare deep into one of the creature's eyes. The orb burst in a spray of wet, warm fluid.

The creature shrieked and jerked its head back. Caught up in the flux of her emotions, Katie kept hold of the flare; it slipped free of the thing's eye socket, the light now extinguished by thick gore.

From the sounds it made, the creature was in unbearable agony. Owens had been escalating the pain it felt by the second. Now its eye was destroyed, the socket a burned-out crater. It all proved too much.

With a guttural snarl and a clumsy bite at the old man's face, the creature broke free and retreated into the darkness.

After dropping the flare, Katie fell to her knee next to Owens. She reached out, found his arm, followed it down until she held his hand.

His flesh felt cool and dry despite his efforts against the creature.

"Are you okay?" Her voice was loud in the sudden silence. "Mr. Owens, please. Say something."

His hand moved, his fingers closed over hers. "Didn't anyone," he said gruffly, "every teach you to listen to your elders?"

She grinned in relief, though in the near dark she doubted he could see it. "How long has it been since you've dealt with a teenager? We don't listen to anyone."

"Well, you're going to listen *now*. Help me up. We've got to get out of here before that thing returns."

"You're not hurt?"

"Not anything a little time won't fix. Come on, let's get moving."

She helped him to his feet. "Where to?"

"Anywhere but here," he said and led her into the dark woods.

They had gone what seemed like several hundred feet, moving as silently as possible and listening for sounds of pursuit, when Owens stopped. "This is far enough."

Katie had no idea where they were. The forest looked much the same in the day. At night, it was worse: visibility was down to a few feet, and any landmarks disappeared as soon as they moved. Unless Mr. Owens could see in the dark, they were seriously screwed.

"We need to find Nat's mom and Mr. Vincent," she said. "That thing's still out there."

Mr. Owens' voice floated out of the darkness. "They should be all right for the moment. You hurt the creature badly. Unless Darryl's control over it is stronger than I suspect, it's probably off nursing its wounds."

"'Suspect,'" Katie said, angry at the old man's words. "'Suspect.' That's what you're hanging our friends' lives on?"

Owens didn't say anything for a moment. She could feel him staring at her. Then, in a voice so low she could barely hear him: "You want to tell me what's wrong?"

She struggled for words. Her nerves were wound so tight, they hummed. "I just stuck a flare in the eye of something that shouldn't exist!"

"Katie—"

"In the last three days," she continued, the words spilling from her along with a torrent of emotions, "I've been shot at, chased by a monster, and confronted by people with powers you only see in movies. I watched a man I respect try to kill you, my boyfriend got the shit beat out of him, and my best friend is still missing." She shook her head. "And you want to know 'what's wrong'?"

"I understand it's been—"

"No, you *don't* understand. I lost my father, and now my mother's dead." Her eyes felt hot with tears. "I don't have anyone left in my life. I'm alone."

She felt Owens grip her shoulders, gently but firmly. It was something she would expect a father to do, but she'd rarely experienced that. Her father had decided death was a better alternative than staying with his daughter.

"No, you're not," he said. "You never were, and you never will be. Remember what we talked about?"

Last night, when she had sat alone with him in the police station, believing he had given up on his life, they had discussed her father. She remembered the conversation. Owens had surprised her. He'd spoken passionately about the sanctity of life, how each person was precious beyond measure, and that despite what her dad had done, he was still loved. And she was, too.

And then, as they'd sat there talking, he had healed. Or, she thought, he'd *been* healed. But that would mean....

"Something happened to *you*, didn't it?"

His dark shape grew still. "What do you mean?"

Katie pulled her jacket more tightly around her. "You can inflict pain just by touching someone. You recover from injuries that would kill normal people. And then there's your age. I'm not stupid. You can't have been born this way. You were changed somehow, made into who you are."

"You don't—"

"Which means other people can be changed. Am I right?"

Owens was quiet for a moment. "So that's it," he said, releasing her. "You would give up all that you hold dear, just to be like me."

"You really think I can go back to my old life? Forget everything I've seen? Walk around school pretending there are no monsters or magical old men? Live in a house filled with painful memories and little else?" Bitterness flowed through her veins like molten copper. "I have nothing left that's dear to me. I have nothing left to hope for."

"This existence isn't the answer."

"Why not? Because I'm a kid?"

"No," he said, not unkindly. "Because what you're asking is impossible."

"I don't believe you. Whatever machine or drug made you can do the same for me."

"It doesn't work that way."

"You're lying!"

"Katie, listen to me—"

"Don't do this. Don't turn me away, too." She lifted her eyes to where she thought his would be. "Don't leave me without hope."

Owens fell silent. After several seconds, he spoke. "There's something you need to understand. I was there, Katie. When the plague killed half of Europe, and when men like da Vinci and Galileo emerged from the ashes to change the world. Later, I witnessed the crushing poverty that ignited the French Revolution. What happened to me happened a long time ago. There was no drug. No machine. I'm sorry."

Katie wanted to shout, to accuse him again of lying; that his claim of being centuries old was another diversion. But she didn't—he sounded too sure of himself.

"Then how did you...?"

"Get this way? Some secrets are held closer to the heart than others. That's one of them."

Katie pressed her lips together. One door had closed on her. She tried another.

"Take me with you, then," she said. "Let me be your Webber. Let me help you."

"No," Owens said flatly. "I told you, I won't risk anyone's life. You saw what happened back at the police station. How long do you think you could survive that?"

"I have. *Twice.*"

"It's too dangerous. I won't have it."

"These people came into my town, into my *life*, and took away the only thing I had left. If we don't stop them, they'll do it again and again. And then one day, some other kid will end up like me. I don't want to see that happen."

"This isn't your fight."

"Webber made it my fight when he murdered my mother. Face it—I'm part of your world now. Take me with you."

"So it's about revenge. You want to strike back at the people who hurt you."

"Partly," she said, though the admission made her feel cheapened somehow. Payback wasn't going to return her mother. And it was a sentiment she thought her father might have embraced. "Mostly it's about doing the right thing, about making a difference. One day, I want to be able to look back on my life and feel proud about what I'd done. Is that so wrong?"

"No, it isn't," he said. "Look, you don't understand. A man once died horribly because of me—because of his association with me. After that, I vowed I'd never put someone in such a dangerous position again. What you're asking for is a death sentence."

"You don't know that," she returned. "And besides, it's still my choice. If I want to do some good in the world, then I will. With or without you."

Owens didn't respond. He stood in the darkness, and Katie could almost hear him thinking. Finally, he spoke.

"Selflessness is one of man's greatest virtues. Or in this case, woman's. Let's hope you live long enough to make a difference."

Katie waited for him to continue. When he didn't, she said, "Wait, does that mean—?"

"No promises. We still have to live through this" His dark from shifted. "I don't see any flares. We need to find the others."

"Lead the way," she said with a grin, and followed him into the darkness.

CHAPTER
34

"Izzy," whispered Gene. "Can you hear me? Are you okay?"

Out of the black void he heard a low groan, and he began crawling in that direction. Snow leeched the warmth from his hands, making them ache.

"Izzy!"

"Here," she said, her voice weak.

"Where, damn it?"

"Use a flare."

Gene grabbed the one in his pocket and soon had it glowing. It threw off enough light that he could see Izzy getting to her feet. He hurried over to her. "Are you hurt?"

She shook her head. "Nothing's broken, but I twisted my ankle. And I'm sore as hell. That thing hits like it's made out of concrete."

"Tell me about it. Can you walk?"

"I think so. Owens and Katie—?"

"That way," Gene said, pointing with the flare.

"My flashlight?"

He shook his head.

"Doesn't matter," she said. "I've got two more flares. Let's go."

From deep in the woods, a wretched howl ripped through the night.

"Sounds like Owens is doing his thing," he said.

"Come on," Izzy said and set off, following the old man's tracks through the snow. With her injured ankle, she had to lean on Gene, half-limping, half-jogging alongside him.

"Those cops you cuffed to the ambulance," he said. "Think they might be able to help us?"

"Frenz will take his time freeing them. Besides, as soon as de la Rosa shows up, he'll arrest me." She put too much weight on her ankle and winced. "That'll be the extent of his help."

"Can he do that? Arrest you?"

"Assault. Assault with a deadly weapon. Obstruction. And those are just for starters."

"What does that mean for your job?"

Izzy snorted. "I don't suppose you have an opening for a waitress?"

Gene's pulse quickened at the thought of Izzy working at the Lula, at being able to see her each day. There could be worse things in his world.

"Look," she said, pointing.

Gene brought the flare low. The snow had been flattened, the tracks obliterated. Izzy stepped into the middle of the disturbance and crouched low, running her hand over the ground. "The snow's uneven. See how it's pushed up in places, like someone was rolled or shoved?" She paused for a moment. "I think this is where Owens caught up with Katie and the creature."

He stepped around Izzy, swinging the flare in a wide arc. Trampled snow packed the ground like a second skin. "So where are they?"

"Good question." Izzy stood. "Since they're not here, I can only hope—wait, stop."

He froze. "What?"

She took several limping steps forward. "I need more light."

He hurried to her side. The flare's glow revealed two deep channels dug into the earth. They were about four inches deep, four feet long and roughly two feet apart. Clumps of dirt and dead leaves littered the ground.

Izzy bent down and pulled something out of the snow. It was a flare. One end was blackened and covered with some kind of fluid or gel.

"What is that stuff?" he asked.

Izzy shook her head. "Don't know," she said, then tossed it aside. "Come on."

They began pacing the area, looking for tracks that led away and not in. Whatever had happened here had been frantic; they found several trails that ran around trees or changed directions. One ended at another flattened area of snow, only to lead back to where they'd found the flare.

He and Izzy were getting ready to follow another trail when she put a hand on his arm, stopping him.

"What?" he said.

"Over there." She gestured off to his left. "I think I see a light."

Gene stared into the darkness. "I don't see anything."

"Here, give me the flare."

He handed it over. Then she turned her back to him, blocking its glow. "Now look."

The darkness became deeper. It took a few moments for his eyes adjust. Then he saw it.

"Yeah, it's faint—really faint. And white, not red."

Izzy returned his flare. "That's our destination."

"Owens?"

"He's got a flashlight."

"But the light's so still. If he was walking around, it'd be moving."

She nodded. "I know. It could also be Webber."

"Still want to head that way?"

"What other choice do we have?"

Gene gave her that lop-sided grin. "All right, then. I've got your back."

"Yes, you do," she said, returning his smile.

Her expression made him pause. "Something else?"

She reached up and touched his bandage. "You know, it's not often a guy gets shot for a girl."

"Izzy—" He wasn't sure he could get the right words out, or even what the right words were.

Her hand moved to the back of his neck, and she pulled his face down to meet hers. When their lips touched, it was soft and sweet. He hesitated, then slid his arms around her, drew her in tight and kissed her back. He wanted this moment to last forever.

The kiss ended too soon, and Izzy leaned her head on his shoulder. "Thank you for everything."

"Anytime," he said, reluctantly letting her go.

"Let's check that light out," Izzy said and walked away.

Gene set off after her.

Gene crept through the woods, shadowing Izzy's footsteps, the darkness once again concealing their movements. They had decided to extinguish the flare. The glow would draw the attention of anyone nearby, and while they wanted to find Owens and Katie, Webber and Jack were just as likely to see it. Besides, if that white light *was* Webber, then walking up blazing like the Statue of Liberty could get them killed.

Izzy halted. Gene took two steps and came to a stop next to her. When she brought her head close and spoke, her breath warmed his cheek. He fought the urge to kiss her again.

"There's a clearing up ahead," she said. "The light's coming from there. It's too bright to be a flashlight. I guess that means we found Webber and Jack." She paused. "What're they doing out here?"

"Could be some kind of safe house, a place where they can hide out for a while."

"That'd make sense—if they'd done a better job at covering their tracks. They didn't care who followed them." She stared at the light for a moment. "I don't think they're hiding."

"Then there must've been something out here Webber needed to pick up. Something he couldn't afford to leave behind. And now his plans are all screwed up. Score one for the good guys."

"Maybe not," Izzy cautioned. "A cornered animal will fight more fiercely than a rabid one."

"So how do we handle this?"

"*We* don't," she answered. "*I* do."

"No," Gene said. "We're doing this together."

"It's not up for a vote."

"I'm not going to—" He realized his voice was climbing and lowered it to an urgent whisper. "I'm not going to stand by and watch while you risk your life!"

"It's my job."

"You're not facing this alone. So unless you plan on shooting me, you may as well accept it."

"Why are you being so stubborn?"

"The same could be said for you."

"You're not coming."

"Yes I—"

She stiffened, and began making small, terrified gasps.

"Izzy, what's the—?"

Something hard jabbed him in the shoulder.

"You should learn to keep your voice down," Webber said from the shadows.

Before Gene could react, his head exploded in pain and he felt himself falling to the cold ground.

* * *

The old man stood at the edge of the clearing. He and Katie had spotted a faint white light and had followed it here.

Across the glade, the earth rose steeply to form a small hill. Snow covered the ground, reflecting the dim moonlight; brighter light spilled from an opening in the hillside.

Darryl Webber knelt a few feet from the opening. He was working on something near the ground, his shoulders hunched and his arms flexing. Whatever he was doing, he must have finished. He stood and looked to his right.

Bart followed his gaze. At first he wasn't sure what he was seeing. It looked like Webber had trussed up a dead deer and hung it from a tree branch. Then he peered closer. No, it wasn't a deer. He could make out arms hanging down, fingertips grazing the snow-covered ground. The shape was tall and broad. It wasn't a woman.

Webber had strung up a man.

The figure coughed weakly and groaned.

Bart stiffened. It was Gene.

Next to him, Katie drew in a sharp breath.

"No," he whispered. "Say *nothing*. Stay here until I call for you."

Then he entered the field, and, with a raised voice, called out to Webber. "Remember how you failed in Denver? I don't see this ending any better. You may even end up with more than a scar."

Webber spun around, his face hidden by shadows. "Ah, there you are." The words were raspy, as if they barely had the strength to scrape past his vocal chords. "Thought you'd gotten lost."

"You sound tired. Long day?"

"Fuck you."

"Be nice," Bart said. He stuffed his hands into his pockets and took a casual half-step forward. "What are you doing out here? It's risky, especially since you've already got the boy."

"One man's risk is another man's reward. But you're already familiar with that concept. Or are you so old you've forgotten?"

"Bright are the paths of my past." A quick shrug and another half-step. "My memories are writ in blood and pain. I'm not allowed to forget."

"Oh, stop it," said Webber. "That highbrow shit gets under my skin."

Bart nodded. "I remember."

"And you, old man? You know what the boy can do. I'm surprised *you'd* take the risk of coming this close."

Nod and step. "Yet here we are, both fighting over him. Here's a novel idea: why not let him decide his own fate?"

"You know I can't do that."

"This is about your fate, too," Bart said, taking another step.

Webber reached a hand into his pocket and removed a small, white knife. He pointed it at Bart. "There was a lesson my sister learned from you. I swear it was the only time you made any sense. Care to guess which one it was?"

"Your sister—"

"'The more power you're given, the less freedom you really have'."

"—would never approve of what you're doing."

"So according to your own profound wisdom, this boy has no freedom!"

"That's not exactly what I said. I told Jesse that the more power someone is given, the more others will expect of him. It has to do with responsibility, not freedom. Power isn't limiting. It simply makes the consequences of your choices more significant."

He risked another step forward.

Webber crouched down and put the knife to Gene's throat. "Keep your distance, old man."

"More killing? Didn't you learn anything from me?"

"You never stop, do you?"

"What you've done can be undone. All of it. Let this be your first step."

"And give up everything I have?"

"What—lies and gimmicks? Smoke and mirrors?"

"Power, Bartholomew. Something you never offered."

"Jesse never needed power."

"Stop it."

"She'd weep at what you've become."

"Shut up!"

"She never stopped loving you."

"Quit talking about my sister!"

Webber gripped Gene's hair and bent his head back. "Let's see how you deal with choices," he said. "You can save him, or you can save the cop. But you won't be able to save both."

"No!" Bart shouted. "Don't!"

Smiling, Webber drew the knife across Gene's throat. The skin split open and blood began to spill down his face.

Then Webber sprinted into the cave.

CHAPTER
35

Izzy pried open her eyes.

Cold light surrounded her. She was lying on her side, facing an uneven dirt wall that rose toward her at a sharp angle. Her arms were wrenched behind her back and bound at the wrists. Looking down, she saw her legs bound at the ankles with duct tape. Her head pounded thickly. A stench assaulted her nostrils, bringing tears to her eyes.

She tried to blink away the confusion. What happened? She'd been talking to Gene, and then—

What?

Determined, she pushed past the pain and forced herself to remember. Yes, she'd been talking to Gene, and then the woods had just *disappeared*. She'd found herself lost in a maze of obsidian tunnels veined in fire. Nightmare creatures, wrecked and wretched, had chased her and she'd fled, hurtling down dark passages. Propelled by her fear, she'd run, turning and turning.

Then pain. Pain—and nothing else until she opened her eyes.

Owens's words came back to her. *Don't believe everything you see. Darryl is a magician of sorts. He can create hallucinations.*

So, Webber had found them. But then, where was Gene?

And where was she?

Izzy opened her eyes again. The dirt wall hinted that she had been taken from the woods. But how long had she been out? Long enough to be taken out of the forest entirely?

Only one way to find out.

Gingerly, she rolled onto her back. Pain swept down from her throbbing head, and she groaned.

"Ah. Finally awake."

Izzy turned toward the voice, but whoever had spoken was hidden behind the bright glare of a pair of Coleman camping lanterns sitting on the ground within inches of her face.

"Who—?" Izzy croaked, then licked her lips. "Who's there?"

From behind the curtain of light stepped Jack Sallinen. "Surprise, you miserable bitch." His voice had an odd, echoing quality.

She saw movement and barely had time to roll away before Jack's kick landed across the base of her spine. The blow sent intense pain coursing through her body. Not wanting to give Jack any satisfaction, she locked a scream behind clenched teeth.

There was a rustle of fabric and then Jack's hand gripped her chin, pulling her head around. He had crouched down with one arm resting across his knees. He was smiling.

"You really thought you could beat me? A nosy, Be Nothing cunt like you?"

Ignoring the pain, Izzy shook her head free. "Where's Gene?"

"Always concerned with the little guy, aren't you?" His grin fading, Jack unzipped her coat and spread it open. His eyes caressed her body. There was a hunger in them that sent icy shivers along her spine. "Never concerned with what's important. Never concerned with *who's* important."

"Jack?" When he didn't look at her, she repeated his name until he met her gaze. "What happened to Gene?"

Panting, Jack leaned in close to her. "Why, *he's* the Tar Baby now, I expect," he said. "Bait for Little Black Sambo."

What? They actually *wanted* Owens here? This was a trap for *him*?

"You've lost, Morris," Jack continued. His hand snaked out and groped her breast. "And you're going to lose so much more."

Disgust filled her. She tried to swing her legs around to defend herself, but Jack had wedged himself close, cutting off her angle. Falling to his knees, he used his other hand to pin her shoulder to the dirt. Then he swung a leg over her so that he was straddling her hips. He looked down at her, helpless under his bulk, his eyes gleaming with lust.

"It's time I knocked you down a couple pegs," he said, his hand kneading her breast. She could feel his rising excitement and wanted to vomit. "Or maybe I should knock you up." His lip curled into a sneer. "You know, since you're childless and all."

Izzy stiffened. "That's a lie."

Jack's hand left her breast and started fumbling with his belt buckle. "The nose knows," he said. "I'm sure you've smelled her by now."

The stench—she recognized it now: the low, rancid stench of a rotting corpse. And according to Jack, it was the dead, decaying body of her daughter.

She'd found her baby but had been too late to save her.

As tears stood in her eyes, Izzy gathered her most precious memories of Natalie and forged them into a steel-hard shield for her shattered heart.

She would grieve later. For now, her thoughts turned from rescue—

—to revenge.

During her brief silence, Jack had managed to unclasp his belt buckle and was working at the button on his pants. With his hand shaking like a nervous teenager, he had lifted his hips to ease his access. His chin was tucked down against his chest as his focus shifted to the stubborn button.

Glancing past Jack, she saw a shadowy form shift behind the light.

"Hey, asshole," she said. "Are you really going to fuck me in front of your son?"

"Wha—?" Startled, Jack lifted his head, then sat back and threw a glance over his shoulder. When she felt his weight settle on her legs, she tensed her muscles and waited.

"Nice try," he said, turning back toward her. "He'd never understand anyway."

As soon as Jack's face came into range, Izzy used his weight on her legs as a fulcrum and shot up, driving her forehead into his mouth. The impact sent more pain crashing through her head—but this time she welcomed it, embraced it, used it to drive her further.

Without pausing, she reared back and lunged forward again. But Jack had brought up his hands to protect his face, and her head only struck a glancing blow to his cheek.

"You goddamn *BITCH!*" Jack roared, his hand covering his bleeding mouth.

Knowing her headshot ploy was spent, Izzy crunched down further and plowed the top of her head into Jack's chest, shoving him off balance.

The bastard did exactly what Izzy had hoped: he sat up, overcompensating to regain his balance. With his weight off her legs, she dug her heels into the dirt and pushed. Her body slid across the ground. When her knees were clear, she bent them, drawing her legs out from under him. Then she drove them forward, her heels slamming hard into his chin.

Jack's head snapped back and he collapsed onto the ground, unconscious.

She worked her way to a sitting position. Looking from above the lanterns' glare, she found herself in some sort of cave.

It wasn't very big, maybe six or seven feet high in the center and a little more than twice that in width. The rough walls sloped sharply, making it impossible for a person to stand upright along the periphery; from where she was sitting, her head came only a handspan or two from the ceiling. The entrance was a jagged crease barely wide enough for a person to slip through.

Kevin Sallinen stood across the narrow span of light, his vacant stare wandering the cave. A heavy jacket covered his thin shoulders; his cheeks were ruddy from the cold. Absently, he wiped his nose with the sleeve of his coat. The boy seemed unaware of what had just happened.

A few feet away from Kevin, a body lay on the ground. And next to it, something had been heaped into a broken pile and was covered with patchy frost.

Izzy's gaze was drawn to the body and she immediately recognized the billowy shirt, the jeans, the white Sketchers, though the clothes were stained with dirt and sweat and far too much blood. Wanting to deny what she was seeing but knowing she couldn't, Izzy took in every familiar feature and angle and nuance—all in one unkind, unforgiving moment.

She had found Natalie.

Her beautiful baby girl, cold and lifeless—

On the ground beside her, Jack moaned and began to stir. Opposite his father, Kevin maintained his peculiar emotional detachment, humming quietly to himself as he acknowledged no one and nothing.

No time. She had no time. Rolling onto her side, Izzy dropped her shoulders and tried to work her bound wrists down beneath her hips and bring her arms to her front.

"Shut up!"

Izzy froze. That was Webber's voice, coming from outside the cave. If he returned before she got free....

Desperate to escape, spurred on by her urgency, Izzy wrenched her shoulders lower and pulled her wrists forward. But whatever bound her arms—she had to believe it was the same duct tape that secured her ankles—had been fastened above her wrists; there wasn't enough room to clear her hips.

Coughing and sputtering, Jack lifted his head from the ground. The flesh around his hate-filled eyes was already bruising from the blow to his face.

"Bitch." He spat the word at her. "Miserable *fucking* bitch."

Nearby, Kevin began humming louder, a melody as disjointed as his personality.

Izzy gave Jack a sharp kick to keep him at bay. Then she brought her knees up hard against her chest as she jerked her arms down. With her muscles corded from the strain, she pushed, pushed, and was rewarded when the bound juncture of her arms slid under her left hip. Grinning, she heaved her arms forward—

—and found they wouldn't move.

"No," Izzy cried. "Please, no."

Outside the cave, Webber was yelling again.

"Quit talking about my sister!"

Jack reached out and grabbed her ankle. "Time's up, you whore."

Standing near Natalie's body, Kevin's humming grew until it couldn't be contained. His mouth opened and he let out a cracking, disharmonious wail.

With her heart laboring in her chest, Izzy tried to yank her feet free. But Jack clung stubbornly to her ankle.

"Come here, Morris." Jack wrapped his other hand around her leg. "We have unfinished business."

She ignored him, started to straighten her back. Wedged as they were under her hip, her arms were pulled tight, the duct tape that bound them digging sharply into her skin. Then she lifted her shoulders, straining, the pressure building as her muscles and tendons were stretched, drawn taut. The pain grew, a hot agony—hotter than grief, hotter than hate—building and building, until she cried out through clenched teeth and then—

Pop!

She'd dislocated her shoulder.

Two quick, hard kicks to Jack's face freed her from his grip. With another cry, Izzy wrenched her arms forward, the added space from her torn shoulder enough to bring her arms under her hips and in front of her.

Before Jack could react, Izzy brought her hands to her face and started tearing at the tape with her teeth. The movement made her injured shoulder burn like a piece of iron in a forge.

A new voice from outside—Bart Owens.

"No. Don't!"

She couldn't waste time wondering what was happening outside the cave. She needed her hands free. Her teeth worked at the tape.

Kevin's wordless singing scaled the cave's walls, climbing dirt and frost and despair.

With fresh blood dripping from his mouth, Jack surged to his feet and spit. A tooth fell to the dirt. From his jacket pocket, he withdrew his .38 and pointed it at her.

His hand wavered as he said, "To hell with Webber and his orders. I've had enough of you."

He brought his other hand around to steady the gun. But before he could squeeze the trigger, Webber charged into the cave. In his hand he held a small white knife, its blade coated with blood.

Seconds passed as Webber stared at Jack, then Izzy. Frowning, he threw an irritated glance at Kevin, whose voice continued to buffet their ears.

Turning his attention to Jack, Webber said, "Put away the gun."

"She broke my fucking teeth!" Jack shouted.

Izzy grabbed a frayed edge of duct tape with her teeth and yanked. The gray tape ripped like a noisy zipper and suddenly her hands were free.

"I'll do more than that," Webber warned, "if you don't put that gun down."

With a dislocated shoulder, her wounded arm hung uselessly at her side. So Izzy reached down with her good arm and tried to tear the tape around her ankles. But it was hard to find a purchase with one hand.

Eyes darting between Webber and Izzy, Jack seemed to weigh the consequences of his choices. He lowered the pistol.

"That's good," Webber said. "Very good."

Sweat slicked Izzy's skin. Her fingers kept slipping, couldn't find a firm grip on the tape.

Like some kind of insane opera singer, Kevin's melody was reaching a crescendo.

Webber turned to Izzy. "Oh, no you don't," he said, racing over to Izzy. Placing the knife at her throat, he added, "Hands off the tape."

Izzy ignored him. He was responsible for Natalie's death. She was going to kill him.

"Don't try my patience, Morris. I *will* cut your damn throat."

"Go ahead," Izzy choked out, her hand still working at the tape. "I can't hurt more than I already am."

"Crazy bitch, I tried to warn you—"

Webber didn't get a chance to finish his sentence. Three things happened at once.

Bart Owens emerged through the narrow crevasse, his face a mask of anger.

Jack pivoted and raised his gun, pointing it at Bart.

And Kevin Sallinen stopped singing. From his place near her dead daughter, he spoke. His voice was high and clear. Two syllables were all he uttered, but they chilled Izzy to her core.

"Uh-oh."

CHAPTER
36

"Watch out!" Izzy shouted to Owens. "It's—!"

"Jack," Webber yelled. "Kill him!"

Grinning, Jack fired, the sharp crack of the pistol turned explosively loud in the confined space of the cave. He wasn't used to gunfire; the barrel lifted and his shot went high and wide.

Owens rushed Jack. At the same time, Izzy tried to roll away from Webber, but he reached down, gripped her hair and jerked upward. She cried out. He yanked again, and she had little choice but to work her legs beneath her. She stood awkwardly, her balance hobbled by the duct tape binding her ankles.

Once she was on her feet, Webber dropped his knife, drew a gun from his waistband. He jammed the barrel hard against her temple.

Without hesitating, Izzy dropped her good hand to his groin, grabbed a fistful of denim and squeezed. When she felt his testicles come together in her clenched fist, she wrenched her hand around, bearing down with all the strength she could muster.

Webber paled, his Adam's apple stuttering as he tried to expel air. His knees buckled as if he'd been felled by a sledgehammer. In his pain, his hand clenched reflexively. The gun fired, but his collapse had pulled the barrel from Izzy's head. The round grazed her arm, tracing a line of fire along her flesh

Owens slammed his body into Jack's, his open hand smacking the man's arm upward. Another gunshot shattered the air. Dirt fell from the ceiling. Tiny fissures formed along the uneven surface.

Next to Jack, Kevin stuffed his fingers in his ears and began to cry.

Izzy was hindered by the duct tape around her ankles and couldn't prevent herself from tumbling to the ground with Webber. She landed on her injured shoulder, this time almost passing out from the pain.

Webber, writhing on the ground, clutched at his groin. In his agony, he'd dropped his gun. It lay on the ground on the other side of him, out of Izzy's reach.

Fighting back waves of nausea, Izzy watched as Jack tried to bring the gun down, tried to get a shot off at his attacker. Owens, his lips pulled back from his teeth, had grabbed hold of Jack's wrist, forced the man's arm down and sideways, away from his body. Both men shook from the effort, and Izzy wondered how Jack could continue wrestling with Owens. How he could endure the pain?

With a frustrated cry, Jack drove a heel into Owens's instep. Then he followed up with a stinging blow to the old man's jaw.

Owens grunted, shook his head. He drove a fist hard into the banker's gut, doubling the man over, then brought his knee up to connect with Jack's cheek.

All the while, the old man never let go of the arm holding the gun.

The blow hardly seemed to register with Jack—he fought with the frenzy of a rabid animal. Pulling himself upright, blood seeping from a cut on his lip, he latched onto Owens's throat with his hand. His eyes bulged as he tried to choke the life from his foe.

This has to be it, Izzy thought. There was no way Jack could take much more of the pain from Owens's defenses. Now she would get the opportunity she wanted, the opportunity she *needed*: the chance to put down Webber and Jack forever.

The chance to avenge her daughter's death.

Instead of releasing Owens, Jack levered his taller frame over the other man. Owens gripped Jack's wrist and twisted, trying to break the chokehold on his throat. Jack simply redoubled his efforts, his thick fingers pushing deep into the dark flesh of Owens's neck, closing off his airway, cutting off his circulation.

Stunned, Izzy couldn't understand how Jack could withstand his attack. The escalating agony coursing through Jack's body should have incapacitated him, but the bastard showed no signs that he felt *anything*.

She was going to be robbed of her vengeance.

Webber stirred next to her. Using her good arm, she drove an elbow into his jaw and felt his teeth come crashing together. He grabbed her bad arm and twisted—but she was so far gone into a fury that the pain barely registered.

Then they both lunged for the gun.

* * *

Thunder pealed through the dark clouds surrounding her.

Run. She needed to run. She *had* to run. Only she couldn't remember why. She ran anyway. She ran as if her life depended on it.

She felt no ground under her feet, could not discern a sky above. Nothing. Only clouds. Or perhaps it was fog. Thick whorls of putrid-smelling mist swirled about her, spinning wildly like a cyclone, making her dizzy, making her weak.

And cold. Oh God, she felt so *damn* cold, as if the marrow in her bones had frozen solid.

Still, she ran.

Memories threatened her, floating out from the grayish mist. But no, the memories *were* the mist. Nebulous vapors came together to form a monstrous head.

A face. Unfriendly, angry, screaming silently, its mouth gaping impossibly wide and dripping red saliva like arterial blood—Jimmy Cain.

Then he was gone, swallowed by the fog.

The head swirled, turning madly, and a second face emerged on the opposite side, wide and smiling, familiar wrinkles etched in the mist. It was her father.

She wanted to call out to him, but like Jimmy, he was consumed by the mist.

The head rolled and spun, a mad carnival ride, and another face surfaced, eyes wide with concern, panic flowing through the fluid swirls of fog. Her mother's searching face.

The head pulsed and her mother's face was gone, dissolved. In its place, a monstrous shape, lupine and feral, formed. It loped along on swells of foul fog, pursuing her, huge jaws snapping soundlessly at her heels—

Her mind skittered away from the terrifying image. She didn't want to remember.

Still she ran.

Another thunderclap tore through the air, louder this time, cascading down from the mountainous heavens that weren't there. Not really.

Then the shape dissolved back into the mist.

She could now hear voices. Whispers. Susurrations which beckoned to her, far in the distance—whatever distance *meant* in a place like this. And while she couldn't make out the words, she knew they were important: they were the first remotely human sounds she had heard in how long?

Running, running, she tried to locate the voices, but they surrounded her, echoing through the mist. When she turned—or did she? It was hard to tell in this shapeless void—the voices remained diffused, directionless. She pushed herself faster, chewing up ground that didn't exist. Fog parted before her.

Ahead, she spotted a bright spot, brighter than the fog. She bolted toward it.

Closer. She was closer.

The mists thinned. The light grew like a nascent star. The light exploded into a supernova—

—and Natalie pried open her eyes.

* * *

"Mom?"

Startled at the sound of the voice, Izzy stopped struggling and looked toward the back of the cave.

Webber snatched up the gun and pushed Izzy off him. As he got to his feet, Owens released Jack's wrist and drove his knuckles into the man's throat. The impact stunned the banker into releasing him. Owens began retching, trying to draw breath into his lungs.

Removing his fingers from his ears, Kevin walked over to Natalie, knelt down, and ran his fingers through her hair. Brushing a few strands from her face, he said, "Pretty lady."

Natalie, her eyes open, drew in a shuddering breath, then blinked.

"Oh God. *Mom.*" Her voice was weak, trembling. But she was speaking.

Her daughter was alive!

How? No, she didn't care how.

"Say goodbye, Bartholomew," said Webber, leveling the Glock at the old man.

"No!" shouted Izzy and kicked at Webber. Her heel connected with his thigh just as he fired, shoving him off balance, causing him to almost shoot Jack. The smell of burnt gunpowder filled the cave. Her ears rang solidly.

Webber spun to face her, eyes wide with rage. Then she was looking up the barrel of a .40 caliber death sentence.

"Mom!" cried Natalie.

"Shut up, kid." Then Webber jerked his head at the banker. "Let's do this different. I still need you, Jack. So, step away from the old man. *Now.*"

Rubbing at his throat, Jack threw Owens a baleful glare and then backed away. As a parting shot, he said, "I don't know why everyone's so afraid of you. I almost killed your ass."

Owens, his face bruised, his lip bleeding, returned Jack's glare. The man was breathing heavily, his shoulders bent. Fatigue deepened the lines on his face. For the first time since Izzy had met him, he truly looked like an old man.

With the gun still pointed at her, Webber said, "Wrong, Jack. If it weren't for your son, you'd be in worse shape than him."

"Kevin never touched him," Jack said. "All he did was stand there."

"All he *had* to do was stand there."

Lying on the ground, Izzy knew she had to do something or they weren't going to get out of this alive. She edged herself closer to Webber, drawing her knees up. Her eyes sought Owens. She'd only have one chance—

From the other side of the lanterns, he met her gaze, gave her an almost imperceptible nod. Then he focused his attention on Jack.

"Your son," Owens said. "He has von Kliner's Syndrome."

Jack frowned. "What does that matter?"

"You know it's a rare condition."

Webber's lifted the gun, aimed at Owens. His knuckles whitened. "Shut up, 'Forever Man'."

Jack glanced curiously at Webber. "What—?"

"It's so rare," the old man continued, "that Darryl and I have only seen one other von Kliner child. And that didn't end well.

"That person was Darryl's sister, Jesse. He killed her for having it."

Webber's eyes flew wide with rage and he fired. At the same instant, Izzy drove her legs forward and smashed Webber's knee back at an unnatural angle. Cartilage shattered and Webber collapsed to the ground.

Take out the knee and you take out the man.

Webber lay on the ground, his mouth gaped open, the veins in his neck throbbing. But his eyes had gone strangely blank.

Izzy looked over at Owens. He was on the ground, blood seeping from a gunshot wound to his chest.

With his recuperative powers, he should be fine. Then again, why hadn't Jack invoked the old man's defenses? What if his other abilities weren't functioning? Were they somehow lies?

A shadow moved across her. She looked up to see Jack standing over her, his gun pointed at her head.

"That wasn't nice, Morris," he said, gesturing to Webber with his gun. "He's my ticket out of this place. And I'm not going to let you ruin it for me."

Izzy scrambled for an idea. She couldn't let Jack win. Natalie depended on her.

Owens, his voice weak, called out to Jack. "Wrong.... Darryl never wanted you. Your son...has powers. Abilities. Darryl...I don't think he ever planned on taking you with him."

Jack's face spasmed in rage. He spun and aimed the gun at Bart.

"No, it's me! This is about *me!*" Jack was snarling now. He straightened his arm, the hand holding the gun trembling.

Before Jack could shoot, Izzy propped herself up with both hands— her left shoulder hurt, oh damn it *hurt*—and dug her bound heels into the dirt. Then she launched herself at Jack. He saw the movement and spun, snapping the gun around and firing.

The round punched into her side like a fist of burning coals. But she wasn't going to let this bastard get her. She wrapped her arms around Jack's waist, her good hand gripping the bad, her dislocated shoulder screaming in agony. She shoved hard against the ground. The momentum threw Jack off balance. But his stance was too strong. He remained standing. He aimed the gun at her head.

Izzy loosened her arms and slid down to Jack's knees and his shot missed. Before he could fire a third time, she squeezed again, twisted, rolling, dragging Jack's legs with her. His knees buckled and he fell. He squeezed a fourth shot, but the round impacted into the cave's ceiling. Dirt fell onto the lanterns. More cracks spread along the surface.

Jack landed hard onto the ground, the air whooshing out of him.

From outside the cave, Izzy heard a scream. It was Katie.

Then, through the opening, the monster charged into the cave. One of its eyes was a charred black hole.

Webber called out, his voiced heavy with pain: "Bartholomew! Kill him! Now!"

The creature seemed to hesitate; maybe it remembered the pain Owens had inflicted on it before.

In that moment, Izzy clawed over Jack and wrapped her hand around his gun. With an effort that she felt would break her, she brought her wounded arm around, gripped the gun with both hands. Pointed it at the monster. Slid her finger over Jack's. Squeezed the trigger.

The round caught the creature in the neck. Flesh and fur exploded.

"Again," said Owens, his voice urgent.

Izzy fired again. The round blew half the creature's shaggy head apart. Bone and blood splattered the cave wall. The monster's left jaw came unhinged and hung loose, its tongue escaping between broken teeth. Then it fell wetly to the ground, its massive girth sending vibrations through the stone floor.

Jack, his breath regained, abruptly convulsed. His hand splayed open. Izzy grabbed the gun.

On the ground next to her, sweat streaming down his face, Webber lifted his gun. Izzy kicked, knocking Webber's weapon aside.

She brought Jack's gun around.

She'd learned there was the justice she'd always believed in, the one that lead her to be a cop. And then there was Justice—one she'd always known in her heart existed but had been afraid to embrace. That had changed.

"This is for my daughter," she said and fired.

* * *

Her round hit Webber in the chest, punching a hole through him the size of a baseball. She fired again. And again. Each shot made Webber's body jerk like a marionette with a couple of strings missing. His chest disintegrated into a mass of crimson gore. He raised an arm, fingers twitching. Then it fell. The life drained from his eyes. His body sagged.

Dead. Darryl Webber was finally dead.

She ripped the tape from her ankles and stood. Adrenaline had reduced the gunshot wound in her side to a painful ache.

"Izzy."

She turned. Bart Owens gestured toward Jack.

The banker had stopped convulsing. He was lying on the ground next to Webber, trembling, the heels of his shoes drumming against the ground. His face was flushed, feverish. Sweat oozed from his pores. The muscles of his neck were corded. His eyes had rolled back until only the whites showed.

But his skin—

She blinked, not sure of what she was seeing. His skin was moving, shifting, as if bugs were crawling under it.

Izzy frowned at Owens. "What's wrong with him?"

"Get out of here. Fast."

"But—?"

"Go," he repeated. "Please, *now*. Take Kevin and your daughter. Hurry."

Jack's jaw creaked open with a tortured sound like someone loosening a rusty lug nut. From his open mouth spilled a thin, reedy sound . His hand snaked out, grasped Webber's leg.

And the corpse twitched.

"Right," said Izzy, horrified. "Time to go."

She limped across the cave, her hand held over her gut.

On his knees next to Natalie, Kevin seemed blissfully unaware of what was happening to his father. He continued to stroke Natalie's forehead.

Her daughter's eyes were closed. She appeared asleep. But after days without water, lying on the cold ground with her wounded abdomen, she must be near death.

"Hurry," gasped Owens. He coughed. Droplets of blood flew from his mouth. "Get Kevin away from me."

Looking questioningly at the old man, Izzy stretched out her hand to Kevin and felt his tiny hand slip into hers.

"Von Kliner's," wheezed Owens, "negates my abilities."

Izzy's eyes widened. That's why Jack could attack Owens and not get hurt.

"The boy," Owens said, his face coated with sweat. "Get him away...or I *will* die."

Oh, shit. Galvanized by his words, Izzy helped Kevin to his feet.

"Katie." Owens lifted a hand toward the cave opening. "Outside. With Gene."

Kneeling down, Izzy lifted a hand to Kevin's face, cupped his chin, forced the boy to look at her.

"Kevin, honey. You need to go outside. Katie's there. Remember Katie? J.J.'s girlfriend? Please, go find Katie." She gave him a gentle push toward the cave opening. "Go, Kevin. Go find Katie."

Kevin stopped after a few steps. He looked back at Izzy—then broke into a smile and scampered through the opening.

With Kevin safely outside, Izzy threw a wary glance back at Jack. The man had managed to somehow drag Webber's corpse over so that it lay partially on top of him. Still emitting its reedy hiss, Jack's mouth had stretched to impossible dimensions: his chin rested on the middle of his chest. Just beneath the surface of his skin, his flesh continued to boil.

Webber's corpse twitched and shook like a man having a seizure.

When Jack lifted one of Webber's hands and stuffed it into his gaping maw, Izzy turned away, revulsion rising in her throat.

Natalie lay unconscious on the floor. Izzy bent down, eased her arms under her daughter, and lifted. Somewhere in the back of her mind, her injuries shrieked at the effort. Her weakened left arm could barely support Nat.

Holding her daughter for the first time in days, she whispered, "Time to go, honey."

As she struggled toward the cave opening, she heard Owens call her name. She stopped and turned her head toward the old man.

"Hurry back," he said. "I'm going to need your help."

Nodding, Izzy stumbled out of the cave.

CHAPTER
37

Locked inside his convulsing body, Jack's mind wailed in terror.

He was burning, his body an inferno, a living pyre. Incandescent, the heat consumed him. Muscle and sinew, blood and bone. He felt it all: every rupture, every blazing reformation, igniting his nerves.

No! he screamed silently. What's happening? It wasn't supposed to be like this!

Then he was gagging, his throat violated by something squirmy, like a sack of worms. Reflexively he retched, tried to clear the object from his airway—but more was shoved down his gullet, crammed until the passage stretched to accommodate the writhing mass.

Choking and unable to breathe, his panicked heart raced faster. It strained against the confines of his chest, hammering until the muscle buckled under the pressure: with a harsh kick, it hesitated, stuttered for a few helpless, clinging beats.

He knew his time had come.

Your drawings, Kevin. I always loved them...and you.

I'm sorry.

And then Jack Sallinen died.

For a long moment, nothing. Then his heart clenched. Relaxed. Clenched. Blood flowed. The gagging subsided—

—and was replaced by hunger.

His jaw gaped wider. Thick saliva oozed into the orifice, coating his burning membranes, cooling them, making them slick, slippery. His esophagus flexed, a rhythmic peristalsis, forcing more of the twitching mass into him.

Gradually, he swallowed, though he still could barely breathe. Eventually, he ate. The burning pain faded until it was no more than an ache. And was replaced by noise. Harsh and caustic, like the tortured screams of a thousand—

Be Nothings.

Chew, swallow—savor. He couldn't get enough.

Noise was pain. And pain. Pain was power.

The power he wanted. The power he demanded.

The power he deserved.

The noise grew. It called to him.

He could not refuse.

* * *

Stumbling out of the cave with Nat in her arms, Izzy almost fell into snow. Only the sheer determination to save her daughter kept her from collapsing.

Katie was kneeling not far from the cave's entrance, the long frame of Gene's body lying prone on the ground beside her. She had a blood-soaked cloth pressed to his neck. Her face was knotted with worry.

Kevin stood near Katie, bundled in his jacket, his small frame shivering from the cold.

Izzy had to set Natalie down. Her wounded shoulder wouldn't support her daughter's weight any longer. She managed a few more halting steps toward Katie before she fell to her knees and laid Natalie on the ground.

With her dislocated shoulder aching and the gunshot wound in her abdomen a searing tooth biting into her flesh, she crawled to Katie.

"What happened?"

Katie looked up. "Webber cut his throat. I've tried to stop the bleeding, but there's so much." Tears began rolling down her cheeks. "I think he's going to die."

"Let me look," Izzy said, lifting the cloth from Gene's neck. She drew in a sharp breath. The wound was angry looking, the skin curling back from the cut. He was indeed bleeding heavily, but there was no tell-tale spurt of a severed artery. Perhaps Webber's knife had skidded across Gene's trachea, preventing the killing stroke. Regardless, he needed medical attention or he would almost certainly die.

As would she and her daughter.

Izzy shook her head. She didn't make it this far to let them die in the woods.

She removed Gene's shoes and socks. She handed a sock to Katie and placed the other over Gene's wound. It was far from perfect, but it was all she had.

"Keep pressing on this. If it gets soaked with blood, use the other sock. I've got to get Owens. After that, we need to get everyone to a hospital."

"Natalie?" asked Katie, her hand now back on the make-shift bandage.

"Alive," Izzy replied. As she tried to stand, she cried out, her hand clutching her side.

Katie frowned, then saw Izzy's blood soaked shirt. Their eyes met. "Hurry."

Izzy nodded, then charged back into the cave.

* * *

Izzy pushed through the narrow opening and spilled into the cave.

Several feet away, Jack Sallinen continued his morbid feast. A thick, clear fluid ran from his mouth. Obviously corrosive, it flowed over Webber's body, liquefying him into a vile slurry. Even so, Jack's belly was swollen, the fabric of his clothes ripped and frayed.

She looked away, fighting the urge to vomit. Just get the old man, she thought, and get out of here.

She hurried to Owens's side. His eyes were closed. She touched his shoulder and he opened them.

"Can you move?" she asked.

He nodded. "Gene?"

"Katie's trying to keep him alive."

"Good. Help me up."

She extended a hand, grimacing as she pulled him to his feet. "Jack?"

There was a strangled, gurgling noise. They both looked at Jack. The last of Webber's body slid effortless down the former banker's monstrous gullet. The man's jaw creaked close with the same grating noise she'd heard earlier. Then his ponderous stomach heaved.

"It's not just him," Owens said. "It's both of them."

"But what's happening?"

"You don't want to see. Let's go."

Izzy took a step back, intending on moving out of Owens's way, when her foot caught on something. She stumbled but managed to put a hand on the dirt wall to keep her balance. She looked down at what she'd almost tripped on.

Covered in frost, it looked like a pile of dirty clothes. She remembered seeing them earlier. After giving them a cursory glance, she'd dismissed them as harmless. But now that she was closer, she saw mottled skin, a couple gnarled fingers, a milky eye, and—

She bent down and picked something up. It was a torn and bloodied checked cap.

"Chet Boardman." She looked sadly at the heap on the floor. He'd been a harmless old drunk.

Owens stretched a blood-coated hand to her. "There's nothing we can do."

"But—"

Before Izzy could finish, the ground began shaking, a deep rumbling that she felt in her bones. Like a charging locomotive, the tremors grew violent and loud. Cracks spread across the cave walls, loosening dirt and sticks and raining debris down on them.

Then the ground shifted, knocking them off their feet. Owens managed to catch himself with his hands, sparing his body further injury. Izzy fell hard onto the stiff, mutilated corpse of Chet Boardman. Her hand punched through dead man's bloated skin and sank wrist-deep into his putrefying organs.

All around Jack Sallinen, the ground broke into fissures. From the openings emerged dozens of small snakes. Long and thin with bright viridian scales, they slithered over Jack, tore at him, opened up wounds—and slid into them.

Then his body swelled.

Horrified, Izzy didn't register that Owens had pulled her to her feet until he shoved her toward the cave opening.

"Out!" the old man yelled. Then he scooped up one of the lanterns and followed her. "Now!"

Jack's body swelled further. His taut skin rippled. The last shreds of his clothes fell away.

At the cave opening, Owens stopped her. "Your gun!"

"What?" Izzy didn't think she had heard him right.

"Do you have your gun?"

From her pocket, she removed Jack's revolver.

"Hurry! Shoot the ceiling!"

Beyond the remaining lantern, Jack's body distended, bloating until he was so massive his flesh could not possibly bear the stresses. With a sound like ripping fabric, his entire skin disintegrated into bloody ribbons, revealing the wet fur and scales lurking beneath.

Stunned, Izzy shook her head. "That can't be."

"I need your help." Owens faced the cave, eyes locked on the ceiling, hands raised and palms out. "Shoot the ceiling!"

The creature that had once been Jack Sallinen and Darryl Webber scrambled to stand on all fours. Its broad, shaggy head swiveled toward her. Jack's hateful eyes bore onto her. Black lips flapping, revealing teeth like knives. Then it threw its head back and howled. To Izzy, the dual-toned cry was eerily reminiscent of Jack and Webber—the two men who now seemed to comprise the creature.

"Izzy!"

When she heard Owens shout her name, Izzy shook herself out of her immobility. The old man had closed his eyes, a look of concentration on his brown face. His hands shook. He was trying to do something.

Lifting the gun, Izzy slipped her finger onto the trigger.

Above her, cracks spanned the ceiling. Dirt streamed down from the seams, weakening the integrity of the structure: large sections of the cave were starting to crumble.

A dozen feet away, the creature crouched, thick muscles bunching, its malevolent glare fixed on her.

As the creature leapt, Izzy fired—and kept firing until the gun was empty.

Lead slugs slammed into the ceiling. The impacts should have had little effect. She was surprised when they shattered the cave's integrity. Like a dam under too much pressure, the patchwork of cracks exploded, releasing a deluge of dirt into the small space.

The creature was still in the air when the earthen flood hit, driving it to the ground. Snarling with rage, its front talons dug in, found purchase on the ground. But the heavy flow of debris and dirt smashed into it, burying it.

Izzy felt a hand on her arm.

Owens gestured to the cave's exit.

Nodding, Izzy turned to leave. With Owens pushing her on, she raced through the opening.

Just as they stumbled into the moonlit glade, Izzy heard the creature scream, a sound so full of rage that it made her want to weep at the fate of the two men trapped within it.

And then the cave collapsed, burying everything inside under tons of rock.

CHAPTER
38

Izzy sat crossed-legged on the damp ground. Her daughter huddled next to her, wrapped in the jacket Owens had offered to help contain what little warmth she had left. Natalie had lapsed back into unconsciousness since being brought out of the cave. The wound in her side was infected. She was dehydrated and weak from starvation. Her lips were cracked, the flesh under her eyes bruised. Her eyes raced beneath their lids.

Natalie needed a hospital, as did Gene.

Not that Izzy didn't need one, too. Her left arm hung uselessly at her side, the shoulder joint still out of its socket, not to mention the ankle she'd twisted less than an hour ago. And she'd been shot twice. One injury was minor, just some torn skin and muscle from where the bullet had grazed her. The wound in her side, where Jack had shot her a second time, throbbed with each beat of her heart. Fortunately, the round had entered at a shallow angle and seemed to have missed any major organs. It hurt like nothing she'd experienced before, but as long as she wasn't going to die, she'd deal with the pain.

The irony wasn't lost on Izzy that she and her daughter now suffered similar wounds.

Owens stood next to Izzy. After emerging from the cave, he had rushed over to Gene and helped Katie tend to the man. It meant coming near Kevin, who would not leave Katie's side, but he wasn't near the boy long enough to threaten his healing.

"What did you do back there?" Izzy asked Owens. "In the cave? There's no way bullets would bring down a cave like that."

Owens gave her an uncomfortable look. "Remember when you asked if there was anything else I could 'do?' My answer wasn't entirely honest." He turned his head and looked back at the cave. "I was redistributing the weight of the earth in there. I needed the bullets to break apart the surface and start the collapse."

"But that's—?"

"Yes, I know. Impossible. I did the same thing with the gun your husband pulled on me. Made it too heavy for him to lift." As he spoke, he scanned the glade, his eyes fixing on the tree line opposite them.

Izzy shook her head. This was too much information for her to process right now. There were other, more important matters at hand.

She checked her watch. "We have a few hours until dawn. After that, de la Rosa will be coming for us in force. We should leave before he gets here."

When Owens didn't respond, when he continued to stare off into the woods, Izzy said, "Is there a problem?"

"Sorry," Owens said, turning to face them. His cheeks puffed out as he exhaled through pursed lips. "I'm afraid it's not as simple as that."

Katie walked up to them. Kevin came with her, his small hand in hers. "Gene's neck has stopped bleeding. His pulse is a bit stronger. But he's still going to need a doctor."

Izzy nodded her thanks. Then to Owens: "What did you mean?"

"We have two unconscious people. They'll have to be carried. That means two adults for each person. You've been shot. And your shoulder's dislocated. Kevin can't help anyone. We don't have enough people. We can't get everyone out."

"So we work in shifts. Carry one for a while, then another. It'll take longer, but no one has to be left behind."

Owens was shaking his head. "That would take *too* long. The only reasonable answer is to have all of you stay behind. When the Lieutenant finds you, he can get you the medical care you need."

Katie opened her mouth to protest, but Izzy held up her hand.

"Why does it sound like *you're* going somewhere?"

"Kevin's not out of danger yet," Owens replied. "Others will come looking for him. Not soon. Not after what just happened. But eventually, he'll become a target again. So he and I will have to disappear."

"Hold on," Izzy said. "You can't just take a child away like that. What about his mother?"

"His parents are divorced," Katie said. "His mom lives down in Grand Rapids. And don't forget J.J. He has a brother, too."

Owens's face grew serious. "You don't understand. If Kevin stays with his family, then they'll all be in danger. At any time, someone, or some*thing*, could come after him."

"Okay," said Izzy. "I get that part. But what do you think his mom's going to do if he goes missing? Ignore it? No. She'll contact police. The news. They'll set up searches. And if they think someone has taken him out of the state, then you'll have the FBI involved. You'll have the entire nation glued to their televisions as they watch the hunt for the young autistic boy lost in the woods. I'm guessing that's a little more attention than you're comfortable with."

He nodded. "You're right. Like I said, he can't stay with his family. That would put them and everyone else around them in danger. And yes, his mother would come looking for him—if she thought he was alive."

Izzy caught the implication. "You're going to fake his death."

"What choice is there?" Owens asked.

"You'd do that to his mother?" Katie said, clearly uncomfortable with the idea.

"I regret the cruelty of it," Owens said. "But it's the only way to keep them all alive. If the world thinks Kevin Sallinen is dead, then the world won't come looking for him."

"I suppose you're right." Izzy still had her doubts. "But will that work with whoever is after Kevin?"

Owens said, "No, it won't. That's why Kevin will have to come with me. I have a network of friends that will help. They're used to this kind of thing."

Izzy stared at the old man. "I'm not sure I like that idea."

"It's for the boy's safety. Once I get him out of here, my friends will help hide him until I can find someone to watch him."

That got Izzy attention. "What do you mean, 'someone to watch him'?"

"He can't stay with me. I'm often a target myself, and that would put Kevin in more danger. When I get home, I'll have one of the friends I mentioned start looking for a person who will agree to raise him."

"You're going put him in the care of a stranger?" Katie asked.

Owens shrugged. "Again, what choice do I have?"

Izzy thought about poor, sweet Kevin, destined to be raised by someone he didn't know. By someone who had simply agreed to the job as a favor to Owens. That was no life for a little boy. He would need love and attention, not just protection. A person he could turn to when he had nightmares or skinned knees. Someone to hold him and hug him and tell him he would be all right. No, he deserved a normal life. Not some isolated existence in a strange Witness Protection Program.

"He's not going with some stranger," she said evenly. "He's coming with me."

"No," the old man said. "I'm sorry, but I can't allow that. Think this through, Izzy. Not only will Kinsey be one of the first places anyone will come looking for the boy, remember that he's supposed to be dead. How are you going to explain his presence?"

"I won't be in Kinsey." She paused, afraid of her own next words.

"I'm leaving." She hugged Natalie closer. "I'm coming with you."

"What?" Katie exclaimed.

Owens said, "Izzy, you don't—"

Izzy brought a hand up. Everyone quieted.

"Listen to me," she said to Owens. "My life here is over. When de la Rosa arrives, I'll be arrested. I've just gotten my daughter back. I won't leave her again to go to jail." She looked at Kevin. "Besides, you say he's important."

Owens nodded. "Important enough to have drawn the attention of some very dangerous people. You saw that he could blank out my abilities. And Darryl's. That may just be the start of what he can do."

There were implications in that statement that Izzy wanted to pursue, but she let them slide. Owens was right. Now was not the time.

"If Kevin's that important," said Izzy, "then you don't want to leave him with a stranger. You want someone he knows raising him. And I've already seen what can happen. I'll know to keep my guard up." She shrugged. "I'm the perfect choice."

"What about your husband?" Owens asked. "Are you just going to leave him?"

She thought about Stanley. Their marriage had been failing for years. Her leaving would give him a chance at a new life, provided he lived.

She nodded.

"And Natalie," Owens continued. "Doesn't she have a say in this?"

"After what she's been through, I don't know what she'll think. But for now, she's best off with me, too. I can deal with her choices later."

Owens opened his mouth to say something, but then closed it. He scratched idly at one cheek. Then his eyes found Katie.

"What about you? What do you intend to do?"

"My parents are dead." Katie's tone was firm. "I have nothing to keep me in Kinsey."

The old man nodded. "All right. But then there's Gene. We can carry Natalie out, but we can't carry both."

Izzy looked over at Gene. Owens was right: he was too hurt to be carried out. And he's already been through so much.

"We'll stick with your original plan for him," she said quietly. "He'll stay behind for de la Rosa to find. Then he'll get the medical care he needs."

"He's not going to like that," said Katie.

"I know," replied Izzy. "But at least he'll be alive to get over it."

"So now what?" asked Katie.

Izzy nodded in the direction they had taken earlier. "We can't go back the way we came. We might run right into de la Rosa. I'd say follow the moon west until we reach the road. It won't be easy, but I think we can make it."

"And then?" Katie asked.

Owens said, "And then I'll arrange to have us picked up. And for medical care for Natalie and Izzy. But that'll take time. We'll need a place to hole up."

"There's a motel up the road," said Izzy. "Owned by the guy Denny tried to kill. Deke Frenz. He's much sharper than he looks. I bet we could trust him to put us up and keep quiet about it."

Owens nodded, then threw a glance back at the tree line. When he turned back, he said, "That'll have to do for now. You guys start for the road. I'll be right behind you."

Katie knelt down in front of Kevin. "Hey, buddy. You ready to go?"

A shiver ran through him and he sneezed. Then his random gaze fixed on the tree line. His expression darkened.

Izzy followed his gaze but couldn't see anything. Shrugging, she turned back to Owens.

"You're not coming with us?"

"In a bit," Owens said. "First, I'm going to make sure Gene gets found. Also, I want to make sure that it looks like we all died in that cave-in. I've picked up a few tricks over the years with this sort of thing, if you can believe it. Can each of you give me something you're wearing?"

After they had obliged—Izzy had to tear off bits of Nat and Kevin's clothes—Izzy gripped Nat under one armpit; Katie got a hand under the other. Together, they stood Nat up. Then, hooking each of Nat's arms over a shoulder, they began walking away.

Kevin didn't move. He continued to stare off into the woods.

Stopping, Izzy looked back. "Kevin, honey. Come on. We're leaving."

For a moment, it didn't look as if he was going to listen to her. But he turned to face Owens. The boy stood, regarding the old man with steady eyes. Then, without saying a word, he scurried over to Izzy and Katie.

After a few steps, they stopped next to Gene. With Katie supporting Nat, Izzy bent down, whispered, "You and I aren't done yet," and kissed him on the lips. Standing up, she wedged her good shoulder under Natalie, and they walked into the woods.

Once they were out of sight, Bart scattered the pieces of clothing around the site. He had to adjust two of the pieces, but he was soon satisfied. It looked like bloody murder had happened in the glade.

He had to wait almost an hour. He checked on Gene. The man's vitals were stable but he was clearly passed out. Then he took a deep breath and turned toward the tree line.

"You may as well come out," he said. "I know you're there."

* * *

A woman emerged from the tree line. She wore a long leather jacket over dark pants and knee-high boots. As she walked toward him, the lantern light gradually dissolved the shadows obscuring her face, revealing dusky features accented by high cheekbones and full lips, hair like raven's wings swept back from a high forehead, dun-colored eyes that slanted slightly upward.

She stopped at the edge of the light and nodded a greeting.

"Hello, Bartholomew."

Bart nodded in return. "Marbæs."

"It's good to see you again," she said, almost affectionately.

"Wish I could say the same."

The ghost of a smile haunted her lips. "Ah, let's be civil. After all, it has been a long time."

Bart squared his shoulders. "What do you want, Marbæs?"

Her smile slowly faded. "Want? My dear Bartholomew, I already *had* what I wanted. But you came along and took it away."

"Pardon me if I don't shed a tear."

"Very funny." She arched one eyebrow and angled her head just so. Bart couldn't mistake the challenge in her look. "Suppose I simply decide to take it back?"

"It? We're talking about a boy."

Marbæs gave a disaffected shrug. "If you say so."

Gesturing to the collapsed cave, Bart said, "Darryl tried to take Kevin. That didn't work out so well for him."

"Darryl, Kölbe, Behraam, Anala...." Marbæs replied coolly. "Imperfect tools from an imperfect world. You break one, you simply find another. Oh, and speaking of tools, I found your little spy at Dr. Westwood's office. She won't be feeding you any more information."

Bart's nostrils flared. Mai Li was an intelligent, resourceful, and brave woman. Put in place by Phillip, she was the one who had alerted them about Kevin, and Darryl Webber's interest. For almost a decade, she'd done an excellent job in a dangerous situation. And now she was gone, of that Marbaes's words left no doubt. He felt a familiar hollowness in the pit of his stomach.

"I've upset you." Marbæs nodded. "Well, you deserve it, after robbing me of my prize."

"Yes, you've failed...again." Bart's words cut through the night. "Germany, Turkey, Armenia, Ethiopia, Mesopotamia. You keep losing battles, Marbæs. You keep coming in second." It was his turn to smile. "To me."

Her expression darkened. "The boy is nearby. It would only take me moments to find him."

"And then what? Would *you* approach him? Would *you* risk death? I doubt it."

"Or maybe I should just leave him for now," Marbæs replied. Her eyes seemed to have vanished entirely, leaving only empty, black cavities. Bart had seen her this way before; she was losing her temper. "Maybe I should just kill you."

And then she was standing before him, closing the distance in the span of a second. Her hand flashed through the air. It had elongated, the skin now dark and leathery. Fingers tipped with long, blade-like claws attempted to decapitate him.

Bart had anticipated her attack; after so many centuries, her patterns had become predictable. He ducked, and her arm passed harmlessly over his head. Bringing his hands together, palms out, he put his own considerable strength into his own strike. The impact sent Marbæs flying. She landed on her back, rolled to her feet. Her jacket had come open. Above her blouse, the skin on her neck had also taken on the leathery appearance; the transformation climbed up to her face, her cheeks. When she smiled, her teeth were small, sharp.

"Do you remember, Bartholomew? On the shores of the Caspian Sea, when you first awoke?"

Her voice was compelling, hypnotic—it pulled at his memories. He gathered his will, tried to resist, but she was far stronger than Webber.

Images flashed through his mind.

Albanopolis...the hot wind blowing off the Caspian...hard sky and a blazing sun...water lapping at his prone form...his body in pain, wracking agony....

"No," Bart muttered, shaking his head. His vision cleared. Marbæs was advancing. He edged away, keeping his distance.

"Yes," she said. "You remember. Long ago, when we first met."

He had cried out, his back arching, shoulders digging into the sand...and then she was there...kneeling beside him with words of comfort..."let me help you"..."care for you"....

A flash of movement. He threw an arm up, barely deflecting her attack. He lunged forward to grab her, but she spun out of his reach.

"But even then," said Marbæs, stepping to his left, "you were a stubborn man."

He peered up at her...an oval face framed in black hair...a smile...but her eyes, they were wrong...something inside her was wrong....

"You refused me." Her voice was barely above a whisper as she swept in closer. "And what a revelation it had been, discovering who you had become—what you had become. You and the others."

Others—

The present snapped back with a clarity that was brutal. The woods hurtled into focus. The cold air scraped his skin. Oblique shafts of moonlight cut across the glade, leaving pearls of light glinting on the snow.

"That discovery nearly killed both of us." Bart's eyes lit on Marbæs, and she stopped her advance. Her transformation was complete—her outer beauty had surrendered itself to the ugliness of her soul.

"I grieve for you, Marbæs. How you must have hated yourself, giving everything away for this." He gestured at her corrupted form.

"Yet here we are, the two of us—ageless walkers on an aging world." He heard voices coming from the forest, shouts of men searching. Marbæs heard them, too: she began retreating toward the tree line. "Spare me your pity, Bartholomew. We are more alike than you care to admit."

"In some ways, I would agree." He hooked a finger around the chain at his neck and pulled out the tiny piece of wood attached to it. Raising it in front of his face, he added, "Then again, to become truly great, one has to stand among people, not above them."

Marbæs had reached the edge of the woods. She paused, her gazing lingering on him or the piece of wood. He couldn't tell which.

"The Nazarene was right about one thing," she said, an ancient bitterness creeping into her voice. "There is no deception in you."

And then she was gone.

EPILOGUE

The old man found an empty seat near the back of the bus.

Carefully, he secured his guitar case in the upper storage bin. Next to it he placed the army duffel—Dexter Grant's duffel. Then he took his seat and tried to get comfortable. It was going to be a long ride back to Nashville.

From the pocket of his jacket, he pulled out a new paperback. He'd just gotten into the first chapter when someone stopped in the aisle.

"I'm sorry. Is this seat taken?"

Bart Owens looked up and smiled. "It's all yours."

Katie Bethel plopped down next to him. She wore a nondescript blue jacket, jeans, and a plain gray sweatshirt; clothes which would be hard to recall if anyone came around asking questions. Her dark hair had been cut short. Large sunglasses hid part of her face. A tan backpack went on the floor between her feet.

"Did you have any problems?" he asked.

Katie shook her head. "Kept my eyes open. Didn't see anyone following me. Just to be sure, I walked past the stop, went down two blocks. Nothing. No one hanging back or window shopping. Still, I took a side street and hooked around. Figured I'd come up on the stop from a less obvious route. I think we're safe."

Bart nodded. The girl was a quick study.

"And our friends?" asked Katie.

"They're as well as can be expected. Others are looking after them now."

"Gene?"

"I called the hospital. He's out of ICU. Looks like he'll be okay. Besides, Dr. Morris is going to need his help. The man believes his wife and daughter died."

Stanley Morris had finally woken from his coma. When told about the fate of his family, he had broken down and cried.

Still, Katie looked uncertain.

"Something wrong?" Bart asked.

"It's just…." Katie's voice trailed off.

"You don't like leaving Gene behind?"

Katie shrugged, then nodded. "He almost died helping us. It doesn't seem fair to go on without him."

Bart turned to face her. "Life is rarely fair, Katie. If you stay on this bus, you'd better be prepared to learn that—often the hard way. If you don't think you can handle it, there's still time to get off."

He hated being so blunt, but this was a crucial moment in her life.

Katie's unflinching gaze held him for a dozen heartbeats. "My mom died for no good reason." She looked around to make sure they were alone, then added, "Torn apart by that creature. Was that fair? My dad killed himself, leaving me behind to wonder why he wanted death more than me. Was *that* fair?" She settled back into her seat. "Don't talk to me about fair. I'll handle anything you throw at me."

Bart smiled. "I had to be sure."

Katie's shoulders slumped. "Sorry. Guess I'm still a little on edge."

Settling into his seat, Bart said, "Aren't we all."

The End

<<<◇>>>